Priya Basil was  in Kenya. She now lives in L... ...el, *Ishq and Mushq*, was sh... ...Writer's Prize, and longliste... ...e for Young Writers and t... ...ward. Priya's novella, *Strangers on the 16:02*, was one of the annual ten Quick Reads published in February 2011. In 2010 Priya co-founded Authors for Peace – a platform from which writers can actively use literature in different ways to promote peace. Please visit her website: www.priyabasil.com

www.**transworldbooks**.co.uk

The Obscure Logic of the Heart

Priya Basil

BLACK SWAN

TRANSWORLD PUBLISHERS
61–63 Uxbridge Road, London W5 5SA
A Random House Group Company
www.transworldbooks.co.uk

THE OBSCURE LOGIC OF THE HEART
A BLACK SWAN BOOK: 9780552773850

First published in Great Britain
in 2010 by Doubleday
an imprint of Transworld Publishers
Black Swan edition published 2011

Addresses for Random House Group Ltd companies outside the UK
can be found at: www.randomhouse.co.uk
The Random House Group Ltd Reg. No. 954009

The Random House Group Limited supports The Forest Stewardship
Council® (FSC®), the leading international forest certification organisation.
All our titles that are printed on Greenpeace approved FSC® certified paper
carry the FSC® logo. Our paper procurement policy can be found at
www.rbooks.co.uk/environment

Typeset in 10.5/13.5pt Giovanni Book by
Falcon Oast Graphic Art Ltd.
Printed in the UK by CPI Cox & Wyman, Reading, RG1 8EX.

2 4 6 8 10 9 7 5 3 1

To my mother, Gudy, with love and gratitude

'We are our own demons, we expel ourselves from our paradise.'

Johann Wolfgang von Goethe
(from a letter to Ernst Wolfgang Behrisch,
10 November 1767)

I

Waiting

S HE IS LATE.
Anil expected this and has come prepared. A newspaper lies by his side, but he doesn't touch it. He just sits on the black leather banquette of a corner table at Café Lafin and watches the glass doors. Waiting.

His eyes flicker on to the white tablecloth. He admires the squared elegance of the shining cutlery – he notices such things because shapes have always fascinated him; often he thinks more clearly in forms than words. Beside the glinting knife is his phone. When they'd first started seeing each other all those years ago – his heartbeat stumbles as he tots up the decades – few people had a mobile. How often he'd waited with no notion of when she might arrive, imagining all the things that could have gone wrong.

He stares at the doors; calm, knowing he'll be here alone for a while, and still ready to forgive her bad habit. He won't check his watch again or strain his eyes to scan the street outside the café. No, he tells himself, I have learned patience. It's all those rammed earth walls I've built. He smiles, thinking of the ancient pisé de terre construction method, the central motif of his architecture, for which he's become renowned. Such walls made of earth need days to dry and harden. Sometimes it can take up to two years before they're fully cured. By then the earth is hard as rock. Yes, he knows how to bide his time. Unlike that younger self who used to pace and sweat and worry when she didn't turn up on schedule. How different I am, he thinks, from the Anil who waited to declare his love for her one autumn day. He can still remember that afternoon, pacing outside St Paul's Cathedral, glancing left and right, expecting her to round the corner any moment . . .

He looked at his watch and rapped its face suspiciously, ready to accept it must be wrong, he must be too early, or else the minutes were trickily swelling in proportion to his anticipation. He still believed she was capable of punctuality – though she had already held him up twice, each time for more than half an hour. But then, even the seasons had been tardy that year. Spring had arrived in June, summer in August. And in late November, autumn was hurrying to an end. The trees, tipsy on an excess of wind, swayed and wantonly shed their leaves.

In three days he would be flying back home to Kenya. At the thought, something fluttered in his chest. Something that needed to be spoken, that would not sit quietly within him for another month. He'd considered staying back, spending Christmas alone in London, lying to his parents about his workload – just so he could see her. Only he'd discovered she was going home to Birmingham for the holidays. Then he'd decided he couldn't leave without telling her – though it was hard to believe she hadn't guessed.

Since the beginning of that semester, when they'd met at a concert, he'd been turning up at the places she frequented, and joining the organizations of which she was a member. His close friends were not impressed by his new-found preference for South London crêperies and halal curry houses. They were even less persuaded by his novice zeal for Amnesty International and Greenpeace. 'Can't believe you're picking up all this sissy stuff because of a chick,' they said. Grudgingly they followed him to venues where he might meet her, because the habit of childhood meant that they banded together regardless of the strange inclinations one of them might have.

The first time he had seen her was in a crowded room at the student union, where members of the Asian Society were seated barefoot on the floor around a group of qawwali singers. At the beginning of the performance, phrases had spilled from the performers into the crowd, like torchlight being cast around a dark room.

Who can measure the distance between two hearts?

Anil listened, enthralled, though he could not comprehend all the Urdu. Soon, sound sparkled from each of the players. Many in the audience shut their eyes against the music's luminosity, afraid to see glints of their own yearning. But Anil kept looking, and his reward was the vision of her.

She was sitting diagonally opposite him, a short distance away, legs pulled up to her chest, arms resting on the summit of her knees. Her bottom half was swathed in a flowing lilac skirt embroidered delicately along the edges with black thread. It was her slim ankles he noticed first. The hem of her skirt cut just above the shapely ankle bones, the left one circled by a thin gold chain. Then he saw the elegant feet. Each second toe, distinctly longer than its neighbouring big toe, seemed to be pointing at him. The painted nails, shimmering silver, were like the heads of arrows aimed at his heart. He felt impelled to bow his head before this stranger. The sheer loveliness of her limbs made him want to pray; something he had never done before. Throughout his young life, everything had come easily to him: each need was fulfilled, each wish granted. There was nothing to ask God for.

But, as he sat at that concert, Anil sensed the possibility of prayer as praise – not supplication. This was the essence of the music pulsing around him: worship not as a petition for something, but as an exaltation of the divine for the desire of itself that it inspired.

The chief qawwal, raising his hand upwards, called out:

Oh my beloved!

Anil could only appreciate the phrase in its most secular sense. No matter how many qawwalis he listened to, he would never understand how such adulation could be heaped on an invisible being, the purported Almighty. For him, the word love was associated first and foremost with romance. His gaze moved over the clothes concealing the stranger's body to her head. In that instant, with the first glimpse of her face, he began to comprehend all the lyrics.

Your body is the map of my longing.

He felt his destiny was written in the folds of the fabric that fell over her frame.

I am a prisoner of your sighs.

People were clapping. He was clapping, though he did not know it. He only saw her hands turn into the wings of a bird.

Your hair is the thread of my memories.

Anil was oblivious to the slumped figure beside him. It was his best friend, Merc, who'd drunk heavily before coming: 'Otherwise, there's no way I can sit through that matope, mazeh.' Merc was asleep, but still swaying and snoring to the beat of the tabla, as if the music had invaded and colonized his dreams.

The qawwal slipped from song to speech and back to song again, praising the beloved, pleading for recognition, and then rebuking his lover while seeming to revel in despair. Shaking, sweating, the singer heaved himself, from time to time, off his large behind and on to his knees. Thus raised, he almost shouted at his tormentor. His pupils dilated, his cheeks quivered, his lyrical voice was frayed by passion:

Who else will weep when you turn away your face?

Glancing around, Anil was surprised to find that the whole audience was not fixated on the stranger in lilac but remained in thrall to the qawwal, whose tan-coloured, tussore-silk kurta was turning dark brown in patches under his arms. Anil wanted to live for ever in the poetic preludes that had borne him to this point – and yet he needed the music to stop so he could find out her name. But the qawwal was on his knees again, beseeching, warning:

After me, who will you torment?

When the music stopped Anil could not move. Merc staggered to his feet with the help of two other friends, but Anil remained cross-legged on the floor.

'I told you we shouldn't have come. This stuff just wastes you, mazeh. Look at Anil, he's turned into a Buddha.' Merc prodded him with a toe.

'I can't believe *you* slept, man – that's the waste,' Jateen said.

'Ah, shut up, JT.' Merc extended a hand to help Anil up. 'Come on, let's get out of here. You said we'd go to a club afterwards.'

'No.' Anil didn't take his eyes off her. 'We have to do something first.'

'What?'

'I need to find out who that is.' He pointed.

'Her? Why, mazeh?' Merc looked down his small, flat nose and blew impatiently out of his full lips. 'There'll be way hotter chiles at the club. Come on.'

'She looks pretty young.' JT nodded. Her thinness and the bounce of her ponytail gave her a girlish air.

'Well, she can't be underage. You need ID to get into the union,' Hardy spoke from behind the beard and moustache cultivated to fence off the world from the spots that raged on his face.

'That's some dowdy outfit she's got on.' Merc's eyes became thin slits of scorn. She was wearing a cream, long-sleeved and collared blouse, which was tucked into the lilac skirt. But even Merc could see that her attire didn't matter. There was something in her carriage that made clothes irrelevant. The litheness of her long limbs was apparent even though she was all covered up.

She turned away just then, leaving Anil and his friends with a view of the thick hair cascading down her back in big, loose curls.

'We need to find out before she goes.' Anil rose quickly

as she started walking towards the exit. 'Come on, help me. Do something.' He turned to his friends.

'Just go up to her. What's the big deal? And hurry up, man. I've hung around here long enough for your sake.' Merc stretched ostentatiously, flexing his muscles, enjoying the glances being thrown in his direction. He was striking in an unidentifiable way. People looked and looked again, trying to work out the riddle of the shaved head and blue eyes and skin the colour of strong black coffee browned with a drop of milk.

'I don't know what to say.' Each word Anil uttered felt grey in his mouth. She had stopped by the exit and was chatting to another guy.

'You spend hours listening to love songs and you still can't tune a chick.' Merc shook his head and started making his way towards her. The rest of them followed, in height order – first Anil, who was a head taller than the others, then Jateen, and then Hardy. Anil ran a hand through the short, dark spikes of his hair and checked that his collar was turned up.

As they approached Merc recognized the guy she was with as someone from his art history course. He knew the face but not the name. He charged up and administered a punch on the shoulder as greeting, 'Hey, I didn't expect to see you here.'

While they talked Anil took the chance to look at her more closely. She was very tall. Perfect for me, he thought. If he stood straight, looked ahead and pulled her close, she would slot right into him: the dome of her head a shelf for his chin. He noticed a white line cutting through the twin peaks of her upper lip. It was as though her creator, stunned by the beauty he'd chiselled, had momentarily let his scalpel slip – and marred his own perfection. Anil could not tell if the scar was from a rectified harelip, or some other accident. He felt only its devastating poignancy – the pain it implied even when the mouth stretched into a smile. As it did momentarily, in response to Merc's brief introduction of the three friends pressing up behind him.

'This is Hardeep, who we call Hardy. And Jateen, who's JT. And this . . .' he gestured as if to usher someone on stage, 'is Anil. Except tonight he deserves to be dubbed Nil, because that's what I'd give him out of ten for dragging us to this concert.'

'Don't tell me you didn't like it?' The art history student, Zahid, gawped at Merc.

Hardy and JT weighed in with their own approbations. 'The guy's a fool.'

'Where's your soul, bwana?'

'All I hear is a fat man straining his voice until it begins to crack. And I can't ignore the fact that the lyrics are religious. Just knowing that is enough to put me off.'

As Merc continued to defend himself, the girl's gaze started to wander, scanning the rows of shoes lined against the wall. Then she slipped away while Anil watched in a state of poised tension. He was ready to race after her if she went out of sight. She found her flat gold shoes and put them on before being surrounded by a group of girls. After a moment she turned and beckoned. 'Zahid!'

Her voice was like a tickle across Anil's senses: the full, throaty depth of it unexpected.

'Hey, I better go,' Zahid said. 'Look, what are you guys up to? A few of us are heading down the road to my flat. Why don't you come along?'

'Nah—' Merc started, until a kick in the heel stopped him. 'I mean, I don't know.' He turned to his friends. 'Are you up for it?'

'Sawa. Why not?' Anil tried to sound casual. The other two shrugged.

'Good. Come on.' Zahid started towards the group of girls.

'I thought we were going clubbing.' Merc lagged behind and hissed at Anil. 'That was the deal, mazeh.' He clutched at the upturned cuff of Anil's slim-fitting, charcoal shirt. 'It's the only reason I agreed to come to this sing-song of yours.'

'Who says the night is over? We can go later.' Anil doubted they would, but it was all he could say to ward off Merc's irritation. His eyes skimmed the crowd furtively. She'd moved! Within seconds she had drifted to the other side of the room and was standing in a queue of people waiting to speak to the qawwals.

'Lina!' Zahid called and waved to get her attention.

'Who is she?' A hint of dislike was already tugging down the corners of Merc's mouth.

But Anil heard nothing else. He saw, instantly, that her name was the mirror image of his. LINA ANIL LINA ANIL LINA ANIL. He ran the sounds through his mind. Her name was the confirmation of his instincts. She is the one, he thought.

Rush

A MESSAGE FLASHES UP on Lina's computer screen, obscuring the document she's trying to read.

Terror alert in Piccadilly.
Severe disruptions to many underground services.
<u>More details.</u>

She frowns; a little pi-shaped symbol appears in the crook between her brows. She puts her finger on <u>More details</u> and a new window slides into view, describing the discovery of 'suspect packages' left lying on benches at various tube stations in central London. The site reports that most underground services have been suspended.

There's less than an hour to go before Lina has to meet Anil. 'Shut down,' she says, and her computer begins to turn itself off. Normally, the journey to Café Lafin takes about twenty minutes. But if there really are delays with transport it'll be longer, and she can't be late today, no matter what.

On her desk the debris of the day lies scattered, washed in by the tides of post and meetings and unfulfilled intentions. She has been distracted since morning: read documents without taking in a word, come off the telephone only to realize she can't recall what the conversation she's just finished was about. Now she pushes things into piles suggestive of order, and wonders at the slight tremble of her hands, the tremors in her heart. She gives herself a disapproving shake before leaving the high-ceilinged, blue-walled sanctuary of her office.

'You should make a move soon,' she advises her colleagues as she passes by and tells them about the alert. 'It's not going to be a smooth journey home.' She could probably walk the whole way if it wasn't for her high heels. But then again, she doesn't want to arrive for their rendezvous a damp, dishevelled mess. She has to look her best.

I'll get a taxi, she decides, as she enters the bathroom and eyes herself critically – though not without some satisfaction – in the mirror above the basin. She remembers what her father once said: 'At the end of your life, your face will show how you've lived.' She's not doing too badly, she thinks, for someone who's about half way through, though she does wish her eyes were brighter. The golden green of each iris has darkened over the years to a more sombre shade. Maybe her tearful twenties leached all lustre from her gaze. That decade of crying. Ya Allah. She has not wept so much since; in fact, has hardly been able to cry at all. Except when – her body stiffens. No, she can't think about that now. She uses an index finger to smooth out the crease of pain that's furled at her brow. She doesn't see, despite her father's words, the pertinence in the shape of that wrinkle, that pi-like sign. She is now stamped with this irrational number, which, if written out in full, would never end. A symbol of her own irresolution, the endless contradictory impulses of her heart.

She leans in over the basin, moving closer to the mirror to apply some lipstick. The synthetic colour slides over the contours of her mouth, almost rubbing out all trace of that

21

scar from a childhood accident. She recalls the first time Anil touched it – and she is a student again, running, in flat sensible shoes, towards the moment when everything really started.

Lina came out of St Paul's tube station and hurried towards the cathedral, pushing flying hair from her mouth and eyes. Crisp red leaves skittered diagonally across her path, like panicked crabs. In her mind she rehearsed apologies, trying to find excuses convincing enough to turn her own weakness into something accidental. Having started off with a day unencumbered by any appointments except the late-afternoon meeting with Anil, she had somehow managed to string the hours with a succession of commitments, which ended up jostling each other like too many pendants on a chain.

She still didn't understand how her plan for a quiet day working at the university library had been transformed into hours of unfruitfulness: an unsuccessful hunt for a research paper, a long lunch with someone she didn't especially like, and then an impromptu meeting with her tutor just as she was leaving to meet Anil.

She'd ended up chatting to her tutor for longer than expected, and was already running late when she got on to the tube. Then she'd missed her stop and had to backtrack, losing another fifteen minutes – all because a senseless story had grabbed her attention. She'd picked up a discarded newspaper and started to read an article under the headline: 'NUDE SWORDSMAN SLAYS WORSHIPPERS'.

A naked man brandishing a three-foot-long samurai sword charged into St Andrew's Roman Catholic Church in Thornton Heath, Croydon, during the Sunday service. The

22

man randomly attacked the congregation, injuring several of them before he was finally overpowered.

Witnesses said there was screaming and panic during the incident, and many people ran from the church into the adjoining hall. One parishioner apparently attempted to dissuade the attacker by thrusting a large crucifix in his face.

An off-duty policeman, Tom Tracey, eventually overcame the attacker by using a six-foot long organ pipe. 'Five minutes previously I was singing the psalm – the next thing I was fighting with a sword-wielding madman,' he said.

Victims were taken to a nearby hospital where their injuries were described as 'horrific'. It is not yet clear why the crime was perpetrated.

Slowly, she'd folded up the paper, put it to one side and tried to stem the rush of associations the article had triggered. Here was another story to undermine her old assumption that one was always guaranteed safety in any house of God. There had been enough examples recently. The destruction of the Babri Mosque in Ayodhya, India; the crushing to death of Tutsis in a church during the Rwandan genocide. In the wake of these atrocities her father, Shareef, had said, 'There is only one place no one can ever touch – and that is your conscience. Only a man's conscience cannot be defiled by anyone else.'

Only one's conscience cannot be defiled by another . . . Lina was turning this over in her head when a voice on the train had warned: 'Mind the gap.' For an instant she wondered if it was an exhortation to watch out for the great chasm between aspiration and reality – between her notions of how she must live and the increasingly strong impulses of her heart. 'Please stand clear of the doors. Mind the doors.' The 'beep beep beep beep beep' that followed the announcement had pierced her reverie and had her bolting towards the exit. Except that the doors had shut before she could reach them, and she'd seen the red letters spelling ST PAUL'S start moving away, faster and faster, until the train entered the dark of a tunnel. Lina had wondered if this was meant to be a sign: if the doors should be closed on the friendship she'd started with Anil, if missing the stop was an indication that she shouldn't go to him at all now. But her conscience had pleaded against standing him up – the same conscience that questioned why she was seeing him at all.

Back at the right station, she ran towards St Paul's Cathedral as if the two minutes she might gain would make all the difference. She wondered if Anil was alone. The first time he had invited her to meet him, outside Lloyd's of London, his three friends had been there and had trailed behind them, arguing about the merits of the building while Anil extolled its virtues and revered its creator, Richard Rogers.

'What do you see that's unusual about this structure?' Anil had asked Lina, one thumb hooked under the strap of the messenger bag that hung over his left shoulder.

Unsure what she should be looking for, she'd studied the armoury of steel girders, pipes and stairwells that dressed the building. She'd found herself wanting to please him with her answer, despite knowing nothing about architecture. Tentatively, she'd described what she saw, and he'd encouraged her like a teacher: 'Exactly. Yes. What else?'

All the while, they were accompanied by a symphony of sarcasm and sniggers. Merc's voice was the loudest:

'Whose idea of romance is a lecture on postmodern architecture?' But Lina was moved by the rapture in Anil's words and the novelty of what he showed her.

'What's brilliant is the way the architect has completely redefined the concept of space. He's turned utilities into ornamentation,' he said. His chin jutted upwards, the jaw bordered by a thin line of sideburns that met at the cleft of his chin. 'Just think of the space a lift takes inside a building and then consider the genius of putting it outside, so that it becomes a beautiful piece of glass jewellery decorating the façade.'

'You have one crazy notion of beauty.' Merc sneered. 'This whole inside-out approach just looks gimmicky to me. And rather messy.'

Anil turned calmly to his friend. 'This from the guy who's doing his dissertation on the aesthetics of violence? You like your human beings better with their blood and guts on display, but the façades of buildings have to be pristine?'

'Weh-weh.' Merc narrowed his eyes. 'I will smack you to the point that you remember your forefathers!'

Lina pulled at the sleeves of her coat. The lingo used by the guys was impenetrable to her. Worried that a fight might break out, she cleared her throat to say something. But she was pre-empted by laughter as they gave each other high fives to celebrate their rudeness. At such moments she felt incidental – then Anil would look her in the eye and start talking and, suddenly, nobody else counted.

It had been almost the same another time when she'd met him at the National Gallery. Merc had come along and escorted them for a while before heading off to do some research. 'Don't bore her with your running commentaries! Make sure you show her all the nudes!'

he'd called to them, as if heaping bawdy blessings on a newly married couple. People turned and stared, alerted first by his loud manner and then arrested by the body displayed under his 'look at me' clothes: a long-sleeved tight black T-shirt and narrow trousers pinned to his hips with a designer belt. Even Anil, who stood out in most crowds as the niftiest dresser, could look shabby beside his slick friend.

Lina felt uncomfortable in Merc's presence. He was not especially friendly and even his changing contact lenses couldn't mask the distrust in his eyes: blue, green, grey – every hue was tinged with doubt. Anil told her that Merc, who was doing an MA in art history, was the best person to visit the gallery with.

'He knows so much about the paintings and the artists. You see things differently because of what he tells you. These, for example . . .' Anil gestured at the walls, '. . . begin to make full sense only if you know your Bible stories well. Of course, when they were painted, society was highly religious and so even a peasant would recognize the scene. Nowadays fewer people know or care about the content of such works, even though they might appreciate their beauty.'

Like me, Lina thought, stopping in front of a large oil painting. 'I would guess this is a religious painting because that's Jesus.' She pointed a finger at the central long-haired and bearded figure. 'But I have no idea what it's about.'

'Didn't you do Bible studies at school?'

'Well, we had to learn about all religions at my state school, but we only got a basic insight into them.' Outside school, Islam was the faith in which she'd been instructed, learning the Koran by rote from the age of five. By the time she was ten she could recite vast chunks of the

Arabic text from memory, though she'd had little idea what they meant.

'OK, but I'm sure you know enough to be able to work out some things about this painting. Here, let's sit down.' There was a bench facing the image. They perched on it side by side. He pulled at the strap of his bag so that the bulk of it rested behind him. Several folds of her long, pleated skirt bunched up against his jeans, and the tassels of her red scarf brushed the sleeve of his butter-yellow cashmere sweater.

'Now, just look at it again.'

Lina's eyes zigzagged over the canvas. She concentrated so hard on discovering some mystery that the obvious eluded her. When she didn't speak Anil prompted her.

'How many other people are there in the picture?'

She counted. 'Twelve men – oh, so they're his disciples?'

'Exactly, you see? You've already been able to figure out a bit more by using your knowledge. Now look again, more carefully.'

'I don't know what to look for.' She kept whispering, even though Anil wasn't. She hadn't been to many art galleries but had a sense you weren't supposed to talk in them. A bit like how you had to be quiet in temples.

'What do you notice about Jesus?'

'The holes? In his hands and feet?' She felt stupid for not having seen them immediately. 'He's been crucified, right?'

'Yeah, so now you can probably guess what the scene is.'

Lina shook her head in mortification. Though Anil was being nice, she could detect his surprise at her ignorance. But she ventured another shot at interpretation because his patience reminded her of her father, who always encouraged her to keep at things. 'There's no failure in trying,' he liked to say.

'I'm still not sure. I mean, all I know is that Jesus was crucified and then he came back to life. So presumably this is after that?'

'Well, after his resurrection Jesus appeared to his disciples, but one of them, Thomas, wasn't there and didn't believe the others when they told him. So then Jesus reappeared and showed Thomas – that's him, the one in front wearing red and green – his wounds and let him touch them. That's when Jesus said: "Blessed are they that have not seen and yet have believed". See?' Anil gestured at the little plaque on which details of the painting were listed. 'It's called *The Incredulity of Saint Thomas*.'

'How do you know all that? Have you seen this before?'

'Sure, I've seen it several times, but I recognized the story in the painting the first time.' Anil said this as if it was the most natural thing to do.

'How come you know the Bible so well?'

'I went to a Christian school. We had proper Bible study classes and full on prayer services every morning. We even had a few hours a week devoted to hymn practice. So I know more about Christianity than any other religion.' He leaned back on both hands, taking advantage of the wide wooden bench.

'Did you like it?' She turned to face him properly and her softly curled hair spilled over one cheek.

'I was totally seduced! I joined the Bible Club and decided I wanted to be a Christian.' He was studying the painting again, as if some idea had just occurred to him.

'No way!' Her mouth hung open for a moment.

Suddenly Anil pulled his bag around and undid the

buckle of one pocket. He took out a pen and a tiny pad of plain white paper. 'Sorry,' he smiled at Lina. 'I just need a sec.' He balanced the pad above his knee and began drawing.

Lina noted the over-new shine of his black leather trainers. The white stripes along the sides were so pristine they had the glare of neon. Her own suede boots were in need of replacement. She quickly drew her feet under the bench.

The abstract lines on Anil's pad accumulated to form a multi-faceted prism like structure. The sapphire at the top of his platinum pen gleamed. His thumb pressed over the stone as he clicked the nib back in. 'I had to get that done before I lost it.'

'That's OK.' Lina had seen him break off doing things and start jotting before. 'So, um, what did your parents say, when you converted?'

'I only told my mum, but for some reason she mentioned it to my dad. She thought he'd be amused.' He snorted. 'He threatened to throw me out of the house unless I "renounced my faith", as he put it.'

'Oh, my God. So what did you do?'

'I was only nine years old, so the easiest option was to say I was no longer a Christian. Though I think I did remain one in my heart, for a while.'

'Are your parents really religious?' She couldn't keep her eyes fixed on his.

'No! The only Sikh things about my dad are his turban and his kara. And the only day in the Sikh calendar that we ever celebrated was Diwali, just because it was a great excuse to have a party and shoot fireworks. But, for some reason, he was outraged that I could reject the religion of my birth.' He stood up.

'That's so weird, isn't it? That they would be against you changing faith even though they don't really practise it themselves? I mean, I could understand it if they were really devout . . .' She rose slowly, still caught in the net of their conversation. Their most important one yet, she felt, coming so close, as it did, to what troubled her each time she thought of him. 'But you're not a Christian any more?'

He shook his head.

'Or a Sikh?'

'You know what? I'm not inclined any particular way as far as religion goes.'

She'd hoped he'd turn the question around and ask her what she believed. It would have been a chance to make their differences apparent. But he seemed more eager to resume the subject of art.

The subsequent hour was the loveliest she'd spent with anyone. They went through doorways framed in carved dark wood, and elaborate hallways where the walls were hung with rich Venetian fabric. Lina noticed the colour of each room before the paintings hanging there: blue, green, gold and a red so deep it could have been a backdrop of fresh blood. They passed ornate marble pillars, and paintings so large that Lina felt a lifetime of looking might not suffice to see the whole image.

Anil showed her the masterpieces, which, he claimed, 'You have to have seen at least once.' He couldn't believe she had never visited the gallery, though she'd been living in London for almost three years. And she was surprised by how much his astonishment upset her, making her feel stupid. So she listened intently to what he told her, trying to memorize the names of painters, and the styles he described. Yet immediately afterwards, she could only recall half of it. And a week later, only a couple of images still remained in her mind: Van Gogh's mustardy yellow sunflowers and a painting of Venus and Mars by Botticelli. Mars sleeping with his mouth tenderly open and his body extended gracefully towards Venus who, serene and contemplative, was watching him. 'What I adore about Botticelli's women,' Anil had said, looking at her as if she was one of them, 'is how they are so elegant, so sensual and, still, they have an innocent, spiritual aura.'

How different he had been that afternoon from the broody person she'd met at Zahid's flat after the concert. Then he had seemed awkward and tongue-tied amidst his bantering pals. He had spoken only when she asked him directly what he thought of the concert, and even then he'd been hesitant, as if speaking English for the first time. It transpired that they loved the same music, the same singers. He told her he had seen Nusrat Fateh Ali Khan perform live in Nairobi and, when she begged for every detail, he was able to describe the colour of the kurta that the maestro had been wearing, and the order in which he'd sung each qawwali. When Lina tried to discuss the nuances of the lyrics with him, she learned that Anil did not speak Urdu.

'So what do you talk at home?' she wondered.

'English,' he said, scratching one of the long, thin sideburns that looked as if they had been meticulously measured and drawn along his face. 'My parents sometimes speak Punjabi, so I've got a basic grasp of that, which can help with figuring out Urdu. But mostly, when I really like a qawwali, I get my mum to translate it for me. She's fluent in Urdu, and I'm picking up bits from her.' He joked that he had acquired a foreign vocabulary of infatuation and devotion, intoxication and loneliness.

'The essentials,' Lina had said.

31

*　*　*

'I'm sorry,' she said, running up the steps at the main entrance of St Paul's Cathedral. Anil was standing, with arms crossed over his broad chest, in the narrow gap between a pair of Corinthian columns. The collars of his shirt and coat were turned up, the stiff edges almost grazing the lobes of his ears. Worry, which had started to flare across his body like a bad itch, melted into dampness across his palms. He was suddenly thankful that they wouldn't shake hands in greeting. To date, they had acknowledged each other only with smiles and hellos. When they touched it had been accidental: a brush of knees or elbows while sitting beside each other. And once, when she was leaning over to point out something, her cheek had grazed his arm: a fleeting, teasing caress.

'My God, it's huge.' Lina took in the two tiers of columns and the great bell towers that rose up from each end of the cathedral. One of them bore the time and announced in golden Roman numerals that she was over an hour late. 'I'm *so* sorry.' Her eyes and mouth shrank in embarrassment. 'Thanks for waiting . . . so long. I just . . . I don't know. It was one thing after another. And the time just . . .' She snapped her fingers.

'At least you made it. Shall we go in?'

'The others?' She glanced around. 'They're not here?'

'No, they were busy.' Busy wondering where he was, probably. Anil wiped his hands on his brown corduroy trousers as they entered the nave of the cathedral. He'd made vague claims about a project deadline to get out of the game of squash the friends had been scheduled to play. He hadn't said he wanted to see Lina alone. It would have meant putting up with jokes beforehand and facing an interrogation afterwards. And, for the first time, he felt a need to protect a little part of himself from them.

Suddenly, Lina was nervous. She fingered the ends of her hair. Tousled by the wind, it had more volume, and emphasized the thinness of her face, making her chin seem longer. For all the minor irritations having Anil's friends around entailed, they had provided a convenient buffer against the slowly unfolding truth that she was trying to deny.

When she gasped it was more at being dwarfed by her own feelings than the tremendous dome under which they had arrived. The floor of the cathedral was shaped like a cross and they were standing at the heart of it.

'Incredible, isn't it?' Anil spun around and opened his arms. The cuffs of his striped shirt rode up, revealing strong wrists. There was a thick gold kara, a symbol of Sikhism, on the right one. 'It's the second largest cathedral dome in the world.' Then he started pointing out different features and telling her about the architect, Sir Christopher Wren. 'He took inspiration from everywhere. Remember those twin columns at the front? Well, they're based on ones at the Louvre. And the dome, the porches – they're all taken from what he saw at other churches. The genius lies in the way he combined everything so harmoniously. And he did it against so much opposition. The church hated his original design! They thought it was too modern. He had to keep watering down his vision until they approved it. But he was clever, he got sanction from the king to make variations on the agreed plan, and basically constructed the original building he wanted right under the noses of the clergy. Of course, by the time they realized it was too late!' His face opened into laughter. The gums above his top teeth were exposed and shone pink.

The fine down on Lina's face stood to attention as a

light spray of mirth sprang from his mouth and landed on her forehead. 'You could apply to be one of their official tour guides.'

'Thanks. It's good to know there's something I can fall back on if my other plans don't work out.'

Afraid to ask about these, Lina turned slowly to take in the murals, the ornate gilding and the galleries that lined the dome. When she looked down again, the black and white tiles on the floor seemed to slide into the vortex at her feet. She put a hand on Anil's arm to steady herself. 'You seem to admire people who do things differently.'

He closed his eyes for a moment and appeared to think before replying. In fact, he was trying to reclaim his body, all of which had become inconsequential in relation to the burning patch under her palm. 'I like it when people dare to challenge the prevailing orthodoxy.' Her hand slipped away and he could breathe again. 'I believe in fighting for what you want.'

His conviction persuaded Lina, who didn't know that he'd never had to struggle for anything.

'Come.' Anil took Lina's hand. 'I want to show you something else.' Both were quiet at this first deliberate pressing of flesh against flesh. Around them people were starting to fill up the pews. 'I think the evening service might start soon. We need to be quick, otherwise it won't work so well.'

He took her up an endless staircase. The higher they went, the more his grip on her tightened. Towards the top of the 259 steps it was the strength of his clutch that propelled her along. Her legs had become woolly leaden things, inordinately heavy, and yet trembling like thread. There was a tightness in her chest which couldn't just be attributed to the strenuous climb.

Then they were in the Whispering Gallery. Anil explained that it got its name from a quirk in construction, which made a whisper against its walls audible on the opposite side. He led her to a section where there was no one else. 'Stay here.' He left her standing in front of a wall and disappeared behind the one directly opposite.

Lina?

His voice wafted softly towards her. A moment later his head peeked out from the edge of the wall, eyebrows lifted in enquiry. She nodded to confirm that she'd heard him. Once he was out of sight, he spoke again. At the same time, below them, a priest began a rumbling welcome to the congregation.

. . . FIND IN THE WORDS OF THOMAS À KEMPIS . . .

I've been wanting to tell you for weeks.
I think you can guess –
LOVE IS A GREAT THING, YEA, A GREAT
AND THOROUGH GOOD.

Anil worried that whatever he said might be drowned out by the microphone-enhanced voice that was blowing through the cathedral. But he went on:

I felt something from the first time I saw you.
Like, I can't explain – it was meant to be. Even our
names . . .
LOVE FLIES, RUNS AND REJOICES;
IT IS FREE AND NOTHING CAN HOLD IT BACK.
The more I know you, the more I want to know.

Lina's hands were joined, palm to palm, with the index fingers pressing hard against her lips and the thumbs digging into the soft valley beneath her jaw. The simultaneous boldness and shyness of Anil's gesture moved and amused her. She wanted to skip in response to his

35

adoration, but a history of compliance was binding her feet. Her mother's face loomed before her, a finger wagging in warning as she mouthed her favourite saying, 'Don't put a question mark where Allah has put a full stop.' There was no way around the great bulwark of Iman's expectations. But then, Lina saw her father with his gentle equivocations. Shareef's way of applying pressure was to say, 'You must do the right thing. It is always either the easiest or the hardest course of action. Usually, the latter.' Lina found herself wondering if succumbing to Anil could possibly be the rightest of all rights, because it felt at once supremely easy and excruciatingly hard.

> LOVE FEELS NO BURDEN, THINKS NOTHING
> OF TROUBLE,
> ATTEMPTS WHAT IS ABOVE ITS STRENGTH,
> *I can't go away and not speak to you for a month.*
> *I guess what I'm asking, if you agree, is . . .*

No. Oh no! Lina thought.

> *I've fallen –*
> LOVE DIVINE ALL LOVES EXCELLING
> JOY OF HEAVEN TO EARTH COME DOWN

He appeared again as the Charles Wesley hymn filled the cathedral. As he walked towards her, she felt a strange amalgam of elation, guilt and ominous premonition.

Anil was in front of her. They stood face to face – him looking down, her up – and read each other's eyes for all the feelings that words could not measure. Then his finger pressed against Lina's lips – as if to silence any objection.

'Does it hurt?'

For a second she thought he'd glimpsed the agony of indecision in her heart – until his finger started to trace the scar on her upper lip.

'No.' She couldn't explain that the spot was at once

supremely sensitive and strangely numb, because – suddenly – his lips were on hers.

Astaghfirullah! Allah forgive me! She begged quietly.

Certain moments come to stand out in memory like rocks rising treacherously from the sea. I am repeatedly tossed against these pernicious outcrops of the past. I lie broken, like a wrecked ship, after the storm of deceit that you unleashed on me. One image, above all, continues to haunt me: you in the doorway, your face half-turned away as you gave me the most pathetic justification anyone can. Four words which claim the weight of aeons and offer the impression of finality. Four words which millions around the world use as benediction, consolation or excuse. Four odious, if not to say otiose, words, which ruined my life: It is god's will.

Your revelation seemed to come out of nowhere. It had the suddenness of an accident: impact – pain – followed by the stunned sense of having survived. In the days that followed, I was shocked at how you just hit and ran. Now I know you must have been mulling over the decision for months, preparing yourself, while I was given less than one hour to absorb it. And then you were gone.

You boarded a plane and headed East, towards a country you called home but didn't want to live in. A woman you were meant to marry but hadn't ever met. A family you loved but had avoided visiting for years. And a future over which you were content to let god's will, instead of your own, preside. Who are you? Surely not the man I had loved and lived with for five years?

How could this have happened to us? Of course, now it's easy to find portents everywhere. One reverse glance, and warnings flash at me like road signs picked out by a car's headlights.

Your last four words continue to echo in my ears, a mantra of irrationality that I am going half-mad trying to fathom. I can't quite bring myself to write them down again. The way I can't write your name, or any of the variations on it that I used as endearments. That's why there's no addressee at the top of this letter – or accusation, or attempt to understand, or – whatever it is.

I suspect there's nothing behind those four words except cowardice. Nevertheless, I can't stop examining them, hoping their convoluted mystery might yield a glimmer of sense. Logic is its own justification. I'd accept logic, even if it confounded my heart.

Stop trying to work out what happened – my brother, Lucas, said – it'll never be clear. Religion and logic don't mix. They're like oil and water. However much you try shaking them about together, they separate eventually; the oil spreading over the water, the way faith does over reason, asphyxiating it.

I could only wonder how come I didn't notice that slimy film of unreason before. Because I was in love and blind! Lucas insisted.

But Lucas is wrong. I fell for you because I saw our differences. More than all our similarities, they were what fascinated me: your quiet piety in the face of the careless abandon of that time, your Indian accent which occasionally transformed the most banal English words into moments of delicious scandal – like when you once asked for a 'cock' instead of a coke and got a gallant offer from the flattered waiter. How we laughed! I was so impressed by the way you effortlessly socialized, managing to discuss or dance through the night, without ever taking a drop of the drink that fuelled everybody else – but damn it, this isn't meant to be any kind of tribute, least of all a list of your virtues.

See how memory creeps up and tries to sugar the bitter truth. I long for a brain enema that could purge you from my thoughts. I half-hope writing might be a kind of exorcism: unsticking the words from my mind and binding them to the page. Perhaps on paper my bewilderment will find some kind of coherence. And if not, there is always the possibility that you might, your dear god being willing, of course, read this one day and be ashamed.

Palazzo Mayur

INSIDE A BIG VILLA in the Loresho district of Nairobi, fenced in by high walls and electric wire, Minnie Mayur reclined on a white leather chaise longue. One arm was thrown back over her head, the other out-stretched with cupped palm. Sunlight poured in from wide French windows around her and filled the bowl of the room like a light, clear consommé.

'It's too hot, really.' Minnie sighed and pushed away the book on her lap. *The Love Sonnets of Ghalib* fell open on its spine, and its pages fluttered gently in the eddies of air being hummed by the air conditioning. Beneath the book, the pleats of Minnie's yellow and orange sari had fanned open over her legs. She looked around and was satisfied by what she saw: shelves filled with books arranged according to the colour of their spines, and a huge earthenware vase – almost as tall as her – engraved with hundreds of different faces. That was it. The rest of the large space was empty, just metres of marble floor extending towards the walls. Minnie wanted it this way so there'd be room to think.

'How big are your thoughts?' her husband, Pravar, had wondered. But it was here, lying on her chaise longue, that Minnie did most of her reflecting and, what she called – though there was rarely evidence for it – composing. She believed she had always been at her most creative while horizontal (her husband, if asked, might have asserted otherwise). Minnie claimed her best verses came to her during sleep. The sad thing was, she could never remember them on waking.

'All the masterpieces that have come to me and then – gone!' she would complain to those in her literary circle. One of them had joked that she ought to publish a blank book of verse under the title *Paradise Lost*. Behind her back, worse things were said: 'You know that warning, don't let your imagination run away with you? Well, Minnie Mayur's has run without her.'

Outside, the water sprinklers were wooing the lawn to ever more lush expressions of green. Above this a clicking sound could be heard, like nails being clipped. The noise came from Joyce, who was sitting cross-legged on the floor and shelling pistachios. She dropped the shells into the pocket of her white apron and put the kernels into Minnie's waiting hand. The nuts were then tossed, with spectacular speed, into Minnie's mouth. Joyce could not shell fast enough to keep up with her mistress's consumption.

'Where is Anil?' The words emerged through bouts of crunching.

Joyce pushed out her lower lip and shook her head. The ruffled knot on the scarf tied around it twitched like a small bird.

'But he's home, nah? Or has he gone out again?' She had little to do except worry about him. 'Oh God, what will become of this boy?' Her days were spent following fitness regimes, planning parties, and reading or trying to write Urdu poetry. This left plenty of time for speculation about her only child, to whom, she detected, something wonderful had recently happened. She knew it involved a girl, though Anil refused to give her any details, as if they were too precious to be shared. Minnie had, however, managed to extract the girl's name from Merc, who dismissed her as 'just another one of Anil's infatuations'. The friend, for all his closeness, could not know better than the mother. Something was different this time. Minnie spotted it in the qawwalis Anil selected for her to translate, and in the extra attention he was paying to learning Urdu, instead of being content just with a translation, as he had been before.

'Anil is he-ah. Sum-weh-ah,' Joyce said. She'd picked up the sound of flip-flops slapping the marble floor – everything echoed slightly in this huge house with its minimalist furniture. The pace and force of the footsteps told Joyce they must be Anil's. Her ears were more sensitively tuned to his whereabouts than his mother's. She had looked after him since he was born.

'Coming, going. Coming, going. This boy is making me restless.' Minnie chewed more fiercely.

Anil walked in with Merc. Both were wearing shorts. The muscles in their lean calves rippled as they moved. Merc was the lither of the pair, his physique boasting a natural athleticism.

'There you are!' Minnie opened her arms and waited for him to come and hug her. 'I was just asking Joyce about you. My goodness, I've hardly seen you since you came back from London. Always you're in and out without a word, like this is a hotel or something.' She ruffled the carefully gelled spikes of his hair. 'Oh my God, Anil, how much wax have you used? Every strand feels like copper wire.'

He eased out of her grasp, using his fingers to plump up the hair which his mother's touch had flattened. 'Why don't you buy ready shelled nuts?' He sank down on the floor next to Joyce, winked at her, and took a handful of pistachios from the half-full plastic bag.

43

Merc had stopped at a bookshelf and was scanning the row of violet to blue spines. He had learned when and how to keep his distance in this family, who had treated him kindly and yet, in spite of their best efforts, had not been able to forget that he wasn't one of them. If it hadn't been for the tragedy with his mother, and Minnie's subsequent guilt, perhaps he would not have been quite so welcome here. Only Anil's affection was completely genuine, he suspected, untainted by considerations of race and history.

'Have you tasted the shelled ones? Soft as raisins, usually. Nothing can stay crisp in this heat.'

'Then you should shell them yourself.' Anil concentrated on prising open a stubborn nut. 'Don't you agree, Mama Jo?'

Joyce pretended not to have heard him. She knew that his disapproval of Minnie, though sincere, was superficial. In a moment he would be issuing his own orders without a thought. But Joyce did not mind. She would do anything for this boy who had grown up playing amongst her own children, and still called her mama.

'I can't. I had a manicure yesterday.' Minnie stretched out a hand to admire the pink ovals gleaming at the ends of her plump, brown fingers. 'And I don't want to ruin my nails before tonight. I hope you're going to be here. I'm having one of my sorries.'

Anil resisted the impulse to say 'soirée'. Even a series of French lessons hadn't corrected Minnie's pronunciation. Her Indian accent was spread as thickly across her words as the gloss was over her lips. When Anil had suggested that she refer to the monthly gatherings as a salon she had refused: 'No thanks, *please*, that would make me sound like a hairdresser.'

'I don't know if I'll be there, Ma. I'm not in the mood.'

'Why? Have you sealed up all good moods in the letters you write and post every day to your new London-Low?' She made love sound like something cattle did.

Anil rolled his eyes. She'd been teasing him incessantly about these missives and their mysterious recipient. 'I just don't feel like socializing with a bunch of people I don't know.'

'Oh my God, what nonsense does this boy talk? You know the whole crowd almost, since you were a small boy. There are only a few new faces. Bring me some water, Joyce, please. These nuts have just dried out my mouth.' Minnie licked her lips. 'Here, you have the rest.' She passed what was left in her hand to Anil.

'Anyway,' Anil examined the little lime-green pods, with their rosy bellies. 'I'm supposed to be going out with Merc and all tonight. Isn't it?' He called to his friend, who pretended to be too absorbed to reply.

Minnie shook her head. 'Almost every day you go out with the boys and today I am asking you specially to give me some time, and you want to tell me no. Merc? It's not right, is it?'

'You should listen to her, mazeh.' Merc spoke without looking up from the book he was flicking through.

'I've invited your dad, Merc, so I hope you will come as well. At least this one can't complain that he won't have company.'

'I don't know, Ma. Like I told you, I'm not really in the mood.'

'You haven't been in the mood for anything, mazeh. Except moping.' Merc looked up. His eyes today were a frosty pastel green.

'Really, it's true. Even the post office, I think, has seen

more of you this trip than your mother. Now I know the meaning of that saying: a daughter is yours all her life, a son is yours until he finds a wife. You have only found a girlfriend, and already parents don't matter. That's what I think.'

'Oh, Ma, come on. Don't be so over-dramatic.'

Minnie reached for the tumbler of water balanced on a plate that Joyce was proffering. She sipped thoughtfully, as if some kind of inspiration might come to her. 'I wish you had a sister. She would be here when I needed her.'

Anil frowned at another uncooperative shell. He could feel his mother's expectation bearing down on him, trying to crack his resistance. Refusal, he knew, would dent her feelings, the way the unyielding shells had the tips of his fingers. 'OK, I'll come – just don't expect me to contribute anything.' When he was a child she'd displayed his paintings or got him to recite a poem on such evenings. And the last time he'd been home for one of the soirées, she'd taken some rough architectural drawings from his room, and without asking him, passed them around her guests saying, 'Anil has just done summer internship with Forrester and Partners in London.'

'The only thing I want from you is an opinion,' she now told her son. 'Don't sit there like a dullard. Let people see you've studied in the UK . . .'

'As if that in itself qualifies me for anything.' Anil absently dropped empty pistachio shells.

'I should hope it does. Why else did we send you there?' Minnie handed the glass back to waiting Joyce, then turned and propped herself on an elbow. Now that most people in Minnie's circle had equally big houses, cars, businesses and art collections, they sought to distinguish themselves by comparing their children's achievements.

'So, please, huh? Put away the low-sick face for tonight, and let everybody see Anil the artitech. And wear something white, Neelu, you always look best in white. At least, I think so.'

'I'm going to phone the other guys.' Anil pushed down on his heels and went from sitting to standing in one easy move. 'I'll tell them to come as well.'

'Can't you do anything without that bunch for even a few hours? Really, Anil. What about when you go see your girlfriend, do they tag along?'

'I wish you would stop making assumptions about my relationship status. And what's the big deal if some of my friends come? You're going to be surrounded by loads of people anyway. You won't even notice.' He started to walk out of the room with a briskness that suggested annoyance. The commitment between him and Lina was vague. She'd agreed that they could keep in touch over the holiday, but wouldn't give him her home phone-number because, she said, her parents would become suspicious if he called. He couldn't email either because her family didn't have a computer or the internet at home. So they had exchanged addresses, and subjected themselves to the delayed gratification of the postal service, and the excruciating ambiguity of words on a page.

Minnie sat up and tossed her head so that her hair swayed before settling in neat drapes over her ears and forehead. 'Oof, look at the mess he's made. Joyce, please, will you clear up all this.' Minnie waved at the residue of husks and nuts that Anil had left in his wake. She thought about his comment that she wouldn't notice him. How could she not? He was like a part of her that had wandered off outside the boundaries of her own being. Even when he was thousands of miles away, doing his own thing, she

47

was conscious of him, the way she was of the tiny, circular, grey floater on the periphery of her vision.

That's the difference between parents and kids, Minnie thought. Children can forget about parents, act as if they don't exist. While parents remain trapped by the perpetual and impossible desire to protect their offspring from the more painful consequences of living. It was sometimes crippling, this feeling, especially when you knew their weaknesses and intuited the scope for disaster. Anil, Minnie was aware, had one grave flaw: he was not a gracious loser.

She remembered how sullen he would become after school sports days if he didn't win every race. She had stood on the sidelines – it was always just her, because his father, Pravar, had been too busy – willing his victory; not because she cared if he came first, but because she couldn't bear to see the gloomy, withdrawn boy that second or third place would turn him into. Even these days, she could tell when he returned from a game of squash what the outcome had been. Either he'd mumble a greeting and disappear to his room, or he'd be punching the air and ready to do anything she asked.

Minnie used to think this competitive streak was inherited from his father. Now, she sometimes wondered if she was also responsible for it. In trying to give Anil everything, both she and Pravar had left him unable to accept any kind of setback. And, more than that, Minnie knew, she had been guilty of trying to manipulate things in her son's favour. At his birthdays, for example, when the kids played musical chairs or pass the parcel, she'd often stopped the music while Anil was near a chair or holding the parcel.

She would never forget overhearing a comment from

one attending mother to another: 'Since when does a birthday mean you win every prize at your own party?'

'Well, this *is* Pravar Mayur's boy we're talking about.'

After that Minnie had tried to be more circumspect about arranging things to Anil's advantage. And in fact, as he got older, it became harder to do so, anyway, for she didn't have the same control over the world as she did over the 'stop' and 'play' buttons of a stereo system. Fortunately, Anil was proving bright and determined enough to do well on his own. It was this Minnie preferred to dwell on, and not the incidents when things didn't go as he would like.

In the past, she had, amongst other things, caught him stealing from the bank during a spot of trouble in Monopoly, and surreptitiously moving the pieces on the chessboard to outdo his father. Once she'd confronted him over a sly chess manoeuvre.

'Anil! What are you doing?'

A knight had fallen over as his hand had leapt from the board. 'Nothing.'

'Will you really get any pleasure from such a false victory?' Minnie stared at him, her lips pursed in stern rebuke so that her face wouldn't betray any of the sympathy she felt. Pravar never let him win a single game.

Resentment rose off Anil like steam. With hands on thighs and shoulders pushed up to his ears, he continued to focus on the chessboard.

'You are almost good enough to beat your dad, now. All you have to do is practise more. Please move the pieces back like before. Quickly, huh, before he comes.' Minnie would have left it at that, but just as Anil was about to follow her advice, Pravar returned. He sensed the tension in the room – a rare thing between mother and son, who were normally on cosy terms. He looked at the board and saw the toppled knight.

'Cheating?' He said it like a gangster who anticipates his opponent's move only because it would have been his own next course of action. That question from his father, complicit in tone, had disconcerted Anil more than his mother's rebuke. Pravar started to laugh and held out his hand for a high five. Anil wasn't sure how to respond.

'The boy is like his father, he knows a little bit of heraferi is what gets you to the top. I've caught many cheats in my time, and do you know why? Because I know how they think. What do you call a Singh who's good at conning people?'

'Pravar!' Minnie's eyes narrowed in her oval face. 'This is not the time, really.' While she was relieved that Pravar didn't seem inclined to punish Anil severely, she didn't think launching into a frivolous word game was appropriate either.

'Come on eenie-Minnie-miney-mo, I'm sure you know the answer already. You're the expert amongst us.' She certainly had a wide vocabulary, even though her pronunciation sometimes faltered. 'Look at Anil, he has no idea!' Pravar clapped his hands and hooted. He wouldn't have known the word either, if an irate supplier hadn't accused him of it earlier that day.

Minnie knew, but didn't want to say.

'Come on, people, where are your brains today? What do you call a Singh who's good at conning others?' Pravar paused before revealing the answer. 'Flee-*cing*!'

'This is silly, Pravar. Are you teaching Anil that it's OK to cheat?'

'I don't need to teach him, Minnie. Anil already understands the way of the world. And what can I say but –

50

good! The sooner he learns the better.' Pravar sat down, easing the waistband of his trousers. 'Come on, high five,' he said.

Anil's hand came down slowly.

'Properly!' Pravar ordered. And the next instant his palm was red from a stinging smack. 'Ah-ha-ha, he's turning into a man.'

'He's only twelve years old.' Minnie twirled the diamond stud in her right ear lobe. She did not doubt that some guile was necessary to get on in life, but that wasn't what you told children. They had to be instructed in honesty, and then left alone to discover the deviousness in themselves and others. 'Pravar, please.' She spoke quietly. It was not often that she contradicted him. After all, Pravar Mayur, whose name translated as Chief Peacock, and who was known across town simply as Chief, always knew best.

Pravar looked from his standing wife to his seated son, whose bony knees jutted like promontories on either side of the chessboard. He smoothed his beard and shook his head. 'No, no, no, no. Absolutely. I'm not saying it's OK. I'm just explaining that in certain situations, if you really want something badly, you have to act outside the rules.'

'Honesty is always the best way. That's what I think.' Minnie directed this at Anil, who was looking into his lap and regretting that one unchecked impulse had led to this back and forth between his parents. He did not feel sorry for what he'd done, just annoyed that he'd been caught.

Pravar frowned and the wrinkles went all the way from his forehead to the apex of his turban. 'Oh, Minnie, who wouldn't prefer to be truthful?' Though, in fact, he rarely considered truth and was more influenced by convenience. 'Today my name is on the door, but in the future Anil's will be. He needs to have an idea of how things work. And I'm pleased to see that he's got the right instinct.' Pravar turned his attention back to the game. 'Now, my boy, let's see what you've done. Oh, I see, you've checkmated me. That's probably a little bit extreme. Next time you want to pull such a stunt . . .' He started rearranging the pieces, '. . . you have to be more subtle about it.'

'Oh, Merc? You're still here,' Minnie suddenly noticed that he hadn't left the room with Anil.

'I hope I'm not disturbing you. This book is quite fascinating.' He held it up for her to see.

'I haven't read that one.'

Merc knew as much. She hadn't even looked at many of the volumes that lined her walls. For many years she'd had an agreement with the owner of a local art bookshop that he would send her all the latest and most interesting publications. Perhaps she liked to collect them, as indications of intent.

'It's about faces. The history of portraiture.'

'Take it if you want, Merc. Have it.' She was always ready to give things away. Only someone who hadn't read and loved a book could let it go so easily.

'Maybe I'll borrow it.' He used the bookmark ribbon to mark his place in the book and then snapped it shut.

'This Lina girl,' Minnie ventured. 'What does she look like?'

He shrugged. The stretchy T-shirt he had on showed off his strong shoulders and narrow waist.

'She must be something special for Anil to be so taken with her. That's what I think.' She was always working the word 'think' into her sentences, as if to emphasize her cerebral processes.

Merc shrugged again.

Minnie realized he wasn't going to give away more. 'I have a feeling this one's got him good and proper.'

Upstairs in his room, Anil flopped on to the bed and stared at the ceiling. The afternoon sun bounced off the white walls and marble floor. After a moment Anil reached for one of the switches by the side of the bed. His touch produced an electric whirr, and then grey blinds began to unwind at each window. Soon the huge space around him was subdued by shadows, just like his days without Lina. His life in Kenya was a faded version of itself. 'Mazeh,' Merc had warned him that morning, 'you're going up way too fast.' As if love was a lift from which Anil could get off at a lower floor, instead of hurtling riskily to the zenith of feeling.

Since they'd all returned to Nairobi for the holidays two weeks ago, Merc had dubbed him: 'An-ill the Lovesick'. But the humorous aspect of Anil's condition was starting to wear thin for his friends. This became clear during a three-day trip they'd all made to Tsavo. Anil, despite much back-thumping and blanket-snatching each morning, couldn't be persuaded to get up for the early game drives. He didn't want to sacrifice the quiet hours of dreaming, when the idea of Lina seemed to melt into a skin-close reality, for the rowdy confines of a combi filled with squabbles over who got to have the binoculars, who really spotted the giraffe first, and whether that hump in the distance was a sleeping lion or the felled trunk of an acacia tree.

'If this is what love does to you, man, I'm going to avoid it. And please . . .' Merc brought his hands together as if praying to the circle of friends. 'If I start to get sucked into the quicksands of devotion, drag me out. I give you permission to pull me to my senses. I swear, you are all my witnesses.'

It had been the last evening of their safari and they'd been lounging in canvas folding chairs on the terrace of a hilltop lodge, overlooking a valley of sun-scorched bush into which, it seemed, a fragment of the moon had accidentally fallen: the watering hole had shrivelled to a puddle and, that day, cloudy skies had turned its surface opaque. A herd of springbok were grazing nearby, their ears twitching.

'Yeah, yeah. This from the guy who can't keep his hands off any woman – let alone one he might be in love with,' JT said. 'You've got chiles on the mind day and night, bwana.'

'I'm not denying that I'm . . .' Merc massaged his square jaw and searched for the right word, '. . . susceptible. But at least I don't get all mopey and dopey like this one here.' He pointed at Anil.

'Maybe you should sign a document giving us the authority – hey, what's it called?' Jateen nudged Hardy, who was studying law.

'Power of attorney.' The words emerged through a veil of smoke. Cigarettes were Hardy's other defence, deflecting the pitying stares of strangers from his acne.

'Yeah, give us power of attorney. I'd want it on paper from you, Merc. Otherwise I wouldn't trust you not to overreact.' Once Merc had punched Jateen for trying to stop him from driving when he was too drunk. Another time, he had broken Jateen's squash racket by thrashing it against the wall after his friend had refused to concede, on a final match point, that his serve had been on the line.

'You can say whatever you like.' Anil rocked back in his chair.

'But, mazeh,' Merc leaned towards him. 'You can't just let feelings knock you flat. Love is like a puppy that needs to be collared and taught some commands. Otherwise, I'm telling you, this great emotion you go on about is going to end up dictating to you.'

Anil didn't reply. It didn't seem so bad, to be in thrall to love. And yet, despite readily abandoning himself to it, he was restless.

Back at home in Nairobi, he tried to puncture the inflated hours with trips into town to check the postbox or mail another letter. When there was a reply from Lina, he pored over her words, squinting at the handwriting, looking for clues to the state of her heart in the flourishes of her pen.

He was filled with ideas for buildings and sketched relentlessly. It was as though everything that he could not articulate with language found a different form. He drew quickly, marking the paper with lines, shapes and shadows that bore no relation to the architecture he had learned to design on AutoCAD. In his new world, a skyscraper had the form of the figure eight and a house could be an upturned U. He started sending these sketches to Lina, along with the letters, believing they were the most eloquent expression of which he was capable.

Back at university, even his professors would notice a change in his work. Always technically talented, his drawings would become more audacious. 'What happened to you? Trying to defy the laws of physics?' they'd say. Anil couldn't explain it, he knew only that conventional forms weren't enough to express what was happening to him.

Minnie's Soirée

THE MAYURS' LIVING ROOM was crowded. Insects flew through the windows and clustered around the lights. Much the same way, guests were bunched in little groups around the various stars of the moment. The artist Gideon Lonkiti Ole Tikwa was there, wearing a white tuxedo and dark sunglasses. Nothing about his appearance hinted at his Maasai origins. Instead, perhaps to compensate, he dressed his canvases with the materials traditionally used by the tribe to decorate their bodies. There was one such piece on the wall in the Mayurs' house. A triptych, in which a wave of red ochre rode from one canvas to the next, carrying with it a swell of coloured beads.

In an adjoining room, people jostled and pushed in an effort to reach Aslam Kumar, who was surrounded by fans probing for hints on what he might read that evening. Amidst the fawners were stiff figures, their stick bodies carved out of wood and painted a matt black. These Giacometti-like sculptures of men, standing alone or in pairs, with hands pressed to their brows, were a head higher than their tallest human counterparts. They gazed at the living with sad resignation. In return, people admired the brittle artworks – no limb was thicker than a child's wrist – but kept a distance from them: their fragility hinted at something they were disinclined to face. Even gaunt Aslam Kumar seemed chubby next to the stick sculptures.

Though Aslam smiled and nodded at the praise being lavished on him, his scrawny neck tensed diffidently within the baggy confines of the Nehru collar on his black silk sherwani. He wondered if people subconsciously matched their compliments to the surrounding décor. He always got the most effusive comments here in Palazzo Mayur, as he liked to think of it. The house's mock-Italian exterior belied its ultra-modern interior – though this had not stopped Minnie from commissioning leading artists to paint frescoes on several ceilings. Aslam's eyes darted to the scene above him – a contemporary take on heaven in which God was depicted as a haloed dollar sign.

'You know, Aslam, the truth is, your poems are good for the soul but bad for the waistline,' said one lady, reaching for a canapé from a silver tray. Aslam beamed, his teeth brightening his face, like two strings of fairy lights.

'No, seriously.' The lady finished the rest of a small fried risotto ball before continuing, 'I put on three kilos while reading your last collection. All those references to food! My God, they made me want to eat and eat. I had to go on a diet afterwards.'

Aslam Kumar was a highly trained chef as well as a published poet. He was one of those over-enthusiastic exponents of nouvelle cuisine for whom food had become, primarily, an adornment for the blank plate. He was renowned for the presentation of his food, which also happened to taste rather good. Above all, he was famous for the aphorisms that graced his dishes. While other chefs arranged food and drizzled sauces in abstract designs, Aslam turned each dish into a personal message. Potato might be piped to read: *In every beginning lies a hesitation.* Or, a pale and quivering pannacotta might be encircled by a sentiment in raspberry sauce: *Hunger gives bad advice.*

No one got the same message as anyone else, or indeed the same words twice, for Aslam had a wide enough repertoire. Sometimes he simply used part of a line, either because he'd run out of space on the plate or he liked the cryptic intrigue of words snipped from the chain of sense: *it is all becoming*. People approached his food the way they did Chinese fortune cookies: part cynical, part curious, but mostly hoping for some kind of insight into the mystery of their own lives.

Minnie, naturally inclined towards the esoteric, had been a regular patron of his restaurant. While her husband tucked into the food without even bothering to note its tidings, she pondered the words on her plate as though they could change her destiny. She'd befriended Aslam, discovered that he wrote on paper as well as porcelain, and resolved to help him get published. Ten years later Aslam's slim collections had become local bestsellers. Food featured strongly in all his writing, as though the words had been marinaded in his culinary past before being turned into free verse. He still cooked from time to time, exclusive small dinners for which he created themed menus and poems and charged exorbitant amounts of money.

'Aslam? Look who is here.' Minnie towed Anil through the ring of bodies towards her friend.

'Anil, good to see you.' The two shook hands. 'You must be almost finished at Uni now, heh? How much longer?'

'About six months.' Anil swished the wine in his glass. Its polished surface reflected the gleam of his freshly gelled hair.

'Are you going to come back here afterwards and work with your dad?' It was what most sons did. For many, degrees were just a kind of decoration, extra letters to put after a name on a business card. Few chose to stay abroad and build their careers from scratch when they could come home to Kenya and start as MD of daddy's company.

'I don't know yet.' Anil didn't intend to work for Pravar.

'Oh you'll be back.' Aslam patted the hair curling over the tops of his ears. 'This place gets into your blood. The weather, the lifestyle – it's not easy to give up.'

'Aslam,' Minnie leaned in and whispered. 'Have you tried the wontons? Are they crispy enough?'

'Perfect, perfect.' Aslam kissed his fingers – which hadn't picked up a morsel of food since he arrived. He was fussy, and rarely ate anything that he hadn't made himself. Besides, the wontons put him in mind of greasy money-bags, which was probably why everyone else liked them so much.

'Good. Now, tell me, what are you reading tonight? I want to know if it might inspire Anil.' She smiled conspiratorially. The outline of her lips was drawn in plum-coloured pencil, giving an illusion of fullness.

'Why?' Anil and Aslam asked at once.

'Well . . .' Minnie put an arm over her son's shoulders. 'The boy is in *low* . . .' She dragged out the last word and left it hanging tantalizingly.

Aslam, arms crossed over his chest, bent towards her expectantly, waiting for her to finish.

'Mum! What are you . . . ? You're just . . .' Anil spluttered and shrugged out from under her grasp.

She saw the blush creeping up his throat behind the white collar of his shirt and laughed. 'Why so touchy, Neelu? What's to be embarrassed? Happens to all of us, nah, Aslam? Low?'

'Of course, yes.' Aslam grasped her meaning from Anil's

discomfort. He asked what he hoped was a neutral question. 'Did you meet in London?'

Anil ducked it by saying he was going to get another drink, though his glass was still half-full. He wished he hadn't agreed to be there and would have liked nothing more than to have left right away with his three friends. He could see them outside on the patio, lounging on the rattan chairs.

As he headed in their direction, Anil was intercepted by Pravar, who pulled him into a conversation about a retrospective of the Longonot school of artists at a local gallery. Pravar had not heard of them, and was not especially interested in their mission to paint the Kenyan landscape in thin brushstrokes that veered into abstraction. Anil knew of the group, but did not feel like getting into a debate about its merits. He couldn't just slip off, though, because Pravar had handcuffed his wrist with short, meaty fingers. His father's raisin eyes signalled that he wanted to be rescued.

Not a shy man by any measure, Pravar tended to become uneasy amongst his wife's arty crowd. Anil or Minnie often had to engineer excuses to extricate him from some discussion that had left him floundering. There was little Pravar detested more than having to be helped in this way. He'd rather pretend to know about something and bluff his way through than admit ignorance. He was a man of grand entrances and exits, who liked to make his presence felt and his opinions known. He continued to wear a turban mainly because it distinguished him so effectively from the crowd – not because of any strong allegiance to Sikhism. If he'd liked dogs he would have had a pit bull. Years ago Minnie had talked him into letting them get a puppy for Anil. Pravar had finally agreed on the condition that the dog never entered the house. He had regretted giving into his wife from the very first day, when the cocky springer spaniel, Tamu, had leapt on him and peed down his leg. He hadn't been able to understand his wife and son's affection for the animal. 'Bloody sissy dog,' he'd grumbled each time Tamu had tried to win him over. 'You could at least have got an animal who could defend the house. This bloody creature just wants to make friends with everyone.'

Anil listened to the debate going on between the group in whose circumference Pravar was trapped.

'You can have glossy tourist brochure images of sunsets, beaches and mountain ranges,' Sally Hunter was saying. She had on so many layers it was hard to tell if she was wearing three dresses on top of one another, or a skirt with several tops, or a combination of both. Beaded chains of varying lengths hung from her wrinkled neck. 'Or press photos of drought and flooding. *Or* you find local artists producing clichéd work that they think tourists will like. And none of it captures Kenya's real spirit. The Longonot group are redressing this.' She ran the gallery which represented these artists.

'Me, I don't know how you can talk of capturing the country's true spirit through a medium that is totally alien to its culture and traditions,' said the sculptor Kilempu Ole Nampa, adjusting his spectacles. 'I mean using this kind of abstract impressionistic mode to portray a country that has historically been defined by the stories its peepo told – seems absad to me.'

'Kilempu, bwana, you can't bar any culcha from adopting new forms of expression,' one of the artists belonging to the Longonot school said, sticking his nose into the air with disdain. He was wearing a Hawaiian shirt unbuttoned right down to the navel.

Kilempu looked into his wine glass. Its stem was lost in his big, rough hand. 'The problem with us is that we are too eegah to jump on the Westan bandwagon and discard our own heritage in the name of "modanism". And what we mostly produce is third-rate echoes of Gauguin and Kirkner.'

'Oh come on, Kilempu.' Sally's silver bracelets tinkled as she flicked her hand dismissively. 'You can't expect young Africans to ignore the West or be immune to it. That's impossible, what with globalization and everything. And as an artist, curiosity is all. You can only produce good work if you're willing to look beyond the confines of your own world. You can also be inspired by other cultures – as the artists you mentioned were. And they managed to change the direction of art in their time.'

'Absolutely. No. Completely. Yes,' Pravar agreed, though he had no idea what she meant. He pulled the cream silk handkerchief out of the pocket on the front of his suit jacket and promptly stuffed it back in again. Then he cleared his throat and looked around impatiently. But Anil, who was now enjoying listening, didn't immediately rescue him.

'As far as I can see, globalization means homogeniz-ation. Everyone's just out to copy whoever's been most successful. Curiosity is all very well, but my motto is: You see it, you admire it and then you shed it. You don't bow before it as if it is a betta version of yourself. Eh? Are we together?' Kilempu was taller than all those around him. 'Let me tell you, these eagah young Africans who can't wait to run abroad and visit the Uffizi or the Prado – if they could be bothad to look at their own country propally, their work would improve tenfold. Instead, they come back smitten by what they've seen and ready to become slaves to the white man's idea of art. And so they remain mentally colonized, even though independence was achieved almost fotty years ago. Ahhcch.' Kilempu looked as though he would like to spit, but took a swig of his drink instead.

'Oh, Kilempu,' Sally said, as though she'd just heard he had a terrible illness. His irascibility was not new to anyone, and they all expected it would worsen as the evening progressed and he drank more. By the end of the night he would probably have sworn at Gideon for turning their tribe's rituals into empty, decorative trinkets for rich philistines. But Kilempu was forgiven these eccentricities because his sculptural panels, made of wood or stone, were beautifully carved with depictions of Maasai fables. And he was the only person they knew who had work on display at MOMA in New York.

'I think,' Anil said, leaning forward, 'it could also be that people are seduced by the reverence for art in the West. I mean, some of these galleries are amazing. The collections are housed in beautiful buildings that are like opulent temples where art is sacrosanct. For goodness' sake, a beeper can go off if you peer too closely at a painting. Maybe that's partly why we're all susceptible to worshipping that tradition.'

'Mind you, there are artists challenging that attitude.' Kilempu rattled off a few names. 'They invite the viewer to invade the supposedly sacred space – to step on their art or take a bit of it away with them. This is the kind of work I like. Eh? This . . .' He stuck his middle finger into the air, '. . . challenge to the establishment.'

'Exactly.' Anil nodded, and Pravar copied him. 'I like that, too. But what I mean is, in general, the presentation of art in the West is designed to foster distance between the viewer and the work. And this helps to create the sense of reverence we feel in such places. Almost like we're privileged to be there at all. And, I guess, there just aren't the resources for that sort of thing here.'

'Forget the resources, there isn't even the inclination.' Sally played with one of the necklaces that hung down almost to her groin. 'Most of the population is too pre-occupied with the more important matter of making a living. I think that will start to change though, as the country gets wealthier.'

'Ah rubbish! Stop this trash talking.' Scorn hardened the contours of Kilempu's face. 'There's enough wealth, it's all just misused. Maybe there are a handful of patrons supporting local artists, but there's no chance of a renaissance here yet. Are we together?' He checked. 'And, I would bet you anything, that if funds were suddenly available for a museum of Kenyan art it would be built in some neoclassical or mock-colonial style.'

'Which is a shame,' Anil said. 'Because there are many ingenious building practices used by different tribes across the country. These could be harnessed to create something very impressive. Think of makuti roofs, which have sheltered people for centuries, or the stone buildings and heavy carved doors of Lamu.'

'Exactly, our peepos have been living sustainably for years, and now that "ecological" is a big buzzword we turn to the West for solutions, when they are the ones who have caused all the problems.' Kilempu clicked his tongue against the roof of his mouth. 'In some countries they are starting to patent indigenous flora and fauna so that big international companies can't come in and steal their heritage for profit. We need to do something like that here. Maybe I should file for patents on behalf of my tribe. And then I can frame all the certificates and have them displayed at some venerable institution under the heading "The Art of Preservation". Eh? Did you capture that?'

Anil suppressed a snigger, but Sally was quite taken with the idea.

'You never know, Kilempu. It could work. I mean, it's very *conceptual*.'

'It's exactly the sort of empty ostentation that goes down well in galleries like yours, Sally.' Kilempu looked down at her. Then he raised the phantom traces of his eyebrows at Anil. 'The hope of our country is with people like you. Maybe you will come back and champion the traditional architec-cha? Eh?'

Before Anil could answer Pravar leapt in. 'Of course. Yes. No. Tourists, you know, they are loving this traditional style look. Think of all the visitors who go to these Maasai living settlements. They really have the feeling of novelty, like they've come to the real, old, primitive Africa. Tourists want to experience something different from what's in their own countries. Absolutely. And if we can help to give that impression, why not? No?' Pravar raised a hand to ward off Kilempu, who was making disapproving noises. 'After all, don't forget tourism is our third largest foreign-exchange earner after tea and horticulture.' Now, pontificating on the economy and reeling off figures, he was in his element. 'By all means—'

'Ahch,' Kilempu interrupted. 'I hate the way the enkang have become little model toy villages for tourists to visit. We have turned our traditions into empty entertainment for the white man: we dance for him, we pose for pictures with him, we let him sniff around our hut. And in return, we are very happy to take his squalid banknotes and condescension.'

Everybody started to talk at once: defending the Maasai, accusing Kilempu of wanting to halt progress. Pravar was put out. He arched his short neck over one shoulder and surveyed the room, looking for more interesting prospects.

'Dad,' Anil intervened. 'I think Mum wants you.'

'Oh, excuse me. Excuse, please.' Pravar backed away, but the others were too absorbed in their argument to notice. 'These people like to get worked up over nothing. I don't know why your mother always has to invite that gypsy lady.' He was not a fan of Minnie's soirées and usually tried to avoid them. 'Enjoying yourself?'

Anil pulled down the corners of his mouth.

'You didn't come to my office this week.' Pravar drained the watery gold remains of whisky in his glass.

'I just got too busy, Dad.' He could easily have gone, but hadn't wanted to. He knew his father was a businessman, but was still unsure exactly what Pravar did. The man seemed to have interests in property, construction, tourism, tea exports and politics. The few days Anil had spent at Pravar's office had given him the impression that his father's days consisted mainly of wheeling and dealing and losing his temper. It was not a career path he felt tempted to follow.

'Next week is Christmas, and then you'll be off to the south coast for New Year, and then you're gone. So I think you won't get any chance to come, no?' Pravar jingled the ice cubes in his glass at a hired waiter, to signal a refill.

'Probably not.' Anil tried to look sorry.

'You should start getting more familiar with the place. My name is on the door now, but in future yours will be.'

Anil glanced at his feet. He could never think of a fitting response to his father's boast about the name. And

Pravar wasn't just talking metaphorically. His name (accompanied by the image of a peacock with its tail fanned out in magnificent formation) was indeed on lots of doors – the way mezzuzahs were in Jewish houses. At his companies, PRAVAR MAYUR was emblazoned across the gates, main entrances, lifts and, of course, the door of his personal office. A steel sign bearing his name was welded to the gate of their house, and their front door declared: MAYUR AND FAMILY.

A man came up and slapped Pravar on the back, 'Jambo, Chief!'

It was Merc's dad, Samuel Ojielo, the Minister of State for Defence. He wore a perfectly cut suit, tailored to make him look trimmer than he was. Everything about him was slick. His hair, beard and moustache were sharply trimmed, and speckled with just the right amount of grey. He smiled generously and laughed easily. And yet, it was rumoured that his briefcase and filing cabinets were wired, so that any unauthorized person who tried to get into them would receive an electric shock.

'Heh, Wabenzi!' Pravar addressed him by the nickname he'd acquired due to the fleet of Mercedes Benz cars that he owned. Many people assumed this fetish also explained his son's name, but Merc was short for Mercury – chosen by his mother for its rich associations in Hindu mythology, where, amongst other things, it was considered the most precious of all metals.

'I didn't expect to see you here tonight.' Pravar wrapped both his hands around the one proferred by Ojielo. Two bodyguards flanked the minister, and several others were scattered through the room and those adjoining it. 'To what do I owe this honour?' Pravar played the sycophant with ease.

'Your good wife invited me, so how could I refuse? I can't stay for long, though.' He turned to Anil. 'I take it my son is somewhere on these premises? I've hardly seen him these last weeks.'

'This one's the same.' Pravar's mouth pulled down in disapproval. 'I've been waiting for him to come and spend time with me at the office, but he's too busy.'

'Ati!' Ojielo tutted. 'You should learn a thing or two from your father. It's men like him who are the backbone of this country.'

Anil made sounds of agreement and then slipped off, saying, 'I'll tell Merc you're here.'

Pravar watched him leave. 'At least you have four.' His attention went back to Ojielo. 'Chances are one of them will take after you. Yes. Most probably. Anil is my one and only and . . .' He threw up his hands.

'Ah, he's young. Let him have his fun, he'll come back, don't you worry, bwana. Blood and cash count. You know what I'm saying? He's already inherited the first and, believe me, he'll return for the second. Now . . .' Ojielo glanced around. The two nearest bodyguards, standing with their legs spread and their arms crossed, formed a cordon no one would have been tempted to breach. The minister lowered his voice. 'How are things at Air Mayur?' Pravar owned a plane-charter company specializing in air safaris for tourists and private short-haul flights. 'I hear nothing went out last week.'

'I was only told yesterday.' Pravar lied. He'd got word several days before, but hadn't thought the matter required immediate attention. 'Trouble with a couple of the pilots, apparently. They've been complaining it's too dangerous.'

'Ati, dangerous!' Ojielo snorted. 'You know all concerns about danger can be eradicated with kitu kidogo.' A little something – that was all it took to get things done, no matter how difficult the circumstances.

'We'll sort it out. I'll speak to the guy who's handling everything.' Pravar touched one wing of his bow tie.

'They need to resume right away.' Ojielo clicked his fingers.

'I didn't realize there was any hurry.' Pravar frowned.

'Ati, hurry! It's not a matter of haste, Chief. It's just that the turnover has to be regular. The stuff needs to come in and go right out.' Ojielo's hand flew towards his chest and then away again. 'I don't want it hanging around. Otherwise the wrong people might get their hands on it.'

'I thought you said there was no risk.' Pravar's glass tinkled eerily as he ran a finger round and round its rim.

'Ati, risk!' Ojielo's shoulders shook. 'That's why I like working with you, Chief. You don't take anything for granted. Of course it's not risky, provided we do things the right way.' He scanned the vicinity once more and then drew Pravar towards an emptier corner of the room. People were stealing glances at the two men. Pravar felt his cachet going up. He listened while Samuel Ojielo quickly ran through how things should be run in order to ensure success.

'I thought one of your people would be overseeing it all.' Pravar started getting annoyed. He'd agreed to allow Samuel to use Air Mayur planes, but he hadn't expected to have to nanny every flight.

'Ati! If it's your man or mine – what's the difference? Once a system is set up it will take care of itself. The less we're involved the better. I think we just need to look after the pilots. Make them feel it's worth their while, you know? They're key in this operation.'

Pravar noted the way Samuel said 'we', when it was Air Mayur bearing all the costs. Still, he knew doing this favour would buy him other advantages. 'I'll sort it out. Don't worry.'

'Good man.' Ojielo slapped him on the back. 'I knew I could count on you. Now, where's that son of mine?' He squinted in the direction Anil had headed.

'They must be having their own private party somewhere.' Pravar followed his gaze.

Ojielo wasn't going to run around looking for the boy. He spotted Minnie. It was hard to miss her in the electric-pink trouser suit. 'Let me say jambo to your wife before I go.' He took a step, then stopped. 'Oh, I almost forgot. The President asked me to invite you to State House on the seventeenth. There's going to be a dinner for the Indian Foreign Minister.'

Pravar smiled, knowing the gesture was a reward for his compliance.

As Anil stepped on to the patio he could see the swimming pool glittering in the near distance like a bean-shaped aquamarine.

'Mazeh, can't we get some proper food here?' Merc had already appropriated a tray of tandoori chicken drumsticks from a waiter, and all of them were tucking in. A few minutes later he exchanged the platter of bones for one of spring rolls, and the guys fell on those as though they hadn't eaten for a week.

'Your dad's here,' Anil told him.

'Probably had some work to do.' Merc knew his father never went anywhere just to pay a social call. Every move was calculated with Samuel Ojielo. 'What's with all these snacks?' Still unsatisfied Merc looked around for another waiter whose canapés he could hijack. 'Usually there's a banquet at your house.'

'Not on evenings like this. You should know that by now.' Anil sat down with a spring roll in each hand. 'It's more about satisfying the senses with art than food.' Minnie believed that if people got too full they stopped thinking properly.

Merc shook his head. 'Art can't fill my stomach. I might have to go and raid the fridge.'

'Go on,' Anil said. 'I'm sure Mama Jo will be able to give you something.'

'Hey, hey, hey. Guess who's here?' Jateen stood up and announced, like a game-show host. His slightly chubby round face was filled with mirth. 'If it isn't Preeti Devani.'

They all turned to look at the young woman who had just arrived with her parents. Her jeans were too tight, her top cut too low. Long earrings dangled from her lobes and brushed the tops of her shoulders. She made her way confidently across the room to greet her hosts.

'*You* were *obsessed* with her last summer.' Jateen gestured at Anil.

'No I wasn't.' Anil started fussing around, looking for a napkin.

'Oh my God, you were so into her it was crazy. Remember that time we were at Orna's and you couldn't even eat your lunch because she was sitting on the other side of the room?'

'No way.' Anil picked up a tissue that lay discarded on the table and used one corner to clean his fingers.

'Look at this guy, man!' Jateen turned to the other two, his mouth open in astonishment.

'Short-term memory.' Hardy pretended to be chewing

71

the last bits of satay chicken from a stick, but was actually trying to pick his teeth with it.

'He had to forget her, didn't he? She wouldn't give him a second look.' Merc caught another waiter, but sent him off again after realizing his platter only contained vegetable brochettes.

'Ah, wacha your maneno.' Anil tried to brush them aside. He stood up, as if to defend himself better. 'It's not true.'

'What do you call a Singh who denies the facts?' Merc had learned the family game.

'Confu-*sing*?' JT ventured.

'He's that, too, but it's not the word I was thinking of. A Singh who denies the facts, what is he, Anil?'

'Merc, just because *you* happen to believe something doesn't make it a fact.'

'It's not just me. The three of us find you unconvin-*cing*.'

'Well, you're all deluded.'

His friends began to offer evidence to the contrary. Anil started off denying everything, then accused them of exaggeration, and was finally cajoled into a tiny, reluctant admission. 'OK, maybe I did have a little thing for her, but that's just because there wasn't much else going on.'

'Typical,' Merc said. 'You always do this – go overboard and then later claim it was nothing. Let's see how long this infatuation with Lina lasts.'

'Look, Lina's different.' Anil's tone was enough to dispel, for some moments, the conviviality of the group. During the brief silence between them, the crickets could be heard chirping to the murmuring trees. Jateen and Hardy examined the upholstery of the chairs. Merc picked at the crumbs of pastry left on the empty spring-roll platter.

'Come on.' Anil tried to be normal again. 'Let's go in and see what Mama Jo has to offer. This way.' Instead of cutting through the guests, he headed around the outside of the house.

'What is it?' Merc couldn't stop himself. 'Scared of being singed by one of your old flames?'

Shareef

LINA WOKE JUST AS her father, Shareef, padded past her door on his way to do namaz. The soft spanking of his slippers against the carpet sounded like a mother's hand patting a baby's bottom. She opened her eyes and looked at the clock on the table beside her bed: 7:08 – the luminous green digits beamed out into the dark. The radiator nearby creaked contentedly as heat started to pulse along its long, metal ribs. Outside, all was quiet on their cul-de-sac street, east of Birmingham's city centre. Yet, in almost every house there was one lit window behind whose curtains someone was quite likely performing ablutions or facing Mecca and starting to recite: *In the name of God, the Most Gracious, the Most Merciful . . .*

Pulling the red-and-white striped duvet up under her chin, Lina wriggled on to her side, trying to burrow deeper into the bed, hoping that might help her drop off again. For most of her life she had slumbered through this ritual of Shareef's. Occasionally, the smack of his prayer mat touching the floor had penetrated her sleep, the way a lighthouse does the night expanses of an empty sea: un-obtrusive and comforting. Only during Ramadan did she, her two younger sisters and her mother get up with him to pray and eat something before the sun rose. Otherwise, Shareef alone in their family prayed five times a day. He had never insisted that they follow his example, but his quiet piety had inspired Lina to emulate him.

When she was just six she'd insisted that Shareef wake her early to do namaz with him. Sleepily, she'd imitated his movements, wrapped a scarf over her head as he'd donned a kufi cap, and tried to recite, in time to his utterances, the verses that she'd learned. But finding the words was difficult, for the fog of dreams had still filled her mind, licked the back of her eyelids and lolled heavily against her tongue. She had not risen after the first prostration, but remained curled up on the musalla until Shareef, completing his supplication, turned and saw her foetal form at rest on the mat. He'd been so engrossed in prayer that he'd forgotten she was there. His heart had lurched with tenderness at the sight of her in pink pyjamas, with her mother's green chuni trailing her head and shoulders like a ribbon on a half-opened present. Gently he'd lifted and carried her back to bed, loving her more for her earnest failure. Later, when she awoke, she hadn't been able to remember a thing and only the chuni still bunched around her neck had enabled Shareef to convince her that she had, in fact, got up and tried to pray. 'You were very good. You just need a bit more practice. But I think you should wait a few years,' he'd said.

Lina had not tried again until she was eleven – with much the same result. That time she fully recalled her poor effort at namaz, and she was old enough to know her prayer was invalidated by the yawns, sighs and instants of dozing that had interrupted it. When she'd complained it was too hard, her father had conceded that the regime didn't suit everyone and told her not to worry about it. 'There are other ways to serve Allah. To be a good Muslim, you must, above all, be a decent human being. You just concentrate on staying good.' He'd said it as if he had an inkling, already, of how temptation could sully even the purest heart.

Now Lina heard Shareef roll out his musalla at the end of the corridor and she anticipated the click in his knees that would follow as he knelt and bowed between rakas. Each day, since coming home for the Christmas holidays, she had woken up just in time to hear her father perform his act of devotion. Normally, she would sleep in for another hour or two, but her conscience had become an internal alarm, bleeping with morbid punctuality at this sacred hour of morning.

The stairs strained like out-of-tune piano keys as Shareef went down. In the kitchen he filled the kettle and opened the curtains. Dawn yawned across the sky, colouring the world with its soft, peachy breath. He leaned on the counter and looked through the window, savouring the solitude. Their garden was a little patch of pale, square stone slabs bordered by a thin, muddy frame of failed roses. Above it a line of clothes was hanging out to dry: a whitewash of vests, socks, shirts, towels, sheets and pillowcases. No underwear, because Iman never hung that out in public. If it were possible to read laundry, the way one does tea leaves, this load would speak of a simple, conventional life; a little austere perhaps, and seemingly without complications. His life. And not his life.

Shareef wondered how he might be remembered by posterity. As a young man who'd won a scholarship to study law in the UK, he'd imagined himself capable of making a difference. In England he couldn't find jackets with sleeves that fitted his long arms, but he aimed to amass something that he could one day carry back and pour into the empty, cupped palms of his motherland,

India. And it wasn't money he had in mind – though there had been enough remittances to family there over the years. Knowledge and experience were what Shareef focused on acquiring. He had planned to return to Delhi. It was his obligation as the eldest and only son. He would shake up his own father's ailing legal practice and participate in the development of the country. He'd wanted to help draft laws to improve women's rights and fight for more equitable land distribution.

In the end, he had never returned to live permanently in India. Even before graduating he'd got, on the recommendation of a tutor, a job at a leading legal firm – the first coloured man they'd ever hired. And his race had remained, for co-workers, the most significant thing about him.

He was there for ten years, initially rising quickly through the ranks until he was pulled off an important case. Mumbles about a 'difficult client' were all the explanation he got. After that he was relegated to the background, always called in to assist senior partners when they were in difficulties, but rarely asked to accompany them to meetings or court. Then he started noticing junior colleagues overtaking him. A frank admission from his boss enabled Shareef to understand why this was happening.

'It's nothing to do with ability, Merali.' Gerald Summerfield had that public school habit of referring to people by their surnames. 'Lord knows you're sharper than most. But, as you're aware, it's the clients that keep us in business and they have, well, certain expectations.' He paused and screwed up his mouth regretfully.

In the curl of his thin lips Shareef read: white skin and the right accent. 'Why did you hire me then?' He felt a sudden revulsion for the man, all snug in his waistcoat and armchair and firm partnership – insulated, above all, by prejudice.

'You're good, that's why.' Gerald hadn't added: 'But no one expected you might be better at the job than any of us.' That was the pinch, really. That's where their progressive experiment had gone wrong: the coloured man had proved more talented than most of his colleagues.

Shareef, newly married and with a pregnant wife, had resigned the next day.

The sky was a thick smudge of grey, now that dawn had passed. The day was assuming its typical, dull December hue. It's going to rain, Shareef thought. He remained propped on his elbows, squinting through the window. He ought to bring in the laundry, unpeg the flapping eulogy before its airy eloquence was lost to a heavy shower.

'Slalikum, Baba.'

'Walaikum as salaam.' Shareef, as always, enunciated every syllable in response to the greeting that his daughter clipped down to half its length. He turned as Lina pulled a chair out from the table and dragged it to a spot along the wall, near the radiator. She sat down, managing to get her bottom and feet on the seat. She pulled the old jumper she was wearing – one of his – over her knees and wrapped her arms around them. Shareef was always amazed at how she could fold up her long body to perch on such a small area.

'You're up early.'

'Couldn't sleep.' She yawned into the navy-wool mountain made by her bent legs, and said something else he didn't quite catch.

'Do you want some tea?' He moved towards the kettle.

'Uh-uh.' She watched him throw a tea bag into a wide,

round, chipped cup and pour over the boiled water. He always used that cup, a relic from his university days. While the tea brewed, he started getting out the ingredients for the 'eggy bread' he would make for breakfast as soon as everybody was up. This was their Sunday morning ritual, and one of the things Lina missed most when she was away from home: Baba cooking his extra-sweet, extra-buttery, almost-burnt French toast. It was the only thing he made, and they all loved it.

Lina watched her father's back as he worked. He was always slightly stooped, as if slightly embarrassed of his great height. Or perhaps the stoop was from bending over to talk to shorter people all his life. Methodically Shareef laid what he'd need out, placing things side by side on the counter – eggs, whisk, spatula, butter, knife – as if they were instruments for a surgical procedure. He was meticulous in all ways, scrupulous about keeping time, cautious about taking decisions. Practising the law had made him excessively careful. This fastidiousness seemed to have etched itself into his face as well: the lines in his forehead were all the same length and equally spaced, as if the distance between them had been measured as carefully as the consequences of every choice had been weighed.

'Baba, where did you learn to make this eggy-bread?' It was the first time she'd thought to ask.

He repositioned an egg tenderly. 'When I shared a flat with friends at university, one of my flatmates used to make it.'

'I didn't know you lived with friends then.'

'Well, I wasn't lucky enough to have relatives to stay with. I had to live as cheaply as possible. For a while I was lodging with strangers.'

'Was it a French friend, then, who taught you this?' She

stuck her chin out towards the ingredients. 'I mean it's actually called French toast, right?'

'I don't know if the name really has anything to do with the origin. The girl . . .' His tongue stayed curled over the word for an instant, 'Who used to make it for me – for us – was English.'

'You lived with a girl? Before Ma?' Lina's eyes widened.

'I didn't *live* with her. We just shared a flat: me, her and a few others.' He still didn't turn around to face his daughter, but continued touching the items before him as though trying to place them exactly upon some tiny mark.

'That must have been fun. I would like to do that next year. Some of my friends already share a place, and they have a great time.'

Now Shareef spun around and rested his hands and backside on the black Formica counter. 'Your final year will be intense. Maybe it's not a good idea to have other distractions.' The lines in his head deepened, their perfect symmetry making him look all the more stern.

'I think it will make things easier, actually. I'll be closer to the faculty and library. The trek to Khala Rocky's in Ealing is so time-consuming.'

'It's also a question of money. Why should you pay rent when you already have a place where you can stay for free?' He rolled one shoulder back and then the other, as if trying to loosen some knot in his back. 'And anyway, how come you have this whim now, right at the end of your studies?'

'I've always felt a little like I'm missing out on something by just living at home, Baba. Sharing with friends is a totally different experience. You know that, you did it.' Her eyes, steady and thoughtful, matched the quiet challenge in her voice.

'I'm not sure we can afford it.' His eyes narrowed under his brows. Thick, bushy brows with long hairs that stuck up like silver aerials.

'I will save in the summer, and I can work an extra day during the week. I'm sure I can manage, maybe with just a little help from you.' Lina picked at a loose thread on the sleeve of her sweater, trying to appear casual, though her heartbeat was staggering like a drunk trying to walk a straight line. And it wasn't because she was afraid of his reaction. She was startled by her own guile. It would be easier, she felt sure, to see Anil if she was living with friends rather than relatives.

'Your final year studying law is not the time to be taking on extra jobs and whatnot.' Shareef resumed his breakfast duties. 'Besides which, let me tell you, there are inevitably tensions when you share a space with others. Someone will always be messier, louder or stingier than you can stand. You don't know how easy you've got it at your rock-star auntie's. What is it you want to do that you can't while living there?' He pulled his brows together in a question-ing frown – thick greying eyebrows, with stray long hairs that stood out like silver aerials.

'I just want to experience another side of university life.' She managed to hold his gaze, but was unsettled by the stare of what she deemed his 'third eye' – the ash-coloured, ten-pence-coin-sized callus on his forehead, the mark of prostration. It seemed especially pronounced this morn-ing, and liable to see through her explanations. The mark had this effect on all sorts of people. It had earned Shareef respect and trust. People imagined him forever kneeling on his prayer mat, his forehead piously pinned to the floor.

Only Iman irreverently joked about it. 'Let me tell you,

he has an identical mark on his bum – only bigger, from sitting too long at the office.'

Lina watched her father now, waiting for his answer. 'Baba?'

'Let's see.' Shareef shrugged. 'Let's just hold on and see.' He was always ready to postpone decisions, especially ones which he anticipated wouldn't turn out as he wished. 'You've got two more terms still to go. Get through those and then we can talk about the final year.'

'I can't leave it right until the end.'

He dipped his chin into his chest, stretching his neck.

Above them the stairs creaked out the familiar music of Iman's considerable weight.

'Let's see what the Management thinks.' Shareef's nickname referred, half-tenderly, half-resignedly, to the fact that Iman made many of the decisions in their household.

'You know exactly what she'll say, Baba.'

Shareef started breaking eggs into a shallow porcelain bowl. Lina pulled her knees tighter into her chest.

'Oh what-weh! Why didn't one of you bring in the washing?' Iman hurried to the window. The elegance of her hair, rolled high into a bun, clashed with the worn-out homeliness of her purple quilted dressing gown. She stood with her hands on her hips and considered these two people, her husband and daughter, who deliberated on issues the way cows chewed on cud. She could sense that some topic had been suspended due to her arrival. Sometimes, the two broke off mid-sentence when she entered a room. Even if they immediately resumed their talk, there was always a slight shift in mood, as though she had obstructed the sunlight, leaving the space slightly darker. Lina, she knew, was not as open with her as with Shareef.

'I didn't realize it was raining.' Lina rubbed her long nose with the back of her hand.

Shareef, with broken eggshells in his palm, twisted his head and gazed past the full figure of his wife into the garden. Everything was drenched. The laundry hung limply from the washing line and dribbled on to the shiny stones.

'You two. The sky could fall down and you wouldn't notice.' Displeasure puckered up Iman's pretty face. Her lips wrinkled into a tight ball, like the mouth of a draw-string bag pulled shut. 'Allah only knows what you jabber on about that's so fascinating you forget the world. What was it, weh? The date of your mother's funeral?'

'Ma!' Lina's legs tumbled off the chair as she straightened up in outrage.

'What else could give you such a long face so early in the morning?' Iman's mouth spread generously, setting off a charming ripple of light wrinkles along her cheeks. Then she stepped back, blinked and exclaimed, 'Tobah, tobah, Shareef, what are you wearing, weh?' Her eyes rode up and down his frame, questioning the prudence of wearing one of his best white shirts and a pair of smart grey trousers while cooking. 'Why must you dress like you're going to the office even on a day off? At least put on an apron.' She reached for the flower-patterned one hanging from a hook on the back of the kitchen door.

Shareef, dripping spatula in hand, looked down at himself, unable to see what all the fuss was about. Already there were small specks of splashed raw egg and melted butter on his front. He refused the apron Iman tried to put over him. 'It won't make a difference now,' he said.

'It just means extra washing and ironing for me. You'll have to change before we go out later.' Iman started laying out plates and cutlery. 'Lina, please go and wake your sisters. Tell them breakfast is ready.'

'Ma, you were just up there. Why didn't you tell them?'

'I did, but they'll need another shake before they get out of bed. Go on.'

'I'm sure they'll come when the smell of Baba's cooking wafts up.'

'I hope he won't fill the house with smoke this week,' Iman moved to shut the kitchen door. She flicked on the extractor fan above Shareef's head and pushed the window open despite her daughter's protests about the cold. 'I don't want the fire alarm going off again.'

'At least it would get the girls out of bed.' Lina shivered while butter melted in the pan under which Shareef had just ignited a blue flame.

'You must write that letter for Rizwan today about the plumbing problem.' Iman referred to the friend they were going to for tea later that day. 'I've got all the details here.' She reached for the silver toast rack stuffed with letters that sat on top of the fridge. She sniffed, and shuffled the letters as though they were a giant pack of cards. 'Oh, there's one for you, too. I forgot to say.' She glanced at Lina before examining the thick envelope. 'From Kenya. Who do you know over there? Shanila Mayur,' she read off the back of the envelope. 'Who's she?' Iman passed the letter over.

'A friend from uni.' Lina's heart started to churn. Bread sizzled in the pan and the smell of caramelized sugar filled the air. Thank goodness for Anil's foresight. He'd created that pseudonym after seeing her anxiety about being contacted by him at her parents' home. 'Who's also going to specialize in human rights.' The lies made her tongue feel thicker, like an obstacle in her mouth. 'And has been

84

sending me stuff about the situation in Kenya, press-cuttings and things.' She was aware of the oddness of her genderless sentences. She looked at her parents, ready to meet their eyes and eradicate any doubt. But Shareef did not turn from the hob, and Iman kept on sorting through the pile of papers.

'Yes, I noticed there were one or two others since you came home, also from Kenya.'

One or two. The ones Lina had missed. For there was another reason why she got up so early every day: to be the first one to collect the mail as it dropped through the letter box. Alerted by the squeal of the flap being lifted by the postman, she was usually bending to retrieve the letters just as they hit the floor. And by the time she straightened up, she'd know whether or not there was something from Anil.

'Here it is.' Iman waved a phone bill on the back of which was a handwritten list detailing the particulars of Rizwan's dysfunctional boiler and blocked drains. 'You'll have to do it straight after breakfast.'

Shareef nodded. 'I know some people from Kenya.'

'The Dariwals, right?' Lina hoped he was referring to the family who ran the chemist next door to his office. She didn't want him to know anyone else from Kenya, didn't want any reason to dwell on the subject. 'They emigrated from there, but my friend . . .' She couldn't bring herself to say 'Shanila', '. . . actually lives in Nairobi and is a foreign student.'

'Where shall I put this? So you don't forget?' Iman ran her fingers impatiently along the folds of the paper.

Shareef lifted two browned slices of bread from the pan and set them on a plate. 'Just put it back where it was. I'll get it later.'

'Oh-fo! I know your later, it's usually too late. I'm leaving it here.' She arranged the paper in the middle of the table so that its three folds opened out like a miniature Japanese shoji screen.

'I'd better get the girls to come down.' Lina slipped off the chair, the letter pressed into her palm, burning to be read. She ran up the stairs, ripping the envelope open and calling out to her sisters that breakfast was ready. She went straight into the bathroom and locked the door. Leaning back against it she opened Anil's letter. It started,

> Dearest Lina,
> I am coming back early. Is there any way you can get down
> to London a few days before the semester begins? You can
> reach me at the flat in Chelsea from Sunday 17th.

That was today! Lina noted the telephone number he'd written out. She repeated it to herself several times, her lips miming the words as her brain committed them to memory. She'd have to nip out and try to ring him. She took a deep breath and went on reading. Already, her mind was coming up with convincing excuses for leaving home almost immediately.

Vitruvian Man

A WEEK LATER, they sat side by side on a purple velvet sofa in a busy coffee bar off King's Road in central London. The air was saturated with the rustling of cellophane wrappers and gossip being exchanged over steamy over-sized cups. Lina held a tall mug with both hands and drank her hot chocolate. In between sips she rotated her mug slowly, so that after a while, its rim was garlanded by the pink lipstick marks of her mouth. Anil, who had downed two lattes as if they were water, watched her. She noticed his greedy eyes and held her mug out to him.

'Would you like some?'

He took it and carefully put his lips exactly around one of the creased petal marks left by hers. She smiled as he returned her drink, turning the mug so she could grasp it by the handle. 'So, then, after Tsavo you went to the coast?' She'd been plying him with questions almost ceaselessly. As though, if she could keep him talking about himself, he might not ask how, despite numerous promises that she would get to London tomorrow – tomorrow – tomorrow, she had arrived five days later than expected, with only two free days before the term started. And one of those, she was afraid to admit, she had to spend helping Khala Rocky with her son Yusuf's birthday party.

'We always celebrate the New Year at this place called Forty Thieves on the south coast in Mombasa.' He pushed up the sleeves of his sweater. His forearms were tanned, the normally dark hair on them lightened from his weeks in the sun. 'It's just a really chilled-out beach party. We ended up being thrown out of the place, though, because Merc got into a fight.'

Lina halted mid-sip. 'Why?'

'He tried to hit on some girl who was already with someone. She actually started flirting with him, and then her boyfriend had to avenge his wounded ego by laying into Merc.' Anil threw an elbow over the back of the sofa and slid closer to Lina.

She pressed her legs tighter together. 'He seems quite volatile.'

'Well, he hasn't had the easiest life. His mother committed suicide, and he was the one who found her body.'

'Oh my God!' The milk she'd just swallowed went down the wrong way and she started coughing. Anil patted her on the back.

'When was that?' she asked, after she'd caught her breath again.

'Years ago. He was just four when it happened. But anyway, let's not talk about it now.' His hand stayed on her back and started moving in slow circles. He felt her tense up under his fingers. 'You have to come to Kenya. You'd love it, I'm sure.' His other hand came to rest on her thigh.

She gripped her mug tighter. 'I would like to. Some day.'

'I was thinking about this summer, actually.'

'Is it a good idea to plan so far in advance?' Lina said, after a pause.

'Why not? Plans are how you tame the future.' His breath was warm on her face, and filled her nostrils with the smell of coffee. 'And besides, given that it took you almost a week to get to London after I arrived here, I figure maybe it's a good idea to start planning early. That way you might actually make it on time.' His hand slid to the curve of her waist and pressed into the thick knit of her cardigan.

Behind them, there was a scraping of chairs as a group of girls stood to leave. Nearby, a baby started to cry. But Lina was noticing the scattering of moles, delicate as pollen, across the bridge of Anil's nose. He was studying the golden specks that dotted her green pupils. Their noses bumped before their lips met. Anil shut his eyes, and the next instant – she wasn't there. He opened his eyes to find her clutching the round neck of her jumper, her cheeks a paler shade of its rich maroon.

'Is something wrong?'

She nodded, shook her head. 'It's just . . . there are so many people.'

The place was filling up. A man whose paunch hung over his belt came and squeezed on to the sofa beside Anil. The line of people waiting to order stretched from the coffee counter right down to the entrance, near which they were seated. Cold air blasted in each time the main door was opened. Lina shivered.

'You wanted to meet here.' Anil had suggested she come to the apartment he shared with his friends, which was just around the corner, but she'd declined because they would be there too. He'd managed not to retort that they wouldn't have been, if she'd only got to London earlier, as she'd promised.

'It's not really private.' She had just realized that being anonymous in a crowd wasn't enough to set her at ease with Anil. She needed complete seclusion. Then, she thought, she would be able to relax.

Anil nodded. The air around him seemed to throb, as

though his heart was not just driving his circulatory system but pumping outwards into the world. 'Tomorrow, I'll get the guys out of the flat so we can have some time together. I'll cook you a meal. My famous prawns piri piri.'

Lina reached forward to put her mug on the table. The colour had drained out of her leftover hot chocolate; a skin of milk hung on its surface. She folded her hands together, pulled her shoulders forward and winced. 'Tomorrow, I can't.'

'What?'

She wished she could smooth the disappointment off his face, the way an imprint in sand can be erased with a stroke. 'Anil, I'm really sorry. I have to – my aunt, she needs my help.'

'Your family—' He stopped himself. 'Will I ever get to see you properly?'

The uncomprehending sweetness of his plea was almost harder to bear. 'On Sunday. I promise. The whole day.'

'A whole day? From morning to evening? Real time, not Lina time?'

'Sunday. All day.' She reached out to hug him, knowing only such a gesture would convince.

Sunday came and the morning slipped away. He asked his friends if they'd go out for a few hours so that he and Lina would have some time alone. He believed, fervently, that she would come, as if believing could make it happen. It wasn't just trust in her that persuaded him, but his own unshaken sense that things would always be the way he wanted them.

'So this is love, huh? Chucking your old friends out for a chile?' Merc stood in the doorway between the sitting room and the hallway, his arms stretched out to hold the corners of the door frame. In the room before him the curtains were half-drawn under their heavy silk swags to prevent the sun from reflecting on to the TV. Empty beer cans were dotted about in places where other people might put candles: on the fireplace, the coffee table, the window ledge, by the TV. One wall was covered in an assortment of drawings, posters, photos, receipts, time-tables, letters and recipes – all attached to bulldog clips and hung from nails as thin as pins.

'I'm not saying you have to go. It was just a request.' Anil slouched on the black suede sofa, a copy of *Architectural Digest* on his lap. Across from him JT and Hardy were sprawled on the floor, furiously wielding Playstation controllers. 'It would be nice to have some time alone with Lina.'

'Alone.' Merc gave a low whistle.

'All by themselves,' JT cooed.

'Just the two of you,' Merc sang. 'We'll have to phone before we come back, or give you some kind of signal. We wouldn't want to catch you *in flagrante delicto*.' His tongue curled provocatively over his top teeth.

'I don't think that's likely.'

'Neither do I, you poor bastard.' Merc laughed and leaned forward as though he was about to swing from the frame. His T-shirt rode up his waist, revealing six hard, even lozenges of muscle across his stomach. Striped grey boxer shorts stretched over his tight bottom and the sinuous contours of his thighs. 'No chance of any jigijigi with her. I don't think I've seen her wearing a top that reveals her collarbones. And I definitely haven't even glimpsed her elbows, because she's always in long sleeves.'

'It is winter, in case you haven't noticed. Not everyone's an exhibitionist like you.' Anil flicked the pages of the

91

architecture magazine, hardly seeing what was on them.

'I don't doubt there's some booty under all that cloth.' He thought of the full breasts that weren't entirely hidden by Lina's baggy clothes. 'The question is, when will you get a taste of it? She might as well wear a burka. Thats the ultimate "hands off" sign, isn't it?'

'As far as you're concerned any woman who's not in a bikini might as well be wearing a burka.' Anil snapped the magazine shut and put it on to the pile nearby, under the glass side-table by the sofa.

There was laughter from the two engaged in virtual mortal combat on the TV screen.

'Merc's favourite kind of girl is one who doesn't leave anything to the imagination.' JT turned to leer at his friend, while his on-screen self combusted.

'Yes!' Hardy bent his elbow and balled his hand into a fist. 'Oh, we saw some hot stuff at the club last night. Wa-wa-wa-wa.' He sucked his teeth, remembering the young woman, with silver tassels dangling from her nipples, who'd performed for them at the pole-dancing club they'd visited. 'Oh, bwana,' Hardy looked at Anil. 'You really missed something. Just the sight of those girls' asses made me want to burn down my house!'

'You two should have been around during Mughal times.' Anil balanced one ankle over his knee. The small hump of a bunion protruded from his bare foot. 'You would have loved that, all the courtesans and mujra dancers. It was better then.'

'You make it sound like women dancing for men has become depraved,' Merc said.

'No.' Anil picked some fluff off his trousers. 'But there's definitely a different flavour to the whole business now. It's cruder, almost nothing is left to the imagination.'

'Speak for yourself, mazeh. There's plenty more I can conjure up when I see those girls. *You* would have preferred that mujra era, not me. The women were a bit too over-dressed for my liking, with even their fingers, toes, ears and foreheads covered in jewels. And I couldn't have stood the lamenting love songs they wailed and performed to. Give me the lyricless beats of today anytime.'

'I don't know how you can enjoy that empty music.'

'That's what I like, the emptiness.' Merc closed his eyes. 'The music is a space in which you can just be. You fit into it without thinking. It takes your shape. Everyone's shape.'

'Especially the gyrating shapes of young nymphs.'

Merc's eyelids flicked open. He hadn't inserted any contact lenses yet, so each iris shone its natural dark brown. 'It's better than those heavy ghazals and qawwalis you listen to. They're just overflowing with self-pity. Honestly, I feel like I'm being kabisa wiped out, suffocated almost, when you play that stuff. And that concert we went to last year, the one where you met Lina, that gave me an idea of what it must be like to be buried alive.'

'Oh for goodness' sake!' Anil's gums came into view as his mouth opened in laughter. 'You fell asleep, so it can't have been that painful.'

'I was knocked out, mazeh.' Merc propped himself against the doorframe, one leg crossed in front of the other. 'Seriously, crushed out of consciousness by all that emotion. Why the hell would you want anyone to become like the blood in your veins, or to haunt your heartbeat, or to appear in the guise of flowers? That's just unhealthy.'

'You understand more than me by the sounds of it! Hey, JT, Hardy, listen to the poet revealing himself.'

'I don't get a word. I'm just assuming that's the kind of bullshit they sing.'

'Ah, come on!' Anil pulled a cushion from behind him and chucked it playfully at Merc. 'You must have picked it up somewhere? Maybe even from the stirrings of your own heart?'

'Na na na na na.' Merc kicked the cushion back with one great flipper of a foot. It curved sideways and landed on an antique Persian rug in the middle of the room. 'I only know about the stirrings that go on below the waist. You're the sucker for all this heart stuff. Talking of which,' Merc said, 'coming back to your *girlfriend*. What I don't understand is why there have to be these special conditions for her. We've all asked girls back here regardless of who's home or not. You've done it before without any qualms. So, what's changed?'

'It's just different this time.' Anil stood up and went to retrieve the fallen cushion.

'Obviously.' Merc bent down to pick up the dumb-bell that was serving as a door-stopper. He jammed his heel in its place instead and started pumping the ten-kilo weight with his left hand. 'You've even tried to tidy up. I heard you banging about with the hoover at the crack of dawn.'

'You're the only person I know for whom dawn is whatever point in the day you happen to wake up.'

'At this rate,' Merc continued, as if he hadn't heard, 'we won't need a cleaner any more.'

'Hardly.' Anil shook his head at the towering titan standing before him like some modern variant on the statue of liberty, the upraised dumb-bell proclaiming physical perfection as the ultimate ideal. 'Look at all this.' He started collecting the empty beer cans. 'And Christa's not here until the day after tomorrow.' He meant the Filipina cleaner, who came by twice a week to keep the flat civilized and do all their washing and ironing.

'Yeah, well, let's cancel her. We can say we've got some-one new called Shanila.' Each syllable of the name lingered on his thick lips, as if he were advertising some porn star.

Anil swooped past with his hands full of crushed, glint-ing aluminium. He could hear his friends guffawing as he dumped the cans in the kitchen bin. He wished he'd never told them about that pseudonym.

'As long as you're around, cleaners will never become redundant.' Anil gave Merc a pointed look as he re-entered the room. Merc left traces everywhere he passed: scratch-ing, breaking, losing or forgetting things. 'In fact, I've often thought, what you need is someone trailing behind you with a roller or drag mat or something to smooth over the mess you make. Like they do on clay courts after people have played tennis.'

'Say what you want, mazeh, I fear there will be nothing that can smooth over the mess you're getting into.'

'What mess?' They stood facing each other, two metres apart.

'With this Lina. You can't see it, can you?' Merc watched confusion crease Anil's brow. 'You've just fallen flat for her without even considering that she's a *Muslim*.'

'What's that got to do with anything?' Anil sensed Merc was serious, even though he was trying to act casual, lifting the weight and watching its progress from his shoulder towards the ceiling.

'I wouldn't bring it up if you didn't seem so obsessed. I'm just worried that you're not thinking things through properly.'

'I don't understand what you're trying to say.' Anil stood straighter.

'Oh, come on. This whole religious difference, you can't pretend it's not there.'

'I don't see why it should be an issue. We're not in the dark ages any more.'

'You think I came out of the dark ages?'

'Aw, man, don't hark back to that. Things were completely different in your parents' day.' His eyes went to the two black-and-white photos in silver frames which hung on the wall by the door. One was of Merc as a baby with his mother, Chanda. The other showed Chanda and Samuel Ojielo on their wedding day, a head-shot in which both smiled into each other's faces, confident that their love would surmount every obstacle.

Chanda had committed suicide after society refused to accept her marriage to a black man. She slit her wrists in the bath one morning. Her body lay undiscovered for several hours. It was four-year-old Merc, returning from nursery at lunchtime, who'd found her. He'd run around the house, a parrot mask he'd made in class pulled over his face. He'd entered her bedroom, flapping his arms, believing he could fly: 'Look, Mummy! Look! Mummy?' He'd checked the walk-in wardrobe where she'd often sat at her dressing table, absently pulling a brush through her long black hair. Then he'd entered the bathroom where the water in the tub was red and Mummy lay asleep, her head lolled to one side, her face white.

After that Minnie, full of remorse, had tried to make up for the past by becoming a sort of guardian for Merc. His father had later remarried and had three more children, but Merc remained closer to Anil than his new brothers and sister. He refused to have anything to do with Chanda's family – even when they started to reach out a conciliatory hand. He claimed their interest in him had grown in direct proportion to his father's advance up the political ladder.

'Intermarriage and stuff is the norm now,' Anil went on more gently. 'We all know people in such – hey!' Merc was turning away. 'Where are you going?'

'I want to show you something.' He left the room. The door swung on its hinges behind him.

Anil sighed at the other two who'd turned up the volume on their game to signal that they weren't getting involved.

Merc was back before the door clicked shut. He used the dumb-bell to hold it open again and then handed three newspaper cuttings to Anil. The headlines read: 'GIRL FLEES DEATH THREATS', 'FATHER SLAYS DAUGHTER' and 'COUPLE KNIFED TO DEATH'. 'And in two of the cases, the forbidden boyfriends were *Muslim*. Just think of that. The only reason they weren't approved was because the parents hadn't chosen them.'

'Where did you get these?' Anil kept them at arm's length, as though they were toxic.

'I just came across them in the papers over the last couple of months. I wasn't even looking especially hard – which goes to show. This kind of thing is not as antiquated as you seem to think.'

Anil pulled in his cheeks for a moment. 'Maybe you just have a special eye for such stories.' He handed back the cuttings. 'This has nothing to do with me. Or Lina.'

Merc ignored his outstretched hand. 'You don't even want to consider the possibility of difficulties.'

'You're being way too paranoid.'

'So it doesn't strike you as odd that you can't even phone Lina at home?'

Anil folded his arms across his chest. 'I'm more struck by the number of people I know who are managing perfectly well in similar circumstances. It's not all horror stories, like you're trying to imply.'

'Of course. It's perfectly normal that you can't ever call your girlfriend at her own house and that you have to print a female name on the back of the letters you send her.' He stared at Anil, his eyebrows raised. And there was an invisible spark as their wills – which had hitherto been deftly circling each other – clashed.

'*Look*.' Anil gritted his teeth. 'I don't believe Lina would have got involved if there was that kind of risk. I really don't think it's the big deal you're making it out to be. Now can you just drop it? She's going to be here soon.'

Merc's hand closed over the cuttings. He crushed them into a ball that he tossed into the air and caught. Tossed and caught again. Then he lobbed it on to one of the empty cereal bowls still sitting on the table. 'What do you call a Singh who won't listen to anyone else's opinion, and is never prepared to give ground?'

'Aren't they all like that?' Jateen turned from the game. 'I thought that was the definition of a Singh.'

They all laughed and the tension was eased somewhat.

'Uncompromi-*sing*. That's you, man,' Merc said.

'And what does that make you?'

'Right.' He lifted his chin, convinced about his instincts.

Anil began collecting the dishes from the table, his mouth misshapen by a sulk. 'Can you guys give me a hand? This place is a tip, and she's going to be here soon.'

Merc resisted pointing out that Anil had been predicting her imminent arrival for hours already. Instead, he started to help with clearing up. 'Do you remember what they used to say in Jamaica all the time when we were there?' He grinned. ' "Come soon",' he imitated the accent perfectly. 'Everything was "come soon" – food orders, taxis, bills – and then it took ages.'

Anil nodded, and a silent truce was declared.

'Come soon,' Merc repeated. 'Let's hope she does.'

She arrived with a heavy canvas bag over one shoulder.

'What's this?' Anil took it and ushered her inside. 'Are you staying for good?'

'Books.' She looked guilty. 'I told my aunt I was going to study with a friend.' They made her toes curl, the lies she told. But all discomfort faded at the sight of his smile, the feel of his fingers running along her arms as he helped her out of her coat.

'Such a big flat.' The refurbished modern interior was a surprise after the traditional Victorian façade. Lina took in the spacious entrance hall from which all the other rooms opened. There was a pool table in the middle of it. Her eyes darted along the different doors, wondering if someone might step out from behind one of them.

'It's Merc's place. Well, his dad's. The guys aren't here, they've all gone out.' He took her hand and pulled her towards him. His other arm slipped around her waist, and for a moment it seemed he might lead her off in a waltz. But over the next minutes it was only their lips that danced. When Anil's hands tried to join in, Lina drew back. She managed to make it seem natural, a toss of the head, as if she was getting her hair out of the way. She unwound the scarf that was still looped around her neck until it was just lying across her shoulders.

'It's warm in here.'

'Let me put that with your coat.' He reached out for one end of the scarf and pulled it so that, slowly, it slipped across the back of her neck. Her blood seemed to stall in her veins. She had to move her feet apart slightly to steady herself.

'Will you show me around?'

The kitchen felt bigger than the ground floor of her parents' house in Birmingham. Each bedroom had an en-suite bathroom. She was struck by the colour scheme – the way everything matched, as if all the items had been bought simultaneously. The homes she knew had a décor composed of things accumulated over years as tastes and budgets changed, the older pieces kept through necessity or fondness.

'It's not your typical student accommodation, is it?'

'We're lucky: Merc's dad doesn't really charge us much to stay here. It's like their family base in the UK. I think he's quite glad it's finally getting some proper use.'

'What does his dad do?'

'He's the Minister of State for Defence in the Kenyan government. And this is my room.' He stepped aside to let her enter first. 'I got the biggest one so there would be room for the drawing board. I know it's outmoded now, but I love working at that thing. I do my initial sketches and stuff there.'

The drawing board was almost in the middle of the room. You had to walk around it to get to the bed or desk. The papers on his desk were neatly arranged, the largest ones on the bottom. He had one holder for pencils, another for pens, all with nibs of differing thickness or lead of different grades. Four prints of various studies drawn by da Vinci hung above the desk in a straight line. His books – one wall was covered in shelves – were in alphabetical order. The navy-blue duvet on the double bed was smoothed out and crease-free. If she opened the cupboards she would see that his clothes and shoes were organized with equal care.

'Is it always like this, or did you make a special effort today?'

'I like order. It helps me think better.' He hung back by the door, watching her survey the contents of his room as if they were a window to his soul.

'Me, too.' Though she never quite achieved the level of order to which she aspired. 'I think I've seen that before.' She leaned over the desk towards the drawing of a nude male figure in two superimposed positions with his arms and legs apart.

'I should hope so. It's Vitruvian man, one of the most famous images in the world.'

Here was another statement that unwittingly underlined her ignorance. Lina tensed up. They came from different worlds, that was all, she tried to calm herself. He didn't have a clue about some of the things that mattered to her, like the scale of human rights abuses or the positive effects of micro-finance in some impoverished regions. And that was partly why she adored being with him – all the new things he exposed her to. Although, she *was* quite certain she had seen this image before. 'Why is he in a square and a circle?'

'There are a couple of different reasons.' Anil came to stand beside her, and they both studied the drawing. 'It's actually based on the idea of a Roman architect in the first century BC called Vitruvius. He considered proportion to be *the* major guiding principle of architecture. He also thought that the human body was the greatest work of art, and so he looked to it as a guide. He outlined the notion that the extended limbs of a perfectly proportioned human would fit into both a circle and a square.'

'Oh, wow.'

'No one managed to represent that as well as Leonardo da Vinci. He also believed that man is the model of the world.' They pondered for a few moments in silence. 'It's beautiful isn't it?' His voice was full of reverence. 'Some people also think that Leonardo intended the square to represent the material aspect of man, while the circle shows the spiritual side. So, in a sense, the drawing depicts the correlation between those two facets of human existence.'

'I love the idea of a balance between physical and spiritual.' Her head tilted pensively.

Anil saw in the graceful extension of her neck, and in the soft straightness of her middle parting, lines more divine than had ever been captured on paper.

'I'm sure that the people who manage to achieve an equilibrium between those two areas are probably the happiest. Don't you think so?' Lina asked.

'Possibly. It depends how you define those two categories.'

'I guess physical would be worldly pleasures: wealth, material possessions and different indulgences, like say dancing or drinking or loving.' She meant sex but was too shy to use the word. 'And spiritual would be your faith or religion, the kind of code by which you choose to live.'

When he didn't immediately reply Lina wondered if she'd said something wrong. 'Or maybe, I don't know.' Her index finger went to the scar on her lip and pressed it for a moment. 'I'm not really sure. You ... do you have a different idea?'

'I think of the spiritual more as things that, well, lift your spirit, that inspire you or bring you to a higher awareness of yourself and others. So art and books and music –

these things seem to me the best complement to the physical dimension, which, as you say, is more about bodily gratification or material acquisition. I also have the sense that, sometimes, the two facets merge. There are certain states of being in which you can feel physically and spiritually satisfied, like being in love.'

'But—' Lina started and then broke off.

'What?' Anil brushed her hair off one cheek.

'No. Nothing.' She smiled, then looked down at the wooden floor.

'Come on. Say it.'

'I don't know. It's just . . . I think . . . doesn't spirituality also involve morality?'

'Sure, it can.' He dipped his chin and raised his brows suggesting he didn't see where the contradiction was.

'And that comes from religion, right? As a guide?'

'If you want it to. But I think it can also come from your own understanding and interpretation of the world as informed by experience: your own directly lived experience, and also the experiences you are exposed to through films and books and music and other people.'

'Yes, but surely that's all in the bigger frame of your faith?' She couldn't help posing these statements as questions, her certainty temporarily shaken by the need for his approval.

'For some people, I suppose. Actually, probably for many people that's the case.'

She felt disadvantaged, somehow, at being lumped with the majority. 'Not for you?'

'Like I said to you the other day, the strong Christian influence at school has left me better able to understand many medieval paintings. But I can't say it framed the parameters of right and wrong by which I try to live. Those come from many things – like, I'll never forget the effect Balzac had on me. There's a complete moral universe depicted in *La Comédie humaine*. You get to see just how complex and shady people could be and that, for me, was much more powerful than, say, the Ten Commandments.'

Her hands sought out each other, twined fingers and then hung at her groin. Not sure what to say, she looked at the Vitruvian man again. Her eyes settled on his navel, the very centre of the image.

'Has Islam informed your perspective on everything?' The muscles in his legs tightened.

She was silent. There was no way to describe her faith. No way that did it justice.

'I suppose,' Anil said, 'that even when you believe in certain principles, life is still a process of negotiation.'

'My father says that if faith was easy everyone would have it.' She braced herself for some challenge from him, something that might signal an irreconcilable gulf between them. But what came was a question asked so gently it felt like a blessing.

'Do you think you'll manage to find a balance, then? Between what your faith requires of you and what you desire for yourself?'

'I hope so.' Her gaze melted into his. 'The possibility obviously exists. On paper, at least.' She inclined her head towards the drawing.

He stepped behind her and reached his arms out to hug her waist. She, too, lifted her arms, keeping them raised for a moment, before letting them settle over his. And so, for the briefest instant – intuitively, deliberately – they mirrored the stance of the figure in the drawing. For the briefest instant, there was a promise of perfection.

They held each other and surveyed the image while

Anil recited from memory some of the notes about pure symmetry that accompanied it. They imagined the flawless proportions of their own future were also inscribed somewhere in those ancient calculations. Only, they did not fully understand that the body in the drawing was immaculate, a specimen unknown on earth. Not flawed, like them. Not composed of limbs that weren't identical on the left and right. Not burdened by the history of illness and genes and fractures. Not misshapen by errors of judgement that could never be rectified. Not subject to the magnetic field of love, which is capable of destroying every shape – circle, square or heart.

'One day,' Anil said, 'we'll go and see the original together at the Accademia in Venice.'

'You're always making plans.'

'Because plans are how you tame the future.'

Rage bounces within me like a ball: up and down, up and down, depending on the clues I find to the strange riddle of your departure. I'll be trying to get on with things, when all of a sudden that orb of anger will spring out, triggered by some association with you.

The lease on our flat was due to expire a week after your departure for India. I thought we'd renew, but, at the last minute, you said you didn't want to remain in the small, two-room basement any more. There wasn't much time to find another place before you left. You were working long hours at the firm and I was immersed in my PhD. We decided to leave things until you got back. I would stay with Lucas during your absence. It all appeared reasonable then. Now, every development seems like another convenient manoeuvre in your master plan.

You helped me pack before you left. We had few possessions: none of the furniture was ours, except the bookshelves. You combed through those, pulling off volumes and boxing them. I saw the strange gaps between books and wondered how you were packing them. You said you were doing yours first. And I felt a pang that you had distinguished between yours and mine. Of course, I had a special attachment to all the books I'd bought and read, but I'd started thinking of everything as ours. I suggested that it might be more efficient to pack them by shelf, so they could then be unpacked in the same order. But you said that you'd already started doing things your own way and, in any case, you'd never liked the thematic arrangement we'd established, and maybe it was time to find a new kind of order.

How language can deceive! Now I understand the meaning of that expression: you only hear what you want to hear. All the warnings I missed ring in my ears now, like sirens.

My friends say I loved too readily, generously and thoughtlessly – leaving no room for doubt. But who wants to love with reservations?

The right thing is never easy to do, you claimed. May you suffer long and hard for your bizarre notions of goodness! What was the toss-up in your mind? How did you justify things? Better one jilted woman than a family let down and a God rebuked? Better the flimsy promise of eternity than the warm, pulsing absoluteness of NOW? Better a life half-lived than a death that means damnation?

It's hard to imagine how you – the star of the Debating Society at university, devil's advocate extra-ordinaire, able to argue any issue from any premiss, a man who makes a living from deliberating over nuances – could have convinced yourself that you did the right thing.

Religion is insidious. Faith – Lucas says – is like a form of theatre, all dressing up and ritual. Believers are actors who've lost all sense of reality. Most of them are also hypocrites, but you can't really blame them for it. They set themselves up to fail because all religions ask the impossible: that you submit your will and thought to some supernatural being.

But you always appeared quite your own person. Yes, you prayed and fasted and observed halal, but these acts seemed like benign habits. Stranger, to me, was your tendency to sleep wearing socks, even in summer, or your inability to throw out a newspaper you hadn't read, even if it was days old. I had rituals, too – I say *had* because everything seems to have gone haywire since you left, and who knows if I'll resume my old ways?

Sometimes I'm filled with revulsion for the woman who let herself be duped, but still loves you for crazed, humiliating instants. I watch her with a steely resolve, determined not to capitulate to her emotions. I am ashamed of her weakness. I am frightened of her sadness, which is an endless, floppy thing.

But I was writing of habits . . . my own. Yes. Amongst other things, I used to weigh myself every morning, learn a new quotation each day, soak oats in water at night for the porridge at breakfast, use every tea bag twice . . . So many such ticks peg down the tent of our daily lives. I thought your religion was a few such pegs, not the whole damn tent.

And yet, I know how your god would appear, unexpectedly, in conversations, tagging the end of your sentences like a form of punctuation. The invocation you, tellingly, used most often was 'inshallah'. God willing. It made me feel uneasy, especially when you used it in any talk about our future. Your commitment was always qualified by those two words: god willing. Except, as far as we were concerned, he wasn't, wouldn't ever be. And you knew that all along.

Your deceit was in silence. All the things you never said . . . Until the final hour.

Rockstar Auntie

SPRING WAS IN full stride and reaching out a hand to summer. Tiny green apples hung off the tree in Lina's aunt's back garden. The patch of green was big by London standards and crowded with trees. Through their branches the high evening sun sent a dapple of light that filtered into the living-room window.

'I tell you, Rocky, that girl is killing her parents,' Iman said.

Ruksana tutted. She was sitting on the carpeted floor, knees bent to one side, back against the sofa. Iman was behind her, hands swathed in yellow kitchen gloves, dabbing dye on her sister's thick, wavy hair.

'From day one she's been nothing but trouble.'

'It's a trial, mashallah, Allah has willed it. We all have our burdens to bear. I should know.'

'How can such decent people deserve this? If you ask me, it's not the work of Allah, it's Shaitan's hand at play. That child always had a devious bent. I remember when she used to come over to play with Lina, she'd end up stealing her dolls' clothes.'

'But all kids do stuff like that, Iman.' Ruksana admired her own hands, which were resting on her lap. Along her fingers gem-studded rings protruded like elaborate coral formations. These, together with the stud that shone on her left nostril and the ever-changing selection of jewels that dripped from her ears and jingled at her wrists, had earned her the sobriquet 'rockstar'.

The name evolved from a comment Iman had made years before: 'It's not enough that your name means brilliant, you have to try and dazzle even more by covering yourself in these stones. Really, you're not Ruksana any more, you're "Rocksana". A proper rockstar.' The whole family had quickly adopted the nickname, shortening it to Rocky.

'No they don't, weh.' Iman gently butted one knee into her sister's shoulder. 'But you, of course, are bound to have sympathy after the way you used to help yourself to my things.'

Iman remembered their childhood in Delhi: chasing around the neem trees in the communal courtyard after her older, longer-legged sister, who would have appropriated one of the trinkets they'd been given to share. As they grew up, Ruksana got greedier and Iman learned to make do with less. It seemed a pattern had been set and was bound to continue. Ruksana ended up with a richer husband and a bigger house and extremities studded with diamonds. Even her firstborn, Yusuf, was a son. But then things had started to change: the pretty pattern of Ruksana's life became a complicated tangle. The first blow was that her son had Down's syndrome. Two years later, just before his fortieth birthday, her husband, Abbas, went into hospital to have a hernia repaired and never regained consciousness from the general anaesthetic. There had been some error during the operation. The hospital admitted liability. A huge settlement was made out of court. Ruksana was left very well off. What she ended up coveting, of course, was her sister's simple life: a devoted husband and perfectly healthy children, living in a small semi-detached house on a street where the neighbours didn't wonder what sin you had committed to deserve so hard a sentence from God.

'All I'm saying is not every child who indulges in a bit of pinching from friends is going to end up pregnant before marriage and living in a women's shelter. I've heard stories of angelic children who've turned into complete rascals. Having kids is like throwing dice.' Ruksana flicked her hand, as though she herself was taking a shot in the game of luck. 'You never know what combination you're going to end up with.'

'But with Zara it was clear, I'm telling you, Rocky. There's one thing, astaghfirullah, I shouldn't really repeat it, but . . .' Iman leaned forward and lowered her voice, even though there was no one else around except Lina, who was seated on the other side of the room, at the dining table. 'When she was a little girl, just two or three years old, she had this habit of taking off her underwear and flashing her privates in public.'

'No!' Ruksana's hand flew up to cover her mouth.

'I saw it with my own eyes. Shameem used to check her before, make sure she was properly dressed before they went out. But still, somehow, somewhere along the way, Zara used to slip off her panties.' Iman's eyes brightened as she talked. 'When they got into the shops or arrived at someone's house, she would lift up her dress and curtsey. She did it at our place, in front of Shareef. Just imagine.'

'Very bad,' Ruksana said, though her disapproval was not strong enough to stifle her laughter.

'Poor Shameem tried everything. I heard all the dramas, because they used to live right next door to us in those days. At one stage she even stopped putting Zara in skirts or dresses, and only let her wear trousers. Even those

111

the girl managed to strip off. Finally, Shameem put a belt on Zara's trousers, and she'd knot it in a way that the girl couldn't undo herself.'

'Oh, Ma.' Lina nudged her way into the conversation. This impromptu visit of her mother's had set her on edge. Iman's sudden arrival near the end of the spring semester made Lina wonder if she'd caught some hint of her daughter's doings in the capital. Maybe Khala Rocky had mentioned that Lina was going out more than before and coming home much later in the evenings. 'Kids that age are innocent, and you make Zara sound perverted.'

'Well, this girl definitely had something wrong with her from very early on. It seems Shaitan entered her blood-stream, and, if you ask me, he's still very much resident there.' Iman used a comb to part another section of Ruksana's hair. 'She managed to deceive her parents com-pletely, lied to them for months.' Her words made Lina's breath stall. 'Said she was working in Sheffield, and actually she was living with a man.'

'Still, Iman, you shouldn't be so hard on people.' Ruksana stretched out her legs and then bent them to the other side. Her shalwar rode up, revealing a gold anklet around her thick left ankle. 'Not everyone finds their way by following the rules. Some need to take a few detours before they settle on the right path.'

'What, weh?' Iman's head bobbed with indignation and her plump cheeks wobbled slightly. 'Tobah! Tobah! Listen to you. May Allah protect us from such deviations. He has given us guidelines because He knows what is best for us. We human beings are so fickle, if we didn't have God's will to live by, we'd be tossed like leaves in the winds of all our desires.'

'I don't believe *you* could be blown off course by

anything.' Ruksana couldn't imagine any forecast other than temperate for her sister. Iman knew what was right or wrong, good or bad, and didn't seem to spend any time troubled by eddies of doubt like normal people.

'Some children, no matter what you do, are impossible to control. You know Aziza predicted it?' Iman said.

Aziza Aziz was Shareef's receptionist, and a psychic. She'd foretold the demise of Ruksana's husband. Generally, she spoke beautiful Urdu, but lapsed, involuntarily she claimed, into a broken, plural English when sharing revelations. 'Everythings can be changing with only just the pricks of one needles,' she had told Ruksana, who'd interpreted her words as a reminder that the smallest of actions had the power to alter one's destiny. It was only much later, after the event, that she had realized the precision in Aziza's words.

'But, just because you know something bad might happen, doesn't mean you suffer less when it does. Those poor parents.' Iman tutted.

'Zara can't be having much fun either, from what you were saying before, about the refuge and stuff,' Lina's head tilted to the right, so that she could watch her mother without shifting in her seat.

'She should have thought of that before falling into the kind of life she led.' Iman energetically brushed the purple, toothpaste-textured dye into Ruksana's scalp. 'Any girl who spreads her legs before marriage deserves whatever comes afterwards.'

Lina crossed her own legs tighter and looked down at her textbook, glad that her hair could curtain her burning face.

'I don't understand how these girls can just give themselves up to any man.'

'He can't have been *any* man.' The words were out before Lina could stop them.

Iman, toothbrush poised mid-air, looked at her.

'What I mean is, presumably he was someone she loved.'

'Let me tell you – that word you use, *love*,' Iman said. 'This word you young people throw around like it's a justification for anything – half the time you don't know what it means.'

Iman herself was still learning love's lessons, groping her way through its shocks and disappointments, and clinging to its joys. She had not arrived easily at her present state of fulfilment. The first years with Shareef had been difficult. At the beginning, he had spoken to her solely in English, maintaining that this was the only way she would master the language.

'But I go to the classes every day,' she'd protested in Urdu, hungry for contact in her own tongue after the solitude of a long afternoon.

He would shake his head, as if he hadn't understood. So that she was forced to converse in halting snippets, hating the sounds she made, fearing that this man could not love her while she produced such faulty, ugly words.

She spent hours rehearsing what to say to him, consulting the Urdu–English dictionary he'd bought, and writing her thoughts out on paper. She planned to tell him about the 'well done' she'd got from the teacher that morning, and the invitation to tea that a fellow student had given her, and the man who rang the doorbell in the late afternoon offering to sharpen knives for a fee, and how she'd been caught by rain on the way back from the shops and arrived home drenched. But when her husband was actually there, fixing her with a quiet attention that seemed almost abstract, her day's happenings became trivial and she condensed them into short, dull sentences. So that for a long time he did not know that her grasp of the language was much broader than he assumed. Until one day, over a year later, he noticed the newspaper had already been read, or at least flicked through, and he asked her about it. She noticed his eyebrows rise as she mentioned the articles she'd perused.

'Did you understand it all?' he wondered.

'Most of it,' she said.

He seemed to take her more seriously after that, and began to ask questions instead of just assuming that what she said revealed the limits of what she could express in English.

In spite of this, although she could never reproach Shareef for being in any way unkind, Iman often had a sense that there was a grudge against her tucked under his skin. As if she had caused offence, just by being herself. She did not consider that perhaps he was guilty of some slight that he could not admit, but sought to compensate for through a penance of politeness. She had begun to assume this was marriage: by day a routine of cordiality and measured affection, at night a brief melting of flesh before they both reverted to cold, unshared thoughts on separate sides of the bed – until Lina was born.

Then her husband began to move closer across the distance. He would gaze at the child and the mother, his eyes full of wonder at what had been created. At moments it seemed he'd perceived something previously searched for and not found. Or, perhaps, it had never really been sought, because he had not expected to discover it. In any case, their relationship started to change.

One Sunday, as Iman sat feeding the baby, he came over and knelt beside them. She looked down shyly, embarrassed to have her breast on display in broad daylight. He pushed away the hair that fell over one of her eyes, and let his hand slide down to her throat. Gently he caressed her cheek with his thumb. Then he kissed her on the mouth: long, slow and tender. Longing churned within her to a need so tight she had to clench her buttocks. For the first time she felt something like love pass between them. She was too scared to move and risk losing the feeling. Even after Shareef had got up and went to make her a cup of tea, even after the child turned her mouth away from the inflamed nipple, Iman remained motionless, as if this might safeguard the precious new emotion.

In time, that sensation, the first drops of which had swilled into the bowl of her being, grew stronger. It filled her up and, now and then, would spill from her pores in a brightness that made her beautiful. She would catch sight of herself in mirrors and not believe it was her face, rounder with happiness, staring back. Fulfilment had come unexpectedly after five years of marriage, three of which she had spent waiting in India to join her husband, and two of which had been lived in benign cohabitation. On these glowing days Shareef, also, noticed. He was not a great one for giving compliments, but would admire her openly with his eyes and then later, at night, with his hands, soaking up her radiance with awe and humility. What had appeared so bland now possessed a grandeur that he was desperate to fathom. So Iman began to believe what she had always been told: that real love between a man and a woman grew out of decency, patience and procreation. She did not hold with theories of love at first sight or love as destiny. She was sceptical of blatant displays or dramatic statements of affection. Passion was too precious to be made public. People, her own sister even, assumed she was too correct for any great emotion. In truth, she was too private to show openly what she felt.

'Ya Allah!' Iman stopped midway through dabbing dye on another section of hair. 'I'd better call Shareef and remind him to collect his blue suit from the dry cleaner's. Lina? Bring me the phone.' She pointed at the receiver perched on the sideboard.

'No, don't give it to her, Lina!' Ruksana twisted around. 'Can't you leave that man alone? You've already phoned him three times since getting here. The world isn't going to end if he forgets one or two chores. Come on, please just finish my hair now. I'm getting stiff from all this sitting on the floor.'

Iman resumed with a sigh. 'What was I saying? Oh yes, love is never a good excuse for flouting Allah's will.'

'Iman, what are you doing?' A blob of dye landed on Ruksana's cheek. 'You want to colour my face, as well as my hair? As if I haven't had enough bad luck in my life. Now you want to ruin my looks?'

'If you ask me, there is no luck worse than that of parents who are let down by their children. Parents who deny themselves in order to do the best by their kids and are then rewarded with complete disregard or worse – total humiliation. Because, let me tell you, astaghfirullah, this boy Zara has gone with . . . this . . .' Iman shook her head. She couldn't say it. The man was Chinese. 'I feel very sorry for Shameem. The girl even got an order from court against her parents, a what do you call it . . .' She tried to remember the English term. 'A junction, conjunction something.'

'Injunction?' Lina said.

'Yes, just imagine! Now they can't go near her without being arrested, even if they want to.'

'Why did she do that? Were they threatening her?'

'If giving their opinion or saying how they felt can be called threatening. What did she expect? That they would congratulate her and throw a party?' Iman's purple chuni slipped off one shoulder as she wielded the toothbrush like a wand. 'The father wanted to go and get back all of the items she took when she left home – things he paid for. He wanted to strip Zara of all that she had ever got from them. But Shareef managed to calm him down a bit. He said, "What difference will a few clothes and pieces of furniture make? Your blood is running in her veins – are you going to drain that out?" It's true. You give and give and give to your children and then, with one action, it can all go. And you realize there's nothing you can take back. Nothing that matters. Though Zara's father seemed to think her blood was worth spilling. "Let it be spread across the streets, like my honour, for people to walk all over," that's what he said.'

'So what will they do now? The parents?' Lina wondered.

'What can they do? They'll sit and die slowly of shame.' Iman gathered Ruksana's hair in one fist and twisted it into a knot.

Her sister was holding up her hands and watching the rings sparkle as they caught the last of the sunlight. Ruksana always behaved as though there was a camera nearby secretly capturing her every move. This gave an exaggerated self-consciousness to all her gestures, as if she was trapped in the Indian soap operas to which she was addicted, and not caught in the mundane reality of her own life.

'Can you look down, please? Instead of admiring your-self, as usual.'

'You like to deny everyone the smallest of pleasures.' Ruksana crossed her arms over her chest. 'What else have I got in my life? Why can't I at least enjoy beautiful things without your disapproval?'

Iman pressed her lips together and tugged a little harder than necessary on her sister's hair.

'Ouch.'

'That's why I'm telling you to sit still.'

Lina was rubbing the curved edge of Ruksana's black laquered dining table, leaving smudged fingerprints all over it. 'Maybe when Zara has her baby the parents will feel different,' she said.

'No, they won't. That's for sure.' Iman almost shuddered. 'As far as Shameem is concerned it's over between them, all ties have been cut. They don't even mention Zara's name in their house any more. She's dead for them, that's what her mother told me.'

'You mean they're never going to speak again?' Lina's throat tightened.

'There's nothing left to talk about. What she's done can't be undone. I don't understand why you're so concerned, you're not still in touch with her, are you?' Iman's eyebrows arched.

Lina pinched her upper lip. 'It's just so sad.'

'Sad! What do you know of sadness?'

Iman's words made her chest tighten.

'It can't be easy for Zara either, to have lost her family,' Lina said.

'Easy or not, she's the one who chose this route. Those who take the decisions always suffer less than those who are left to live with the consequences. I sympathize with Shameem, I would do exactly the same.'

If she didn't know her mother better, Lina might think this was a veiled warning. Iman was more a launch-right-in-with-a-drum-roll sort of person. She had no idea about Anil, Lina realized. But the recognition brought no great relief. Hearing Iman talk this way only intensified Lina's sense that her relationship with Anil was doomed. Over the last few weeks she had managed not to speculate about the future too much. It was extraordinary how quickly one could get used to being in a state that had initially felt so disagreeable. Everything seemed to be getting easier: telling lies, accepting Anil's extravagant generosity, being with him in the presence of others. The pangs of paranoia had not diminished, but time was enabling her to adjust to the deepening dichotomy in her life.

And now this.

She stood, pushed back her chair. Her eyes widened to hold the liquid suddenly pooling in them. She left the room slowly, balancing the saucers of her eyes, the way one does a full cup, so that they didn't spill over.

'Lina? Where are you going?' Ruksana asked.

'I'm coming right back!' Her voice was as cheerful as the clinking of champagne glasses. It was only when she reached the kitchen that a sound – half-snort, half-gulp – burst out of her.

Lies

'I would love to go, but . . .'. Lina shook her head. 'It's impossible.'

She was walking with her best friend, Isabel, to the house she shared with four other students in Camden. They were on a street lined with cherry blossoms. The trees were in full bloom and swayed gracefully, like bridesmaids in a long procession. Lina was talking about Anil's wish for her to visit Kenya. 'If only there was some way . . . I don't want to disappoint him.'

'I've noticed.' Isabel looked sideways. Her coppery bobbed hair was roughly pulled back with an elastic band. 'The rest of us have been somewhat sidelined recently, in your efforts to please him.'

'*Isabel.*' The name came out as an apology, a plea for understanding and a delicate remonstration. They had known each other since primary school, grown up in the same neighbourhood, slipped in and out of each other's houses. And then they had ended up at the same university, Lina studying law, Isabel sociology. 'It's not just about pleasing *him*. I *want* to be with him, it makes me happy.'

'Look, I understand that he's your priority right now. That's fine. I accept it.' Isabel couldn't hide what she really thought, unlike Lina who could wear an expression of enchantment while talking to the most boring person on earth. 'But . . .' Isabel's close-set grey eyes widened in her oval, freckled face, 'you still haven't arranged for me to see Merc.'

Lina stopped, her lips a crumple of censure. 'I don't know why you're still interested in him. I've told you how weird he is.'

'Yah, but he's sooo hot.'

'And he knows it. The guy oozes ego.' Lina tightened the straps of her rucksack and began walking again. 'You don't want to get mixed up with him.'

'For goodness' sake, Lina!' Isabel rolled her eyes. 'I'm not like you. Just because I fancy a man doesn't mean I'm planning to marry him. But first let's sort out how I can see more of you.'

'I wish there was some way of being with all the people I care about at the same time.' Lina quickened her pace to keep up with Isabel's strides. Her friend could speed-walk even in high heels. The three-inch spikes of her knee-high boots, into which her long stocking-clad legs were tucked, clopped swiftly across the concrete.

'Well, there isn't. You end up irritating and disappointing people. You've got to learn to say no. That's always been your problem.' Then Isabel's face beamed with amusement. 'On the other hand, it's also why we became friends. Do you remember?'

They both thought of the day in primary school when Isabel's egg mayo sandwich had fallen into the sandpit. As her bottom lip had pushed out in dismay Lina had offered her a potato bhaji. Isabel had accepted, taken a wary bite, smiled, gobbled up the rest and then asked for another. And another. And just one more. Until most of Lina's lunch had been in her stomach.

'Of course I remember, greedy-guts! I practically starved

for the rest of that week with you taking my food every day!'

'I offered you my sandwiches. You said no.' Isabel giggled and jumped to brush at the blossoms hanging off the tree they were passing under.

'You know why! Even you couldn't eat those.' Again Lina had to hurry to keep abreast of her friend.

'Tell me about it.' She started going through the pockets of her cloth satchel, searching for her keys. 'My mum never did get the hang of making things edible.'

'I guess she had more important stuff on her mind.'

Isabel's father had left her mother, Linda, just before she was born. Linda had raised the child on her own while holding down a full-time job as a nurse.

'That's true, but I'm glad I had Iman to educate my taste buds. Otherwise, who knows, I might still not have experienced the pleasures of keema koftas or chicken makhani. But, anyway,' she said as they walked up to the door of the shared terraced house, 'this whole Kenya thing, I think it would be great to go. Can't you just tell your parents you're going to do work experience or something?'

'I don't want to lie more than necessary.' Lina followed her in. It smelled musty, a mixture of smoke and old tea bags and coffee brewed for too long. 'I think making up a job on top of everything else would be going too far.'

'There's no point in analysing degrees of deceit, Leenie. You're lying – full stop. Whether you tell one or ten, whether they're big or small, I don't think it makes a difference.' There was an untidy stack of letters in the long hallway. Isabel picked them up and looked through them before dropping them back down. She headed up the creaky stairs to her room in the attic. The brown carpet was frayed along the edge of each step.

'Maybe. But still, I'd rather not overdo it.'

'Well then, try and get a real job out there. I'm sure there must be organizations that offer internships. Ask Anil. His parents must be pretty well-connected. Maybe they can help.'

Anil liked the idea. He was sure his father would be able to call in favours and get Lina a placement with some non-governmental organization. So they started planning as if everything was bound to work out as they wanted. Lina didn't know that Anil had asked his father to help find a placement for a 'friend' without elaborating on any of the details, not even mentioning that he intended to bring this person to stay in their home. Pravar, surprisingly, had not probed, merely commented, 'I hope you will follow your friend's example and come get some experience in my office.' Anil agreed to this. It was the price he had to pay. Spending a few weeks at his father's company would perhaps also help mitigate the other news he had not yet shared – that he wouldn't be returning to work in Kenya after graduating that summer. He had already secured a job as a trainee in the London office of a prestigious international architecture firm.

Lina had no idea that she wasn't the only one being untruthful. To her, Anil's life seemed like a leather-bound book of the highest quality paper on which he could scribble as he pleased and have events unfold to his liking. Whereas her own existence resembled a jotter pad with the margins already ruled and little space left for manoeuvre.

'Have you told them yet?'

Each time they spoke, this was Anil's first question. And she always had to confess: No. She had not yet managed to reveal that her name was down for an internship at the United Nations office in Nairobi, thanks to Pravar's contacts and his liberal hand with kitu kidogo. Several times she had approached her parents, fully intending to discuss the offer with them, only to stall at the last minute, like a car shifted suddenly into the wrong gear. Anil couldn't understand her prevarication.

'If you don't want to come, just tell me,' he said.

'You don't understand how it is with my parents. I'm just waiting for the right moment.'

'The right moment never just arrives, you have to make it.'

It did indeed come – though it was not of Lina's making – some weeks before she was due to leave for Nairobi, during a weekend visit home. She was thrust into the moment when Iman began discussing plans for a family trip to India that summer. They were in the sitting room, watching a documentary about marmots. Shareef sat on the sofa with his feet stretched out on the coffee table. Beneath it was a stack of old newspapers that he hadn't read but wouldn't throw away because, he claimed, he still intended to go through them when he had time. It drove Iman mad. His tiny office downstairs was almost crammed solid with them. From time to time, she would go in there and heave out one of the older piles.

Iman was sitting beside him, a yellow plastic bowl on her lap, picking fenugreek leaves off their stalks. Mariam lay on the carpet, stretched out on her stomach, flicking through a magazine for young teens. Little Nasra was upstairs in bed with a bad cold that she'd caught after a gruelling week of training to qualify for the county under-tens swimming team. Sunk in the comfortable old single-seater, Lina sat with her knees folded up to one side, her elbow on the armrest and her head on her hand. She was ostensibly watching the programme, but her thoughts were wandering.

'You need to let me know what dates I should book for you.' Iman's elbow winged out to nudge her husband. 'You said you would know by the end of this week.'

Shareef nodded.

A bluish light from the screen crept through the room, turning the pale-brown flowers on the wallpaper violet.

'I think I'm just going to confirm for me and the girls.'

'Confirm?' Lina sat up straight. 'Is it definite, then?' Her mother had been talking about this trip for months.

'Well, *we* are all going.' Iman glanced at her daughters. 'But as far as Baba is concerned, only God knows.'

'I won't be able to come for the full stretch of your trip, that's for sure. But I should be able to manage a fortnight or so. I'll have a better idea next week.' Shareef didn't take his eyes from the TV.

'Oh what-weh? Next week, next week. Tobah, Shareef, *you* are the boss. I don't know why you can't just decide. Well, I'm going to book our seats. If I always waited for you, nothing would get done.'

On screen a couple of marmots were beating up their young female offspring. The voice-over reported that this severe persecution was calculated to make the little rodents abort if they became pregnant.

'How horrible.' Iman made a face.

'Those big ones must have been influenced by maulana Akbar.' Mariam pushed herself up and twisted around. Her moussed and sprayed fringe cut across her forehead in a stiff diagonal line.

'Bismillah! Have some respect, talking about your old teacher like that!'

'Do you remember, Lina, the way he used to say, "A girl will be bitten if she doesn't follow the straight path"?' Mariam imitated his hectoring manner and his mispronunciation of beaten as bitten. 'Or, "A girl should be bitten if she loses her way." And I actually used to think he meant literally bitten, which was somehow scarier.'

Lina nodded. She couldn't tell her little sister that the old maulana had been unwittingly prescient. The sharp bites of reality assailed her regularly, in short vicious bouts, one of which had commenced with her mother's conversation about the family vacation.

The narrator of the documentary went on, saying that although, at first, the marmots' behaviour appears inordinately cruel, there is method in this meanness. It is in the survival interests of a marmot family not to produce too many babies, because they cannot all be kept warm and safe during hibernation.

'Parents know best.' Iman spoke as if confirming a long-known fact. 'It's nature, this instinct which helps you deal with your kids in the right way. Don't you think?' She elbowed her husband again.

'Ssshh. Listen.' Shareef disagreed. The best parental guidance in humans, he thought, didn't come from mere instinct.

Lina shifted on the sofa, set her feet down on the floor and leaned forward. She knew she had to say something, *now*. 'Maaaa . . .' She pulled at the hems of the purple leggings she'd borrowed from Mariam, forcing them to come a bit further down her calves.

'Oh, what-weh?' Iman knew the long-drawn-out

syllables of that address meant some tricky request was going to be made.

'Maybe you should hold off with my booking as well.' Her heartbeat quickened. 'I might not be able to come at all.'

'Why?' Iman frowned and even Shareef turned away from the TV.

'Well, I've been offered a summer internship at the UN—'

'The *UN*?' Shareef was impressed.

'I didn't expect to get it.' Lina's toes dug into the worn brown carpet. 'I applied on a whim, because my tutor suggested it. I never thought I'd even get close.'

'Well, that's very good.' His eyes creased up as his mouth lengthened into a smile. 'Well done.'

His admiration struck her like a dart, and it took willpower not to flinch. 'Well, I don't know, it was just a fluke. I'm not sure how much it had to do with my ability. I think I just got lucky.'

'And this termship, when does it start and how long is it?' Iman asked.

Lina told them, but was too afraid to add that it was in Kenya.

'So then you can join us for a while at the end. I was planning to be in Delhi for six weeks. Mariam and Nasra will be with me. Your father can come whenever it suits him and you can fly straight from London after your work is finished. Oh but . . .' A hand went over Iman's mouth. She remembered that her sister would also be abroad. 'How will you stay alone in that big house of Rocky's? It's not safe.'

'Actually, Ma, the placement is at a UN office in Kenya. And since I'm going over there anyway it would be great to stay on for a week or two after the placement and see a bit of the country.' The words rushed out: flat, too well-rehearsed, desperate to be said and done with.

Her parents looked at each other.

'What-weh? Kenya? Let me tell you, that is impossible. How can you go there on your own? Where will you stay? We don't know anyone in Kenya.' Iman shook her head and set the yellow bowl to balance on the armrest of the sofa.

Shareef moved slowly, looking for the right button on the remote control to turn down the volume. He lifted his feet off the coffee table and set them on the floor before leaning forward with both elbows resting on his knees. 'Why Kenya?'

'It's one of their biggest offices,' Lina said. 'The fourth largest, actually. So it's a major regional hub. And they have an opening . . .'

'What about practicalities? The cost of getting there, living somewhere? Are you paid for what you do? How does it all work?' Shareef was looking at Lina and didn't notice Mariam slither around the coffee table and grab the remote control. Even when the red lights of a music video beamed from the screen on to their faces his attention wasn't distracted from his eldest daughter.

The intensity of her father's gaze made Lina forget her script. 'Um, I'm not sure, I mean yes. Everything is included, Baba. Almost, I mean, they cover the flights. There and back. And they don't pay a proper salary, but they do give a bit of money, like you know, expenses, sort of. To cover daily food and travel, that kind of thing.' It was not going well.

'And accommodation?'

'Oh, um, yes, um, they do offer to help you find

something if necessary, but I'm quite lucky because my friend, you know, the one from uni, who lives in Nairobi? She's said I can stay with her.'

'What-weh? Is this the friend you got some letters from?' The fingers of Iman's right hand pressed against her temples, as if she was trying to pinpoint the memory. 'We've never even met her. And we have no idea about her family. Listen, we can't just let you run off across the world to stay with strangers. Tell her, Shareef.' She moved along and sat closer to her husband, as if to suggest a united front.

'I've got to agree with the Management. I assumed when you said UN that you'd be working in London.'

Part of Lina wanted to stop talking and give in. But another bit of her was thinking about how Anil might react if she told him that their plans had come to nothing and she would be away on the Indian subcontinent for the summer.

'The thing is, Baba—' She took a deep breath. One hand clutched at the flowing white linen top she had on. Already it was a rumpled relic of the crisp, starched garment she'd put on that morning. It was bunched around her, creased with the history of the day, every movement scored into the fabric the way every lie was on her conscience. 'Kenya is what I've been offered. It's so competitive. If I turn it down, there's a waiting list of people ready to grab at it. And I might never have such an opportunity again.'

Shareef sat back, thinking that the tremble in her voice and the clenched hand were indications of how much she wanted the internship.

Lina saw doubt in his silence. 'It will look great on my CV. You're the one who's always told me just a good degree is not enough.'

Shareef nodded.

'Tobah! What shamelessness.' Iman stared as girls in silver catsuits threw their bodies into provocative shapes across the screen. 'What rubbish are you watching, Mariam? Is that where you got the idea to wear these stupid tight trousers?'

'They're called leggings.' Mariam spoke without looking at her mother.

'And that other thing you've got on.' She made a face at Mariam's tank top. 'What's that called? A tumming? Don't you dare even think of stepping out of the house in those clothes.'

Mariam continued to ignore her.

'I'm going to have to start coming shopping with you again, if this is the kind of rubbish you pick up. Now put on that nice animal programme again.' Iman waited for Mariam to obey before going back to addressing Lina. 'Listen to me, tell them your culture does not allow this. If they like you so much, they will find something else for you, something closer to home.'

'What culture, Ma? We're not living in Saudi Arabia.'

'Wherever you live, show me one good Muslim parent who would let their daughter go gallivanting to Africa all alone.'

Lina felt the fight was lost, but kept on. 'Actually, I couldn't believe that I had been selected out of all the possible candidates. I'm still half-expecting them to turn around and say it was a mistake or something. I thought getting the internship would be the hardest bit, not persuading you.' Her green irises fixed on Shareef like suckers. And he felt himself yield to her entreaty.

'It is a very unique opportunity, no doubt about that,'

he said. 'Maybe we can find a way to make it work, inshallah, God willing. Let me think about it.'

'What-weh? Will you go with her to keep an eye?' Iman stood up irritably and accidentally knocked the yellow bowl, which teetered precariously before she managed to grab it. 'It's too hot for cooking.' She started walking out of the room, but turned at the doorway. 'If you ask me, you should forget this whole idea, Lina, and stop troubling your father. Shareef, please, huh, don't sit around debating now for hours.'

As soon as she left Mariam started channel-surfing again.

'Baba? So? What do you think?' Lina asked.

'When do you have to confirm acceptance?'

'That's pretty much assumed. I mean they don't expect to be turned down. But, obviously, I need to tell them as soon as possible if I'm not doing it. That's only fair.'

Shareef watched images jump across the screen as Mariam pressed idly on the remote control and complained that there was nothing good on.

Lina sat still and waited for her father to speak.

'Who is this friend you're planning to stay with?'

She explained that Shanila Mayur was a girl on her course. They had become very good friends over the last year, and her family, who were quite well-to-do, were happy to have Lina stay with them. During the course of this description, her glance wandered, flitting away from him a couple of times.

'I am not against this, in principle.' Shareef scratched his nape. He hadn't gone to the barber for two months and his hair was a mess of tight, greying curls. The ends hung untidily along the back of his neck. 'But you must understand that your mother and I have concerns.' He continued to ponder, taking long, slow inhalations followed by similar extended exhalations, as though he was meditating on the problem. 'Are they a good family?'

She knew what he was asking. 'They are Sikhs.'

'So they're decent, believing people.' He might have been persuading himself. Shareef pressed down the corners of his moustache with his thumb and index finger. 'And does Shanila have any brothers or sisters?'

The sound of him saying that name! It made her want to grind her teeth. 'She's an only child.'

'I would like to speak to the parents,' he said.

Lina hunched forward so that her bottom was perched on the very edge of the seat. This was not what she'd expected. 'Baba, you used to do that when I was nine. I don't see what difference it will make. What can you figure out through a phone call?'

'If your friend Shanila came to us for a month and her parents didn't bother contacting me beforehand, I wouldn't think too well of them. It's a question of politeness. They will have more regard for you, Lina, if I speak to them.' The ash-coloured callus on his forehead seemed especially pronounced. She felt an urge to reach out and wipe it away, the way she had tried to, years ago, when traces of it had first appeared, like the daub of a dirty palm against a freshly painted wall. Right now the rough circle seemed to be challenging her. I've got a black mark on the inside, she thought. A nugget, solid as the night, that was the seed of falsehood.

'I don't know, Baba. Maybe I should just forget the whole thing.' She looked at the floor.

Shareef, upset by the disappointment in her posture, protested. 'Don't be silly. Why are you being defeatist now? What's wrong if I speak to the family? I will feel better, the

Management will be satisfied and it won't do you any harm. So?'

There seemed to be no way out.

Shortly afterwards some visitors arrived to see him and he proudly told them, 'Lina has won a summer internship with the UN.' She tried to deflect the implications of 'won', which boasted accomplishment when she had displayed none, except, perhaps, in acting her way almost convincingly through a fraudulent scenario.

As evening fell and she packed for the journey back to London, Lina's shame seemed to swell like an inflammation. At the bottom of her bag lay the bundle of letters she'd received so far from Anil. They too travelled, back and forth, between her different homes. She felt they were safer with her, rather than left for someone to stumble on. Isabel had offered to store them, but Lina hadn't passed them on to her as yet. She felt for the bundle and pressed her hand around it, as if it was a totem that would give her the strength to go on.

Shareef came in and she quickly stuffed the letters back and shoved some clothes on top. He seemed about to say something when he caught sight of a book lying on the desk, next to her railcard and wallet. He picked it up and ran his fingers slowly over the title, *I Am Another You*, and the name of the author, S. M. Turner. Then he looked at the blurb. Lina went on packing.

'Are you reading this?' He sounded unlike himself. Lina looked up to check if he was disapproving, but he just seemed very surprised.

'Yeah. A friend lent it to me.' Merc had given copies of the novel to her and Anil as a salutary warning. It was the story of an affair between a Muslim and a non-believer that ended in failure. Anil had found the tone pathetic and told Lina not to bother with the book, but she'd been too curious after all the things Merc had said.

Shareef opened the book and glanced at the first page before quickly shutting it again. 'What do you think of it?'

She wasn't sure if there was some kind of trap in the question. 'I'm only halfway through.'

'This author got famous when I was just a little bit older than you.'

Lina returned to folding and putting away her clothes. 'She's been in the papers again because she died recently. Apparently she fell under a train. Might have been a suicide.' Merc had come across various tributes and seen the author's first novel, *I Am Another You*, mentioned repeatedly. That's what had made him want to read it. 'The book is quite gripping so far.' She turned, but her father had already left the room.

II

Different Worlds

WHEN PRAVAR REALIZED that the person for whom he'd arranged the internship was Anil's girlfriend, and that she was coming to stay in their house for the summer and – on top of everything else – that she was a Muslim, he was indignant.

'Since when are we so Westernized that we are allowing this kind of thing right under our roof?' He laced his fingers and then bent his hands backwards so that every digit clicked. 'And why has he gone for a Muslim? Of all the girls in the world, Minnie? Why one of *them*?' As if he'd never had anything to do with Muslims.

Pravar, like many Sikhs, had acquired a hotchpotch sense of his people's history, in which, from Mughal times through to the partition of India and right up until the present day, persecution by Muslims seemed the predominant theme. The prejudice was always there but, like a stain, only showed up in certain lights.

Minnie couldn't understand Anil's choice either, but what could you do? Children acted as they wished these days, and if the parents didn't approve they simply ignored them or, in the worst cases, cut off all ties. She explained this to Pravar as she arranged the milky gauze fabric that hung from the frame of their super-king-size four-poster bed. She had picked a moment, late at night after an enjoyable party, to disclose their son's plans, anticipating that

Pravar would be more amenable while slightly intoxicated. 'With the young generation, I think it's just attraction that counts. You shouldn't get worked up. Anil is young, he's properly in love for the first time, and I don't see any harm.'

'No harm!' Pravar pushed aside the curtains his wife had just arranged. 'What if he decides to marry this girl?'

'Oh, what are the chances of that?' She made it seem unlikely, even though she herself was surprised by the extent of Anil's feelings for the girl. The way he had pleaded with her to collude in the plan to get Lina over, even persuading her to lie to the girl's parents, as if his sanity depended on it. He'd threatened not to come home for the summer if Lina couldn't be there. So Minnie had acquiesced, wondering how long the infatuation would last, assuming it wouldn't be long because Anil's obsessions usually came in short bouts, like colds.

'You never know, if he's so keen on her already. He hasn't tried to bring any other girl over to stay.'

'I don't think it's likely.' Minnie pushed some cushions out of the way and slid into bed. 'How many youngsters these days marry their first love? They all want experience. Everyone has at least one or two relationships before they get settled.'

Pravar grunted and climbed in beside his wife. Too agitated to lie down, he sat scratching at his chest, which seemed to have stolen all the hair from his head. 'What will people say?'

'No one will dare say anything.' At least not to their faces. Money put them above judgement. Or, at least, above its consequences. Others might be ostracized for the scandals in their families, but few people could afford not to be on good terms with the Mayurs. 'I don't think it will

140

come to that, anyway. Anil is a bit like you: if you deny him something he wants it even more. That's why I think there's no point making a fuss. We'll just push him further into this girl's arms,' Minnie said.

'Very funny, that her parents are letting her come. Who sends their daughter off like that to stay with strangers?'

Minnie cleared her throat and pulled the bed cover up under her chin. She hadn't told Pravar about the deception: pretending Anil was her daughter Shanila. Pravar would find it petty – after all he only dealt in false-hood on a grand scale. 'No, no. They seem very decent. The father phoned me, he was quite concerned about Lina coming here on her own. He even asked if he could give us something for keeping her for so long. Very sweet man, that's what I thought.'

'But still, allowing her to go to her boyfriend's place. It's very liberal. I haven't met any Muslims like that before. No. Absolutely not.' His fingers drummed against his temples, as if he was shuffling through memory, to make sure.

'Oh no! They don't know anything about girlfriend-boyfriend. They think the two are just friends.' She decided not to elaborate any further. 'The father, Shareef is his name, was very proud that she got the UN job-experience thing. That's why he's letting her come.'

Pravar yawned and said, 'Shareef, huh?' It meant 'modest', he knew. 'Let's hope the daughter is as well.'

Minnie put Lina in a guest-room down the corridor from Anil. The first night, after everyone had gone to bed, he crept to her, tiptoeing across the cool marble like a thief. What he'd been looking forward to most while she was in Kenya was the uninterrupted flow of time they'd have together: whole days and nights, waking up in the same bed, planning what to do without having to take into account Lina's obligations to all the other people in her life. But when he entered her room she was aghast.

'Anil?' She heard the door click open then shut again.

'Sshhhh.' He held his hands out feeling his way through the dark as if it was a bag, and he was trying to locate something in one of its deep pockets.

'Anil! What are you doing?' She sat up as his weight pressed down on the mattress.

'I want to be with you.' He leaned in, searching for her face. The only visible shape was a faint rim of velvety blue light around the curtains at the window. 'We've never slept in the same bed together.'

'But your parents!' Her whisper was panicked.

'So what? They're asleep. No one knows.'

'But we're in their house!' She pushed him away. 'I can't do this. Please, Anil. What would they think if they found out?'

'They won't.'

'No.' She climbed out of bed, pulling on the sleeves of her long nightshirt. '*Please*. This is *wrong*.'

'You're being silly. My parents don't care. What young couple wouldn't sneak into each other's rooms? As long as we're not obvious about it.' He groped around, trying to reach her, as if his touch might be more persuasive than his words. 'Lina?'

She took another step back and found herself against a cupboard. '*Please*.' It sounded like she was begging an assailant not to attack her. This was what made Anil stop.

'Can I at least have a hug?' He was standing right in front of her.

She realized he was naked, apart from his boxer shorts. 'Not now. *Please.*'

'What's wrong with you?'

'I can't. Not here.' Her face was turned away, her left cheek, like the rest of her body, pressed to the lacquered surface of the cupboard. 'When we're alone . . .'

'Whatever, Lina.' He left quickly.

Anil had not anticipated that she would take her internship so seriously. To him it was simply a legitimate tent under which they could carry on their liaison. He'd thought she would leave work early and skip days without a qualm – the way he intended to for the weeks he'd committed to helping at his father's company. But after her first day at the UN Refugee Agency in Nairobi, Lina started acting like a long-employed, permanent member of staff who was integral to the organization. Each morning Anil would drop her off at work before heading to Pravar's office. She was always ready on time and he would be the one loitering, trying to find excuses to delay. For once, he half-joked, he would have been glad of her tendency to lateness. Thanks to her he ended up in the office even before his dad.

Chauffeuring Lina was worthwhile because they got to be alone together, but she was easily distracted. The matatus that blared past them, an irritant to him and other drivers, were amusing novelties to her.

'Look at that one!' She suddenly pointed, in the middle of a conversation, captivated by a brightly coloured bus with the ridiculous name *Necessary Noise* emblazoned across one side. The vehicle revved on to the pavement in order to overtake them. Music was playing so loudly in the matatu that the bass vibrations spilled into their car. 'How do they cope with that noise?' Lina wondered, gazing at the people crowded into the bus.

'It's a teeny matatu.' Anil explained that these were especially targeted at teenagers or those who were still teens at heart.

'They're like mobile discos.' Lina craned her neck as another one, dubbed *Feel the Flow*, followed the example of *Necessary Noise* and sped along the pavement, over-taking all the stationary cars waiting for the lights to change. A tout, dressed like an American rapper, was swinging from the doors, shouting at pedestrians to get out of the way.

Anil drummed his fingers on the steering wheel. 'They're always playing the latest hits. Lots of Kenyan musicians release their singles on these teeny matatus.' He pressed down on the horn as yet another small bus tried to bypass the traffic by cruising on to the pavement. There was a chorus of hooting as other drivers joined in. Meanwhile, *Necessary Noise* and *Feel the Flow* nipped past the waiting cars as the lights turned green.

Lina laughed. 'This is crazy!' She felt no amount of riding through these streets could accustom her to the strange rules of Kenyan traffic. The matatu now adjacent to them had the words *Jesus Saves* plastered across it in electric blue. It, too, was playing music, though at a less deafening level. If Lina had rolled down her window, she would have caught the sweet sound of 'Yes, Jesus loves you . . .'. On Anil's side, another matatu inched forward. Again, it looked more sober than the teeny ones and boasted the name *Genesis*.

'These two are gospel matatus.' Anil pushed forward, determined not to let *Jesus Saves* cut in front of them. 'They sport biblical quotes and always play gospel music.'

'Are you serious?' Lina rubbed her bare arms. The air conditioning was making the car chilly. Iman would have been horrified to see the bra straps visible on Lina's shoulders alongside the spaghetti straps of her sundress. 'What other kinds of matatus do they have?' Lina tried to spot more of the vehicles. Unlike the anonymous modes of transport at home, these were like individuals with distinct personalities. And the one you chose to ride said a lot about you. 'The funniest so far is the one we saw yesterday which looked like a Louis Vuitton bag.'

'The designer matatu.' Anil smiled. 'It's literally prêt-à-porter.'

'Look!' She pointed to one called *That's That*. 'Is it a teeny?'

'I don't think so. The music's not loud enough.' The lights turned red and they were forced to a halt again. Anil's lips flared as he blew impatiently out of them. 'Unless that driver's been clever enough to spot a policeman.' He looked around for signs of any traffic wardens. 'They make a show of following the rules if they see the police. But mostly they're all in cahoots with each other, anyway.'

'Really?' Lina sat forward and turned to face him. 'How?'

'Kitu kidogo.' Anil rubbed some imaginary money between his fingers. 'And the rest of us have to suffer while these loud machines play at being kings of the road.'

'Hasn't the government tried to do anything?'

A vendor knocked on the windscreen and held up an array of magazines. Lina was surprised to see the kind of titles that you could find in any UK newsagent: *Time*, *Vogue*, *Newsweek*. Anil ignored the vendor while Lina waved, smiled and shook her head.

'Many of these bloody matatus are owned by politicians or senior police officers. A normal matatu might be able to do seven or eight runs along a route in one day. But those with friends in high places can manage ten or twelve with their kata corner practices. And more runs means more money, right?'

'That's awful.' Lina sank back in her seat. 'Is there anything in this city untainted by corruption?'

'Not a lot. The government itself operates like a matatu. Doing as it pleases, breaking the rules and blasting the populace with lies.' They were moving again, nudging out of the worst traffic.

'I don't know if I could live in such a place,' Lina said as they circled a roundabout where there were no lines on the road to divide the lanes.

Anil shrugged. 'You get used to it.' A matatu bearing the words *Dirty Trix* crossed the road in front of them. 'Merc told me some of these are pimped matatus.'

'What do you mean?' Lina's eyes widened.

'A lot of them have TV screens inside and they've started playing porn.'

'My God.' She pulled a face. Who would have thought a city's transport system could offer so much more than just a ride from A to B?

A week after arriving in Nairobi Lina made her first visit to a refugee camp with some colleagues from the UN office. They went to the site in Northern Kenya by plane. Through the window Lina could see the shadow of the small Fokker moving across the earth below them. The land was flat and arid, the vegetation sparse. Acacia trees rose from the ground, their trunks like middle fingers being stuck up at the sky, defying the sun with their resilience. Smaller shrubs were hunched over like old beggars, clinging to the earth. Giraffes and gazelles, startled into motion by the drone of the aircraft, dashed across the plain.

She could not imagine anything surviving in this landscape, and yet, somewhere nearby, thousands of refugees from Somalia and Sudan were living, or at least getting by. The reports she had read about Dadaab in preparation for this trip had been grim. The emptiness made her recall the testimony she'd read of one refugee who had been at the camp almost a decade: 'We have learned nothing in this place, except how to be hungry, and we have nothing other than time.'

Around Lina a conversation was going on between the UN staff who were accompanying the new regional director, Peter Merton, on this visit to Dadaab.

'I've told you before, I think the only way to decrease down the level of violence is by setting up different camps for the different tribes. A-ha?' said Mildred Waraira, head of the local office.

Peter Merton did not believe that further segregation was an option. This had already been done to some extent with the nearby camp at Kakuma, but he didn't feel it should become standard policy. He pulled a handkerchief out of his pocket and dabbed at his receding hairline. 'People have to learn to live together. They've all suffered, they've all managed to reach relative safety. If we keep ghettoizing every group, prejudices and rivalries will be exacerbated. And besides, the more camps we have, the bigger our security problem becomes.' Already it was a huge concern. Besides the internal clashes, the camp was subject to armed robberies by bandits. There were ongoing talks with neighbouring governments about closing borders in order to reduce some of the violence.

Mildred looked her new boss in the eye. 'They go much deeper than you think, these clan differences. Some of these people have been at war in their homeland. They've killed members of each other's communities. So, of course, there is distrust. This is why you are getting confrontations even now in Dadaab.'

'It's a bad situation,' Peter conceded.

'A-ha. Look,' Mildred pointed. 'We're almost there.'

In the near distance, they saw the scrub of the refugee camp, dotted with improvised homes that resembled igloos made of timber and plastic. Around the camp was a halo of nothingness: a sandy belt of land that stood out from its surroundings for being totally stripped of all vegetation.

'What's that?'

'A-ha, that's land which has been totally degraded from overuse. The refugees have cut down all the trees and shrubs for wood and grazed their animals on the grass.' Mildred moved her lips over her teeth as if she was trying to suck something out of the gaps, perhaps the sound – a-ha – that filled her speech.

'Shocking.' Peter shook his head.

'They had no choice, of course. Half the world cooks with wood. And what are they supposed to do if we give them no alternative? But . . .' She raised a finger. 'This is where the solar cookers have started to make a difference. A-ha! I am looking forward to showing you.'

They were welcomed by camp staff and throngs of children, whose excited hellos bounced like beach balls on the hot tide of air. Aside from such displays of goodwill, and the colourful capes wrapped around the women's upper bodies and heads, the camp was even more desolate than it had appeared from the air. Perhaps the meagreness of the place struck Lina more deeply because it was such a stark contrast to the luxury of Anil's home, where she had been just a few hours before.

For the first two days she'd lost her way in the house several times. It felt more like a hotel, with its endless rooms, en-suite bathrooms and uniformed staff keeping order and ready to attend to every whim. The Mayurs even had a vast room for storing crockery and cutlery. Minnie collected dinner sets and had proudly shown Lina the porcelain tableware and crystal glasses that she'd accumulated. Her largest set, which could feed forty people, had been specially commissioned from Rosenthal. It was maroon and black with a gold peacock embossed on the rim. The family ate daily from crockery of a similar quality. There were fresh linen napkins at each meal, even though Pravar and Anil didn't use theirs.

'I hope your mum's not going to all this trouble for me,' Lina had said to Anil. But it turned out this was their usual standard of dining.

Minnie believed in enjoying her good things. 'Most of the ladies, they save the best stuff only for when guests come. I never understood this just-for-show policy.' Minnie claimed to be an artist of the every day, always at work on her immediate environment to make it more beautiful: her home was her canvas.

Lina found out Minnie had been on all sorts of courses; from gift-wrapping to soap-making. And the skills she learned were on display around her house and extended into the garden – not that she got her hands dirty. Three gardeners maintained the grounds under her supervision. Several times she and Lina had strolled there together. Butterflies flitted over the radiance of foliage, and Minnie had told her that some poet, whose name she couldn't remember, had referred to the creatures as 'conscious flowers of the air'. She would regularly reel off odd lines of poetry. Lina was struck by how much Anil resembled his mother. There was a similar intensity about both of them. They demanded your whole attention and assumed your complete interest in whatever captivated them.

The careless extravagance of that life compared with the one in front of Lina at Dadaab was discomfiting. Both were at extremes from the way she had lived. She had been able to enter Anil's rich realm with relative ease, hiding any awkwardness behind her natural charm. But the existence at the camp was harder to adjust to.

There were men who stood around, arms crossed, hips thrust out to one side, turning their idleness into pointless surveillance; women, who risked rape each time they left the camp in search of firewood to cook a meal; children, who raced through dust shrieking to the rattle of rusted old cans, thinking this was the whole world: a place where there was never enough food or medicine or hope. Beside this, even her family's modest lifestyle was opulent, and not just in a material sense. For the first time she truly felt the value of freedom and security.

Lina listened as camp residents and staff discussed the new solar-cooker initiative with the visiting delegation. Women in the camp were being trained to teach others how to use them. But there weren't enough cookers to go around. Peter explained, through a translator, that this was due to a lack of funding.

'But you are from the UN!' people said, surprised to learn of such a limitation. Surely the UN could do anything?

Lina was moved by the way they saw the organization as a force for good with infinite reach. She, too, felt puzzled that it could not stretch to financing the acquisition of a few thousand solar cookers.

During the flight back to Nairobi the atmosphere was subdued. Tiredness, tinged with a degree of hopelessness, made everyone on board seem a little older.

'I wish there was some way of increasing up our budget.' Mildred rolled up the sleeves of her blouse.

'Limits are the one thing you have to learn to accept in this job,' Peter said. 'We can't help everyone in every way, even though that is our objective.'

'How much would we need to pay for all the necessary cookers?' Lina wondered.

Mildred shut her eyes and did a quick mental calculation. 'About thirty thousand dollars.'

'If I could get that money as a donation, would it definitely all go towards getting cookers?' Lina pulled at her seat belt and leaned forward so that she could look down the aisle at Peter.

'Where are you going to get such a large sum?' He smiled.

'I don't know if I'll get it, but I'd like to try.'

'Well, if you manage to get even half that it would be a huge bonus for our effort. I'm going to be pressing at the top for a bigger budget as well. But, you know, in this business we can't guarantee exactly where money will go.' Peter shrugged. 'It depends on priorities at the time. If your money came in and we had a more pressing crisis else-where, say severe food shortages in Ethiopia, we would divert resources there.'

'If you really want to make sure your money goes towards cookers,' Mildred spoke up, 'the best thing – a-ha – to do, is to buy them yourself.'

The easiest option would have been to ask the Mayurs.

151

However, requesting money, after all Anil's parents had already done to make her visit to Kenya possible, seemed too awful to Lina. They'd been good enough not to mention having to pretend Anil was Shanila. Nor had they made any allusion to her being a Muslim. Their welcome had been as warm as if she was a member of the family. It would be wrong to ask any more of them. Lina would never have brought up the issue if Anil hadn't casually introduced it at the dinner table.

'You know, last year Mayur Holdings supported more than twenty different causes.' Pravar poured himself some more wine.

'That's wonderful.' Lina's glass stood untouched, as usual, in frosty, sparkling refusal.

'As a company we are very social-minded. Minnie here . . .' He nodded at his wife, '. . . is always doing little charity things and I regularly give to her enterprises. But many people are coming to me directly. And if I like what they're doing, I donate. Simple as that.'

'Well, I think this refugee cause of Lina's sounds pretty worthy,' Anil spoke while trying to chew the last shreds of meat from a lamb chop. It was only since coming to Nairobi that Lina had noticed his habit of leaning right down towards his crockery while eating or drinking.

Lina looked at her own plate. Two chop-bones made the figure seventy-seven in a pool of leftover gravy studded with a few pearls of rice. She had abandoned her halal principles since entering this house. On the day of her arrival Minnie had served chicken biriyani. As she'd portioned it, Anil had pointed out that Lina couldn't eat any because it wasn't halal. Minnie had suddenly become distressed and apologetic. Lina, sensing something fine in the balance, feeling the weight of all they had done to help her, knew it wouldn't be right to refuse the food. She'd insisted that she was happy to have whatever they did, she didn't want them going to any special trouble for her. Sometimes, smaller sins were necessary in order to avoid larger ones. *Allah will not call you to account for thoughtlessness in your oaths, but for the intention in your hearts.*

'I've given to the UN before,' Pravar was saying. 'In – when was it? I don't remember now. A famine, I think. There's always some kind of disaster or other in this region. It was the biggest single private donation they'd ever received from a Kenyan citizen. There was a notice in the papers to announce it. There's also a photo of me giving the cheque to the UN Special Envoy at the time, I can't remember his name. If you come to the office you'll see it, Lina.'

When she eventually went, she'd find two walls covered with pictures of Pravar shaking hands with different dignitaries or handing giant mocked-up cheques to the heads of various organizations. He was so different from Shareef, who donated a third of all he earned and never mentioned the fact. Even Lina had only found out because Iman had revealed the truth one day while complaining about how he handled money.

'The UN is important to this country, and not just because of their social work and what have you. No.' Pravar's fork sliced through the air. 'They are the single largest source of foreign exchange in the Kenyan economy. And they employ almost three thousand people here.'

'That's all very interesting, Dad, but the thing is, Lina thinks it's better to buy the solar cookers in this case, rather than just give money to the UN. Explain to him why, Leenie.' Anil leaned back as Mama Jo reached from the right-hand side to take his plate.

'We've done it that way before, too, haven't we, Minnie?' Pravar set his elbows on the table. 'Giving items instead of cash? What was it again, that distribution you did?' He turned to her.

'It's every Christmas time. We hand out basic necessities at Kibera: blankets, soap, maize meal. All these kinds of things.' Minnie picked at one of the marble-sized beads on her pearl choker and started to recite some lines in Urdu, 'Put back into the world at least as much as you have taken out, and at the end of your life you may be a rich man.'

'That reminds me of my dad.' Lina's face softened. 'He likes to quote Churchill: "We make a living by what we get, but we make a life by what we give." '

'It's a funny sort of a counting game these fellows are playing.' Pravar snorted. 'If you gave away what you got you'd be left with nothing. Simple mathematics.'

Eventually Lina managed to tell Pravar about the situation at Dadaab. All the while he kept interrupting with more of his own anecdotes. Of course he had already given to a refugee camp, or Minnie had, or someone they knew, he couldn't remember, but anyway, it had involved a lot of his money, much more than what Lina needed. He agreed to help, but wanted his name to be explicitly displayed somewhere – on the solar cookers perhaps? They could be engraved with: *Generously donated by Mayur Holdings*.

Guns

ONE EVENING THEY WENT out for Hardy's birthday. He'd invited friends to join him at a local firing range for a few hours first. It struck Lina as an odd way to celebrate, and she wasn't keen to join in. Neither was Anil, but he felt obliged to support his friend.

By the time Lina and Anil arrived some of the group were already firing away. The others were gathered in a sort of foyer, a grey room hung with framed pictures showing detailed line-drawings of various weapons, from machine guns to pistols. The different shooting ranges and a bar were accessible from this space. There were several people Lina didn't know, including a couple of girls, who looked rather comic: the elegance of their high heels and slinky dresses spoilt by the puffy orange padding of the muffs that sat over their ears like boxing gloves. Lina was glad she'd stuck to jeans. Everyone was relaxed, standing around sipping cocktails and cheering on whoever was shooting.

One of the attendants wearing combat gear came over and handed Lina and Anil a laminated sheet. At the top it said: 'Happy Trigger Shooting Range'. On one side was a 'gun menu' listing various small arms and the cost of hiring them. Each weapon came with a special 'free' drink. If you opted for the AK-47, you got a Black Russian. The M60 came with a Bloody Mary.

'What would you like to start with?' the attendant asked, as if he was taking an order for a meal.

Lina returned the menu with a shake of the head. She didn't want to try out anything. Just the sound of other people's shots was making her jump.

'I don't know.' Anil eyed the options. 'Maybe I'll give it a miss as well.' This really wasn't his thing. He'd never even been able to play combative computer games.

'You've got to try something, since you're here.' Merc nibbled at the slice of apple garnishing the rim of his glass. 'I'd say a Glock is worth trying just for this drink.' He gave the tumbler a little shake. 'The Corpse Reviver.'

'Hey, bwana.' Hardy got up from the ground in the doorway of one shooting range where he'd been lying on his stomach to fire a machine gun. 'You've got to try this. There's nothing like it.' His spotty face was shining with perspiration, and he was breathing heavily after less than a minute of firing.

'I'm not sure.' Anil looked at the floor where his friend had been a moment before.

The range master threw back his head and guffawed. 'Ati, look! He's scared of dirtifying his clothes!'

'That's got nothing to do with it!'

'Just have a go, mazeh.' Merc put a hand on Anil's shoulder. 'We've all done it – apart from the girls, who are too scared. There's a few rounds left. Come on, they're yours.'

Anil unzipped his jacket and handed it to Lina. Then he got into position. The barrel of the gun was balanced on a small bipod, and Anil had to ease his shoulder under the handle. Lina didn't want to watch, but couldn't quite look away. She leaned back, her face half-turned, her eyes half-shut. The range master checked that everything was in order before saying, 'OK, pull the trigger and let go.'

Anil's shoulders jerked as the force of the weapon was unleashed. Lina let out a yelp. The spent shell casings flew out from one side like terrified insects. Everyone cheered after the last shot was fired.

'Wow!' Anil rose, brushing off his cream, tapered trousers. He was in the same state Hardy had been: sweaty and breathless. He hadn't expected to feel such power from handling a weapon. His heart was still racing. 'You just want to keep on pulling that trigger.' His fingers mimicked the action. 'Wow. I can understand how people might get carried away when they're fighting.'

'I told you.' Hardy handed Anil a Bloody Mary as if it was a trophy. 'There's no better way of chilling. You fire one of those things and all your stress is gone. Now.' He rubbed his hands together. 'What next?'

'Nothing for me,' Anil said. 'That was enough.' For a life-time – despite the exhilaration.

Merc went to where Lina was standing. 'Are you sure you don't want to try one of the handguns? Just to get an idea?'

'No, thanks.'

'Might be interesting,' he persisted. 'You'll get another perspective on things. Life can't be one big Peace Corps.'

She didn't like the way he was standing so close, breathing down on her. Luckily one of the other girls pulled him away. 'Leave her alone!'

'We're doing one last round with an AK-47,' Hardy announced. 'Then we'll go.'

As the others lined up to take turns, Lina asked an attendant where the guns came from.

'Me, I don't know. Me, I just work here.' He shrugged.

'I'm sure they're all licensed.' Anil stopped inspecting the pictures on the wall. 'It's a shooting club.'

157

'Yes, but a machine gun?' Lina wondered. 'I thought only governments could get hold of those, not normal civilians. Even the AK-47. It's weird.'

'Maybe some big shot owns this place and has managed to give kitu kidogo and get an OK from the guys at the top. What do you reckon?' Anil turned to Merc.

'Who knows?' Merc was draining the dregs of other people's cocktails.

Later, at Vagabonds, a local bar, Lina listened as the others relived their experience at the range. Hands were turned into mock guns as stories were related. It became apparent that some of the guys carried these weapons for self-defence.

'With all the car-jackings and robberies that go on, you need to be prepared,' Hardy said after Lina asked if it was really necessary. They were all sitting outside, around a large wooden table whose surface was scarred from nights of revelry and excess. Strings of multicoloured light bulbs hung from the trees.

'Have you got one on you now?' Lina couldn't imagine how a weapon might be concealed under the light summer clothes they were all wearing. JT, who was seated next to her, tapped her foot with his. She leaned back to look under the table as he pulled up the right leg of his jeans. A revolver nestled in a holster strapped to his ankle.

'My dad's been nagging me to get one as well,' Anil said. 'But I don't want the hassle.'

'There's no hassle.' Hardy scratched his beard. 'Most of the time you even forget you're carrying one.'

'And hopefully you'll never have to use it,' JT added.

'But what if you killed someone!' Lina was shocked by their blasé attitude.

'You'll only have done so to prevent them from killing you,' JT said, and the others agreed.

'But surely that's the job of the state, the police force or whatever?' Lina put down her bottle of Fanta.

'Not in this country!' Hardy cackled, cigarette smoke billowed from his mouth. 'The police are in with a lot of the criminals.'

Someone started telling a story about how her sister had called the police after being burgled, and it was nine hours before they arrived. And then, the sister had sworn, one of the officers looked just like the guy who'd held them all at knife-point the night before. He had the same scar just above his left eyebrow and the same earring in his right lobe.

'The system is fucked,' Merc said. They all seemed resigned to this.

'But surely the solution can't be for everyone to arm themselves and take the law into their own hands?' Lina insisted. 'It's not right! You guys, of all people, should know that.'

'Oh, for fuck's sake!' Merc lurched forward. 'It's like we're at the International Court of Human Rights whenever you're around. This is wrong, that's not eco-friendly, the other is illegal! You've only been in this country five minutes and you think you know how to fix it.'

Lina looked into her lap.

After a while, she whispered into Anil's ear that she was going to the loo. Twenty minutes later she still wasn't back. Leaving his friends, Anil went indoors and made his way through the clusters of chatting drinkers in search of her. The place was packed: the odd white face stood out amongst the crowd of Africans and Indians. Red bulbs illuminated the room, giving everybody a seedy glare. At the back of the bar, near the toilets, he spotted Lina. She had both hands on the bar counter and was balancing on her left foot, while the other tapped absently on the chrome rail that snaked along the length of the bar. The arch of her foot made Anil shiver, the same way the highest note in a qawwali did. He watched for a moment before noticing the stranger towards whom her head was turned: a tall, blond man with a large Adam's apple. He was lounging with one elbow on the counter, laughing at something Lina had said. Anil walked up to them, smothered by jealousy. He put an arm around Lina and bent his head to kiss her shoulder.

'Anil!' She turned. 'You'll never believe who I bumped into!' She introduced him to Hans Steinmeyer, whom she'd met a few days before at the UN offices, when he'd come in to see one of her colleagues. 'Hans works for Human Rights Watch,' Lina gushed.

Anil noted that she'd never referred to his own profession with such enthusiasm.

'I know I've already said this to you,' she turned back to Hans before catching her boyfriend's eye again, 'but that's one organization I've always dreamed of working for.'

Anil shook hands with the guy, trying to work out how old he might be. Late twenties? Early thirties? It was hard to tell. The man's physique and tan put him in mind of a young surfer, but his charismatically lined face and sunken cheeks made him seem older. Anil was glad he had the advantage of height and could look down on the guy. Meanwhile, Lina was babbling about how she hadn't had a chance to speak to Hans when he'd been in the office and couldn't believe her luck at meeting him in Vagabonds.

'So what are you doing here?' Anil asked.

'Ah, just following the crowd. This place, for some reason . . .' Hans's eyes circled to take in the shabby room, 'seems to be the city's most popular – how to say? – watering-hole?'

'No, I mean in Kenya.'

'Ah-so! Only passing through.' A strong German accent muscled through the syllables.

'I was telling Hans I could introduce him to Merc. And maybe that way he could get a meeting with Samuel Ojielo.'

Anil frowned. 'Actually, Merc and all are already in the car. We're ready to leave, that's why I came looking for you.'

'Oh.' Lina ran a hand through her hair uncertainly.

'We need to go now,' Anil insisted.

'Let me give you my card, Lina.' Hans reached into the pocket of his denim jacket. 'We will see us again, I'm sure.'

'I hope so. It's a shame we have to go right away.' Lina fixed her gaze on Anil, hoping he might reconsider. He showed no sign of budging, so she put Hans's business card into her handbag. 'I'm afraid I don't have one of these, but I'll email you all my details.'

'Yah yah, all is good.' Hans leaned in and they pecked one another on each cheek. 'It pleases me to have met you – and you.' He put out a large hand, which Anil pretended not to see.

'We better hurry, Leenie. The guys are waiting.' He started steering her out of the bar.

At the car she turned to him in surprise. 'I thought you said—'

'I just wanted to get you away from that slimebag. The other guys are still there. But I'm going to phone them and say we're going. I'm tired.'

She watched as he called from his mobile, and then

opened the door of the 4×4 for her, while making his excuses to Merc. Lina didn't get in immediately.

'He isn't a slimebag,' she said when Anil had finished. 'He's one of the head investigators at Human Rights Watch. He's done some amazing work. What's wrong with me speaking to him for a short while?'

'Oh, come on, Lina. You say you're going to the loo, and then you disappear for most of the evening. What am I supposed to think?' He was still holding on to the car door.

'That's not fair!'

'And then proposing that I introduce him to Merc so he can have easy access to his father! How could you even consider that? Besides which, do you know how hard it is to get hold of Ojielo? Even my dad can't see him whenever he wants to.' The gelled spikes of his hair trembled as he tossed his head.

'It was just a gesture—'

'Well, you need to think before you start offering such favours. Expecting me to stitch up my best friend's dad!'

'That's not what I wanted!' Lina's hands flapped at her sides. 'And anyway, Merc's dad has nothing to worry about if he's done no wrong.'

Anil slammed the door shut. 'You don't get it, do you? This is Kenya! You're the one who's given me so many awful statistics about corruption in this place, and now you're being naïve!'

'I just didn't expect, I mean, I'm sure not everybody is guilty. If your family is on such good terms with Merc's dad, then he must be decent. Right?'

'That's some warped logic you've got going there. Think about it. He's one of those running the country.' Anil spoke loudly and slowly, as if Lina was deaf. 'Just consider what that means.' He took her by the shoulders and added more gently, 'Do you see? You can't just offer such introductions to strangers.'

The ride home was quiet. Lina broke the silence only to ask why Anil kept jumping all the red lights. He said bandits often lay in wait at such spots, ready to ambush unsuspecting cars stupid enough to stop at a red signal. When Lina pointed out that some drivers seemed to obey the traffic laws, Anil retorted that that was because those people had nothing worth stealing. Lina could only wonder why anyone would want to live in such a place.

Escape

DESPITE HIS INITIAL reservations, Pravar warmed to Lina. They had long chats during which Anil, who'd rarely sat with his dad for any extended length of time, sat worrying that their exchanges would culminate in antagonism. But they seemed to find a way through their disagreements.

Sunk into the sleek L-shaped white sofa in the living room, Pravar would hold forth, one hand always extended, with the index and middle fingers pointing out like the muzzle of a gun, ready to shoot down any interruptions.

'If you decided to practise law in this country, you could make a fortune. Yes. Most certainly. You would. Definitely.' Pravar's shirt, a dark brown, was the same colour as his turban. This sartorial statement – matching shirts and turbans – was the foundation of his wardrobe.

'Yeah, by bending it.' Anil, at Lina's insistence, was sat at a modest distance from her, though they were on the same sofa, directly opposite his father. 'I don't think Lina is the type for that.'

'The law, as we know, is always open to interpretation. Yes? No?' Pravar looked at her. 'Any good lawyer has to have the stamina to examine all sides, isn't it?'

'You're right, there are always qualifications in every law.' She was sitting right back, and though her long legs hung over the edge of the sofa, her feet didn't quite touch the ground. The soles of her sandals were hanging down from the thong between her toes.

'A good lawyer has to know his way *around* the law,' Pravar said.

'Yes, you're right, it's important to know the ins and outs.' Lina assumed the least incriminating implication of his words.

'I think by "around", Dad means the circumference of the law. In this country lawyers tend to be specialized in how to stay on its outskirts. The more you pay them, the wider they roam.' As if the law was a compass with which you could draw your own parameters. Anil could see Lina was shocked by such blatant talk, even though she was the one who'd told him that Transparency International ranked Kenya as one of the most corrupt countries in the world.

'It's the same everywhere. Law has never meant justice. It's always been about the best lawyer you can afford.' Pravar steadied his hand, as if he was aiming at the heart of the matter, which seemed to be in Lina's direction. 'If you don't yet know that, you may well be in the wrong profession.'

'Possibly.' She sat up straighter. Her hands were in her lap, the fingers folded tightly around each other. 'You have a lot of experience. I'm sure you know much more than I do. But I still believe in law as the best mechanism for achieving the most good most of the time.'

Pravar laughed. 'Wait until you get out in the market place, then we'll see how long these notions last. Money, finally, is the law that governs everything. Yes. Absolutely.' He dropped affirmatives into his speech as though he was heartily agreeing with someone else's sentiments, instead of endorsing his own. 'The type of houses you build.' He pointed at Anil and then Lina. 'The number of refugees you can feed – these things depend on cash. Principles are all very well, I like a person with some, but you have to know when to set them aside.' He said this as if the whole point was that they should be discarded once asserted, like paper plates that have been used.

Anil became embarrassed. He knew it was normal here for people to make corruption seem benign by dressing it up in the language of pragmatism, but Pravar was really going too far, trying to make a virtue out of dishonesty.

'Hmmm.' Lina studied the armrest. 'You're right, it's tricky. My dad always told me that the only sacred law is your conscience.'

Anil shifted uneasily in his seat, but Pravar clapped his hands together. The cave of his mouth flew open to reveal a trove of gold caps. 'A wise man, your father, but not a rich one, I suspect. Yes? No?'

'Don't you think it depends, a little, on how you might define rich?' Lina dared, but then, aware of her own indebtedness to Pravar, she backtracked quickly. 'But you're right. I've never, I mean what you have here . . .' She gestured to take in the room, the house, the grounds. 'This is just something else. I'm very glad to be here. Thank you so much for having me.'

'You hear her?' Pravar targeted his son. 'Don't forget how lucky you are.' He leaned forward and his stomach, sagging comfortably over his belt, looked like thick melted chocolate about to pour down his legs. 'The meaning of "rich", whatever anyone may try to tell you, is the size of your bank balance.'

'That's true, but don't you think there are some things money can't buy?' She crossed one leg over the other, her sandals gaping under her feet like the tongues of panting dogs.

Pravar guffawed again, shaking on his haunches. 'Are you serious?' His eyes narrowed at Lina as though she was a curiosity, the last specimen of some dying breed. He no longer came across people who didn't believe in the supremacy of money. It intrigued him.

Lina sensed Anil tensing up on her left. 'Why?' She smiled. 'Am I wrong?'

'Completely. Yes. Absolutely. Totally. Tell me, how did you come to such an idea?'

'I don't know.' She looked down, as if to shield herself from his astonishment, which felt almost like mockery. And then she faced up to him. 'I suppose it's because we, my family, have never had lots of money, but we have had more than enough of all the most important things, like happiness and understanding and friendship and . . .' there was the tiniest pause during which the word declared itself in a rush of red to her cheeks before slipping out of her mouth, '. . . love.'

'Sure. That's possible. No question. But money leaves you more time to pursue and enjoy all these things—'

'After you've given up your whole life to making enough of it,' Anil interrupted.

'The likes of you,' Pravar's index finger accused, 'are lucky enough to have been born with plenty. That's why you're lounging here with your girlfriend instead of slogging it out at a summer job somewhere.'

Lina leaned forward and appeared to concentrate harder as Pravar continued to pontificate.

'There are two kinds of people who really understand the power of money – those who don't have enough of it, and those who have more than enough. And

I,' he beat a palm against his chest, 'have been both.'

'What do you call a Singh who knows the cost of everything?' Anil suddenly tossed the question up over the coffee table. Its glass top was perched over one large elephant tusk.

'Hanh?' The expression on Pravar's face made him look Neanderthal.

'A Singh who knows the cost of everything?' Anil repeated.

'Your mother is the one who can always come up with the words.'

'Is it bank something? Banking . . .' Lina pretended to think aloud. She'd guessed an answer, but didn't want to say it before Pravar had a chance to.

'Got it!' Pravar clapped his hands together. 'Finan-*cing.*'

'No. That's close, but it's not the word I had in mind.' Anil rose slightly to reposition the sculpture of a woman's head, carved out of malachite, that was on the coffee table. Then he sat back down, using the action as an excuse to get closer to Lina on the sofa.

'Is it, could it be pri-*cing*?' Lina ventured.

'Heh, you've learnt the game already?' Pravar adjusted the tilt of his turban slightly.

'I got a hint from what you said.'

'Pricing.' Pravar chuckled. 'That's a good one. Yes.'

Anil took Lina's hand and stood up, thinking this was a moment to escape. But she tugged on his arm, forcing him to sit back down. 'What you were saying before, Pravar—' She felt odd using his name, but both Anil's parents had asked her to refer to them that way. 'You didn't finish.'

'Oh, yes. No. Sure . . . Uh, what was I saying?'

Anil gave Lina's palm an annoyed squeeze. He didn't

understand why she was so attentive to his parents. Assuming it was politeness, he'd already told her it wasn't necessary, but she claimed to enjoy it.

'How you've had no money and a lot of it,' Lina prompted. The tips of her fingers made tiny circling motions against Anil's hand, trying to pacify him.

'Yes, yes. There was a time I had to go knocking on people's doors, begging for favours and getting turned down because I didn't have the means to persuade them. Now, my name is on the door.'

'When did you realize the power of money?' Lina asked. Now Anil's fingers were tapping against hers, a coded message that she immediately understood.

'Oh.' Pravar rolled one shoulder. 'That I always knew. But I tell you what made me realize that I had to make a lot of money – it was the value other people attach to it. Yes. That was the reason. Completely. People will do anything for money, that's why it's worth having. No?' Then, he cracked his fingers, letting off a series of little detonations before beginning to list all the advantages of wealth, raising a digit to identify each point.

Lina started nodding slowly, as if she'd found some strange, if shameful, truth in his words.

'Even wisdom . . .' Pravar's pinky rose into the air as he concluded, '. . . can be bought – you just pay the best brains to do the thinking for you.' By the end he was sitting before them like some devotee of capitalism, his hands bent upwards at the elbows, his fingers spread to enumerate his arguments, his mouth open in the infinity of 0, his material goal.

After her internship had ended, Lina and Anil went to a lodge in the Samburu Game Reserve, north of Nairobi. An

Air Mayur plane was flying in that direction anyway, and gave them a lift. As they boarded the aircraft Lina noticed large wooden boxes wedged into all the passenger seats, except the row where she and Anil would sit.

'What's in there?'

Anil shrugged. 'A delivery for somewhere, I guess.'

When the pilot appeared Lina asked him.

'Sorry you have to share the cabin with these bulky fellows.' He rubbed the left side of his jaw. 'But the hold is full and I needed to get all these boxes on board.'

'Is it aid?' Lina was curious because of the faded Red Cross symbol on some of the boxes.

'I'm not told. I just know my final destination.' The pilot sniffed and went on rubbing his face.

'Where are you heading?' She wondered if the goods were going to Dadaab.

'Just north. You guys buckle up now. We'll be leaving in a few minutes.' The pilot went to the cockpit.

The ride was turbulent. There were several instances when Lina might have hit the ceiling if she hadn't had the seat belt around her hips and Anil gripping her right hand. Now, with just a few days left before she returned to England, she suddenly felt that she hadn't got enough of him, or given enough of herself. There didn't seem to be any adequate words or permissible actions to express her passion. She pushed up the armrest between them and pressed closer to him. The isolation of the cabin left her able to enjoy his responses: the kisses he kept dropping on her bare shoulder, the run of his fingers along her thigh – hot even through the cotton fabric of her skirt. She felt like squeezing his fist between her legs and rubbing herself against it. Immediately, she bit her lip and turned to look out of one of the windows on the other side of the aircraft.

What was happening to her? It was shocking how her body was ready to throw off the lessons of modesty she had spent her whole life learning. She wondered how far she could let herself go.

The rooms at the lodge were generously spaced out, and arranged so that none of the other buildings were visible from each individual vantage point. The impression of isolation was enhanced by the thickets of bush pressing in around each dwelling. Lina was glad to be walking between Anil and the porter as they went along a narrow stone path to their room.

'How do we know there isn't, you know, a lion or something just there?' She waved a hand at the dense clumps of squat trees, their whitish bark cracked and scabrous. You could hardly see through the vegetation. The bush looked static and unthreatening, but gave off a constant rustling, snapping and cheeping, like the noise of a giant digestive system at work.

'You stick to the paths, madam,' the porter, in a khaki safari suit, spoke without turning, 'and everything will be fine.'

'They have rangers patrolling as well,' Anil added.

Lina cupped her face in her hands and cried out in delight when she entered their room. Its heavy exterior canvas walls, guarded by a couple of flat-topped, thorny acacia trees, had not prepared her for the luxurious interior. She took off her shoes and rubbed her feet against the sleek, dark wooden floor, while exclaiming at the free-standing porcelain bath. Then she went and ran her hands down the huge bed that was draped in layers of beige Egyptian cotton. 'When you said tent I'd imagined something completely different.' Her cheekbones seemed to sharpen as she broke into laughter.

'What? Sleeping bags under a flimsy little plastic pyramid?' Anil stood watching, thumbs linked through the belt hoops on his jeans.

'Yes!' She went to sit on a leather chaise longue and leaned back against the animal-print cushions.

'Do you want to have a rest?' He checked his watch. 'We've got an hour or two before dinner.'

'I don't know.' One of her legs was bent, the other swung over the side of the seat. Her skirt had ridden up to reveal a pale curve of inner thigh. The sudden charge of desire in Anil's eyes embarrassed her. Quickly she brought down the arms that were thrown back over her head. But he was already leaning over her, his knee pressing into the leather between her legs. A moment later she felt the full weight of him. She sighed, amazed by the comfort and thrill of it. Equally astonishing was the way her legs folded around his hips and her pelvis tilted into alignment with his groin: adjustments so instinctive, they seemed to have been practised. She felt she had loved him through many lifetimes and would do so until the end of time.

But the lessons in modesty had not been entirely forgotten: the lines memorized from the Koran forbidding sex outside marriage, Iman's exhortations to keep all flesh covered. When Anil's thumb slid under the thin elastic hem of her underwear, Lina remembered her limits.

'I can't,' she whispered.

He stopped, let his hands slide under her back. His breath against her neck was like hot air being squirted from an aerosol can. She sensed the shift in his limbs from abandon to restraint, the tension of muscles as he took his weight off her and balanced it on his elbows.

'Until we're . . .' Her face contorted at the slip, the heft of assumption in that tiny word. 'I mean, until *I'm* married.'

His lips stretched on her skin as his mouth pulled into a smile.

'Then I guess I'll have to marry you – soon.'

Later that evening they went to the viewing platform, which was on a small plateau jutting out over the ground below. Some people were sitting on deckchairs sipping sundowners, and a group of American tourists were brandishing cameras as if the scene was about to expire.

Lina and Anil leaned on the railing and took in the vastness of the plains stretching out before them. The landscape seemed to have a shiny glaze to it, like a rich dish baked golden-brown by the sun. You had to watch carefully in order to spot all the wildlife teeming in the scrub. Anil was better at it than Lina: he'd find something and then pass her the binoculars – and suddenly the long grass would be busy with gazelles, and dark shadows would reveal themselves as elephants. At one point Lina turned, pushed up the sleeve of Anil's black T-shirt and pressed her lips against his upper arm.

'All the things you've shown me, everything you've given me. I don't know how to thank you,' she said.

'I like sharing everything with you, it all means much more when we're together.'

'No, but still. I know that my world is bigger because of you.'

'And mine too, because of you.' He could see himself reflected in the grey-tinted lenses of her sunglasses. She was similarly mirrored in his. He liked the idea of them being endlessly replicated in one another.

'I can't think of anywhere I've taken you that you haven't been to before.'

He rubbed his chin, pretending to think. 'There is that halal place in Ealing.'

She jabbed him playfully in the ribs and he tried to poke her back, admiring the movement of her shoulders as she wriggled out of reach. She'd changed for dinner and was wearing a knee-length purple silk halter-neck dress. The outfit's expert tailoring honed her slimness to reveal the delicate intricacies of bone and flesh. It was one of the many new things Anil had bought her before they left London.

'You look beautiful,' he said.

'I feel a bit bare.' Her hands crossed one another and reached for her slender shoulders. She'd wanted to wear something over it but Anil hadn't let her, claiming she didn't need anything because the air was like a shawl. For a while, it did wrap them in a soft velvety heat, but that changed quickly.

Darkness came all of a sudden, like a curtain dropped. Immediately, the temperature fell too, as though a few ice cubes had been plunged into the cocktail of the night.

'Shall we go into the dining room?' Anil noticed the goosebumps on Lina's arms.

She took his hand and followed him towards the brightly lit restaurant, whose glow slopped out of huge windows but still wasn't powerful enough to penetrate more than a metre into the night. Even the floodlights used to illuminate the grounds of the lodge revealed just patches of landscape and fragments of buildings: silvery snippets decorating the thick blackness.

'What's that?' Lina pointed at the restaurant's flat roof ahead of them. A nearby floodlight picked out some rectangular protrusions that rose off it.

'Solar panels.'

'Oh.'

'I knew you'd appreciate that.' Anil squeezed her hand. 'I chose this place partly because of its eco-aspect.'

She hugged him, pressing her face against the ribbed cotton of his shirt. 'It's the kind of thing I imagine you designing – stunning and also sustainable. That's how my dream house would be.'

'One day I'm going to build that house.'

She held his gaze, delighting in his promise, marvelling at how natural that prospect now seemed.

So they were standing, facing one another, leaning back slightly, their arms looped around each other's waists, when Anil heard a strange crackle in the bush. His head whipped in that direction, but not much was visible.

'What—?'

'Sshhh.'

Lina felt him go rigid. His face tightened, all the features closing in towards the nose. His eyes scrunched up as if they were trying to drill through the dark. He realized that no one else was around. The guests had all gone in to dinner, and there was no sign of any staff. The restaurant was only ten metres away, but if that really was what he thought it was – eyeing them up, close enough to reach out a paw and swipe at his leg – then ten metres was too far. For one of them, at any rate.

Lina couldn't see what Anil was staring at, but she became as tense as him, every sense straining to work out if there might be some imminent threat.

'Don't move,' he whispered. Yet he began, very slowly, with minute manoeuvres, to position himself in front of her. He could see the creature clearly now, regarding him with the nonchalance of a diva who expects adulation. If it had been standing the other way around, it could easily have brushed him with its tail.

Lina couldn't have moved even if she'd wanted to. She'd spotted it as well through the corner of one eye. Her mouth opened and closed, jerking at the jaw, in soundless screams.

'Start walking – backwards.' Anil took a small step back, expecting Lina to mimic his action. But she remained frozen. He kept his eyes on the animal, whose nose twitched.

'If it comes,' Anil unconsciously ventriloquized, as if that would make a difference, 'you have to run.'

The creature seemed to pulse into hyper-alertness. Anil could feel its might and his own defencelessness behind the cordon of air that separated them. He took another step back, but stopped when his heel encountered Lina's foot.

All of a sudden a ranger was beside them, hissing and waving a baton of fire. In the other hand he held a pistol. The animal slunk off, and was gulped into the dark within seconds. The ranger watched it disappear, and then adjusted his red-checked shuka more calmly than a trader might his tie after playing a rocky market for hours.

'Ai ai ai ai ai.' The ranger shook his head and sucked on his teeth. 'Simba.'

Anil stayed still – not quite sure that it was over – not quite sure that it had happened at all.

'You better go in.' The ranger gestured at the restaurant. 'Tonight many simba around. Don't move alone.' He ushered them ahead and walked them to the door. The light pinged off the multicoloured beads hanging around his neck.

Anil and Lina found themselves seated at a

formal-looking table dressed in two layers: a small navy-blue square of thick, starched linen set over a larger white one. A waiter in a tunic that matched the blue of the tablecloth bent over to suggest an aperitif. Anil nodded, even though he didn't hear what was being asked. It was as if his fear had been put on ice during the incident and was only just starting to melt, trickling through every cell. His hand shook slightly as he took a sip of water.

Lina looked at him. There was a tiny vibration in her lip, near the scar, like the quiver in a bow just before the arrow is released. 'Thank you,' she said.

'It's that ranger we both have to thank. I didn't even give him anything.' His hand went to the pocket where his wallet bulged.

'No but, you know what I mean. If he hadn't come . . .'

He shook his head and rubbed a palm self-consciously over his chest. His actions had been instinctive, but their meaning now struck him, exposing a depth of feeling he had not been entirely aware of.

'I won't forget that. Ever.' Lina reached across the table, weaving an arm through the two wine glasses set at each place. She took his hand in a grip so tight and so tender that he understood perfectly.

You have left nothing behind. No physical relic, except a stray sock, holed at the toes and heel, as yours quickly became, because you wore them twenty-four hours a day. I found it today as I started, finally, to unpack my things and attempt life again. I am with Lucas and will be here for a while, until I finish my PhD, at least.

Notice how I keep mentioning where I am, half-hoping you might come looking for me, yet knowing, all the while, the unlikelihood. How could you, when not a single one of these missives has been sent? I have stuffed them into stamped envelopes scrawled over with your work address, and even walked to the postbox intending to drop them through the grim slit of its mouth – all the while aware of the futility of my actions. If I sent them I would be left waiting for a reply that was unlikely to come. You never once reneged on a promise. So I know your goodbye, too, must be final.

Nevertheless, I resent the clean sweep you made through our things to eliminate any sign of yourself. Who were you to decide what I might or might not want to save? You took even that choice away from me, the way you didn't give me a say in our separation. I remember you speedily packing things away, claiming you wanted to make it easier for me. What did you think? That without evidence I might doubt that you ever existed, or I might move on faster?

Even the few photos we had of each other have

disappeared. I asked you to put them in one of the boxes with 'my' books, but now I can't find them. I would like to imagine that you took them, perhaps in an involuntary sentimental gesture. But I doubt it. I've noticed that you didn't take any of the books I'd given you as gifts. They are here, amongst my things, the adoring inscriptions in them a pathetic vestige of what I once felt. A little library of my loss. You thought it was a sacrilege to mark books in any way. In the ones I received from you, there was never a personal message, instead you spoke one aloud while I opened the present. I have only to flick my eyes across the titles to recall the little dedications that accompanied them. For Sri Aurobindo's *Savitri* you said, half-quoting him – To my darling Sel, the conscious flower of my heart.

Funny how I was the literature student, but you seemed to have more reverence for the physicality of books. For me, underlined sentences and folded page corners were indications of how deeply involved I had become with a text. But you treated all of them the way you did the Koran: with great respect, never setting them on the floor. These were the sorts of quirks I adored. Only now the chivalry seems more like chicanery.

You avoided leaving permanent traces of our love. The presents you gave were ephemeral things: flowers, chocolates, meals in restaurants. We weren't ever apart long enough to make letter–writing necessary, but you never even wrote me a card. You memorized poems or passages from favourite books for birthdays or anniversaries, and recited them to me over breakfast in bed. Actions I once thought romantic I now find devious. How the whole tone of a relationship can alter with one revelation!

If it was your intention to vanish without a trace, you neglected to consider the most incriminating article: me. I remain a repository of our past. On my shoulders: freckles from the day we spent in Brighton just before you left. On my hand: the scar from a cut sustained while clearing up the pieces of a glass we knocked over when I tried to teach you to tango. On my feet: marks from the sandals I wore the day we walked from Regent's Park back to the flat in Battersea.

Physical wounds fade, but what about the scars of the mind? Memory, that old trickster, is cleverer than us all. You must have realized that by now. Even your god, I expect, cannot quell the tide of reminiscence.

Sharing

A T THE END OF AUGUST, after returning from Kenya, Lina
continued nagging her father to let her live with
friends for her final year. In the middle of September, a few
days before term started, Shareef finally agreed. But by
then, people had already formed groups, found flats, paid
deposits and moved in together. Even Isabel, who'd been
keeping one of the rooms in her shared house free, had
given it away shortly before Shareef made his final
decision. It seemed like Lina had no choice but to stay
where she was – until Anil proposed she move in to Merc's
apartment. JT and Hardy had returned to work in Kenya on
graduation, so there was plenty of space. She could have
her own room and bathroom. There would be no rent to
pay, she could just contribute to bills, if she wanted. At first
she'd refused point-blank. It was going too far. She had a
hard enough time keeping on top of all the lies as it was.

Then Anil had started working on her, describing the
sort of life they could have if she assented. As usual, once
the idea was in his head, he talked as though it was sure to
happen. He was always making plans, trying to tame the
future. She could believe in his visions when they were
together, but the minute they were apart, it was as if the
future had been let off its lead. It stood before her, teeth
bared, a wild, obdurate animal that she'd rather not
approach.

Anil had not consulted Merc before issuing his invitation because he was sure he could persuade his friend to accept the arrangement. At first Merc had laughed at the idea, unable to take it seriously. He didn't believe there was any way Lina's parents would let her live with two men.

'Of course she's not going to tell them,' Anil said. 'They'll think she's staying with Isabel. That was the original plan anyway.'

Immediately, Merc began to issue warnings. There was no way Lina's parents wouldn't find out. Moreover, he refused to live surreptitiously in his own flat, trying to defend the girl – whom he didn't especially like, anyway – against the possibility of being discovered. Anil dismissed these concerns. He'd already thought of everything. They'd have a new phone line installed especially for Lina's use, and all her post would be directed to Isabel's address. As Merc listened he was struck by how deeply Anil had become involved.

'Mazeh, that sounds ludicrous. Why should you have to go to all these lengths just to live with her? It's seriously fucked up.'

Anil paid no heed. He went on trying to convince Merc, and even declared he would move out and get his own place with Lina if that was necessary.

'Look, mazeh. I'm not going to throw you out of here because of a bloody woman.' Merc certainly wouldn't allow her to come between them. 'But, seriously, you need to stop and think about whether all this matata is worthwhile. You're going too far!'

'I'll do whatever it takes. I don't care.'

The ferocity in Anil's eyes convinced Merc that he shouldn't be left to his own devices. Better that they remain under one roof, at least he could keep an eye on his friend. He agreed that Lina could move in and have her own phone line, but he was adamant that nothing else about their lives should change because of her. 'I don't want her cooking halal food or anything like that here. We'll go on as we always have. She'll just have to fit in with us.'

Lina was uneasy about agreeing to the new set-up. She decided to do Istikhara, the prayer for guidance. She took a tasbih from the kitchen, where Khala Rocky sat each morning, running the prayer beads through her fingers, while boiling an egg for breakfast. Up in the bedroom that had been hers since she'd started at university, Lina stood by the single bed with its pink polka-dot bedspread and took several deep breaths. Then she closed her eyes and did a two rakat salat. With each prostration her knees clicked as though little fuses were being blown in them. Holding the tasbih in her left hand she began, with her right hand, to move it two beads at a time, while declaring her intention to God:

O Allah! I ask guidance from Your knowledge, and power from Your might,
and I ask for Your great blessings. You are capable and I am not. You know and I do not . . .

She stopped. Her hands were shaking. Taking a deep breath she tried to go on:

O Allah! If You know that this step is good for me,
For my religion . . . for my family . . .

She couldn't. The as yet uncounted turquoise beads on the tasbih hung from her hands promising counsel not hers to receive. How many beads remained? Was it an odd or even number? Was she right or wrong? She didn't need to count in order to know God's will. She didn't need to count to know her own. She pressed the tasbih against both her eyes, kissed it and put it back in the kitchen, all the while repeating astaghfirullah to herself. Istikhara should never be performed for unethical or illegal acts. It was outrageous to try and get Allah's sanction in this instance.

She headed to the bathroom and began filling the tub. Each of the shiny blue tiles reflected her actions as she poured bath salts into the water. Double the usual amount went in, as if using more would help her relax better. She pulled off her clothes and rolled her hair into a high bun before slipping into the tub. The water was so hot she had to lower herself in by millimetres. When she was finally submerged, she closed her eyes and wished someone or something could decide for her. The heat loosened the tension between her shoulders, helped her neck muscles lengthen. Bit by bit the rest of her body yielded to the warmth. By the time she rose, dripping and steaming, to reach for a towel, she knew what to do.

Lina pulled on some clothes and hurried downstairs. The number of eggs in the fridge would decide her fate. If there was an odd number she would move in with Anil, otherwise she'd stay at Khala Rocky's. The tiles in the kitchen were cold under her bare feet. Well aware that this was a ridiculous way to do things, she pulled on the handle of the fridge door. Light spilled out of the open machine, bathing her in its cool brightness. Lina raised a hand and ran her fingers over the delicate ovals nestled in the egg tray. She did it twice. Then she rose on to her tiptoes and peered into the little compartment where the eggs were stored to check once more. There were definitely eight.

So Lina remained at Khala Rocky's, but spent more time away from her aunt's place. Often she'd say she was going to stay with Isabel, because her friend lived so close to the library, and actually she'd end up in Merc's flat with Anil. The absences were justified by the fact that it was her final year, the workload was much heavier and she didn't want to waste time commuting. Since she might have been living with Isabel anyway, neither Khala Rocky nor Lina's parents made a fuss about the fact that she slept away from home sometimes.

Merc's internship at the Institute of Contemporary Arts had introduced him to a hedonistic crowd who thrived on a circuit of vernissages at galleries across London. He was out almost every evening, and Lina was glad of his absence. She could never really relax when he was in the flat. He would often wander around half-naked, and even stripped down to his boxers in front of her sometimes when she was in the living room. It seemed like he was taunting her with his sexuality, daring her not to resist. When she mentioned her discomfort to Anil he dismissed it. 'Don't be silly. He isn't trying to provoke you, he's always been that way.'

One morning, after Lina had spent the night, Anil left the flat before her. He had an early start at the office, and her first lecture of the day wasn't until the afternoon. She had allowed herself a lie-in and got out of bed long after Anil had gone. She was about to take a shower and stood naked in front of the mirror, plucking a few stray hairs from her eyebrows – when Merc walked into the bathroom. 'I'm in here!' she shouted as the door opened. There wasn't even time to pull a towel over herself – suddenly he was standing in front of her.

'I'm sorry.' Merc's eyes rested on her before he took a step back. 'I didn't realize . . . I just wanted to borrow some . . .' She thought she heard the word shampoo as he closed the door.

She locked it and then sat down on the toilet shivering, thinking she had to leave immediately. She'd never be able to look Merc in the eye again. It was only when she finally got into the shower and felt the blast of water hit her head that the absurdity of his excuse struck her. Shampoo! He didn't even have any hair! Lina was sure it was no co-incidence that Merc had barged in on her this morning, of all days, when Anil was not around. As she soaped herself, she wondered what he was trying to prove.

'He wants to intimidate you, of course!' Isabel claimed when Lina rushed to her place after the shower. She hadn't wanted to remain alone in the flat with Merc for a second longer.

'What a creep.' Isabel hugged her. 'Forget anything I ever said about wanting a chance to get to know him. Come on, drink that tea. You'll feel better.'

They were both curled into the cushions that lined the window seat in Isabel's bedroom. Instead of curtains, several batik fabrics hung from the rail above them.

'I can't ever stay over there again.' Lina shuddered. 'I never want to go back!' She balanced the chipped mug, embossed with the logo of a bank, on her knees.

'That's probably exactly what Merc's hoping for!' Isabel said.

'What's the alternative?' Lina sipped the sugary tea.

'Go on as before. Act like nothing has happened.' Isabel

pulled her thin lips into her mouth and stroked the ruffles that tapered down the front of her top.

'You should see the way he looks at me. It's like he's trying to see through my clothes.'

'Yeah, well, he doesn't need to do that any more. He knows now.' Her eyebrows rose and disappeared under her fringe.

Lina's cheeks burned at the memory.

'Seriously, Lina. Don't let him manipulate you.'

'What about Anil? Should I tell him?'

'I wouldn't bother.' Isabel's bobbed hair whipped her cheeks as she shook her head vigorously. 'Merc wants you to make a big deal of this, I'm sure of it. The best thing is to confound his expectations by doing nothing.'

Lina did just that and it seemed to work.

Then, there was another confrontation. One evening, shortly before her last exam, Anil wanted Lina to dine with him and Merc at a restaurant before she headed back to her aunt's place for the night.

'No, Anil. I need to get some studying done, and I don't want to get home too late.' She walked around the living room and picked up a pair of socks that were lying by the sofa. 'Are these yours?'

'I don't know, maybe.'

Lina dropped them again. She certainly didn't want to be handling Merc's dirties. His stuff was everywhere – even in Anil's room. He'd leave things in there – a lipstick, a pair of tights, a hair clip – assuming they were hers. And she had to return them, remarking casually that they must belong to one of his 'friends'. Lina had lost track of the girls he brought home – he must have as well, from

187

the surprise he expressed at the random items that Lina insisted on giving back.

'It's just a meal. An hour or so. I don't see what the big deal is. You need to eat, after all, so you can concentrate.' He sat there unperturbed. When he wanted his way nothing else seemed to matter.

'Why can't you try to understand how it might be for *me*? These exams matter.' She lowered herself on to the sofa beside him. Already she knew she hadn't done as well as she might have without all the juggling that two parallel lives required. The bottomless descent into mendacity appalled her. There seemed no way out. Everything was being corrupted. Each sacred space of her life – family, Anil, God – which the different layers of false-hood were supposed to protect, was being infected. And worst of all, she knew that despite her mental bartering and the compromises she made, the most important person was not being deceived: Allah saw everything. In the moments when it all became too much, she could only tell herself that if He knew and had not allowed her parents to find out, there must be some reason for it. If God had ordained everything, then her being with Anil was also part of some master plan. It would all work out as it was intended to, inshallah.

Anil rose. His shirt had come partly untucked from the waistband of his trousers. 'This is just non-stop hard work, Leenie. Doing the smallest thing with you involves a struggle.'

'We wouldn't need to argue if you could accept my decisions,' she spoke quietly.

'*Your* decisions!' he exploded. 'Your decisions rule this relationship! Everything, *everything*, is based on what you do or don't allow.'

Isn't that what relationships are? she wanted to say – but he was out of the room. Wasn't knowing anyone intimately always a negotiation of boundaries? How many she had transgressed for him! In the corridor she heard him tell Merc he just needed to change and then they could go. She would have followed him if Merc hadn't appeared in the doorway.

In frustration she blurted: 'He always has to have things *his* way!' Immediately she regretted her words. Merc wasn't the one to complain to. He'd never be on her side.

Merc walked over to the window. The fresh, citrus smell of his aftershave filled the room. He looked ready to go and play cricket, dressed all in white. With every movement muscles rippled under his clothes, pressing up against the material, declaring his potency. Lina could imagine his body more clearly than she wanted to. She wrapped her hands around each other and sighed, questioning, not for the first time, the wisdom of her continuing to visit Anil in this place.

'He can be pretty stubborn.'

She looked up, not quite able to believe she'd heard right. Was Merc on her side for a change? Of course he wasn't. The violet lenses in his eyes made them seem particularly cold.

'But for someone so strong-minded he follows a lot of your whims.'

'My whims?' Other people had opinions, her ideas were whims – too insubstantial to be taken seriously, by Merc at any rate.

'He deserves more credit for being with you. I don't know how many guys could handle the catalogue of restrictions that come with being your boyfriend.' He stood leaning against the windowsill, cradled by the evening light that poured softly through the glass, drawing shadows out of the furniture. 'I mean, every woman's difficult in her own way, but you sure make a man hop through some high hoops.'

Puzzlement altered the symmetry of her face: one eye was open wider than the other, one corner of the mouth more pinched. So far Merc had never interfered between her and Anil – although, she suspected, he was always observing and silently judging – and getting it all wrong, obviously. *She* was the one who regularly squeezed through impossible hoops. Anil had it easy because there were no obstacles to anything he wanted, not even financial ones.

'I think we both do our bit. We both know how we – I mean the two of us – compromise.' The pitch of her voice altered as she spoke and by the end of her convoluted sentence it had gone high enough to make what should have been a statement sound like a question. 'How do you think I managed to come and spend time here with him?'

'I'm not saying you haven't both bent over to make things work. But you always bend from the waist, while he bends from the knees. You get me?'

He bends from the knees? What nonsense was Merc talking? And, anyway, wasn't it harder to bend from the waist? More awkward? With a higher risk of injury?

'Anil has learned another language for you.'

He'd always been interested in Urdu anyway!

'He's got his parents to lie to yours. He's willing to eat at halal restaurants for your sake. And he's happy to sit on the rickety fence of agnosticism out of respect for your beliefs.' Merc's mouth twisted in disgust. 'Sometimes I think he might even decide to believe in God, if you needed him to.' And then he ventured on to terrain so delicate that Lina had to turn from his piercing purple gaze. 'The way he's . . . the way you haven't . . . you know – after all this time.' Even Merc seemed discomfited bringing up this subject with Lina. 'It's not natural.' He must have seen embarrassment roll across her features. 'Not that he's said anything to me, but I'm guessing it's the case.'

There was silence. Lina cupped her hands on either side of her face. How many times over the last year had he thought these things? How long had he wanted to speak out? She'd had the impression that a relative harmony had been established between them. An unstated truce: agree to disagree. Now she felt this quiet belligerence coming her way, like an undetected gas leak with the capacity to suffocate.

'What I'm trying to say is that I think Anil is capable of doing or accepting anything for your sake. He thinks he's in control because he always has been. My sense is that neither of you is in the driving seat, and I don't know who's navigating, either. And, what's worse, I doubt there's a road to the place you imagine yourselves going.'

What did he know about where they intended to be? If there wasn't a road, they would make it. That's what they'd done so far: racing forward in thrilling bursts, with a few skids along the way.

Merc walked over to the armchair in front of her. His shadow slunk after him, staying close to his heels, all but stamped into nothingness with every step. She wished his words could be similarly crushed. But they started flowing again, just like the shadow, which reared up and sprawled across the chair he perched on.

'I don't think you realize how much everything you stand for is incompatible with his world. I just hope you won't ask too much of him.'

191

Her hands dropped into her lap. 'I love him,' was all she could say.

'When was love ever a guarantee for anything? Except irrationality. He's already lost his heart to you, don't let him lose his head.'

Crisis

Aziza Aziz was a petite woman in her forties. She wore the hijab, but in her own individual fashion. Instead of covering her hair with the customary black scarf, she improvised with all manner and colour of materials: sometimes the hijab sat high on her head like a sultan's turban, sometimes it flowed softly from her forehead and down her back like a bride's veil.

She had become divorced at the age of twenty-three when her husband uttered the word 'talaq' three times because she had failed to get pregnant during their four years of marriage. The ex-husband, who ran a market stall on Soho Road, went back to Pakistan and wed another young woman, who also failed to reproduce and was similarly dismissed. This same scenario was repeated two more times before the man seemed to get an inkling that the failing might be his. He then settled on a widow who already had three children. Meanwhile, all the exes, apart from Aziza, returned to their families and small villages abroad. She was not permitted by hers to rejoin them. Better that her dishonour remain thousands of miles away in England than return to roost on their doorstep.

Alone in a country where she did not speak the language, amongst a community who regarded her with disdain, there did not seem to be much hope for Aziza. The fact that her eyes were different colours – one dark-brown, the other pale-green – also made people suspicious. Shareef, who had taken on the legal matters relating to her case, hired her as his receptionist.

'Oh, what-weh? But you don't have a reception,' Iman had said.

'I'll put a little desk near the door in the entrance hall, and she can sit there. It'll be a good way for her to get to know people. That fellow hardly let her out of the house the whole time they were married.'

So Aziza became a member of staff at Merali Legal Services. Two years of English classes and a lot of patience later she was a competent and lively addition to the team. Iman's initial reservations about her were laid to rest when she realized Aziza could be her ally in trying to ensure that Shareef didn't overwork. Aziza defended her employer tenaciously, manning the entrance of the office like a bouncer at an exclusive club. If people turned up without appointments she sent them away, trying to be authoritative by putting her hands on her hips, speaking English and peppering her sentences with the legal jargon she had overheard colleagues using: 'Boss is busy. You can't just be turnings up. There are caveats, procedures, you know? *Preliminaries?* Always appointings first *then* meetings. These is the covenant.' She would purse her thin lips together before letting them spread into a small smile. 'So please, Mr, *tells* me please – when is goods times for you to be summoned again?'

Aziza's powers of divination slowly became apparent. People began to notice that things she casually intimated came true. Some started to approach her for advice and pretty soon word got around that she had special powers. She didn't charge for her forecasts, merely asked people to make a donation as they saw fit. In time her pariah status in the community was forgotten, and she became a respected augur. As Shareef's firm expanded and moved to larger premises some speculated that his success was the result of Aziza's powers. But he was dismissive of her ability. He believed all types of prophecy that did not come from God Himself were haram, and he disapproved of the way his wife sometimes consulted Aziza.

'If you trust in God, you don't need human predictions,' he told her.

'But just for the little things, I think it's OK. God doesn't want to be bothered with those, I'm sure. And besides . . .' Iman ran a hand over her bun. 'He is not always so clear.'

'Mrs Aziz is not exactly explicit.' Shareef cleared his throat. 'Some of the things you've repeated to me seem rather cryptic. Statements you can interpret any which way.'

'No, I tell you, that's her style. She doesn't show you precisely. She just suggests to you, kind of, so you *know*.' Iman's wrist circled in the air to elaborate her point.

'I think you also *know*, Iman, that the Book says only Allah has the keys of the unseen, no one knows the unseen except Him.'

Shareef was in the middle of a meeting when he suddenly noticed the top of Mrs Aziz's face appear through the small glass window in his office door. She had to stand on her toes to look through the porthole. Seeing that she'd caught his eye, she mouthed his wife's name and gestured with her hand that he should come out. Shareef only wondered why she was gawping at him and waving frantically. He turned his attention back to his client, Aisha Huzoor, who had obtained a divorce through the civil courts, but was worried that she was still married in the eyes of Allah because her husband had not consented to the rupture, as required by Islam. Moreover, under sharia law, she was entitled to get back her dowry, a condition not enforceable under UK civil law.

She was one of many who sought Shareef's help in reconciling the dictates of their faith with those of their country. He worked closely with local imams to allow members of the community this possibility. He saw himself as a mediator between the two legal systems. There were many who felt sharia was the true way to which they owed allegiance and that, therefore, it ought to take precedence. Indeed there were groups lobbying the government to introduce some aspects of sharia into the country's statute books. This Shareef found excessive. He saw sharia as something complementary to UK jurisprudence, a means by which people could be granted the broadest sort of justice – one that satisfied the intellect and the spirit. He proceeded to reassure Ms Huzoor that he would speak to the senior imam, and also try talking to her husband, who had already rebuffed the attempts that had been made to negotiate with him. In the middle of this, Mrs Aziz flew in.

'Very sorries, Mr Merali boss, sir. And Aisha begum, many apologies, many apologies. Please excusing the challenges but very importants notices is comes for you.' She fixed her mismatched eyes on her employer.

Shareef was momentarily speechless. Mrs Aziz had never interrupted him like this. She usually fended intruders off.

'I must requesting adjournments of this meetings. Please, Mr Merali, sir, you must to give counsels right immediately now.' Her body was coiled tight with whatever news she'd heard. She stood by Shareef's desk, hunched forward slightly, elbows pinned to her sides, hands knotted over each other.

'I'm almost finished, Mrs Aziz. I'll be out as soon as I'm done with Ms Huzoor.' He smiled sympathetically at his client, who was sitting across the desk from him, fidgeting under her chador.

'Oh buts this won't waiting! You must to comes now!'

'I can't just leave my client, Mrs Aziz. You know that.'

Ms Huzoor expressed disapproval by looking away, out of the window, behind which a plane tree stood clutching at its tatters of yellowing leaves.

'You knows I don't interruptings unless it is criticals. You are havings very importants summonings.'

Shareef wondered if Iman had perhaps received bad news from India. She was due to fly there in two days to visit her sick mother. He stood from his heavy wooden desk and apologized to Ms Huzoor, offering to ask one of his colleagues to take over if she had any more questions. She declined. So Shareef asked Mrs Aziz to give her another appointment as soon as possible. His client got up slowly, her chair squealing as it scraped back along the floor. He escorted her out personally and then turned to the receptionist.

'What is it, Mrs Aziz?'

'Your wife's is phonings and sayings you must going homes right straight aways. This is alls. She soundings very upsets. There must be some damages. You should goings now this instants.'

He found Iman upstairs in Lina's room, sitting cross-legged on the floor with her back against one side of the bed. Her eyes were puffy from crying. Balls of used tissues were scattered around her. A suitcase lay open by her feet.

In it were four small white cotton drawstring bags and one larger silk one, all filled with things. And there was one plastic bag from which papers protruded. There were more papers in Iman's lap, and she was going through them, reading. She waved one of these at her husband.

'The worst thing has happened. The worst.'

'Your mother?'

His question befuddled her for a moment. 'No, no, it's not my mother. No, this is too bad, Shareef, I tell you. Too too bad.'

'Lina? Is she OK?' The fact that they were in the girl's room made him deduce Iman's state might have something to do with her.

'She is ruined!' Iman flapped a few pages at him again.

Shareef saw that it was a letter she was handing over. As he took it and knelt down beside his wife he spotted, 'My dearest Leenie', at the top of the page.

'You're going through her things?' The unease that had been churning within him solidified in his chest.

'Oh, what-weh, Shareef? Don't start implying anything before knowing nothing. I just found all this. I came in here to get the suitcase to pack for my trip, because I realized the zip on mine is broken. I thought, I'll take Lina's. She has more time to buy another one. And then' Iman broke off, sobbed a bit and blew her nose. 'There were some items in there. You know . . .' She flicked her hand. 'Things she obviously didn't want just lying around. I started to take them out. And then I realized that in these little bags, these white ones, there are shoes.' She took them out of the suitcase and plonked them on the bed. 'So I looked at them, because I thought – what kind of shoes come in their own bags? And, Shareef, astaghfirullah, such shoes! *High* heels, *tiny* straps, I don't know how the foot stays in them or how the body balances. One pair is gold and the other is red. Where does she wear them?' The thought was enough to start her tears flowing again.

'Probably it's just university fashions.'

'Fashion, tobah! Listen to you, Shareef. You have no idea. Then I opened the other bag – this pink silky one.' That too was now picked out of the suitcase and dropped, with a soft plop, on to the duvet. 'You won't believe what's in there.' One hand clamped over Iman's mouth as if to stop her from going on.

'What?' Shareef glanced at the bundle. It looked pretty innocuous.

'I can't say it. You have to look for yourself.' And then as he reached out she pulled back his arm. 'No! Actually. You can't.' No father should know this side of his daughter, Iman thought, as both her hands closed over her face.

'Iman, what is it?' She was frightening him.

The word 'underwear' emerged from the fleshy cordon of her fingers.

Shareef eased himself on to his bottom, frowning. What was wrong with underwear? He didn't know what to make of the situation. He hadn't seen Iman in such a state since her father had died. 'Underwear?'

'The kind you see in *magazines*,' she whispered, and then squeezed her eyes shut as visions of colours, lace, bows and frills filled her head. When she opened them again she saw that Shareef was still confused. Oh, God, how could she explain? How could she say what had happened? It was too upsetting. She, who had never discussed lingerie – let alone the more intimate parts it covered and all that was associated with *them* – was having to tell her husband what their own daughter had been up to. She gulped. 'The kind which no woman buys for herself. Lina has *someone*.'

'How do you know this?'

'Because then, *then*, I found all the letters, didn't I? In the zip pocket of the suitcase. I had a feeling something was wrong. That's why I looked at them. Most are from Kenya.'

'She has that friend there, Shanila.' He still wasn't sure what Iman was building up to.

'There is no Shanila.' Iman's mouth crumpled again.

At first, when she had seen the letters with that name on the back of the envelope, she had put them to one side. But as she'd pondered on where the stylish shoes and extravagant underwear might have come from, she'd reached for the letters again, and examined them more closely. She'd tugged off the thin black velvet ribbon that held them together. Most of the envelopes had borne Kenyan stamps and had the name and address of Shanila Mayur written on the back.

Iman had opened a couple of the missives at the top of the pile. After just a few sentences she knew she was reading the words of a person in love. Turning them over she spotted the sign-off: Anil. *Anil*? She whisked several more letters from their envelopes and found they too were from an Anil on the inside but a Shanila on the outside.

Iman had put the letters to one side and wept. They were tears of shock, disgust and a not insignificant measure of self-pity. What had she done to deserve this? Where had she gone wrong-weh? Always inclined to find a moral diagnosis for every problem, she began to conjecture how this state of affairs might have come to pass. She blamed herself for, she had heard, deficiencies in a child usually have their root in some parental failing. She had not prayed enough. She had resented Shareef giving so much to charity. She had not been patient enough. She had envied her sister once upon a time. She had been too lenient. She was in the wrong country. But there had never been a sign from Lina – never! Once or twice Iman had suspected her of having too much of an interest in the sons of some acquaintances, and she'd made sure to keep Lina away from those boys – they had been Shias, after all. The girl must have been corrupted at university. It had been a mistake to let her go and live away from home. How would they live this down?

Without the slightest compunction, Iman had begun to read every letter. For some reason, she took pains to return each one to its envelope and to maintain the chronological order in which they had been stacked. She had read romantic novels and seen many love stories played out on film and TV, but none of them had affected her the way these forbidden dispatches did.

A slow reader in English, it had taken her a couple of hours to get through about half the letters. By then it had become clear that Lina had stayed with this Anil person during her trip to Kenya the previous year. At that point Iman had got up and telephoned her husband. Her message to Aziza had been a hysterical insistence that he needed to come home right away.

'What do you mean "there's no Shanila"?' Shareef now said. 'I've spoken to her mother.'

'I don't know who you spoke to, but Shanila is actually a boy called Anil.' Iman pointed out the name at the bottom of a letter and the one on the envelope. And while Shareef continued to stare in bewilderment, she explained her theory that the girl's name had been created to prevent them from seeing what was going on right under their own roof. She shared some more facts about the relationship, but didn't repeat any of the intimate talk she'd come across: words describing longing, touch and smell. Scandalous stuff that normal people didn't mention, even if they felt it. Nor did she mention the sketches that were in some of the envelopes: abstract lines suggesting something she was too embarrassed to decipher.

Shareef shook his head. He was drooping with incomprehension: his spine curved forward, his arms were limp in his lap. One aspect of the whole situation unsettled him above all. It wasn't anything Iman had mentioned, but a particular that he recalled from a past conversation with Lina. If this Anil was indeed the character his daughter had referred to as Shanila, then he was not a Muslim.

'You don't want to believe it, I know.' Iman reached out and touched his leg. 'Neither did I.' But the evidence was written on paper and now also in her mind. 'Let me tell you, if you read these,' she grabbed the rest of the bundle from the suitcase, 'you'd be convinced.'

'Did you go through all of them?'

'Shareef, what are you implying? She has done this terrible thing, and you are making me wrong?' Iman pushed herself up so that she was now sitting on the bed.

'I understand that you had to check, but . . . think how she will feel knowing you've read about her most private experiences?' His lips retreated under his moustache as Iman raised her voice to defend her actions. Shareef crossed his arms over his chest and sighed as she went on.

'You're so concerned about her feelings, but what about me?' She started crying again.

He came and sat down beside her, reminding himself that his wife had no experience of such matters. She was similar to him in her belief that if something was private it stayed in your head or heart, and didn't get translated into a form that might be discovered by anyone who wasn't supposed to know. 'All I'm saying is, it's awful just to find out this is going on. The details don't make it better or worse.'

Iman's shoulders heaved. She was like a soft, shaking mound in Shareef's arms.

'What's done is done,' he said. 'We need to figure out some way to handle this.' Iman pushed out of his grasp. 'Look!' She picked a wad of pink Post-it notes from the carpet and waved it at her husband. 'I know what we can do.'

Shareef saw something was written on the first page. 'Have you been taking notes?'

'There was a number in one of the letters. The boy writes the phone number for where he lives. You can call him.' She shoved the rectangular block of paper at Shareef. 'You must tell him to leave her alone – or else!'

'Don't be silly, Iman.' Shareef took the wad from her, tore off the top page with the number on it, and pushed it into his pocket. 'Ringing up strangers and threatening them is no way to handle things. We have to make Lina see that she's wrong.'

'What if she doesn't listen?'

Shareef was silent. He ran his thumb repeatedly over the longer edge of the pack of Post-its. The pages purred as they skimmed along his skin.

Iman dug her fingers into the flesh of his upper arm. 'Then she must come back home and we have to get her married straight away! Before anyone finds out.'

'Now you're overreacting.'

'The problem is, Shareef, you always underreact. Even

now, look at you, you have hardly squeaked at the news, except to tell me off.' She was irritated by his self-control. She knew that swift leaps into anger were not his style, but she wished he would lose his temper now. 'You've always over-indulged that girl. Letting her go away to study, letting her fly abroad alone, letting her stay with strangers – and now you're ready to let her go to New York for this new job with the UN.'

'I've allowed her a normal life, Iman. That can't be a crime.'

'Then why has it come to this? Secret doings with who knows what kind of unsuitable boys. Other people protect their daughters. And you—' She clamped her mouth over the accusation, but it sprang between them, spinning like a top.

'Maybe we should wait and speak to Lina before assuming any more.' He started gathering the letters. 'Let's put these back the way they were.'

'Ya Allah! She's the one who has sinned and you're trying to cover our tracks like we are the baddies. I don't understand you, Shareef. Put aside your lawyer self for one minute and consider that this is your daughter!'

'So what? Should I treat her less fairly than the rest of the world?' He passed Iman the mail and watched as she retied the letters with a ribbon.

'When will Lina be back?' He knew she had taken her sisters to watch a film.

'Who knows? You know what she's like. Your ability to keep time is one thing she didn't inherit. I hope you don't play the softie, Shareef.' Iman stood up, almost losing her balance. Her left foot was numb and heavy. Shareef put out a hand to steady her. She grabbed it and started pointing and flexing the foot and then stamping against the floor to revive the circulation. Behind her, the packages that had incriminated Lina lay side by side on the bed.

When Iman had regained control of her limb, Shareef picked up the empty suitcase and took it to their bedroom. She hobbled after him.

'I don't think I should bother packing. I can't really go anywhere now, can I?' From his reaction so far she didn't trust Shareef to deal with it alone.

'Of course you must go. Your mother is expecting you. This might be your last chance to be with her.' He put the suitcase on the bed and caught sight of the clock on the bedside table. He had missed the afternoon prayer slot. 'We can speak to Lina together this evening and then we just have to see.'

'Are you mad?' Iman's hands grabbed at her neatly tied-up hair. 'What do you mean "talk to her and see"? We have to make her follow our wishes. For a start, she can't take that New York job.'

Shareef went and stood in front of his wife and put his hands on her shoulders. 'Calm down, Iman.' The pink tassels of the light shade grazed the top of his head. 'We should discuss things with Lina before throwing around ultimatums. Once she sees our disapproval she will end this relationship, inshallah.'

'What if people find out?' Iman grabbed at Shareef's cardigan. 'What will they say?'

'There's nothing to find out. This is between us. We will sort it out. Inshallah.' He squeezed her shoulders. 'She's a good girl.'

'That's what I thought too. But you know what they say, "Give Shaitan an inch, and he'll be a ruler."'

Shareef turned and headed towards the bathroom. 'I would like to pray now, before they get back.' He started washing his face and hands.

Iman decided to do the same. She went on to the landing at the top of the stairs and moved a loaded clothes horse out of the way. Then she rolled out a mat alongside Shareef's. Even though the prayer began to unfurl within her as effortlessly as breath, she couldn't concentrate. Bits of the letters kept coming back to her. These, together with her own speculations and fears, interrupted her recitation. Besides, her body wasn't used to such extended prostrations: her knees and back creaked with reluctance. Pretty soon her left leg had fallen asleep again and she had to get up in order to limp around. The phone rang a couple of times, and she might have rushed to answer it if she hadn't been temporarily disabled.

Meanwhile, Shareef exuded calm. His bending, kneeling and bowing had the smoothness of a ballet. Iman envied the release that such discipline could give him. He had trained himself to shut out the world when he prayed. It struck her again that she had not done that enough. Too often she'd let worldly concerns or pleasures trump spiritual obligations. She had been lazy, preferring sleep over communion with God. She had failed that small test, and now He had set her a bigger one. She thrust herself back on her mat and started a silent delivery at a pace so fast it kept her full attention for a couple of minutes. There was a blunt relief in the hasty churning out of verses. For the first time in hours her head was empty of everything except God's words. But then she became aware of Shareef stirring beside her and, suddenly, desperate to discuss how they would confront their daughter, she brought her prayers to an abrupt end.

The phone rang all evening. Word had got around, from clients whose appointments had been cancelled, that

Merali Sahib had left the office because of a crisis. The callers hid their curiosity behind expressions of concern and a lot of inshallahs. Those who knew why Iman was shortly to depart for India assumed, as Shareef had, that there was some bad news about her mother. Neither husband nor wife corrected this misunderstanding.

'You see how quickly news spreads?' Iman said. 'And this time there isn't even anything to report.'

The two sat at the table picking at their dinner. The salad Iman had hastily cut lay untouched, a mess of oddly sized cucumbers, tomatoes and onions. Shareef watched the oil from the keema pool at the edges of his plate.

'One hint of drama and everyone is talking,' Iman went on. 'Especially the people who have little else to say. Like those Alis, husband and wife. I tell you, the only time they speak to each other is when there's some outside calamity to share. The mess in their own backyard they don't see. Did you know the son is taking drugs? He was caught shoplifting from Haq's store the other day. You should eat something, Shareef.' She forced herself to take another bite.

Lina sensed something was amiss as soon as she parked the car in front of the house. Her parents, who'd heard the purr of their Citroën, opened the front door and hovered there as the girls approached. Iman's hair, which had been neatly braided and rolled up into a bun when they'd left, was now a dishevelled rope hanging down her back. Stray wisps stuck out at the border of her forehead.

'Is Nani-ma OK?' Lina asked.

Shareef nodded, while Iman immediately dispatched the younger girls upstairs. Mariam protested with a drawn out 'Why?'

'Your father and I need to talk to Lina.'

'So? Can't you go upstairs or into the kitchen? I wanted to go on the Playstation.'

'Do as you're told!' Iman pointed at the stairs. 'I swear you girls are just out of control.'

Her tone was enough to ensure a sullen trudge up the steps.

'What's wrong?' Lina was starting to feel nervous. She followed her mother into the sitting room. Iman was staring at her, as if looking for clues to something. Shareef shut the door behind them and Lina's gut started knotting up.

The parents didn't answer, but looked at each other, perhaps to check which one would speak first.

'I think maybe you have something to tell us, Lina?' Shareef sat on the armchair, leaned forward and rested his elbows on his knees.

'You have been lying to us!' Iman exploded and the truth came out in a frenzy of hair-clutching and tears. 'I tell you, Shaitan must have entered your blood – how else have you managed to look us in the eye all this time? Coming and going like there's nothing wrong. And all the time cheating us.'

Lina was stunned by Iman's reaction, even though she had known this was exactly how it would be.

'You've been deceiving us – for months, years, God knows how long – about this—' It was still hard to face. 'This *boy*.'

'I didn't want to lie.' Lina started crying.

'Why did you do this?'

'I don't know. It just happened.'

'Don't talk nonsense!' Iman pounded the sofa with a fist. She was turned sideways, one buttock half-hanging off the sofa, so that she could direct herself better at Lina, who was seated beside her. 'Something like this doesn't "just happen". Getting that boy to write here under another name, travelling around the world with him, and doing who knows what else. Duping us non-stop. It has been very deliberate, Lina. Those letters say it all.'

Oh God! Had Iman been into her suitcase? Lina had only put the letters, shoes and lingerie there yesterday, ready to take to New York. They'd been kept safely at Isabel's house throughout the summer vacation.

Iman was still going on about the letters.

'You read them?' Lina glanced from mother to father.

'Don't you look at us like that. Reading is nothing compared to what you've been up to. It's shameless the way you've behaved. Shameless! And so selfish. We have to live with the consequences of everything you do. Did you consider that even once?'

Lina's face was hidden behind her hands.

'You must know, Lina, that this relationship can't have any future,' Shareef spoke up.

Why? She couldn't get the word out.

'This boy is not a Muslim, is he?' He was hoping to stand corrected.

'Astaghfirullah! Astaghfirullah!' Iman wailed.

Lina could not speak. Could not move. She was locked behind the wall of her hands, the palms were practically stuck to her face by the suction of sobs.

'Your being with that person goes against everything we are. You will have to cut all ties with him immediately,' Shareef said.

'You have to promise right now that you will do it,' Iman added. 'I want to hear it from your mouth.'

Lina sank deeper into the sofa.

'As far as I'm concerned, the only way to put a stop to this is by having you stay home until this whole mess is out of your system.' Iman delivered the sentence like a judge issuing a final verdict.

That made Lina sit up. Her hair was plastered to her face in places, like streaks of mud.

'Swear by God. Say Wallahi, I will never see that boy again.' Iman wagged a finger. 'Say it!'

Lina's jaw trembled.

Shareef squatted so that he was at eye level with his daughter. 'I trust you to do the right thing.' His sincerity was crushing. 'Your mother needs some sign of your determination to change things. For her sake, please renounce that boy in a way that will convince us, otherwise we will not fund you for the year-long internship you're starting in New York.'

Lina could not bear the liquid that beaded in her father's lashes, quivering against the imperative of gravity. She swallowed. 'I will leave him. Wallahi, I will do it.'

III

New York

SEVERAL MONTHS INTO HER internship, Lina was grabbing a late lunch with a colleague in the UN cafeteria. The 1 p.m. rattle of the place – tables packed with people conferring in a dozen different languages – had been overtaken by the calm of a few, mostly solitary, late diners, flicking through newspapers or reports as they ate. Lina sat on one of the blue chairs, gazing out of the large windows. The overcast sky lent its seasonal drabness to the East River. On the other side of the water, billboards advertising Pepsi and Greyhound buses splashed a commercial brightness into the dull day. The view still exhilarated Lina. In fact, everything about the UN headquarters inspired her. Lina's attention was brought back to the table as her boss, Susan Hempel, flapped a hand at her.

'That guy there has been staring at you for, like, a minute.' Susan lowered the coffee she was sipping and tilted her head to the right. 'There. D'you know him? He's hot. You gotta introduce me, hon. Oh my goodness, he's coming over!' Susan put down her cup and flicked at her red curls. 'Have I still got some lipstick on?'

'You're unbelievable, Suz.' No wonder people called her 'the maneater'. Lina dropped her fork into the bowl of her half-eaten fish pie and stood up because Hans Steinmeyer was standing by their table.

'Lina?' He leaned forward and lowered his chin slightly.

He knew it was her. The question in the name was asking permission to intrude.

'Hans!' Her eyes glinted with pleasure. 'I can't believe you're here already. I thought you'd be coming next week!' They'd kept in touch via email.

'Neh, it was always today for my arrival.' He let his tray hover just above the table. 'May I join you?'

'Please.' She moved her scarf and bag from the adjacent seat. 'It's so good to see you again.'

'You also.' Hans kissed her on both cheeks, then removed his coat before sitting down. Underneath it was the same denim jacket he'd had on the night Lina had seen him in Nairobi.

Susan pretended to cough.

'Oh, this is Susan Hempel.' Lina gestured. 'She's also working for the UN Development Programme. She's my boss, actually.'

'Hi there.' Susan blinked slowly. 'And where have you come from?' As though he might have been dispatched by the gods.

'I was in the Ukraine.' Hans pulled his chair closer to the table.

'You look like you've been somewhere much sunnier than that. Check out that tan and those highlights.' Susan's eyes ran up and down his frame.

His hair was longer and blonder than it had been the last time. It fell over the tops of his ears and down the back of his neck, softening the solid contours of his deeply browned face.

'You're right. I've been moving around very much.' He tore the plastic wrapping off a BLT baguette.

'Hans works for Human Rights Watch,' Lina said.

'No way! I did my first internship with them.' As Susan

went on to quiz Hans about where he'd worked and what people he knew, Lina was filled with disbelief – as she had already been countless times – that she actually had this job. Her CV was so staid compared to that of others, like Susan, who'd done several internships around the world, volunteered at shelters in South America, gone on sponsored walks across treacherous terrain to raise money for various causes, and even had a stint at a research and policy think-tank in Washington.

'So what were you doing in Ukraine?' Susan was asking.

Hans finished chewing before replying. 'Trying to follow up on a few leads.'

'Are you based in that part of Europe?' Susan pressed her arms against her breasts, and arched her back, so that her cleavage was displayed to its best advantage through the open buttons of her shirt.

Lina had to look down to hide her amusement. Hans seemed more focused on the flesh in his sandwich than on what was being offered across the table.

'No.' He took another bite. 'Sorry.' He put up a hand to cover his mouth. 'I'm starving. Haven't eaten since landing this morning.' He swallowed a mouthful before going on. 'I'm mostly in Africa, the Eastern bit.'

'East Africa and Ukraine? Well, we all know there can only be, like, one connection between those territories, right?' Susan craned over her elbows and forearms, which were now resting on the table.

Lina watched, not quite sure what was meant. From across the room someone called a greeting and she waved in response.

Hans shrugged, and quickly finished the remaining third of his sandwich.

'Look at this guy!' Susan tossed her head as if she was

doing an advert for some shampoo. 'Why so coy? It's not the FBI you're working for!'

'I don't understand what this connection you're talking about is,' Lina admitted.

'Arms, of course,' Susan said. 'Did you come for the Arms Exports Conference that was going on here this morning?'

Hans nodded.

'Oh.' Lina's eyes widened. 'Is that what you've been researching?'

'Yah, so to say.' He wiped his mouth with a paper napkin. 'Can I take this, please?' He reached for the unused sachet of sugar on Susan's tray.

'Be my guest.' She sounded like she was offering him something else, and watched with a kind of longing as he poured the contents into his coffee. 'Did you have any luck with the lobbying? I guess you spent the whole time stalking people to the loos?'

Hans laughed. His teeth were uneven, the front ones overlapping each other slightly. 'It was a little bit like so.' Delegates were not supposed to speak to other representatives during such sessions. So lobbyists like Hans had to grab candidates in between, during coffee or toilet breaks. He'd press notes into people's hands with the details of his petition and urge them to bring up a specific issue.

'Arms trafficking was, like, my special subject when I did my MA. I guess you know what Eisenhower said on the subject?' Susan glanced from Lina to Hans.

Lina shook her head, but Hans nodded. 'I think I've read it somewhere.'

'Oh, it's such a powerful statement. If I had my way it'd be enshrined in our constitution.' She paused for a moment and recited a few words: ' "Every gun that is made, every warship launched, every rocket fired signifies, in the final sense, a theft from those who hunger and are not fed, those who are cold and not clothed."'

'Yah.' Hans seemed more impressed by that than by all Susan's other wiles. 'Those are great words.'

'They really are,' Lina agreed. Being able to have conversations like this was another thing she loved about being at the UN.

'I wanted to get into that field when I started,' Susan said. 'But then other opportunities came along.' She raised her arms and crossed them behind her neck. 'You realize there are lots of problems in this world that need attention.'

'What are you doing now?' Hans asked.

'You mean right this minute?' Susan's eyes became teasing slits. When he failed to respond her arms dropped again. 'I've been doing some work for one of the refugee coordinators on the treatment of women. I'm examining the notion of rape as a weapon of war.'

'It's not so new, this phenomenon,' Hans said.

'I know! Women have been victims of such sexual violence throughout history. I worked for an NGO in Bosnia after the Balkan war. Mass rapes were part of the Serbs' strategy against Muslim women. The Russians did the same to the Germans at the end of the Second World War. Ditto the Japanese at Nanking, the Indians during Partition . . .' One of her hands made spirals in the air, signalling that the list was endless.

'That's so awful.' Lina pushed the rest of her fish pie to one side. 'Is rape some form of triumphalism?'

'You mean like the spoils of war?' Susan's mouth curled. 'It's worse than that. Rape is a strategy, a way for one side to declare their superiority, and even to redraw

217

ethnic boundaries. Forcefully impregnating women is a way of destroying another community.'

Lina turned to Hans. 'I read the recent report you did about human rights abuses in Sudan. According to that, rape is a huge problem there as well.'

'Yah.' Hans cleared his throat. 'It's not really my special area. The report was co-authored, as you probably saw. My focus was more on other security issues. But, Susan is correct, rape is a huge problem. For this reason, in modern conflict, it's more dangerous to be a woman than a man.'

A lanky guy, wearing a jacket whose shoulders were too broad for his frame, came by their table to say hi to Lina.

'You made a lot of friends already, in just some months, or?' Hans said as the guy walked away.

'Yeah, she's Miss Popularity, all right.' Susan piled her empty crockery on to a tray. 'Even Kathleen Starbright loves her,' she said, referring to the notoriously demanding head of the UNDP. She stood up. 'That's what you get for being the one who's always ready to come in early and stay late. There's nothing like commiserating by the coffee machine at midnight for forging friendships.'

'Please stop exaggerating, Suz,' Lina said, though it was true, her schedule had been intense since day one.

'Do you have a card, Hans?' Susan offered him her own.

'Yah.' He reached for his wallet and gave her one.

'So, get in touch next time you're in town.' Her eyes gave a stronger invitation, opening as if they might get wide enough to suck him in. 'Or even this time, if you like.'

'Thanks. Maybe I will.' It was impossible to tell if he was being serious. As the sound of Susan's heels faded away, Hans crossed one leg over the other and turned to Lina. 'You're quite settled, or?'

'I know my way around, but that's about it! Everyone here is an expert on something. I feel I have so much to learn.'

'You'll find your niche soon enough. Or maybe you know already which field you might follow?' He slung one arm over the back of his chair and shifted so that he was facing her fully.

Without being conscious of it, she also moved so her pose mirrored his. She mused for a moment, playing with the pendant on her necklace. The butterfly collar of her shirt flattered her long neck. 'Well, these last months I've done a lot of stuff on crisis prevention and recovery, mainly to do with conflicts, but also covering natural disasters. I could imagine continuing in that direction.'

'Stopping illegal-arms trading would prevent all kinds of crises.' He seemed about to go on but stopped himself. 'So you'd like to work in Africa? You have a special attachment to Kenya, or?'

She looked away, turned her head completely so that she faced the river again. Boats and ferries moved along the choppy waters. 'I'd like to work wherever I can make a difference. But, please . . .' She twisted back towards Hans. 'Tell me more about what you're doing.'

'Right now I'm trying to get a better idea of the small-arms trade in East and Central Africa.' He went on to explain how various regional conflicts, such as those in northern Uganda, the Democratic Republic of Congo and Sudan, meant there was high demand for weapons in the region. Small arms were easy to smuggle and were flowing across the porous borders between these countries. 'Insecurity because of armed conflict is one of the greatest obstacles to development in such regions.'

'I would have thought it was bigger stuff, you know,

missiles and tanks, that are the major problem. And surely you can't easily smuggle those around?'

'Believe me, you can.' Hans began gesturing, getting into the obsession that dominated his life. 'There's currently no international legally binding treaty to bring the arms trade under control. This is why I'm here today. We're trying to get the UN to table, for all member states, such a treaty.' He became more emphatic with each sentence. 'In the moment, even an arms embargo doesn't make a difference. Countries like the Ukraine ignore such laws in order to make a profit. All the old Soviet weaponry that was left there – about seven million small arms and light weapons – is being shipped to fuel conflicts around the world. So, yah, the big stuff is a problem, but small arms – AK-47s, hand grenades, machine guns – are the most deadly.' He smacked his palms together. 'They are responsible for ninety per cent of total conflict deaths. Half a million people die each year from small-arms fire – that's almost one a minute. This is why we need to stop the merchants of death who are profiting from the business.'

'Do you have any idea who they are?'

'It's a very murky world.' Hans exhaled heavily. 'Governments are involved, rebel leaders, lots of middle-men, false paperwork, corrupt officials, front companies, fake end-user certificates.' One palm rose and fell on to the table as he spoke, punctuating his speech with emphatic little taps. 'It's really complicated. One deal can involve at least a dozen different players. We know it's happening – there are people in this building with lists of names and details of incidents, but still the Security Council won't act.' His palm formed a fist on the tabletop. 'The US is blocking progress. They refuse to get on board. Without a major player like that it's hard to get any momentum. This country is too much in love with guns.'

'And I guess it's not really a priority for them after September the eleventh.' The attacks had taken place two months before Lina had arrived in New York to begin her internship.

'It should be though! Terrorists get hold of weapons more easily because of the lack of accountability. This organization . . .' his index finger pointed at the ceiling, 'needs to act.'

'But I guess the UN also has to be careful. Implicated governments might refuse to let us do aid work,' Lina said.

'We can't let corrupt regimes hold us to ransom with threats to make their own people suffer even more. Small civil conflicts are turning into wars because of the ready availability of guns.' He told her how nomads and cattle herders from different clans, who'd traditionally coexisted on the same lands, were fighting over territory since the illegal acquisition of arms. 'People are starting to believe that owning a weapon is not just necessary, but normal.'

Recently he'd been to a village in Jonglei State, South Sudan, with a couple of other researchers. They'd gone from hut to hut, talking to villagers, trying to gauge how many civilians owned a firearm. In the dusty compounds between dwellings, children in dirty shorts and torn T-shirts had been playing war games with imaginary weapons.

At each hut Hans had ducked to dodge low thatched roofs, which sat over the mud walls like straw hats. Inside they would encounter the same scenario over and over again: a family in possession of at least one gun. This weapon was the most prized item. Children believed they were magic. Mothers thought they were lifesavers. Fathers saw them as status enhancers. Nothing Hans or his colleagues said had been able to persuade these people that they might be better off without a rifle. Some tribesmen had said they'd rather lose a child than lose a gun – because with a gun they at least had the chance of protecting the rest of their family.

'Oh my God.' Lina sighed. Sometimes she couldn't help becoming depressed at the sheer scale of the problems in the world. She thought of the sculpture just outside, which she walked past daily before entering the building: a handgun whose barrel was twisted into a knot. Its aspiration seemed unrealistic. 'So, where are you off to next?'

'Back to Nairobi in a few days. That's now my main base. The only place in the world I have a space where I can leave my things and expect to find them when I get back.' He tousled his hair and laughed. 'My parents have converted my old room in Osnabrück into an aquarium – and I'm not a good diver. Not that I'm keen to go home, but I might not have a choice. I have maybe to go and retire there one day, with the fish. Yah.' His shoulders rose and fell. 'Nobody, I think, does this job for the lifestyle.' He was thirty-two years old and did not own a car or a flat. He'd even had to borrow a suit for his grandfather's funeral last year.

'I know what you mean.' She was on a tight budget, too. 'There's something I wanted to ask you. Have you heard of the Happy Trigger Shooting Range in Nairobi?'

He didn't look as if the name was familiar.

She shifted around on her chair and then told him about what went on there.

'Unfortunately, some old models of machine guns can still be acquired by civilians.' Hans looked disgusted. 'I don't understand people who get fun from this kind of thing. In some places it's becoming a kind of a tourist attraction. Someone told me that in Indonesia you can kill a cow with an anti-tank rocket launcher by paying $200.'

'No!' Horror convulsed Lina's body.

'Could be that the guns at that range in Nairobi are illegal. But you know how things work there: if you pay you can play any game. The Kenyan government itself is involved in arms dealing. A lot of illicit arms come into the port at Mombasa. Kenya has upgraded its military hardware recently, and we have reason to believe that instead of being destroyed, the old arsenal is being sold illegally. What's clear, at least, is that those in power are arming their own tribes. When trouble comes to that place, it's going to be bad.'

Lina smoothed her pencil skirt over her knees before asking, 'Does Samuel Ojielo know about this?' She held her breath.

'He's the Minister of State for Defence. He's also a Kikuyu. It would be extremely strange if he had no idea.'

'But how can you be certain?' She didn't know why she felt a need to stand up for this man she'd never met, the father of a son for whom her feelings were ambivalent. She couldn't believe that a chain of crime might possibly start just a few links from herself.

'I am sure so far as logic takes me. But the truth still needs to be verified – though sometimes I have my doubts that a thing like so is even possible in that country.' Hans shook his head. 'Usually it only happens when someone who's been on the inside blows the whistle. I remember you said you knew Ojielo's son, or?'

'Yes, not very well, though.' She'd spent so much time in his flat! The place had probably been paid for with money from the trade Hans was hinting at. Lina felt sick.

'Hey, don't look so worried!' Hans put a hand on her

arm. 'The son is not necessarily like the father. He probably doesn't even know what's going on.'

Lina took a deep breath. 'It's just weird, you know, that such corruption could come so close. I mean I know so few people in Kenya. Who would think one of them might be involved?'

'Yah, that's one of the hard things about this job. It tests your loyalties, sometimes. But then, what would be the value of life if it was all easy choices?' Now he paused. His Adam's apple bobbed as he swallowed. 'I also have something to ask you. Since you have access to Ojielo's circle, I wondered if you might keep your eyes and ears open. Anything we could get on that man would help our case. But he's so well insulated by all his henchmen that someone like me is never going to get close enough to catch him out.'

Lina was pale. Her cheeks looked whiter than the shirt she was wearing.

'Just think on it. There's no pressure.' Hans kept moving his hands: palms facing down then up, fingers opening and closing. 'It's not often you find someone so committed to the cause who also has access to potential perpetrators. You understand, or?' His blue eyes beseeched. 'Think on it. That's all I'm asking.'

Iman

IMAN'S EYES RAN OVER the spines of hundreds of books, searching for – she wasn't quite sure what. Except that she would know when she saw it. There was a musty smell in this windowless corner of the library. A black plastic plate, announcing 'Theology' in fading white letters, hung above the shelves. Iman's gaze wandered, taking in the volumes dedicated to the world's many faiths. A sticker curled over the lip of every shelf, identifying the religion of the books on it. Christianity, with all its denominations, took up the most space. There were some faiths Iman had never heard of, like Juche and Shinto. She was also surprised to see a couple of books dedicated to Rastafarianism. Wasn't that a hairstyle? Finally, she spotted a couple of little white labels bearing the word 'Islam'. She craned her neck. The section was consigned to the uppermost reaches of the wooden frames imposing arbitrary order on this vast subject.

She was looking at the stepladder and considering whether to drag it over and climb up when one of the librarians, Harriet Tweedie, suddenly appeared.

'Oh, Mrs Merali! Hello! What are you doing here?' Ms Tweedie knew Iman as a regular: she'd been coming to the library for more than ten years, and was usually to be found in the fiction section, near the romances. Or else, by the DVDs. 'Are you all right, dear?' said Ms Tweedie. A sheet of A4 was held close to her chest, pinched, on each side, between thumb and index finger. Her pinkies stuck into the air, as if in practice for taking tea with royalty.

'Oh, fine.' Iman stood to attention like a schoolgirl. 'Just looking.'

'What for?' Ms Tweedie peered over the top of her bifocals. 'Can I help?'

Iman smiled nervously. 'Something on Islam and, um, parents or, um, children.' Put yourself in Ms Tweedie's hands and you might end up with more than you bargained for. Iman had once sought her help locating a book on pregnancy and ended up going home with a sex manual.

'You should take a look at our family section. Round that way, six shelves down and then left.' Ms Tweedie's wiry body curved and twisted, following the directions her mouth was giving. 'You know, dear, the bit where the sofas are. We've got a lot of books on parenting.' She rolled her 'r's so prodigiously it made Iman's own tongue want to curl.

'Oh, yes. Thank you. I might take a look.' Iman nodded, though she had just come from that very area, having spent an unsatisfactory half-hour trying to find something which might show her how to turn her unruly daughters into obedient ones. Most of the books she'd flicked through had advocated letting your children be, allowing them to make their own mistakes. Complete nonsense.

'And you know our Islam section is being expanded?' Ms Tweedie's silvery mullet bounced with the news.

'Oh?'

'Yes.' Ms Tweedie stepped closer to Iman. 'Requests on the subject have just rocketed since the . . .' Ms Tweedie paused, tucked in her chin and spoke more

226

quietly, as if the very word was taboo, '*attacks* on New York.'

'Oh.' Iman's voice went up several octaves.

'I suppose people are just trying to *understand*. And they hope the books might help in some way.'

'They might.' Iman unconsciously pulled at one of the pearly buttons on her pastel-blue sweater.

'Well . . . perhaps. Anyway, that's why we're giving the topic a whole area of its own. It'll be right at the front when you come in, near the DVDs. An entire aisle, on Islam.'

'Oh!' Iman wasn't sure whether to feel pleased or disturbed. Barely eight months had passed since 11 September and already Islam was becoming all sorts of things she didn't recognize: a phenomenon, an accusation, a threat, a weapon, a misunderstanding. And now a special updated and enlarged section in the local library.

'We've got in a lot of new books and documentaries, and I don't know how many different translations of the Koran. If you come back in two weeks, Mrs Merali, the display will all be set up and you'll find a much better selection than what's up there.' She raised a pert nose in the relevant direction. 'Though I wouldn't have thought,' she ventured, 'you'd need much in the way of information on the subject. Being a practising Muslim and all,' she added hastily.

'There is always more to learn, even about the things you know well.' Iman rearranged the chuni around her head and shoulders.

'Of course. Mind you, much as I love books, I'm not sure they can explain *everything*. This whole terrorism issue, for instance.' Her tone became plaintive and confiding again. 'I'm confounded in spite of all I've read and heard.' Her shoulders inched towards her ears before

227

falling abruptly. 'In fact, the *more* I find out, the *less* I understand.'

Nowadays, Iman felt the same about life in general. She murmured agreement. But that wasn't enough for Ms Tweedie. 'What's your opinion of the men committing such crimes in the name of *your* God?'

'Um, I'm not sure.' Iman examined the sleeve of her sweater. No one had asked for her view on the matter so directly before. And besides, she didn't like the emphasis at the end of Ms Tweedie's question. 'I also don't understand.' She went on to repeat an opinion shared amongst her acquaintances: 'They are using Allah's name in the wrong way and making Islam bad.' And then, to make sure she'd covered all bases, she offered the view which the mullah was expounding at their mosque: 'But also America has done bad things to Muslims around the world. They want to make us all like them. Some people get very angry and so they do these kind of things.' Confronted with Ms Tweedie's wide-eyed silence Iman felt compelled to go on. 'It is terrible. But what can you do?'

'Hmmm.' Ms Tweedie sucked some air in through her teeth and touched the high-necked collar of her blouse with one hand, pinky still outstretched. 'Well, like I said. In two weeks we'll have our new Islam area up and running. All government-funded.' She raised her eyebrows. 'Haven't had an extra penny out of them for three years, and then all of a sudden we get a yes on this request.'

'I might just have a quick look anyway, since I'm here.' Iman reached for the stepladder.

'Take care now, dear. Mind!' Ms Tweedie pulled the end of Iman's chuni from the second rung, where it was about to get trampled. 'That's a very nice scarf.' She rubbed the blue chiffon between her fingers before throwing the dangling corner towards Iman who was already halfway up the ladder. 'I'd best get back to work now.' She pursed her lips and narrowed her eyes at the text on the A4 paper she was still holding. 'These inter-library loans . . .' she muttered, heading off towards a collection of books on scientology.

Iman left the library with a fat hardback sticking out of the bag that hung from two leather straps off her right shoulder. With each step the bag knocked against her hip, flew out a fraction and then swung in again. Iman didn't notice this. She was too busy scrolling through the contacts list on her mobile phone. There were only seven numbers – all for immediate family members – not a single one of whom was answering her calls. Her mouth tensed with indignation. She looked up for a moment, and then ran to cross the road before the lights changed. Her trainer-clad feet were at odds with the flowery femininity of her shalwar kameez.

During the first two years of her life in the UK, she had worn chappals all year, even though Shareef had bought her a pair of boots for the winter. As far as she'd been concerned, Western shoes didn't go with Eastern clothes. And besides, though she'd never have admitted this, she liked having her feet on show. They'd often drawn compliments. But after one particularly fierce winter, when frostbite threatened the loss of several toes, despite the fact that she'd worn socks with the chappals, she'd given in and pulled on the clunky boots. Now all prejudice had been replaced by pragmatism.

Iman tried calling Mariam – on her mobile and the landline at home – several times without success. Where was the girl? As she pushed the phone into her bag, Iman's hand rubbed against the spine of the book. She glanced at her watch. Maybe she'd get a few minutes to read before starting preparations for dinner. The tome she'd picked, *Islam and the Family: A Rule Book*, had not been borrowed from the library for sixteen years. Iman had selected it solely on the strength of its contents page, which listed chapters with ominous headings like: Father's Word is Final and The Principles of Punishment. It seemed the proper antidote to the liberal tendencies currently manifesting in her household.

The closer she got to home, the more people Iman recognized in the streets. By the time she was on Ladywood Road she was saying hello or as salaam alaikum to almost every person she walked by. Kids on skateboards whizzed past her and took screeching jumps off the sloping pavement on to the main road. One young girl in low-slung jeans and a hijab hurtled along, almost crashing into Iman. Further up, a small group was kicking a football around. Only a couple of years ago Mariam and Nasra had been part of this crowd, content with playing by the kerb in front of the house. Now they wanted to go off and meet friends all over town. They were monosyllabic with her, but spent hours on the phone, conversing in low voices and giggling incessantly. All the bad phases which Lina had gone through seemed to be manifesting themselves earlier and more severely in her sisters.

Iman turned her key in the door and was annoyed to find it was still double-locked. She was the first home. A glance at the clock at the end of the hallway justified the irritation suddenly throbbing at her temples. Mariam should have been back at least an hour ago. Iman pulled off her trainers, then strode up to the phone and dialled her daughter's mobile number. Again there was no answer.

She tried three more times before throwing the receiver into its pocket. That girl was going to get it today.

The moment she heard a key in the door, Iman put down the cup she was using to measure out rice for dinner. She hurried out of the kitchen.

'Where have you been?' she erupted as Mariam walked in.

'I was auditioning for the school play.' Mariam slipped off her hoodie and slung it over the jackets and scarves that hung from the wall-mounted coat rack. 'I told you about it this morning.'

Iman remembered, but was too angry for this to make any difference. 'I expected you home at five! I don't know how many times I tried your mobile.'

Mariam sidled past her mother. There had been seventeen missed calls on her phone when she'd checked it after the audition. Far from being alarmed that something must be terribly wrong, Mariam guessed that her mother must have forgotten about the auditions and started panicking about where she was. This happened regularly these days.

Iman followed her daughter into the kitchen and stood with her arms crossed while Mariam took a carton of juice out of the fridge.

'What's the point of having those expensive phones if you're never going to answer them?' Iman had bought mobiles for both the younger girls after her discovery about Lina. She was determined to keep a close eye on them now, so that nothing else could go wrong. 'Didn't you hear it ringing?'

'It was in my locker.' Mariam kept her back to her mother while she poured some juice into a glass. Her initial pride at being one of the first at school to have her own mobile had quickly worn off because of the way Iman used it to keep tabs on her. Now Mariam deliberately tried not to have the phone with her. Several times a week she even pretended to forget it at home, leaving it somewhere obvious so that Iman would realize.

'Why can't you keep it in a pocket? They're enough of them on those clothes.' Iman looked at Mariam's black tracksuit bottoms, with pockets in front and behind. She couldn't understand her daughter's idea of fashion: wearing sports clothes all the time when her cupboards were full of nice trousers and long skirts, which Iman had picked from Marks & Spencer. She had no idea that under the baggy disguise, which was stripped off at a suitable distance from home, Mariam was usually wearing a pair of brightly coloured skinny corduroys and a tight little top. 'Do you hear me? Are you even listening? You're supposed to keep the phone with you!'

'OK, I will next time!' Mariam drained her juice and wiped her mouth on her sleeve.

'What-weh! Where are you going now?' Iman shouted as the girl dashed past her again.

'Why can't I even walk around the house without you questioning me?' Mariam yelled and ran up the stairs.

'Get back down here!' Iman put a hand on the wooden cap of the bottom banister. 'Eh, Mariam! Listen to me!'

The only response was a slamming door.

Iman sat down heavily on one of the lower steps and let her head hang. Ya Allah, her daughters were out of control. She would have liked to possess them completely, as she had never possessed anyone, not even her husband, who, for all his love and kindness, gave her only tiny slivers of insight into his thoughts. The girls had been hers, for a while, at the beginning, when they had sucked at her breast and melted, warm with sleep, into the crook of her arm. Their eyes had been wide with belief in her omnipotence. They had wanted her comfort after accidents, and her approval for accomplishments. And she had luxuriated in the voluptuousness of their need. But, too soon, they had begun to close up, to hide some things and see too much of others. Then she had grabbed them, or furtively watched them at play, trying to fish out their thoughts and secrets, as if knowing might somehow bind them to her for good. As more and more chunks of their existence eluded her, she had alternated affection with sternness, because the latter was a reliable form of control.

Suddenly, Iman felt the vibrations of a loud bass quiver down the staircase. She rose and stomped up in her stockinged feet, determined to teach Mariam a lesson.

'Turn that down!' Her knuckles hammered against the door, whose frame was shuddering in time to the music's beat. When Mariam didn't comply Iman pressed down on the handle – but the door was locked. 'Eh, Mariam! Open up!' Iman's fists banged at the wood. Still the girl did not oblige. 'Bismillah! In the name of God! Will you open?' Resignation already lined her voice. She turned and headed down again. Shareef would have to deal with this when he got back. That girl needed to know who was in charge.

Four steps from the bottom Iman's shalwar got caught under her heel and she slipped. Next thing she was flat on her back at the foot of the stairs.

When Shareef came home with Nasra half an hour later, Iman was still lying on the floor.

'Ma?' Nasra knelt by her moaning mother. Her hair, still wet from swimming practice, had dripped patches of water on to the shoulders of her shirt.

'Iman, what happened?' Shareef also hurried to her side. 'Did you fall?'

Mariam's music continued to thump through the house.

'Shall I call an ambulance? What can I do?' Shareef hovered anxiously.

'No,' Iman said weakly. She'd been trying out each limb, cautiously checking if everything still worked. The pain was concentrated in her lower back. 'Help me. Get up.'

Shareef put one leg on either side of his wife's splayed body. His red-and-brown-striped tie flew forward as he bent over. She started whimpering even before he touched her. 'I don't think this is a good idea, Iman.' He straightened up. 'If something is really wrong I might do more damage.'

Nasra picked up the end of Iman's chuni, which was still strewn on the steps.

'Well, I can't. Just stay this way!' She kept squeezing her eyes shut between words.

'How long have you been like this? Where's Mariam?' He looked up in the direction of the noise. 'Go get your sister to turn that off,' he instructed Nasra.

'First soak the rice,' Iman interrupted. 'It's by the sink. In the little—' She winced. 'Saucepan. Fill it. With water.'

'Iman, I'm calling an ambulance.' Shareef stood with his hands on his hips. 'This doesn't look good.'

'Can't be so bad. Everything. Works.' She moved her arms and legs as if to prove it.

'Well, let me ask Dr Hussein. He's just down the road. I'm sure he won't mind popping over.' Shareef moved aside to let Nasra go upstairs. 'Tell Mariam to turn it off and get down here right away.' He went towards the phone, ignoring Iman's protestations. When he'd finished talking to the doctor the music was still blaring.

'I told you. That girl is—' Iman tried to shift again but pain shot through her back. 'Ouch!'

'Dr Hussein said not to move. He'll be here soon.' He crouched down and held her hand. 'And he's calling an ambulance to be on the safe side.'

Nasra reappeared. 'She can't hear me, Baba. She won't open.'

'She didn't. Listen to me. Either. And then I came down. And this.' Iman pointed at herself.

Shareef leapt to his feet and ran up. He kicked the door so hard it jumped in its frame. A second later the music went off. 'Open up!' he hollered.

Mariam came out slowly, shoulders rolled forward, mouth pinched.

'What do you think you're up to? Blasting music like you're the only person in the world?'

'It wasn't—'

'Shut up! Do you know what you've done?' Shareef grabbed her by the arm and hauled her down the stairs. 'Your mother's been lying here shouting for help for God only knows how long.' Shareef felt unbearably hot. One hand went to loosen his tie. 'What if she'd broken her neck, huh? What if she'd died? It would be your fault!' He jabbed a hand in Mariam's direction.

She bit her lip and looked at the floor. 'I didn't—'

'All you think about is yourself!' His hand wagged, moving faster as his voice grew louder. 'You don't realize how lucky you are. All you do is complain and come up with excuses for your bad behaviour. Look at your poor mother! Look what you've done to her!'

Both girls began to cry.

'Shareef, please. Leave them now.' Even Iman was startled by his reaction.

Shareef stood glaring and breathing heavily.

The doorbell rang.

'Must be Dr Hussein.' Iman smoothed her hair. 'Shareef, you better. Let him in. Girls go to the kitchen. Mariam, put the rice. To boil and then. Heat the sabzi in. The microwave. Nasra. You lay the table.'

'As salaam alaikum.' The doctor came over to Iman, skirting around the wooden sideboard. Its drawers were stuffed with hats, gloves, scarves and cheap plastic sunglasses, its cupboards full of old board games that no one had played in years.

The doctor had rushed over without changing and was still in his kurta pyjama. 'So, what happened here?'

'Nothing, doctor-sahib. You know. Just running around. After the children and then. I slipped.' Iman indicated where the pain was most severe.

'Ah, you should know by now that you can't keep up with them.' The doctor turned to Shareef. 'Can we have some more light?'

Shareef went to the switch. He hadn't noticed how dark it had become.

The doorbell rang again and Shareef stood to one side as three paramedics, dressed in electric-blue scrubs, trooped in. Together with Dr Hussein they lined up alongside Iman, each positioned at one point along her body – head, chest, hips, legs – to do a logroll.

'OK,' the head paramedic, a lean black man, gave the signal. 'One, two – three!'

Iman cried out as they turned her, in one smooth flip, so that she was lying flat on her stomach. Nasra and Mariam appeared in the kitchen doorway when their mother shouted, their faces pale. Sweat broke out on Shareef's forehead. He went and nudged the girls back into the kitchen, then shut the door.

The head paramedic proceeded to press against each of Iman's vertebrae, starting at the neck. Everything seemed to be OK until he got to the bottom of her spine. Then the screams started.

'We're almost there. Stay still for me, now,' the medic went on pressing. When his fingers grazed the very base of Iman's spine, she gave her loudest yell yet.

'All right. We've got you.' He signalled to one of his colleagues, who began filling a syringe from a small glass phial.

The medic turned to Dr Hussein and some impenetrable medical-speak ensued, from which Shareef recognized only the word 'coccyx'.

'What's wrong?' He stood with his hands behind his back. 'Is she going to be OK?'

'Well.' Dr Hussein turned to him while someone else gave Iman an injection. 'We can't say for sure until she's had a scan, but it seems to be a fractured coccyx.'

'What does that mean?' Shareef looked at his wife, who was already visibly relaxing thanks to the morphine.

'It means she has to take it easy for a while. With this kind of injury rest is the best medicine. Inshallah, all will be well.' Dr Hussein turned to Iman. 'The coccyx is a tiny, triangular-shaped bone right at the base of your spine. It's really a pretty useless part of our anatomy, but – as you now know – can be excruciating if damaged. I think it should heal up just fine, but we'll know better after you've had a scan.'

The paramedics were already packing up.

'Let's get you on your feet before we leave,' the head

medic said to Iman. Two of them gripped her under the arm from either side and hoisted her up so she was standing against the wall. Her shadow was a weak blur against the patterned brown wallpaper.

'I feel better.' She blinked rapidly. 'Just a little. Dizzy.'

'You might not feel so good when that shot wears off.' The head medic waved a plastic pot of pills at Shareef. 'Give her these if she needs them during the night. But no more than two every four hours.'

'Thanks.' Shareef took the pills and then showed the medics out.

'You should be back to normal in a few months – as long as you don't overdo it.' Dr Hussein gave Iman a knowing look. 'Sitting is going to be the tricky thing for a while. You'll be more comfortable standing or lying down.'

'Ya Allah.' Iman suddenly said: 'What about my prayers?' She'd started praying five times a day since they'd found out about Lina.

'I'm sure Allah accepts the sincere prayer no matter what position it's delivered from: vertical, horizontal or diagonal.' The doctor started towards the door. 'Khuda Hafiz. May God protect you.'

'Won't you stay for dinner, doctor sahib?' Iman tried to hobble after him, one hand supporting her back. 'It's ready. The girls were just warming it all when you came.'

'No, no. Thank you. The wife has everything prepared at home. You go and rest now.'

Iman nodded and turned towards the kitchen.

'What about you, Shareef?' The doctor looked him up and down. 'Are you all right?'

Shareef's face was flushed. His side parting was lost. And he was still wearing his coat on top of his suit. 'Of course.' There was an uncharacteristic edge to his voice.

'Make sure Iman takes it easy,' the doctor called as he headed into the night.

Shareef closed the door and leaned against it for a few moments before slipping off his coat and jacket.

Back in the kitchen Iman used the counter for support while giving orders. The girls moved quickly to comply with every instruction.

'Please sit, Shareef,' Iman said as he walked in.

'You're the one who's supposed to be resting. Shouldn't you lie down?'

Iman tried to ease herself into one of the chairs at the round pine table, but gave up. 'The doctor was right.' She sighed and propped herself against the counter again.

Shareef picked up one of the plates. The flowers that once decorated it had faded to pale abstract smudges of pink and green. He covered the surface with food and took it to Iman.

'Oh, what-weh? This rice is overcooked,' she pronounced. Every grain was withered and broken. She wasn't hungry, anyway. A strange nausea was overtaking her.

'I obviously can't do anything right.' Mariam circled her ribs with her arms.

'Stop feeling sorry for yourself.' Shareef spoke without looking at her. He helped himself to some salad and aubergine curry.

'Shareef, can you tell these two again that they have to keep their phones with them at all times?' Iman was still more concerned about them than her own condition.

Shareef stopped eating and looked around for the box of tissues. He spotted it on the counter, under a desk calendar festooned with images of different mosques around the world. He passed a tissue to everybody and then took one for himself.

'You've heard your mother.' He wiped the corners of his mouth and glanced from Nasra to Mariam. 'It's not too much to ask that you remain contactable at all times.'

Nasra nodded, wide-eyed. Her hair had dried into light curls that fell over her ears.

Mariam set down her fork with a clatter. 'She makes me look like a waste girl.'

Shareef frowned, not comprehending her street lingo. 'Wasting what?'

Mariam rolled her eyes. 'You don't get it.'

'No. *You* don't get it.' Shareef glared.

'I didn't even do anything wrong!' Mariam's eyes swung from father to mother. 'I told her I was going to be home late this evening. She just gets hysterical.'

Iman clutched at the counter and took a deep breath.

'Don't talk about your mother like that,' Shareef said.

'Both of you! Ever since Lina left you've just— ' Mariam clamped her mouth shut, unsure whether to go on.

There was silence – as if they were all waiting for her verdict.

'It's not fair! Why do we have to suffer?'

'Listen to this girl, weh.' Iman slapped her forehead. 'Tobah astaghfirullah.'

'You have a strange idea of suffering.' Shareef struggled to stay calm.

'Shareef, please help me to bed.' Iman made a move towards the door. 'I can't . . . this is too much.'

Once they were upstairs, she started crying. 'I'm so scared, Shareef.' She sobbed as he held her. Ceaseless worrying about the future was wearing her out. And now this accident. She felt exhausted and helpless. 'What will become of these girls? See the way Mariam talks? Lina was so quiet in comparison, and look what happened with her.'

'It'll be OK.' He tried to soothe her, though he was equally worried. 'Inshallah, we'll find a way.'

'What way?' Iman eased out of his arms and then froze for an instant as her back protested. 'You always say that and then do nothing.' They'd had some variation of this conversation every single day since Lina's departure: either a full-blown argument or needling little asides.

Shareef ran a hand over his beard. 'I don't know what you expect! You want me to start hiring detectives to follow them around?' He went over to the window and pulled the curtains shut, the rings from which they hung screeched along the metal rail.

'If we don't sort things out with Lina, then the other two will always use her behaviour as an excuse for their own.' Iman wiped her eyes and began undressing. Her shalwar was easy enough to slip out of, but she had trouble with the kameez. 'Shareef?'

He came up behind her and tugged off the top.

'And can you remove the necklace?' She stretched her neck downwards. Some hair had become entangled in the clasp of the gold chain. He pulled it out abruptly, and then felt a rush of remorse when Iman yelped. He had to get hold of himself. Anxiety was spilling out of him in all sorts of ugly ways.

He held his wife's shoulders and gently kissed the back of her neck several times. 'I'll think about what you've said, Iman. We'll figure it out, OK?'

He left the room repeating 'As-Sabur' quietly to himself. It was his favourite of Allah's ninety-nine names – As-Sabur, The Patient. He invoked it often, as though by doing so the quality might percolate into him. The repetition of the name literally affected the pace of his breath, slowing it down, calming him.

*　*　*

Downstairs the girls were clearing up and messing about. The normally spotless kitchen was in disorder despite their efforts to tidy up. Mariam splashed a handful of water at Nasra, who responded by swatting her with the dishcloth. Shareef stood in the doorway, watching them. He wished he could keep them like this for ever. He felt as though it might be possible if he could find the right words. They welled up inside him, his heart flooding with what his mind was unable to process. If he could only say it, every-thing might be all right. But he could not give it the substance of language, this thing that was tightening in his throat. Instead, he started coughing. The girls heard and became serious again. They went on quietly with their chores. When he felt able to speak Shareef told them to go say goodnight to Iman after finishing up.

'And make sure you both apologize to her.'

'But I didn't—' Nasra started to say, until Mariam's foot stamped down on hers.

'Yes, Baba,' Mariam said. And Nasra echoed her.

As he headed to his small study, Shareef heard the older sister tell the younger: 'Sometimes you just have to pretend to agree with them.'

Only fifteen years old, he thought, and already so wised up.

He shut the door of his study and turned on the desk lamp. He stretched out in his chair, using a stack of old papers as a footrest. Over his crossed ankles, his feet tapped against each other. They were clad in woolly brown socks despite the early summer heat. What were his options? He stared at his cluttered desk and found his eye drawn to the items picked out by the spotlight glare of the desk lamp: the telephone with its blipping green light and, next to it, the Rolodex he still used for storing telephone numbers and addresses. He sat forward and rested his elbows on the desk. Slowly, he began flicking through the rotating index cards, passing through each letter of the alphabet until he came to L. There, amongst other contacts, were Lina's current details in New York. A spasm of anger passed through Shareef. The number blurred before his eyes as he continued to gaze at it. Then he gritted his teeth and reached into the drawer under his desk. His hand went automatically to the back left-hand corner and drew out a crumpled pink Post-it note. He held it between his fingers for a while. Then he smoothed out the small scrap of paper. A number was scrawled across it in Iman's slanted handwriting. He took a deep breath, reached for the phone and dialled.

Merc was in the living room doing press-ups in a pair of Lycra shorts when he heard ringing. Pausing mid-push, he turned his head towards the phone, which sat on a low and narrow carved African table. Merc got to his feet, pectorals heaving. He was just about to pick the phone up when it fell silent. He stood, with sweaty hands resting on his hips, over the cordless gadget whose green light winked at him. The trill of the phone started up again and he answered it before the first bell was finished.

'Hello?' Uncertainty and foreignness permeated the caller's voice.

'Yes?'

'Is Anil Mayur there?' The man sounded as if he was in a hurry.

Somehow, Merc knew, without a doubt, who it was. 'I'm afraid not.' One side of his mouth curled upwards, transforming his smooth face into a sadistic mask. 'He's in New York at the moment. Can I take a message?'

There was a sharp intake of breath. And then the line went dead.

Merc replaced the receiver, amusement radiating off his cheekbones. His heart was beating faster than it had been while he was exercising. He almost whooped when the phone rang again.

'Has he gone to see Lina?' the man asked right away.

'Yes, Lina Merali.' Merc didn't want to leave any space for misunderstanding.

'I wonder if – can you help me?' The man sounded old and choked. 'This Anil – who is he? What is he like?'

'You're Lina's father, right?' Merc didn't even wait for confirmation. 'I wouldn't worry about Anil, if I were you.' He cradled the phone and slouched against the wall. 'It's not going to last between them.'

'What do you mean?'

'They're not right for each other. And they're going to discover that soon enough.'

'What? Who are you?'

'Anil and I have been friends since we were boys. I know him well enough to realize there's a lot about him that doesn't fit in with your saintly daughter's ideas of how things should be.'

'What exactly are you talking about? Tell me.'

'Not so fast, old man.' Merc's mouth stretched wider, his teeth and eyes beamed. 'I can tell you whatever you like, but only if you do things my way.'

Surrender

HE KNEW IT WOULD happen from the way she let him touch her. She didn't twist in his arms or guide his hands elsewhere. She didn't cover up bits of herself while his attention was on other parts. Her body moved against his, like a river that knows its course.

They climbed out of the tub and, without drying off, led one another, kissing and dripping, to the giant bed. The thick pile carpet held the imprints of their feet with the same tenderness that the earth grants the snow – cherishing it the more for its temporary presence.

They were in a hotel near Madison Square, because the room Lina rented uptown was small and not very private. Their suite was all coffee-toned, the muted furnishings set off by splashes of black and purple. They rolled over the bed, limbs entwined, then stretched in pleasure, then curled again with need. The bed linen became a painting of wet marks: a modernist array of arms, legs, heads and the tangled shadows of damp hair. The squelch of their skin made them laugh, and they lowed between kisses like contented cows. It was all so effortless that afterwards Anil could not understand how they'd delayed for so long. Then again, maybe this easy intimacy was the reward for restraint. He lay on top of Lina, luxuriating in it. He looked at the painting hanging on one wall, a cross-section of an orchid in all its voluptuous detail. That magenta explosion was surely the shape of pleasure.

Suddenly Lina's chest jerked unnaturally beneath him. He raised his head and saw that she was crying. He slid off her to one side and propped himself up with an arm.

'What is it, Leenie?' He brushed her hair off her face.

She pulled the covers up over herself. 'My parents.' She wouldn't look at him. 'My mum's really ill because of me.' That morning, just as she'd been about to leave her flat to meet Anil at the airport, her father had called. He had told her Iman had almost been paralysed the previous night by a fall that was caused because of worry about her. He'd said neither of them could function normally any more. He'd claimed they wouldn't be able to breathe freely until their eldest daughter was settled with a good Muslim. He'd informed her that they were going to start looking for a suitable husband.

Lina now repeated all this to Anil. 'I don't know how we can be together any more,' she whispered.

The contrast between her actions and her words confounded him. She ventured a glance at him, but his expression made her look away again.

The curtains were still open. Through the window the rounded corner of the Flatiron building was visible. Its limestone and terracotta-glazed façade gleamed in the afternoon sun.

Anil sat up and leaned back against an army of cushions. When they'd decided to stay together after her parents found the letters he'd thought their love had passed its hardest test.

'So what was *this* all about?' He kicked at the sheets with one foot.

'I wanted you to know how much I love you.'

Anil was out of the bed in one move. 'Do you really

believe that's what counts for me?' The painting of the orchid flashed into sight again – its magenta now the colour of pain. 'You think now that we've had sex I won't mind if we don't have a future together?' Anger creased the corners of his eyes, gave his mouth a crooked slant.

'No! That's not what I meant! I wanted to give myself to you. Now I'll always be yours – whatever . . . happens.'

'Stop talking like that.' He went into the bathroom and came out wearing one of the black hotel dressing gowns. 'Why does this have to change anything between us?' He returned to the foot of the bed.

'I can't keep lying!' Her fingers dug into her kneecaps. 'How am I supposed to avoid meeting whoever they want me to marry? I've got no excuse, Anil. If I refuse they'll know I'm still with you – and then?' She shuddered. 'It might give one of them a heart attack.'

'You're afraid for their health, but you don't care if our love dies?'

Lina muffled her face with the sheet, pressing its folds to her streaming eyes.

Anil started pacing the room. 'What about my health, Lina? What about yours? What state would we be in without each other? Why are they more important? It's *our* life.'

'I don't want it to be like this!' She cut a pathetic figure crouched at the head of the vast bed, surrounded by a swell of linen. 'But what's the alternative, Anil?'

'We go on and we find a way to make it work.'

'I don't think they'll ever change their minds.' She spoke so quietly that he had to come closer and ask her to repeat the words.

He took her in his arms, squashed her pale skin against the black satin of his gown. 'They'll come around. You wait and see, everything will be fine.'

247

Who's the Terrorist?

A FEW MONTHS LATER, Lina flew to see Anil in London. They decided to go to a peace concert that was being held in Regent's Park to commemorate the first anniversary of the attacks on the World Trade Centre. By the time Lina, Anil and Merc arrived there, thousands of people were already assembled. The air buzzed with heavy vibrations emitted from giant speakers and was perfumed by food stalls. The area around the stage was so packed, you couldn't have spotted a blade of grass between audience members. Then the crowd started to thin and, where the three eventually decided to sit down, there were lots of little groups, strewn across the ground like bunches of grapes.

Lina was in town for a weekend visit, coordinated with Anil who'd flown over from Kenya. Pravar had finally lured his son home with an offer to design and build a block of offices right in the city centre. The promise of this freedom to pursue his own visions was too strong for Anil to resist, despite the fact that it took him further away from Lina.

Anil pulled a tartan picnic rug out of their hamper and unrolled it. Merc immediately kicked off his flip-flops and lay back with his hands under his head. Lina knelt to unpack the hamper, which Anil had ordered from some exclusive deli. It was filled with food and drink, but also

248

contained other practical necessities for comfortable out-door eating. Except the things weren't really practical, Lina thought, as she lifted out the china plates, crystal glasses and silver cutlery. She couldn't see the guys re-packing everything, taking it home, cleaning it and then using it again. They were likely to dump the whole lot in with everyone else's rubbish in the nearest bin. She didn't understand why they couldn't have just bought a snack from one of the stalls here. She looked around: people seemed perfectly happy sitting on the grass, eating soggy food from collapsing paper napkins. Only they were posh-ing it up on this little patch of park. Foie gras! She pulled out a ceramic terrine – Anil didn't even like the stuff!

'Why did you order this?' She waved it in Anil's face.

'What?' He read the label. 'I just asked for their luxury hamper. I didn't check what was in it.'

That explained the other contents, too. There was a lot of pork, including a whole platter of cured stuff. Lina put the terrine down roughly. His extravagance! She both loved and deplored it.

'When's Nitin Sawhney on, mazeh?' Merc rolled on to one side and propped himself up on an elbow. 'I don't like this rap stuff. What language are they singing in? Arabic?' He squinted at the stage, a few hundred metres in front of them, where another band was playing.

'Sawhney's one of the last acts.' Anil unscrewed the top from a bottle and poured two glasses. 'We'd better drink this. Another half hour in this heat and it'll be mulled wine.'

Merc sat up and took his drink. His gaze shifted from the stage to the giant screen beaming out a magnified version of the performances. Along the bottom of the screen was a translation of the lyrics currently being sung.

'What are those idiots saying?' White text flowed over the images:

> You say I'm the criminal?
> Where's the crime in taking back what's mine?
> You call me a thief,
> When you've stolen my land?
> You make me the killer!
> When you've strangled my hope!
> Who's the terrorist?
> Who's the thug?
> You are you are you are
> Motherthugger!

'What the fuck? Have you seen this?' Merc turned to Lina and Anil.

Anil watched as more of the translated lines appeared. 'I read that there was going to be some Middle Eastern rap group performing. This must be them.'

Lina stopped and shifted her attention to the screen as well. She pushed up her oversized sunglasses and craned a little to see over people's heads.

'What audacity! These people have got it all wrong.' Merc looked ready to get on stage and throttle the rapper. 'Mazeh, I'm telling you, these people just want to take over the world. You get me? They won't be happy until every woman on the globe is dressed in a chador, so that our streets look like they've been filled with a plague of black clouds.'

'This isn't the place for your wasi wasi, bwana. Speakers' Corner is in Hyde Park.' Anil kept his tone light, but he was conscious of everyone around them. There were all kinds of people in this crowd, including some who wouldn't stand for such opinions.

'I might try Speakers' Corner, if I could get a word in edge-ways. There's probably some Muslim already standing there, proclaiming the innocence of all his fellow brethren.' Merc seemed unconcerned that he might be overheard.

'OK, bwana. Just take it easy, yeah?' Anil glanced at Lina. She was sitting on her heels, her biscuit-coloured sundress rumpled under her bottom. There was disbelief on her face.

'All these slighted Muslims are hogging the pulpits at the moment. Poor them!' Merc raised the pitch of his voice. 'They feel upset and offended that everyone is associating Islam with violence. What a strange and unreasonable thing for people to do, huh?'

'Can we discuss this another time?' Anil was thankful the music was masking his friend's statements. He'd just noticed a group of young Asian guys sitting a couple of metres away. They could be Muslims, for all he knew.

'Calling other people terrorists after what they themselves have done. These people are unbelievable.' Merc drained the wine from his glass and reached for the bottle to refill it.

'I wish you'd stop saying "these people". You're always lumping all Muslims together!' Lina's bottom lifted off her heels and her arms went to her hips. For a moment she was looking down on Merc, but he changed position too, so that he was squatting in front of her. Just then the act came to a close and the crowd started applauding. Many of them even rose to cheer the singer – including, Anil noted, the Asians to their left.

Merc waved a hand dismissively at the stage. 'They can rap all they like, calling the rest of us names. As far as I'm concerned "Muslim" is a word that pretty much means "terrorist" now. You get me?'

'Merc!' Anil hissed. 'You need to watch what you say, bwana. That's a complete exaggeration, and a dangerous one.'

'It's exactly the kind of thinking that causes more friction.' Lina shook her head.

'I'm telling you, if these people don't stop their sick stunts in the name of Islam, the religion is going to remain synonymous with terror, the way "German" still has a Nazi association.' A few heads turned in their direction, but Merc was oblivious. He bent over to break the end off a baguette and then jumped to his feet.

'So I'm a terrorist for you, too?' Lina watched the sunlight reflect off Merc's shiny pate.

'Why are both of you looking at me that way? Suddenly I'm unreasonable for making assumptions on the basis of fact. This is the problem.' He bit into the bread. Crumbs fell, like hail, on to his shorts and the picnic blanket.

Lina and Anil exchanged glances. He could see blame in her eyes. She hadn't wanted Merc to come with them this afternoon. He was beginning to regret it as well. He wished the next band would hurry up and start so that Merc wouldn't be so easily overheard.

'Instead of getting upset with me,' he was off again, 'why aren't you getting upset with those terrorists who claim to do all this shit in Allah's name?'

A couple of the guys on their left began openly staring.

'I can't believe it! You sound like you hate all Muslims. That's so stupid.' Lina got up.

'I'm certainly not feeling too kindly disposed towards the Allah-fans right now. Don't give me that shocked look. Why should I pretend?' Merc got even louder. 'I feel aggrieved that you're not more anti those bloody fundis. Your fellow believers are so ready to take offence and burn

252

effigies of anyone who criticizes them, but why don't they have the same reaction to Osama bin Laden and his crew? Why aren't any of you burning his picture?' Merc lifted his eyebrows and pulled his lips together.

'You can't make Lina or any other decent Muslim personally responsible for what some fanatics do.' Anil deliberately raised his own voice. From the corner of his eye he could see the Asian boys conferring and sending more ugly stares their way.

'Why don't you let her speak for herself?' Merc reached down and cut himself a slab from the log of goat's cheese.

Lina wondered how he could keep on eating while pursuing such a topic. 'You know,' she said, 'these actions don't come out of nowhere—'

'Just stop right there.' He pointed the cheese at her. 'Don't start giving me any bullshit about deprivation, globalization, American military bases or any of that maneno. Nothing – *nothing* – justifies killing innocent people. You get me? Whatever your cause, there are legitimate outlets for the expression of frustration. Murder, as far as I'm concerned, is not one of them, not in any-body's name.'

Anil was hardly listening any more. He was focusing on their neighbours, one of whom had just muttered some-thing like, 'Come we bang dem.'

'I agree with you but—' Lina began.

'Stop fucking butting!'

'There's a context for every action,' she persevered. She was standing rigid, her cheeks flushed. The V-neck of her dress revealed a bit of cleavage, where more emotion showed as red speckles on her skin. 'We all need to take responsibility—'

'Hey – you all right?' A big guy with a faded haircut and

253

two slashes through his left eyebrow was suddenly standing next to Lina.

'Y-es.' Lina had to lean back to take him in. He was a huge cube of a man. Two of his friends were lining up behind him, one tall and lanky, the other a bit shorter than Lina.

'These boys givin' you trouble?' He narrowed his eyes at Merc and then Anil, who was scrambling up from where he'd been seated.

'No. No. Everything's fine.' Lina managed a fake smile.

But the guy didn't budge.

'Go have your own party, man.' Merc jerked his chin. 'Leave us alone.'

'Watch, bruv.' The tall one – punier, but with a more menacing face, stepped forward. 'We heard dem tings you been saying about Muslims.'

'So?' Merc bit another hunk of his bread and ate noisily, as if he was chewing gum.

Lina's fingers gripped each other at her chest. It looked like she might be about to start praying.

'If we're so bad, why you runnin' with one of our girls?' The one with the slashed eyebrow pushed out his chest. 'Why don't you move to one of your own kind?'

'Shut up! If anyone needs to move it's you. Interfering where you have no business. Just leave us.' Merc made a shooing motion.

'Oi, batty-boy.' With one move Slashed Eyebrow had his six-pack pressed against Merc's. 'What you on about? Coming here, talking like you're a big man. Who are you, blud?'

'None of your fucking business.' Merc pushed him.

The other two jumped forward to defend their friend.

254

Anil also joined the fray, stepping off the picnic rug on to the grass.

'Look this isn't necessary.' He tried to come between the two parties. 'This is a misunderstanding. My friend's drunk. He doesn't know what he's saying.'

There was a tussle and then Slashed Eyebrow was on top again, pulling at Merc's T-shirt. 'I'm gonna burst you, blud. Watch what you say. Don't go chatting shit about Muslims again.'

'I'll say what I want.' Merc spat in his face.

Slashed Eyebrow headbutted him. 'What you on, blud? Who are you? I bet your mum was some hoe who got battered by a black boy.'

Merc lunged back. Sliced Eyebrow landed on the hamper, crushing the food and breaking the plates. When he got up there were strawberries smashed into his trousers and two pieces of salami stuck to his bum.

An announcement on stage was followed by applause. Lina didn't hear any of it. The only sound in her ears was the violent thudding of her heart.

'Stop it!' she begged. 'Please stop.'

The short one obliged by coming to threaten her instead. 'What you doing with these waste guys? Are you dumb?'

'They're my friends.' She clutched at the sides of her dress.

'Leave her alone, Shorty!' Anil knocked him to one side.

'Friend! That's some next friend you've picked,' Shorty snarled. 'I bet he's put it in you. Good Muslim girl that you are. If you were my sister I'd give you an honour killing *now*, man, no long ting.'

'You little shit!' Anil punched him. He stumbled,

stepped on to a wine glass, and then came back with a counter-blow. Lina screamed. By now a couple of onlookers had intervened. Just as the guys were separated the police arrived. All of them were handcuffed and driven to the station to give statements.

Afterwards, Merc had to go to the hospital because his lip was still bleeding. He needed three stitches. Lina hoped the injury would keep him quiet for a while. No chance. In the taxi, as they headed to drop him home before going on to their hotel, he started up on his anti-Islamic theme again.

'It's all you believers who are making a mess of the world. You get me?' His speech was slightly mumbled because of the stitches and the lingering effects of a local anaesthetic.

'Be quiet now, please. You've got us into enough mess for one day.' Anil had a big bruise on one cheekbone. There was also blood on the front of his shirt, probably from Shorty, whose nose had been broken during the fight. 'You're really starting to sound racist.'

'How can I be racist for stating the facts? Muslims are involved in all the worst conflicts in the world. Kashmir – Muslims. Palestine – Muslims. Even the problems in Sudan now – those Janjaweed, they're Muslim.'

'That's not a religious conflict. It's more about Arab supremacism. Most of the victims are African Muslims.' Lina rolled down her window, determined not to be drawn into another argument. They were all seated in a row, with Anil in the middle. She wished he would make his friend stop.

'Well, there you go. They can't even stop fighting each other. All that Sunni and Shia nonsense.' Merc pressed three fingers against one side of his mouth while speaking.

'I think all religions are as bad as each other, but Muslims seem to be the most belligerent.'

'You're so quick to judge.' Lina couldn't hold back. 'But do you realize none of these groups would be able to engage in such violence if someone wasn't selling them the weapons to do so in the first place!'

'What?' Merc was thrown for a moment. 'Oh that's great! Don't blame the killer, blame the guy who sold him the gun. That's really logical.'

'You just have half the picture, Merc.' A vein in her neck stood out, throbbing. 'I bet you've got no idea that your beloved enlightened Europe is the largest exporter of arms in the world. This isn't just the continent of high art, they make hundreds of millions of euros a year by exporting death to other countries. And places like Kenya are complicit in this industry because arms are illegally trafficked through there.' Her heart was thumping, spurring her on. She shot him a look of pure reproach. 'So next time you start to blame someone for expressing their views more forcefully than you like, spare a thought for those who gave them the means to do it.'

Merc sucked his teeth and shook his head. 'You don't understand what I'm saying. You're confused.'

Lina wished she could put her hands to her ears. She was tired of his constant attempts to undermine her. Besides which, it was rich to see this talk of confusion coming from a guy who was half-Indian, half-African, lived in England, had the name of a German car, changed the colour of his eyes every day and was ignorant about what his high-flying father might really be doing. She couldn't believe Merc was as much his own person as he purported to be. Why else had he turned his back on Kenya? He must be running away from something.

'Listen—' Merc began.

'Will you leave her alone?' Anil shouted. 'Just stop now!'

The worst things in life are somehow more bearable if
you can plot their course: see what led to what, and
why. Once the world was fully mapped it became more
easily navigable. So I trace the landscape of our past
hoping to chart my way to understanding.

Joy, my PhD supervisor, came to see me after I
missed an appointment with her – the fourth that we'd
scheduled. I'd had every intention of going but it turned
out to be one of those days, less frequent now but still
regular, when misery shackled me to my bed, its weight
a leaden blanket I could not throw off. Until, that is, the
doorbell started ringing. The repetitive, high-pitched
screech, like the trill of an angry parrot, went on and on.
Eventually I crawled to the front door, thinking Lucas
must have forgotten his key. Only to find Professor Joy
Stern, in all her impeccable optimism, standing on the
doorstep. She looked me over and pronounced: Good
heavens, dear girl! You're a mess! She sounded almost
impressed.

She thinks my present condition is a gift. Lest you
start to find any solace in this, or take any credit for it,
let me stop you right now by saying that I disagree with
her completely. The suffering you inflict on someone
can never be justified – whatever they might eventually
learn or gain from it. Nevertheless, her premiss interests
me. She claims that losing you has taken me beyond the
bounds of ordinary experience, and let me glimpse

the tremendous capacity for feeling within each human being. Generally, she says, from day to day, we operate within fairly limited emotional parameters.

Oh! I interrupted, what I wouldn't give to be back within those. If contentment is the bullseye of being, I would happily remain within its placid circumference. I would sacrifice all highs to avoid such lows.

No you wouldn't. Joy shook her head. Every person or circumstance that pushes us, in a good or bad way, beyond quotidian boundaries is doing us a service. They give us a chance to learn what extraordinary vessels we are, what abilities we have to feel beyond anything we might be able to imagine. Especially as an artist, she went on, experience is the best way to increase your vocabulary. To know the true meaning of words, she said, you have to live them. How much more power they have then, than when they lie in neatly defined columns within the sterile pages of a dictionary.

I told her I could have done without becoming overly familiar with the more dismal reaches of language. Words have weight; some of them can crush you.

She grabbed me by the shoulders and gave me a little shake. She's quite strong for a small woman in her fifties. One day, she said, you will look back and see that this was the time when you first began to grasp the glorious spectrum of life. You want to be a writer? She looked at me hard.

Possibly, letting this fact be known has been an error. It is one of my weaknesses – or, as you liked to put it, a symptom of enthusiasm – to declare my intentions before taking any steps towards achieving them. This was certainly not your style. You quietly weighed things up, mulled over them, prevaricated and then, when no one expected it, decided. Sometimes you'd evade a question and then come up with an answer weeks later. I valued this oddity, liking the way you took the time to reflect on things, and didn't feel obliged to have an immediate opinion on all matters.

As Joy was talking, I remembered that you once said: It's better not to state your purpose until you are quite sure of fulfilling it.

The sentiment seems laudable on the surface, but is selfish at the core.

Joy went on to say: Suffering is the writer's stock-in trade – the key to open the casket of our common humanity. What you have here, young lady, amidst all the heartache, is material that can become a story.

That made me jump off the chair. Arms flying, I railed: Ours wasn't a story! At best it was a few incomplete chapters.

How could I not have noticed our incompatibility sooner? I suppose I was complacent because your piety seemed to coexist with worldliness. So it didn't spook me that you got up at strange hours of the night to pray or that you only drank from a glass while holding it with your right hand. When I questioned you, wondering what such an insignificant act could have to do with god and belief, you explained that it was a question of awareness. Through such small gestures, one remembered and felt closer to god even during the mundane moments of life.

God is not just to be called on in times of celebration or strife, you said. God is always there, waiting to sustain us. And such rituals, you said, looking at me, your eyes full of a profundity I almost envied,

261

enable me to do that. They are important for me, these modes of connection to him.

It seemed quite plausible, the way you put it, quite harmless. But even then I had a niggling sense that there was a dimension of your life from which I was being excluded – by my own scepticism, I know, but excluded nonetheless. I told myself it didn't matter. I didn't believe in god and so I didn't imagine he could be my rival. Now I wonder. If I had tried to know him better, his books and laws, maybe I would have been better equipped to fight back when you decided to subjugate us both to his will. Instead, I'm left alone, struggling with this invisible adversary whose flimsiness makes him no less formidable. Whichever way I lurch, however I grab, I cannot pin down this opponent, cannot flesh him out with reason. So I must conclude he is a figment. I must accept that you abandoned me for an illusion.

Hans

THE QUEUE SNAKED slowly from West 11th Street around the corner on to Bleeker Street. People – sporting varying degrees of tan, all manner of summer wear and every conceivable size of sunglasses – waited patiently to purchase their sweet fix from the tiny bakery housed on the ground floor of a tenement painted the colour of aged red wine. Lina and Isabel were close to the front of the line.

'Will you hold these, please?' Isabel handed over a couple of shopping bags. 'I want to take a picture of that.' She pointed to the fire escape hanging on one side of the building, a zigzag of metal platforms connected by steep ladders. Hovering alongside the actual escape was its thin, slatted shadow, picked out with delicate precision by the sun.

Lina watched as Isabel crossed to the other side of the street and stood with her camera pressed to her right eye. The short frill on her friend's top fluttered as a light wind flounced through the street. Her hair was also blown back, baring the small ears, which had little silver hoops hanging from the lobes.

'It's like a line-up for a Benetton ad,' Isabel said, getting back into the queue.

'When are you going to stop seeing the whole world as an advert?' Lina reached out to adjust Isabel's sleeve so that it covered her bra strap. Her friend was doing a PhD on

263

how media had influenced man's self-image in the late twentieth century.

'Hmmm.' Isabel tapped her chin, pretending to think. 'Maybe when you stop seeing it as a social project?'

Lina swung her small handbag from its strap, playfully swatting her friend with it.

The queue moved forward, and soon they were able to see trays of iced cupcakes through the windows. Row upon row, topped with pastel shades of buttercream and decorated with sprinkles or sugared flowers.

Isabel's eyes grew big with greed. 'We have to get one in every colour.'

'The colour of the icing doesn't make a difference to the taste. Besides, there's a limit on how many each person can buy. Look we're almost in!' Lina's shoulders did an excited little jig as they approached the shop door.

'Well, there's two of us. We can buy stuff separately. And maybe we should get your friend to buy some, too, if he gets here soon.'

Lina lifted her wrist to look at the thin platinum bracelet watch, a gift from Anil. Hans was supposed to be joining them at any minute. 'He's always punctual. I'm curious to see what you make of him.'

'I don't know if I want to like him too much, after what you said about him flitting all over the globe. Didn't you say he's flying back somewhere tomorrow morning? That's hardly enough time to start anything. And anyway, I'm not keen to get involved with someone who lives on the other side of the world.' Isabel ran a hand under her bob, lifting it off her hot neck. 'I mean, look how it's been for you.'

Lina didn't answer. Her eyes followed several people leaving the bakery bearing big white boxes.

'What's the limit, anyway?' Isabel looked worried.

'A dozen cupcakes.'

'What?' She held the door open for Lina and they stepped into the smell of sweetness. The air felt sticky, as if it, too, was wearing an invisible coat of frosting. '*Per person?* How is that a *limit?*'

'This is America.' Lina's lips glided across her teeth. 'Everything comes in bigger sizes, even restrictions.'

A hand tapped her shoulder. 'Hey, Lina!' It was Hans, in three-quarter-length khaki shorts and a white vest. His hair was even longer, and now came down to his shoulders, an unruly blond mass tucked behind each ear. 'I'll wait for you across the road, near the park. Maybe I can get us a place to sit.'

'OK,' Lina said. 'What would you like from here?'

'Whatever you're having. I don't mind.' He reached into his pocket and drew out his wallet.

'No!' Lina pushed him towards the exit. 'I'm getting this.'

Several pairs of female eyes, including Isabel's, lingered on the doorway as Hans left. She turned to Lina, who was already placing an order. 'I might have changed my mind about the long-distance thing. And about half a day not being long enough to get to know somebody.'

Lina giggled. 'Choose now, Isabel. The lady's waiting.' She gestured towards a woman poised with a cake box in one hand and kitchen tongs in the other. Isabel started selecting, and soon their dozen box was full. At the counter they ordered three fresh lemonades before paying and squeezing their way out.

'I can't believe his visit has coincided with mine. Are you sure he's single?' Isabel balanced the cake box carefully.

'I'm pretty certain he is.' Lina was juggling the drinks as well as Isabel's shopping.

'He looks like an Australian lifeguard.' Isabel sighed.

'Well, he's a German human rights activist.' Lina crossed the road, glancing over her shoulder to make sure Isabel was following. Hans waved at them from one of the few shady spots, under a linden tree. They set their purchases down on the concrete table while Lina made quick introductions.

'So you are Lina's first visitor from England?' Hans said as the two sat on the concrete bench opposite him.

Isabel nodded while sipping her lemonade. 'I can't believe it's taken me so long.'

'Everyone's trying to squeeze in before I go. Just as well I stayed longer.' Lina's internship, which had been extended by six months, was ending in a few weeks. 'Even my dad's coming next weekend.' She had taken the cover off the cake box and gestured for everyone to help themselves. 'Oh God. I forgot to get napkins.'

'Doesn't matter.' Isabel reached for a lilac frosted cake. 'We can lick our fingers.'

The shrieks of children on swings and slides drifted down from the nearby playground. On the adjacent table, two men, one Arab-looking, one black, were embroiled in a game of chess. Five hangers-on hovered around them, passing around beer in brown-paper bags. Behind, two drag queens bickered while a third stood by, belting out 'La donna è mobile'.

When Isabel and Hans started on their second cupcakes Lina was still picking at the decorations on her first, sucking at each sugared flower until it melted on her tongue. She peeled off the paper case and scraped at the icing round its perforated rim with the tips of her long fingers. Then she proceeded to take delicate bites, savouring each mouthful, as if she was eating something holy.

'Is yours different?' Hans checked to see if there was another one with sky-blue frosting.

'You ask that every time we come here!' She'd been there twice before with Hans over the last months.

'Yah, I don't know. Whatever you're eating always looks better.' He went for a chocolate cupcake. A third of it disappeared with the first bite. 'I don't think I'll be in town again before you leave. Maybe the next place we meet will be in Sudan. They don't have anything like this there, for sure.'

'Sudan?' Isabel frowned at Lina. 'So you decided to take that job and not the one in Kenya?'

Lina's bite went down the wrong passage. She tried to stifle her coughs with sips of lemonade. Hans stopped eating and glanced from her to Isabel.

'You have a job offer from Kenya?' The pitch of his voice rose, buoyed up by surprise.

'No, well, yes. But, no, I mean, it's nothing. I didn't mention it because I knew I wouldn't take it. So it was kind of, you know, irrelevant.'

Hans nodded but uncertainty continued to pinch his sun-bleached eyebrows together. 'What sort of work?'

'It was basically to help set up a small charitable foundation.' Lina played with the straw in her drink.

'Not just set up,' Isabel added. 'You were supposed to run the whole thing, too. Weren't you?' Lina shifted on the bench. One of her hands brushed against Isabel, but her friend still went on, 'It sounded really interesting.'

'Was it a private enterprise?' Hans asked.

'It was all a bit vague.' Lina flicked her wrist.

'Yes, but you probably could have made what you

wanted of it. From what Anil said—' Isabel felt a kick under the table. She shot a sideways glance at Lina before casually changing tack. 'The Sudan opportunity is probably better, anyway. Things seem to be pretty bad there. It was on the news before I came.'

Hans's nostrils flared as he exhaled out of them in a contemptuous puff. 'What? Some thirty-second bulletin, from which all you remember is the word Janjaweed?'

'Actually . . .' Isabel combed her fingers through her copper fringe and then flicked out the hair at her shoulders. 'What hit me most was the fact that they said what's happening there could be genocide.'

'Ah, the dreaded G-word.' Hans had both elbows on the table and a half-eaten cupcake stranded in one palm. 'Let's see how long it takes for the world to react this time.'

'That's partly why I want to go there,' Lina said. 'It's important to start doing something to help.'

Isabel directed herself at Hans. 'The job came through you, right?'

'Well, so to say, yes. Of course, Lina had to apply and be interviewed, but I told her about the vacancy, and recommended her to the head of the humanitarian relief mission there.'

'Hans has been so great,' Lina said to Isabel.

'Ah, come on.' The deltoids puckered along his lean shoulders. 'I had selfish reasons for helping as well.' He looked at Isabel. 'I'm hoping Lina will assist a small-arms disarmament initiative that I'm involved with in that part of the world. But she would have got some other post easily, too. They offered you a chance to stay on here permanently, didn't they, Lina?'

She nodded.

'I would have stayed.' Isabel looked around wistfully.

268

Along the pavement, there was an endless parade. Women so well made-up they looked airbrushed. Groups of elderly Chinese tourists with neatly tucked-in shirts and the latest camera strung around their necks. Dads with stylish haircuts and ripped jeans minding toddlers while their wives popped into a nearby spa. Handsome gay couples strolling, their arms crossed at their backs as each pushed a hand into a tiny, tight pocket on the bum of the other's trousers.

'I love it, but it's so far away . . .' Lina trailed off. She went back to eating her cupcake.

Hans finished his and crushed the empty case. 'From your family? Sudan is not exactly close to the UK, either.'

'Oh no!' Isabel cried out as her third cupcake fell into her lap. She picked it up and made a face at the splodge of green icing on her white skirt.

'We need some napkins.' Lina looked around as if they would miraculously appear.

'I'll see if I can find any.' Hans jumped up and headed back across the road to the bakery.

'What a mess.' Isabel made a face at the greasy mark near her crotch. 'I guess I have an excuse to go and buy a new dress, now. I can't walk around like this for the rest of the day.'

'It'll be fine. No one will notice.' Lina tore a bit of card off the cake box and tried to clean Isabel's skirt with it.

'No one will notice!' Isabel threw her hands into the air. 'Everyone in this city is so spruced up because they expect to be noticed.'

'What I mean is, no one will care.'

'I can't walk around like this with Miss Glamour beside me.' She ran her eyes over Lina's outfit: the green sundress set off by strappy orange sandals with a matching bag and an amber necklace. 'Especially if Hans is going to be with us for the rest of the day. Not that what I'm wearing would make the slightest difference. He seems to have eyes only for you. The way he was watching you eat . . .'

'Don't be silly.'

'Why hadn't you told him about the job in Kenya?' Isabel kept on rubbing at her skirt with two fingers.

'There was no point.' Lina exhaled heavily. 'I could never have taken it, anyway. I'm afraid of what my parents would do if I said I was going back there.' So far Lina had managed to keep them onside by feigning interest in the men whose profiles her mother regularly sent. Iman had signed up for a computer course at the library, and learned how to handle internet and email just so she could expand the search for a suitor. 'They'd probably marry me off to the first sucker who said yes.'

'Is your mum still trying to link you up with someone on shaadi dot com?'

'She's registered me on every site going. She'd be happy for me to marry an elephant as long as he was Muslim.' One corner of Lina's mouth stretched ruefully.

'You're really in a mess.' Isabel brushed at her lap. 'This isn't going to come out without a proper wash. So what does Anil think about you going to Sudan instead?'

Lina looked down at the table. The shadows of leaves fringed by sunlight flickered over its surface. 'I haven't told him yet.'

'What?' Isabel's hand froze halfway to the cake box. 'Why not?'

'I just . . . I'm waiting for the right moment.'

Isabel cocked her head. 'What about your parents? Are they happy about you being in a country that borders Kenya?'

'They don't know about it yet, either.' And then, as if to stall the incredulity springing across Isabel's face, she added, 'I thought I'd tell my dad face to face, when he's here.'

'Hey.' Hans was back. He squatted down by Lina's side of the bench and reached over her to pass Isabel a bundle of paper napkins.

Isabel noticed Lina pull in her stomach and lean back ever so slightly while Hans, oblivious, basked in her closeness.

As Isabel dabbed at her skirt Lina made as if to stand up. Hans had to move so she could slide off the bench.

'I might see if I can slip into the toilet at one of these places.' She pointed to the cafés and restaurants along the street.

Isabel scooped an ice cube out of her drink and sucked on it for a moment before rubbing the slippery nugget against the mark on her skirt. Then she went at the wet patch with a napkin again. By the end it was a faded brown smear.

'That's not so bad.' Hans went back to sit opposite her. The sunlight crept stealthily through the branches above and spilt over his left arm, making the hair on it shimmer white-gold.

'Won't you have another one?' Isabel gestured at the box, which was still almost half-full.

'Maybe in a minute.' He slurped at his lemonade. 'This Anil . . . is Lina together with him?'

Isabel chewed slowly, swallowed, brushed the corners of her mouth with a napkin. 'Why? What has she said to you?'

'Not so much.' Small red blotches appeared in the hollows of his cheeks. 'I asked her one time but she said it was too complicated, and then she started talking on another topic.'

'Yes, she is with him.' Isabel ran her tongue along her teeth and studied Hans, who seemed to be concentrating really hard on getting some more liquid up his straw.

After a minute he worked up the nerve to probe some more. 'Is it serious? Will they get married?'

'They would like to, but it's not simply a question of what they want.' Isabel thought how the state of her skirt, let alone anything else, definitely didn't matter as far as Hans was concerned.

His neck craned forward. 'I don't understand.'

Isabel decided to tell him the truth. It didn't make sense to let the guy think he had a chance.

After her explanation, Hans's mouth fell open. 'So the parents don't accept him because he's not a Muslim? Probably then they would not like her to be with anybody who is not of the same faith?'

Isabel nodded.

'And Lina agrees to this?'

'Well, you know, she's torn.' Isabel absently gouged a blob of icing from her cupcake and then sucked it off her finger. 'She loves Anil, but she's very close to her family as well. If they knew she was with him she'd lose them, and if she goes along with what they want – then . . .' Isabel turned her palms up to face the sky.

They were both quiet. Isabel dug another ice cube out of her drink and popped it into her mouth. A little round protrusion appeared in her left cheek before she crunched the ice away. Hans stared into the distance, and didn't even see Lina approaching until she was standing at their table, waving into his face.

'Where did you go, Lina?' Hans rose. 'I might do the

272

same, and then maybe we can head downtown and get the ferry?' They'd planned to take the ride to Staten Island and back so Isabel could get a good look at the Statue of Liberty and enjoy the sight of Manhattan from the water.

As he walked off, Lina began gathering up their rubbish.

'Hans has got quite a soft spot for you, huh?' Isabel said.

'Isabel! Will you stop this! You're always seeing more than there is in things.' Lina picked up the mess of napkins and empty plastic cups and went to dump them in a nearby bin. 'And anyway . . .' She came back, brushing her palms against each other. 'He knows I'm with Anil.'

'Then why was he just asking me about him?' Isabel stood up and slung her floppy patchwork bag over one shoulder.

'I hope you didn't tell him everything?'

'It didn't seem fair to let him think you might one day share his feelings.' Isabel watched as Lina's fingers knotted up.

'What did he say?'

'Well, of course he was surprised . . .'

'You see!' Lina's hands fell to her sides. 'That's why I don't like telling anyone. Nobody understands. Now he probably thinks I'm some kind of weakling whose parents control their every move.'

'Oh, come on, Lina. People who really know you realize it's not that simple.'

'No one understands.' Lina could see Hans coming back towards them. 'Even you – the way you said, "Of course he was surprised." Like any normal person would be by my state of affairs.'

'Come on, Lina. You know that's not what I meant.'

273

'Doesn't matter.' Lina picked up her woven leather purse from the table. 'Please don't tell Hans or anybody any more, even if they ask.'

United Nations

SHAREEF STOOD BACK waiting and watching while Lina went through the security check for visitors to the United Nations. One of the duty officers, a strapping man in the organization's standard blue police uniform, recognized her.

'Hey! What you doin' here?' He was often working at the staff entrance in the Secretariat Building on East 43rd Street.

'Just keeping you on your toes, Larry.' Lina dumped her cream leather rucksack in a plastic tray and pushed it towards the scanning machine. 'Making sure things are as rigorous at this end as they are on the other side.'

'You betcha!' He grinned, a perfect streak of white spreading across his face.

The metal detector blipped as Lina stepped through. Larry tutted in mock disapproval.

'What you trying to sneak through today, lady?'

'Oh you know . . .' Lina touched her ears and then her throat. 'Earrings, a necklace, two or three fillings. Really dangerous things.' She stayed by the metal detector, expecting to be sent back into it or searched by the female officer standing nearby, but Larry waved her through. As she reached to pick up her bag, his eyes strayed to her hips, loosely sculpted by the red shirt-dress she had on, and then to the slim calves visible under its hem.

Shareef cleared his throat and hurried up to the metal detector without being asked.

'Step back, sir.' Larry turned and raised a palm. 'Await your turn.' He pretended to check something before deigning to motion that Shareef should come forward.

'Any mobile phones, keys, coins, jewellery? There.' He gestured at one of the plastic trays. 'And please remove your coat, sir.'

Shareef put his wallet and jacket where directed and then went through the metal detector, which bleeped.

'You'll have to go back around, sir.' Larry's tone had become severe. 'Take off your belt and put it in one of the trays. The same with your shoes, sir.'

Shareef glanced at the people going through the parallel security check, and then at Lina who was waiting on the other side of a glass screen. 'No one else has had to remove their shoes.'

'Please do as you're asked, sir. There are people waiting. If you don't want to follow the procedure, you're welcome to leave.' Larry put his hands on his hips and tapped the tip of one foot impatiently against the floor.

Shareef clenched his teeth and bent down to untie his laces. Then he padded through the magnetic field created between the tall panels of the detector and, once again, it bleeped.

'Step over here, sir,' Larry motioned like a traffic warden. 'I'm going to have to search you.'

Shareef pressed his lips together. He wondered how much of his forty-eight hours in New York would end up wasted this way. Already at JFK airport his passport had been subject to half an hour of analysis because an immigration officer had felt that his identity photo didn't quite match his real-life face. It was the 'tattoo' on his forehead that caused the confusion. The officer had wanted to know how come it wasn't so prominent in the passport picture. Normally, the officer had argued, tattoos faded over time. Shareef had been forced to give a long explanation, including a physical demonstration of how he prayed, in order to persuade the officer that the mark had darkened due to years of prostration.

Larry ran his hands along each of Shareef's arms and then patted down his back. Other visitors began to pass through the security check, casting sidelong glances their way. Lina realized that something wasn't right and edged forward.

'Larry.' She smiled. 'He's my dad.'

He looked dubiously from father to daughter and shrugged. 'I'm just doing my job.' He became a little less rough with Shareef, but remained aloof. 'Aha, what's this?' The hand-held metal detector he was using started flashing red at Shareef's chest. Larry touched the front of Shareef's shirt. 'You wearing a chain, sir? I warned you at the beginning to remove all jewellery.'

Shareef pulled off the tasbih that was hanging around his neck. He'd completely forgotten about it. 'It's not jewellery.'

Larry clicked his tongue against the roof of his mouth. 'I do not wish to get into a debate about definitions with you, sir. The point is all such accessories are supposed to come off. Now please collect your belongings and go through.'

'Thanks, Larry. Bye,' Lina said.

He acknowledged her with a sullen jerk of the head.

Shareef went to get his possessions without a word.

'Sorry about that, Baba.' Lina squeezed his shoulder. 'I don't know why he was being difficult. Sometimes they get so fixated on doing the job all common sense deserts them. If he'd paid attention he would have realized we're together. It's obvious.'

Maybe, if he'd paid the right kind of attention, Shareef thought. He ran his eyes up and down her elegant frame and then glanced down at his own staid grey suit.

Lina suddenly regretted wearing the dress. The three-quarter sleeves and below-the-knee hem had made it appear modest compared to the kind of clothes she'd been wearing throughout the summer. But to her father it probably seemed a bit too short and fitted. She certainly wouldn't have put on such apparel in Birmingham, but being on her own turf had somehow skewed her judgement.

'Um, I'll leave my bag, and then we can get started. Do you want me to hand in your jacket as well?'

He made as if to remove the jacket, but then hesitated and decided to keep it on. Lina disappeared into the crowd, promising to be back shortly.

All around people were forming groups for official tours. There were a few guides in their country's national dress, including one woman in traditional Nigerian garb, with an elaborate headdress. The rest wore navy-blue suits, with light-blue blouses or shirts, and a scarf or tie adorned with the United Nations emblem. All were divulging an impressive deluge of facts and figures to do with the physical history of the structure. Everything about the place reflected its international character. From the eleven architects who'd collaborated on the design, to the materials sourced from around the world for use in the building's construction, to the globally inspired art and furniture that filled each space.

As he spotted Lina coming back, Shareef's breath

stalled. How sophisticated she'd become! Gone was the modest girl he still expected to see, with an open face and a simple middle parting cutting through her mass of curls. Instead there was this person who smelled of perfume, and whose tresses were cut into choppy layers that emphasized her cheekbones.

She took Shareef on her own improvised circuit of the building, including some bits not normally seen by visitors, like the floor where she worked. Shareef trailed behind, and Lina kept having to slow down or stop and wait for him. He seemed pensive, and said little. Worried that he might be getting bored, Lina kept up a commentary about everything they passed. Every so often she would wave or smile at somebody, and she introduced Shareef to a couple of her colleagues. He expressed surprise at how many people were at work on a Saturday.

'It's always like this. I'm often here on the weekend as well.' Lina adjusted her belt, loosening it a little. She looked ready to get right down to work, with her UN identity pass hanging from a cotton ribbon on her neck. At one point she was indeed prepared to rush to her desk and find some document mentioned by her boss, Susan Hempel, whom they met in the corridor outside her office.

'No! It isn't urgent. I can wait until you're back. Please!' She grabbed hold of Lina's wrist to restrain her.

'It won't take a minute! I don't mind.' Lina tried to pull away.

'Really. There's no need. I just wanted to make sure you had it.' Susan turned to Shareef. 'You better keep a hold of her. Seriously.' She made him take Lina's hand. 'There's no trusting this girl. I wouldn't put it past her to sneak back and email me the document. Don't let go of her.' Susan winked at Shareef. 'She's a stubborn one.'

When had he last held Lina's hand? Shareef wondered. The pressure of it against his own had changed. Her palm didn't simply yield to his any more. Her hand did not seem to want guidance. Rather, it pulled him along. Forcing a faster pace than suited his reflections.

'This is my favourite artwork here.' Lina let go of his hand. They had arrived in front of a large mosaic, entitled *The Golden Rule*, depicting people of every creed and colour. Along the bottom a line read: '*Do unto others as you would have them do unto you*'. Without looking at her father, she said, 'I guess it's telling us that we can't be that different if we're all essentially striving for the same thing.'

Shareef studied the picture with his arms crossed over his chest. Lina stole a glance at him and saw the muscles near his ears pulsing as his upper and lower teeth ground against each other. She shifted on her feet. The low-heeled, open-toed slingbacks that she was wearing, normally so comfortable, seemed tight today. She could feel the thin leather strap cutting into the back of each heel.

'I'm not sure that is the message.' Shareef spoke calmly, but there was a hard undertone in his voice.

'Oh?' Lina felt uneasy.

Shareef pressed down the ends of his moustache with thumb and index finger. 'I have another interpretation. I think the artist is recognizing difference, even celebrating it, and simply pointing out that it shouldn't be a reason for us to mistreat one another.'

'Yes, but I meant—'

'I know what you meant.'

Lina swallowed, startled by his abruptness. She took a couple of steps, seeking to move away from the mosaic, but Shareef remained rooted in front of it. His eyes travelled from the figure in the long, white seamless robe typically worn during the hajj, to the old man in a black skullcap, to the Buddhist boy-monk, to the red-headed girl holding a rosary.

'I don't think it's right to pretend that every difference is bridgeable just because we're all human beings who might share some of the same fundamental hopes. And, in any case, not everything is improved by being the same. We shouldn't underestimate the value of disparity – it's also the means by which we measure progress and achievement.'

Lina wound some strands of hair tightly around one finger.

'You know . . .' Shareef kept his eyes on the picture, his arms pinned to his chest. 'Difference doesn't matter when every man is secure in his convictions. But give uncertainty a variety of options and see what a mess you end up with.'

Lina wished she hadn't shared her take on the image.

'And as far as doing as you would be done by goes, much as I agree with the sentiment, I don't think it can be applied indiscriminately.' Shareef was leaning back slightly, rocking on his heels. 'People have distinct value systems and preferences. Christian Scientists, for example, refuse any kind of medical intervention because they don't want to interfere with what they believe is God's will. You can't force a life-saving operation on such a person just because that's what you'd want.'

'So what's right for you,' Lina seized on the chance, 'is not necessarily what's best for me. Or vice versa.'

'Maybe.' His eyes briefly met hers. 'But if we both follow Allah's guidance we will always find common ground. That is the beauty of His grace.'

Lina experienced a small jolt, as if her insides had shivered. Keen to end the conversation she moved away again, and this time Shareef followed, dragging his feet.

'Lina?' he called. 'I might—' He pointed to the sign for the men's room.

She started to say something, but the pressure in his bladder was suddenly so strong that he didn't wait to hear her finish.

A cleaner was mopping the tiled floor in the toilets. He kept looking in Shareef's direction and finally said, 'As salaam alaikum.'

'Walaikum as salaam,' Shareef replied, soaping his hands and enjoying the rush of cold water over them. He knew the man had identified his faith from the mark on his forehead.

'You here for meeting?' The cleaner leaned on the handle of his mop.

'No, I'm visiting, from London.' He couldn't resist adding, 'My daughter works here.' He undid two buttons on his shirt before splashing his face as well. How nice it would be to plunge his whole body under the running tap, submit his mind to its purifying coolness.

The cleaner pulled a few paper towels from the dispenser on the wall and handed them to Shareef. They spoke for another minute before he left. The corridor outside was empty and quiet. Shareef looked left and right, wondering where Lina was. A security guard suddenly appeared.

'Can I help you, sir?' He walked up and studied the old man, catching sight of the visitor sticker on Shareef's lapel. 'Only authorized personnel are allowed in this part of the building.'

'I'm with my daughter. She works . . . there.' He pointed to the far end of the corridor. 'I was using the men's room. She's . . . somewhere.' He spun around trying to find her.

The security guard raised his eyebrows. He was six inches taller than Shareef. 'Step this way, sir. I'm going to have to escort you back to the public area.'

'But my daughter—'

'Please, sir. Follow me,' the guard said, though it was clear from the way he pointed that he wanted Shareef to walk ahead so he could keep an eye on him.

Shareef resisted the impulse to argue. They went through a set of double doors and there was Lina, talking to another colleague.

'Oh, Baba! I was about to come back!' She said a hasty goodbye to the woman. 'You were quick.' She glanced at the tall figure behind her father. 'Is everything OK?'

'This man with you, ma'am?' The security guard bent and took a hard look at Lina's UN pass. 'Guests are to be accompanied at all times,' he said. 'Good day, ma'am – sir.' He gave a curt nod and went off.

Lina could almost hear the grinding of Shareef's teeth. Her brow creased with sympathy for her dad. 'I don't know what's wrong with the security people today. Maybe there's someone really important visiting.' She wrung her hands, worried that he was going to end up with a bad impression.

'I know the aspiration of this place is towards equality, and there are people from all over fighting for that through this organization. But even in this haven, the cleaners are from Bangladesh, most of the security guards are black, and the man who arouses suspicion is a Muslim. If that happens here, what can we expect from the rest of the world?'

Lina was silenced.

They went into the General Assembly Hall, tailing a tour group to hear what the guide was saying. 'This is the central organ of the UN,' she explained. 'All 190 member countries gather here for discussions.'

A small boy, whose eyes had been running indifferently over the curved rows of desks, spotted the country sign for Jordan and exclaimed, 'Does Michael Jordan sit there?' Everybody laughed, and Lina thought how it was the first moment of levity she'd shared with Shareef since his arrival. She'd never imagined that being with her father could feel so unnatural.

Afterwards they saw one of the permanent exhibitions on disarmament. There were remnants, like coins, bottles and clothes, of the nuclear explosions in Hiroshima and Nagasaki. Various examples of landmines were on display. Shareef caught sight of the Nigerian guide in native dress whom he'd seen earlier. He trailed her group, listening to the harrowing facts about the effects of war. The woman asked her visitors, 'Do you know what an anti-personnel landmine is and how much one costs?' Her eyes searched the faces of the adults, waiting for an answer.

A young girl replied, 'It can cost you your life.' There was silence. Her words gave Shareef goosebumps, and even the guide had to wipe her eyes before she could continue with the tour.

When he rejoined Lina, Shareef was quite animated, condemning the use of such weapons, railing against the people who made and sold them.

'I didn't know you were so passionate about this issue,' Lina said.

'You can't see this and be indifferent! The bloody villains who are involved in the arms trade should all be rounded up and blasted to hell with the exact weapons they're spreading around the world!' Shareef had never talked that way before. Lina told him she would be getting involved in a small-arms disarmament initiative.

'Very good. I will support you one hundred per cent in that.'

She linked arms with him. It was the first nice thing he'd said to her during his visit. Maybe his spirits were lifting. But by the time they reached the lobby near the exit, he seemed subdued again.

Lina went to retrieve her bag from the cloakroom. She'd planned to show him the United Nations gardens, but that no longer felt wise, given the way the place had wound him up so far. She considered going back to the flat on the pretext of having a short rest. But the idea of being in a poky little space while he was in such a mood didn't appeal either. She wished they could do something where they didn't have to talk. Every word she uttered seemed to antagonize him, and everything he said upset her. But it didn't make sense to go to the cinema or see a show when the sun was shining and he only had another twenty-four hours to spend in the city.

When Lina returned, Shareef was leaning against the wall, and she suddenly saw how he had aged: his stoop was more pronounced and the volume of white in his hair and moustache had increased. It occurred to her that his dawdling might have had more to do with tiredness than any psychological cause. As they walked out on to the UN plaza she suggested they go to a nearby department store and buy some of the things her sisters had asked for.

'It's a bit too hot for being outdoors now.' She noticed that the top two buttons on Shareef's shirt were undone. She'd closed those at her own neck, and now felt as if the collar would choke her. 'Then we can try to see something else later, before we go out for dinner.'

'Out to eat? Again?' Shareef slipped off his jacket and draped it over one forearm.

'Baba! You didn't come here to sit in my flat while I cook. Just enjoy it. From tomorrow you'll be having Ma's food again.'

'I thought you said we'd go to the gardens?' She'd pointed them out to him through the window while they were up in the building.

'Isn't it too much?'

'I might as well see all I can, now that I'm here. Maybe we could just stop for a drink somewhere beforehand?'

They walked on to the plaza. Above them the 190 flags of United Nations member states hung limply in the still burn of the afternoon.

'Such a shame I forgot my camera.' Shareef raised a hand against the sun as he surveyed the building they had just left. Behind the low limestone curve of the Assembly Hall rose the high green glass-fronted frame of the Secretariat Building.

Lina didn't say anything. She was still feeling guilty for not offering to let him use hers. But she knew the nifty new digital camera Anil had given her would have aroused suspicion. It was currently hidden away in a large bag in a flatmate's room, together with all the other things that might be incriminating, like the letters which had exposed her before. Lina had claimed the items had to be moved out of her wardrobe to make some room for her dad's stuff. She'd also requested that none of her flatmates mention Anil's name in Shareef's presence. They had all agreed without asking too many questions, but Lina had noticed the surprise in their faces, the discreet looks of incomprehension they had exchanged.

'Was it the right thing for you to come here?' Shareef

suddenly wondered aloud. 'And what next, Lina? You must have some idea by now.'

Over the last months she'd been vague, telling her parents she was waiting to hear back on various possibilities – although she had hinted that she wouldn't be returning to the UK. Last night she'd managed to change the subject when Shareef had probed and he, in the exhaustion of travel and the excitement of arrival, hadn't asked again.

'I'm staying with the UN,' she said.

'Here in New York?'

She shook her head. 'One of their missions in Sudan.'

'What?' Shareef stopped abruptly. They were close to the circular pool in front of the Secretariat Building. The flow of water from its fountain was like a long hiss in the background.

'It's where I'm going to help start up the small-arms disarmament initiative—'

'Are you planning your life around that boy?'

Lina almost dropped the bag which was slung over her left shoulder.

'Is that the big appeal of Africa for you? To be close to him?' One of Shareef's legs swung forward, as if he was kicking at something. His tolerance had been worn down.

'Of course not! The job—'

'Ah, what good is talk?' Shareef fished a hanky out of his pocket and wiped his face. He despised his loss of self-control. He inhaled and exhaled deeply several times, each phase of breath shaped by the silent invocation of God's infinite patience: As-Sabur . . . As-Sabur. 'I can't enforce what I say any more.' The anger ebbed out of his voice. 'You're dependent on us for one more month, and then? My influence is gone.'

'Come on, Baba.' Lina put a hand on his arm. 'Your opinion will always matter to me.' She felt she would faint if they kept standing there arguing, with the sun glaring down.

Shareef took another deep breath. 'Your mother has found two very decent boys who are interested in you. You must come to London for introductions soon.'

'But I'm not ready to get married!' Lina blurted. 'To anyone!'

'Just meet these boys and see what happens. Your mother and I will feel better. Focusing on your career alone won't take care of the future.'

Lina looked left and right. Her mouth twitched. 'I don't even know how often I'm going to be in the UK for the next year or two,' she said. 'And who knows where I'll be based for my next post? It's not fair to any guy.'

'All I'm asking is that you get to know these boys and keep an open mind.'

'I don't see the point.' She sighed. 'But if that's what you want.'

'Good. Your mum will be happy.' It didn't seem to have made any difference to his disposition. He kept frowning, as if there was still something bothering him.

Lina waited, afraid of what else he might say.

But he seemed to collect himself with a tiny whip of the head. 'Is that the way we're going? I could really do with a cold drink now.' He began taking purposeful strides. There was a patch of dampness on the back of his shirt.

Lina limped after him, the strap of her shoe rubbing against a blister on her left heel.

The Arrow

THE NEW OFFICE BLOCK designed by Anil in Nairobi paid homage to one of the city's landmarks, the Kenyatta Conference Centre. a tall cylindrical tower crowned with a pointed concrete dome that resembled a Vietnamese sun hat. Anil's version was a shiny glass edifice that seemed poised to take off towards the sky. Kenyans were proud of the Arrow, as it was called. The president himself was coming to the official opening.

Despite all this, on the actual day of the ceremony, Anil was agitated. Lina had been due to arrive that afternoon, but she'd called to say her flight was delayed. One of the Air Mayur planes had gone to collect her from Sudan, but was apparently sitting on the muddy runway in Juba waiting for the rain to stop before it could take off.

Surprise, surprise, Merc thought. 'Don't worry, mazeh.' He put an arm around his friend. 'If the occasion goes like a typical Kenyan one it'll be starting late anyway, so maybe she'll be here in time.' She wasn't and, as far as Merc could tell, Anil remained aware of her absence throughout the ceremony.

Merc felt irritation more than pity. It seemed pathetic that, at such a significant career juncture, Anil should be distracted by concerns of the heart. Lina's unreliability bordered on the farcical. How Anil put up with it, Merc had no idea. He speedily downed champagne in an effort

289

to alleviate his mood. Across the prism-like room, Anil was uncharacteristically doing the same – and at an even faster rate. Merc thought his friend had made a big mistake in returning home. He should have established himself abroad, where it counted, first. Anil was talented, that was for sure. Merc looked around the glass cube of the lobby, which was encased within the larger glass structure. But Anil was also too proud, impatient and spoilt. For all its impressiveness, the new building lacked soul.

After the formalities of the evening were over, the old crew left the crowd feasting on cocktails and canapés in the lobby of the Arrow and took the lift to the top of the building. From there the whole city was visible: a sprawl of brightly lit and dimmer areas fading to the velvety black patch of Nairobi National Park. Anil took them right up to the huge glass windows.

'Awh!' Hardy stepped back after one glance downwards. 'This is *high*! People won't be able to eat here without being sick.' The plan was to open up a restaurant in the space.

'On a good day,' Anil said, pointing into the distance, 'you can see right into the park and maybe even spot a herd of zebra.' Then he pulled out his mobile phone.

'I don't know why you keep checking.' Merc couldn't hold back. 'She's missed everything anyway.'

Anil put his phone away without a word.

'The rest of us managed to get here in time.' Merc had come from London. 'What's so special about her that she's always on a different schedule? Why was she arriving so last-minute anyway? You'd think someone with her track record would try to leave several days in advance of when she needs to be somewhere.' Merc stood with his hands in his pockets, the sleeves of his shirt and jacket pushed up to the elbow. He was wearing lenses so dark it was hard to tell the pupil from the iris.

Anil's usually stiff, upturned collars had sagged a bit.

'What's happened to you? You challenge people all the time, but with her you've turned into a little yes man. It's always been wait, wait, wait and more wait with her—'

'Eh eh eh, bwana. Just chill, huh? We should head back down,' JT interrupted.

'She keeps her word!' Anil raised his voice. 'Even if she doesn't keep time. She has always kept her word to me. And that's what counts.'

Merc shook his head. 'No, what it all adds up to is that your relationship is going nowhere.'

'That'll change now that she's got the job in Sudan.' It was the first time Anil had stated the fact with any enthusiasm. He wasn't happy about her being in such a volatile area. Nor was he pleased that the post had come about through her acquaintance with Hans Steinmeyer, that weird German whom she'd met on her first trip to Kenya. Anil didn't trust the guy.

'What about the fact that she turned down the chance to set up a charity here? How many people pass up an opportunity like that? Instead she takes some job in the middle of nowhere, as far from the reality of her own life as possible. It's totally fucked up, mazeh. If you don't watch out, you're going to be waiting around for ever.'

'You don't know anything!' Anil's face was deeply flushed. 'Talking like an expert when you've never even been in a proper relationship.' He turned to look out of the window, pressed his palms against the pane. 'I'm not a fool,' he said, like he was talking to the city, the whole world. 'I know Lina better than anyone. You think I can't see her faults? But you forget, Merc, that she has chosen to be with me all this time against much resistance. Nobody commits themselves like that to another person unless they're serious.'

Merc came and stood by his friend, and stared out into the night with him. JT and Hardy made another unsuccessful attempt to urge them back downstairs. When Merc started up again, JT stepped between the two.

'Give the guy a break, bwana. It's supposed to be a happy night, and you're dragging up all this depressing maneno.'

'That's why I'm so annoyed.' Merc kept his profile to Anil. 'This important milestone has been eclipsed by Lina's non-appearance. It's not fair on you, and it's not nice for us because we have to see you in this state. We should be celebrating wholeheartedly.'

Anil remained silent. He was thinking about Lina's tearful voice when she'd called to tell him about the delay. Her regret had been as palpable as the heat coming off a radiator. In fact, she'd been so distraught that he'd had to put aside his own disappointment and console her. He'd even told himself it didn't matter, he would be so occupied with the press and dignitaries at the event anyway. But, for most of the evening he'd missed Lina, and the more he did so, the more he resented her for not being with him. Merc's criticisms were galling because there was some truth in them. And he was still ranting on!

'Even this building—'

'All right, enough is enough.' JT cut Merc off by grabbing his arm and steering him towards the lift.

Hardy did the same with Anil. 'People must be wondering where you are, bwana.'

Anil shook him off. 'What about my building?'

'It doesn't fit here. It's beautiful, but out of place, like a

292

diamond ring on a dirty, gnarled hand.' Merc allowed himself to be led away.

'Will you drop it?' JT hissed.

'Now you're an expert on architecture as well?' Anil approached his friend, swaying slightly.

The lift doors opened. Anil watched the others step into it. 'I'll see you downstairs.' He turned away.

'What the hell?' JT called. 'Just get in here, bwana.'

'I'm taking the stairs,' Anil replied.

'Thirty floors? Don't be an idiot.' Hardy placed himself between the lift doors to prevent them from closing.

'One of us better go with him,' JT said as Anil disappeared.

'Just leave him.' Merc pressed the 'close doors' button. 'You know what he's like when he gets into these moods. Hopefully he'll cool off on the way down.'

'Sawa.' Hardy stepped back into the steel cubicle. 'You need to calm down as well.'

Fifteen minutes after they got back to the ground floor there was still no sign of Anil. The three guys went to the stairwell and started climbing upwards. They found Anil on the seventeenth floor. He'd tripped down a flight of stairs and smashed up his left knee.

For Anil, just seeing Lina again was enough to dispel all Merc's criticisms about her. But his comments about the Arrow continued to nag. It was not easy for Anil to accept that his first project might have fallen short. He had been dreaming of the building, in some form or other, ever since he'd conceived of being an architect. The time he'd spent waiting for it to be completed had been the most frustrating of his life. In retrospect, he realized that it had been naïve to attempt such a venture in a country where the construction industry was propped up by a scaffolding of corruption, and was, anyway, ill-equipped for the scale of the task. He'd had to bring in expertise from abroad, and the project costs had trebled from the original estimates. If it hadn't been for Pravar's deep pockets the whole thing might have floundered. That it had worked out in the end, and even been considered a success, was a huge relief to Anil. He might have persuaded himself of his righteousness if Kilempu, the sculptor, hadn't accosted him at one of Minnie's soirées a few weeks after the building's official opening.

'Me, I had a different idea about you, young man.' Kilempu stood with hands on his hips. 'Didant we spick, once or twice, about honouring local traditions instead of impotting ideas wholesale from the West? Wan't you the one who praised local architectural methods?'

Before Anil could respond, Kilempu leaned forward and looked down his nose at the slightly shorter man. His breath was like a brewery, stiff with alcohol. 'That Arrow you have built. It is an anomaly. It has no relation to its environment.'

'Actually—'

'I don't need to hear your theories.' Kilempu swatted the air in front of Anil's face. 'The true test of a building is how peepo respond to it. They should feel uplifted. And, as far as I can see, peepo are scared inside that place.'

Anil crossed an arm over his chest. The other gripped more tightly on the one crutch he was still using. 'People are often daunted by the new or the unfamiliar.'

'Peepo are not comfortable.' Kilempu might not have heard. 'That building makes them false, they step in there and find themselves struggling to live up to some confused notion of who they are.'

'I see nothing wrong with a space that makes demands of you.' Other guests milled around them, taking turns to appraise the photos of the Arrow, which Minnie had installed along one wall of the room in tribute to her son's achievement. Someone called to Anil, and he was tempted to snub Kilempu by heeding the summons. But he respected the man and felt compelled to make him revise his unfair opinion. 'You yourself know that all the best art challenges and requires something back from those who participate in it.'

'But how? *How?*' Kilempu's eyes widened. The whites looked more like reds with milky bits smudged in. 'That is the question. A building should let you be yourself. However it uplifts or inspires you, it should allow you to be who you are. What you've created is all pretension, and we have enough of that in this country. Peepo trying to be what they're not, deceiving themselves and others, it's a disease in this place.'

'That's why the building is made of glass, actually. It's meant to signify, and hopefully promote, transparency.' Anil kept the defiance in his voice even though he saw some truth in his accuser's words.

'Ahtsch.' Kilempu raised his hands as if to stop a ball from flying into his face. The lines on his palms were like shards of a fractured star. 'Stop this trash talking. The Arrow is all about you, it's a monument built to your ego. Eh? You have discarded the past in favour of what you've learned in the last what? Five, six, seven years? You grew up in this country, it is in your blood – but there's no hint of it in your work! Art that bears no profound relation to its creator can only be banal. I see I am offending you, but I'm telling you what I think because I believe you can do better – if you don't let yourself be smothered by their

295

empty approval.' He jerked his head towards the crowd.

'I think they genuinely like it.' Anil crossed his wounded leg over the other.

'Probably they do.' Kilempu shrugged. 'But how does that make things betta? Eh? They are ignorant, most of them. They like anything that smacks of the West because they think it's bound to be superior to the local equivalent. You are in a privileged position.' Kilempu poked an index finger at Anil's chest. 'Use it well. Teach these peepo how to respect themselves, how to value the richness of this country. Hmmm, are we together?'

'You've misunderstood my intentions.'

'Ach, you are a stubborn one, bwana. I know you have been daring in a way. But I worry about the consequences. You know what will happen, don't you? You will sprout copycats. The next dozen buildings that go up will be imitations of yours. Are we together? And then, what will this city look like? Eh? Just think of that. If you are going to lead the way – and I know that is what you want to do – then at least take peepo in the right direction! Show them what they can be proud of, reintroduce them to what they have forgotten. No doubt what you've done is impressive – but it is not appropriate. Architecture should improve peepo's lives. Ask yourself if yours does that. Just remember, a big chair does not make a king. Eh?'

That last comment had really stung, probably because it spied out Anil's self-satisfaction. He really did feel like he'd done it all with the Arrow. And yet, just a few sensibly raised doubts had him knotted up with indignation. He'd made some excuse and bolted from Kilempu. But as the evening wore on and different people came up to congratulate him he found himself irritated by their compliments.

'We will be rivalling Dubai soon, if you keep up your good work,' someone said.

In time Anil came to recognize that his egoism had indeed distorted his creativity. He came to regard the Arrow as a towering relic of his stupidity. It helped him appreciate the burden of his craft. Other artists, like writers, painters and composers, could hide or destroy misconceived works. That was not an option in his field. As Frank Lloyd Wright said, an architect can only advise his client to plant vines. A forest of jacarandas couldn't have disguised Anil's blunder.

Over the next months Anil refused to take on any of the commissions that came in the wake of the Arrow. He devoted himself instead to travelling and studying architecture outside the West, with a view to clarifying his ideas and finding another idiom. Kilempu's exhortation not to ignore his Kenyan heritage prompted him to revisit memorable spots from his childhood. Everything he saw emphasized the Arrow's sterility. The makuti roofs and timber structures he stayed in while passing through national parks seemed like extensions of the land, as if elements of the earth had assembled of their own accord into a shelter for man.

Driving through the countryside, it was as though he was seeing colour for the first time. It might have had to do with the fact that he was re-exploring these areas on his own. Without the distractions of company and conversation, he was extra-sensitive to all nature's nuances and gradations: the blunt yellows of savannah grass shifting over rusty soil; white lines framing silky brown polygons on the skin of giraffes. At Nakuru he found thousands of flamingos nestling on the lake, like a soufflé of pink cumuli. It seemed as though the sun had dropped into the basin of the lake while the sky took on the liquid blue of water.

Anil returned to his work with a conviction that he must find a way of suggesting the land's richness in his designs. It took him a while to work out a new aesthetic, and his country's heritage came to feature in this much more prominently than he'd expected. Lina's influence on this new phase was also significant. She listened patiently as he outlined the shift in his perceptions. She encouraged his new ideas and showed interest, even when his talk became too abstract or technical. No one else ever heard him out the way she did, looking at him as if he was describing how he might realize her own dreams. Previously, he'd dismissed her preoccupation with the environment, but now it started to filter into his thinking. He saw what was obvious but had eluded him in his zeal for the new: human beings had lived sustainably until wealth and technology gave them the luxury of being impractical.

Sudan

SOMETIMES, BEING IN Sudan felt like being on the set of a strange western. In many towns, there was hardly a paved road in sight. Horses, donkeys and goats wandered lazily through the dusty streets. Almost all the men, whether in civilian or combat clothes, carried guns – as casually as if they were bags. Most had a Kalashnikov, usually hanging from a length of rope, slung over one shoulder. Some even sauntered around with whips. Lina had found this extremely odd until it was explained to her that anybody with one probably had a horse or a camel. These individuals were highly respected because the whip implied they were powerful enough to hold on to their possessions. Most of the population in the south had been terrorized into giving up their land, homes and animals.

Lina had not yet encountered any of the dreaded Janjaweed, the militia said to be responsible for many of the atrocities committed in Sudan. Although she regularly came across men in different military fatigues, she still couldn't work out which group they belonged to. She was barely managing to keep abreast of the political situation, what with the constant splitting and forming of factions and then sub-factions. Colleagues had told her she'd be sure to recognize Janjaweed when she came across them because they were the ones who never smiled.

That wasn't the only thing that set them apart, Lina

realized when she eventually encountered a few. It was at the market in Juba, just before Eid ul-Adha – the celebration held approximately seventy days after Eid ul-Fitr to honour Abraham's willingness to sacrifice his son to God. Lina had gone into town with two colleagues, Jen and Astrid, to stock up on provisions before the religious holidays started. They took a local taxi from their compound because it made them less conspicuous than one of the UN 4×4s. There had been so many car-jackings recently that staff were advised to travel incognito whenever possible.

The market was crowded with people breaking fast and doing their shopping. As usual, there wasn't much in the way of fresh fruit or vegetables for sale. Instead, spread across floor mats or wooden tables, were conical piles of sorghum, groundnuts, sugar and charcoal. The clink and rustle of produce being weighed and sifted into bags was comforting background music to the market proceedings. 'Itfaddal! Itfaddal!' 'Welcome!' People everywhere beckoned with their hands for Lina and the other two women to join them for a bite. Smiling stall owners offered them dates, and drink sellers held out cups of guava juice. A little boy ran up and tugged at Lina's baggy trousers shouting, 'Hawajia!' She could grasp some Arabic because of her Koranic learning, but she'd been told by colleagues that this particular word meant 'foreigner'.

'It's a bit like so in Hamburg, my home town, before Christmas!' Astrid's wide mouth, painted a provocative pink – her face was always fully made-up – opened with pleasure at the joviality that suffused the evening. Even the bleats of the goats sounded festive as they butted their short horns against nearby walls.

Lina, too, relished the warmth being extended their

300

way. It was the first big religious festival she'd ever spent away from home, and she was missing her family. The smell of roasting meat eddied through the air, rising off the whole goats that were being cooked all around town. Lina thought of the barbecue her own family would be having in their back garden. Her mother would be moulding kebabs on to skewers, Baba poking absently at the coals, Khala Rocky balancing a bowl on her lap as she cut a salad, Mariam shirking all work and furtively texting instead, Nasra and Yusuf ready to help in any way . . .

'Look.' All of a sudden Jen nudged Lina. 'Janjaweed,' she whispered.

There were five of them getting crates of soft drinks from a vendor. They wore green khaki uniforms and had white cloth wrapped around their heads and over their faces so that only pairs of cold, staring eyes were visible. The men took the crates and moved towards an unmarked vehicle with no number plates. Eyes and voices were lowered as they walked by. When the men passed the three foreign women one of them paused and leered, 'As salaam alaikum.' The women dutifully mumbled back the greeting, keeping their eyes fixed to the ground. Even Astrid went pale under the raspberry blusher sweeping across her cheeks.

Back at the staff compound celebrations were low-key by normal standards, though luxurious compared to the daily routine of the place. Their meal, shared by international and local staff – believers and those of no denomination – consisted of roast goat and fried eggs with greasy chips, followed by mangoes and chocolate biscuits.

Despite her greed, Lina's pleasure in the food was marred by a hint of grit in every mouthful. 'Is it just me?' She dipped a chip into egg yolk. 'Or does everything here have sand in it?'

'This is nothing. Wait until you've experienced a sand-storm,' Jen said. The first time they'd met, Lina hadn't been able to work out if the short-haired, skinny person with the rather gravelly voice was a man or a woman. The name hadn't been much of a clue, either. Later, Lina found out it was short for Jennifer, but it could equally easily have been a male Scandinavian name. 'After one of those you can't breathe without tasting sand, even for days afterwards.'

'Ah yah, it's true.' Astrid rocked on one of the moulded plastic garden chairs that furnished NGO living quarters around the continent. 'Last time the sand got even into my Chanel cream for the face. It was still in the box, brand new, sealed. But when I took off the cover, the pot was full of grains. It was more like using a scrub than a cream!'

Lina had heard a lot about these legendary storms. It was said that the earth darkened as the sun was obscured by curtains of sand. Everything stopped functioning, even electricity stopped flowing. People shut doors and sealed windows, but the tiny particles still snuck in.

'I have to say, though, the mangoes are always pretty perfect.' Jen reached for one.

There was general agreement around the table. They were, in fact, sitting under a mango tree, the lone specimen in the UN compound. Around them was a high bullet-proof wall that protected against the outside world.

'You know . . .' Bol picked up one of the fruits and held it in his palm. 'This season I go back to my fields just for plant my mango crop.' He was a local volunteer. One of those who had fled his home due to fighting, and was still living in a camp with his family. He'd come by to wish his co-workers a happy Eid. 'I risk – because I think maybe is better this year. Of course . . .' His shoulders heaved under a thin T-shirt. 'Is not. The last many weeks I can't leave here because of all so much shooting. So people from other tribes are harvest my crop. They sell to me my own mangoes in market!'

'It's ridiculous.' Jen shook her head.

'But you know what is more bad?' Bol's eyes grew bigger in his narrow face. 'My father-in-law buyed some mangoes from people who have taken over his fields. Then he walking back home and is jumped on by thugs near camp. They take his money and the mangoes also. Poor man has plant them, paid for them – and still he got no mango!'

This kind of absurdity was not unusual.

Although she was based in Juba, Lina spent a lot of time going out into the field, visiting camps and villages to assist with various projects. At one point, she accompanied a UN officer, Samah Funmi, to a town in Jonglei State for a three-day training course to raise awareness about sexual exploitation. Samah had been running such courses for a while, and Lina wanted to learn about her approach and pass any helpful hints on to others who were being trained in Juba to do similar work.

They travelled there by car, eight of them packed into one jeep. 'Last year we were doing these trips by helicopter,' Samah told Lina. 'But now the UN is too stretched. A lot of aid is being directed towards Darfur. Fuel is being rationed. I'm told there's only enough money for each helicopter to fly about eighty hours a month.' Her hand flapped like a fan the whole time, waving away the flies.

They passed through landscape quite different from the dry areas, infested by apricot-coloured dust, which Lina had begun to think characterized the whole country. Along the route, there were tracts where wadis were swollen, the grass grew waist-high and crops seemed plentiful. The land looked so rich it was hard to believe there wasn't enough food to feed the whole population.

It was late in the afternoon by the time they arrived at the camp for internally displaced people. One local volunteer, a man with a head that seemed too large for his body, and a fat, bumpy scar running from his right temple to his ear, showed them around.

At one end of the camp they came across families crouched together under makeshift huts with barely a scrap of protection against the sun, wind or night-time chill. Most did not even have mats or blankets, and simply huddled on the deep sand. 'These are the newcomers. We do not have enough supplies,' their guide explained.

Back at the staff quarters, a grubby compound surrounded by a bamboo fence, Lina and Samah were shown into a small tukul where two mattresses lay side by side on the floor. Lina had slept in such thatched huts before, but usually on a proper bed. However, the thought of the families exposed to the elements just a short distance away made her grateful for what she'd been given.

As she lay down for the night she recalled how the conditions in Juba had seemed extremely basic when she'd first arrived there. It had taken a while before she'd started feeling at home in her sterile container with its single bed, small desk and tiny cupboard. She still wasn't used to the showers, and screeched each morning when the cold jet of water hit her back. Jen had told her she was lucky not to have arrived six months earlier, when they still had out-door pit latrines. The installation of a flushing toilet was a major advance. It wasn't the same everywhere. Apparently staff at USAID had a swimming pool and fully fitted gym in Juba, and lived in houses with imported furniture. On the other hand, there were smaller organizations whose staff stayed in tents and had no internet access. Lina was thankful that UN standards were somewhere in between. She hadn't told Anil much about the state of the facilities. He was already against her working there. If he knew how she lived he'd probably insist that she give up the job.

The workshop for camp dwellers, which took place during the day, included both men and women. Everyone sat on mats under the shade of gum trees. There was a lot of embarrassment as Samah talked. The men would smile into their shoulders. The women pulled their tobes more tightly around themselves, sometimes giggling into the fabric of the brightly coloured sarongs. During the session on rape one man raised his hand and asked: 'Is it possible for a girl to be "raped" if she is no longer a virgin?' That provoked heated responses from some of the women. Despite this, a few men went on to blame the women for any sexual assaults they suffered: 'She must have been asking for it in that Western-style top.' The men also tried to excuse themselves by claiming their 'urges' were natural and had to be relieved.

Lina, who was sat beside Samah, absorbed the translator's slightly delayed version of the discussion. She waited for Samah to challenge some of the statements more forcefully. Finally, as Samah gently suggested that men had to take responsibility for their actions, Lina could no longer hold back, and blurted out, 'No means no!'

The whole group immediately asserted that the problem lay not in saying no but in saying yes! Women will never say yes, they argued. Only prostitutes say yes. A 'real' woman resists and says no even if she means yes. It was the kind of psychology Lina understood well, but she

305

was dismayed to see how it could be misused. She didn't believe a rapist could truly think a woman secretly wanted his advances if she was screaming in protest at them.

Then one woman, whose left eyelid was sewn down over the eyeball, said quietly, 'How can they think we mean yes when they pull off our tobes and tie our hands up?'

Women often did not admit to being assaulted for fear of rejection by their husbands and families. 'It's not the woman's fault if this is done to her.' Samah stood in the front of the group. 'Why should she be punished once again by her own people after what she has suffered? You hurt your children when you send away their mothers. You break up your own families, and this way you give power to those people who are attacking you.' The listeners frowned, shook their heads or picked indifferently at their feet. Most of them did not seem persuaded.

Lina heard that at larger camps, especially in Darfur, up to twenty babies a month, conceived through rape, were being abandoned by their mothers. One man in the workshop didn't accept this. He raised his voice, interrupting Samah: 'We believe that nobody can become pregnant when raped, because this is unwanted sex and you cannot have a child from unwanted sex.'

Even Samah lost her cool for a minute, 'Sex is sex: the mechanics are the same whether it is consensual or not.' She went on to describe the fundamental biology, and the man who'd questioned her began to look a little sheepish. Some of the other relief workers in attendance estimated that almost every woman in the camps had faced some form of sexual violence. 'Rape is the biggest problem in this country.' Samah sighed. 'It is the worst weapon used against our women. More terrible even than guns.'

Yet government spokesmen claimed that the rape statistics were being falsely augmented by aid workers. One government humanitarian aid commissioner for Darfur issued a statement saying: 'On the one hand the aid workers tell us that women in Sudanese society do not speak of things like rape. On the other hand they inform us that all the women are victims of rape. How can they assume this if the women do not confess it? They are making up figures for their own purposes. There is no rape in Darfur.' Such constant, blatant discrepancies between what was visible on the ground, and what was alleged by the government or reported by the press, wore Lina down. Her colleagues advised her not to get so caught up in the bigger picture.

'If you start thinking about how much there is to do, you won't be able to get up in the morning,' Jen said. 'You have to focus on what is possible within your own limits. Every day, just give yourself to accomplishing the little that you are able to do. Each small thing we do here makes a difference.'

Air Mayur

LINA FLEW TO NAIROBI whenever she had a few days off. Once, when she had a longer break, she zipped on to London, to see her family. The pressure of 'introductions', which now hung over every visit home, made her return less frequently than she might otherwise have done. How much longer could she go on fending off potential suitors before her parents realized she was deliberately sabotaging their plans? Already Iman suspected that Lina wasn't taking things seriously. During their last conversation, she'd told Lina off because one guy, Khuram, had rung her to complain. Lina couldn't be serious about making a commitment, he'd claimed, if it took her more than three weeks to reply to a simple email. He'd then declared that he was no longer interested in 'forging relations'. Iman was unimpressed by Lina's excuses that the internet connections at her base were unreliable. 'What-weh do you expect if you insist on hiding out in the middle of nowhere?'

Usually, aid workers relied for transport on the NGO cargo planes that came in and out of the region. Such rides had been free, but the worsening situation in Sudan, and the extra funds required to cope with it, meant that people were now charged for a seat. About $100 could get you a place on one of the World Food Programme's Humanitarian Air

Services planes. The aircraft often stopped en route to deliver goods and pick up more passengers, so a two-hour journey could end up taking four times as long. Moreover, trying to coordinate days off with the airline schedule wasn't always easy. Lina was fortunate to have access to Air Mayur. She could get a plane to pick her up at a day's notice. Pravar insisted it was no problem because aircraft were often in the vicinity, collecting or dropping tourists or other people who'd chartered a plane.

Anil was always waiting for her at Wilson Airport. Even when his ankle was still in plaster from the fall, he'd sat on the back seat of a car with it raised and got a driver to take him. Anything was worth getting to see Lina a minute sooner. One Friday evening he approached the recently arrived plane as airport ground staff wheeled a staircase up to its door. Through the windows he caught glimpses of Lina as she collected her things before leaving the aircraft. There were other people with her, he noticed. She often gave a ride to colleagues who needed to get to Nairobi. They'd nicknamed her 'Lina Lift'.

She ran down the stairs, each shaky metal step clanking under her kitten heels – the only pair of non-practical shoes she kept at her base in Sudan: for the sole purpose of wearing them on the trips back to Nairobi. She jumped straight into Anil's arms from the third step near the bottom. They squeezed each other, burying their noses in each other's necks, talking between kisses.

'You're all gritty as usual.' He smiled, feeling the odd grain of sand in his mouth. Tiny specks of the stuff were lodged all over her: in the faint creases at the corner of each eye, under the curl of cartilage on her ear, along the minute crevice of the scar on her lip. Freshly arrived, she had what he called her desert smell – an intensified version of her normal body aroma, as though her essence had been dried and pressed like a flower.

The clap of heavy boots on the stairs made Anil look up. He saw Hans looming over them, wearing that ragged old denim jacket as usual: the elbows were worn whiter than before, a button was missing at the left cuff. Behind him was another guy. Anil pulled Lina closer, shutting his eyes against the hovering intruders. She suddenly became conscious that they weren't alone and eased out of his grip.

'Hans came with me from Juba.' She ran her fingers over the round hem of her neckline and glanced from one man to the other.

'Oh?' Anil feigned surprise. He and Lina moved aside so that Hans could get off the portable staircase. A shorter man with a receding hairline and red-rimmed glasses alighted behind.

'And this is Fabio. He's working with Hans.' Lina sounded extra buoyant, perhaps to make up for Anil's indifference. 'Fabio has worked in South Sudan for more than ten years. He's an expert on the area.' No one would have guessed that she'd met him for the first time just before the flight. His knowledge of the issues she was most passionate about had made her feel their acquaintance was longer than the two hours they'd spent chatting on the plane.

Fabio Rossi was a leading member of the South Sudan Disarmament, Demobilization and Reintegration Committee. He and Hans were collaborating on a project to try and trace the origin of illegal arms voluntarily given up by Sudanese citizens. It was proving virtually impossible, because the serial numbers and markings on most of the weapons had been removed. Amongst those that remained, some British-manufactured weapons were identified. These might initially have been sold to Kenya, but both countries denied any knowledge of how they could have ended up in Sudan.

There was as yet no international system to record and track every weapon that was manufactured and sold. Fabio had got worked up during the flight, blinking rapidly behind his sleek glasses. He had said it was outrageous that you had more chance of tracking a genetically modified tomato or a suitcase than you did an AK-47. A piece of lost luggage could be traced from San Francisco to Sierra Leone within hours, yet deadly weapons disappeared on a daily basis.

The two men were heading to Geneva in a few days to participate in a UN conference calling for an international, legally binding arms-trade treaty. Hans had been campaigning for this when Lina had first met him three years ago – and yet so far, very little had been achieved.

'How many lives have been lost in that time due to small-arms fire?' Hans had stared out at the clouds they were flying through. 'I don't even like to think on it.' He had squeezed his eyes shut for a moment. 'One a minute. Sixty an hour. Tens of thousands every month. Half a million each year. Too many. I have the feeling,' he'd gone on, 'that we're mopping the floor while the tap is still open. One day we disarm a group, and a week later they have already fresh arms and ammunition.'

'Do you have a stronger case to put to the UN this time?' Lina had asked.

'We're taking a different line.' Fabio's hands and arms had risen and fallen. 'We'll be arguing that unless the world acts now to limit arms trading they can forget meeting any of the Millennium Development Goals. You

311

remember all those targets, for health and education and stuff? Which are supposed to be met by 2015? Well, few countries are on course to do so. Two-thirds of the thirty-four countries least likely to achieve the goals are in the midst of, or emerging from, conflict. So what we're going to highlight is the fact that irresponsible defence-spending by governments is a drain on resources. We need tougher international laws to vet all arms transfers.'

'Did you know that a fifth of all developing-world debt is due to arms purchasing?' Hans was always throwing new facts at Lina. As if she needed to be convinced. Now that she was in Nairobi more regularly, Hans assumed that, given the chance, she would try to get hold of, and pass on, any suspicious information about Samuel Ojielo, Merc's father.

'You think it'll be hard to get agreement on new legislation – even with all this information?' Lina asked. She was glad Hans was seated on the other side of Fabio, across the aisle. It made it easier to avoid the emotional pressure he was putting on her.

'Oh, most of this already they know, and still they're stalling.' Fabio pushed his glasses further up his nose with an index finger. 'We just keep throwing more stats on the fire and hoping the issue will get too hot for them to sit on.'

'The best thing would be if we had an informer leaking information on a high level.' Hans looked directly at Lina. 'They'd be shamed into acting if we had solid facts about a standing government. The public relations effect would be huge.'

Lina turned to face the window, fully aware of what he was implying. She'd tried telling him that she was hardly on the inside, that Merc actually disliked her, and would probably get suspicious if she suddenly started trying to get closer to his family. But Hans didn't understand how she could pass up such a chance to help their cause. And given the urgency, the scale of it, maybe he was right. Shouldn't she be doing more?

'I don't know, Hans.' Fabio removed his glasses and massaged the bump on the bridge of his nose. 'Think of that Ukrainian ship which was hijacked by pirates recently. You know the story?' He pointed one leg of his spectacles at Lina.

Somali pirates had taken control of the ship, *Yeva*, which was carrying a large consignment of arms, including thirty-five battle tanks. The US Navy, who'd managed to free the *Yeva* and its crew, were now asserting they had reason to believe that the cargo was not due for Kenya, as the Kenyan government and the Ukrainian shippers claimed, but for South Sudan – which was under an arms embargo. They had allowed the BBC to publish the *Yeva*'s freight manifest. The contract number on the manifest included the initials MOD/GOSS – which stood for Ministry of Defence/ Government of South Sudan.

The Kenyan government had contested that interpretation, saying GOSS stood for General Ordinance and Security Supplies – a division of the Kenyan Defence Ministry. Yet Kenya had declared no arms imports or exports to the UN for that year. Moreover, so far, Kenya had failed to produce what would be the conclusive document: an end-user certificate, which would show whether it was keeping the tanks for itself or re-exporting them to Sudan.

'I read about it.' Lina rubbed her nails against each other.

'There you have a clear case of something bad going on and still we get no major reaction from the international community.' Fabio had thrown up his hands. 'I don't think you can get more high profile than that.'

'It makes me crazy!' Hans had twisted in his chair and leaned over the aisle towards Fabio and Lina. 'On one side Kenya is hosting peace talks for the warring parties in Sudan, on the other side they are selling arms to them!' He had jabbed an elbow against the armrest. 'I won't stop until those responsible are behind bars.'

'So this is your plane?' Fabio peered over the top of his spectacles. He and Anil were facing each other on the shimmering tarmac, the diagonal line of the plane wing's shadow cutting across their torsos.

Anil frowned, not quite sure what the question was implying.

'You like the minimalist look?' Fabio took in the body of the aircraft. It was plain white: no logo on the tail, no colour or letter markings, no numerical code.

'Some of them have a peacock on the tail,' Lina said. 'Like that – look.' She pointed to one that was taxiing nearby. There was a troubling flutter in her chest. Fabio had commented on the lack of any identifying features even as he and Hans had been boarding.

'Anil, is it OK if we give them both a lift to Hans's apartment in Lavington?' she asked quickly, as if she might be able to slip it by him if she said it fast enough.

'I'm not sure we've got time, Leenie. It's not exactly on our way.' Anil tugged at her hand, drawing her towards the car, which was parked nearby. 'We've still got to go home and change before we head to Merc's party.'

Lina followed him, her body half-turned towards the other two men, her face etched with apology.

'Doesn't matter.' Hans came after them, carrying Lina's

314

small suitcase. His own rucksack was slung over one shoulder. 'We can get a taxi.'

'Yeah, bene.' Fabio followed.

Lina started to say something, but the sound of her voice was lost as a propeller plane took off. She massaged Anil's palm with her thumb as they strode to the car park. He pulled the keys from his pocket and pressed at the electronic pad to unlock the car. Lina's eyes darted in Hans's direction as the lights on the Discovery flickered on. He'd stopped, set down Lina's suitcase and swung his own rucksack off his shoulder before proceeding to unzip it.

'Do we have to go to Merc's?' Lina lowered her voice and twined her arm around Anil's. His skin was slightly damp from the heat. Through the corner of one eye she could see Hans kneeling on the tarmac, shuffling through his things. Fabio had pulled out a mobile phone and was calling someone.

'It's his dad's sixtieth birthday,' Anil said. 'I told you about it weeks ago.'

'I know, but . . .' So far, she'd managed to avoid attending any sort of event hosted by Merc or his father.

'Merc's come over especially – he's expecting me to be there. And anyway, it's bound to be a good bash.'

Hans rejoined them, holding out Lina's suitcase which Anil grabbed without a word.

'Lina, I didn't realize you had plans.' Hans looked at her intently. 'You should attend definitely this party.'

Her gaze dropped to the ground before flitting back to Hans again. She wished he hadn't heard Merc's name.

'It's really no problem for us to take a taxi,' Hans repeated. 'That's what I do normally. Already we're lucky we got the flight here with you, otherwise we would have

been stuck for another day in Juba. So, please don't worry.'
He took a step towards her to say goodbye.

Anil put Lina's case in the boot and then slammed it
shut.

'Maybe you'll feel better in a cab, anyway – it's probably
more sustainable than this thing.' She inclined her head
towards the car.

'I'll see you soon, Lina.' Hans kissed her twice on both
cheeks, and waved a long arm at Anil before going off.

'Yeah.' Fabio pumped Lina's hand up and down. 'We'll
meet again, no doubt. Ciao bella.'

Anil opened the door for Lina and shut it firmly after
her. Back in his own seat, he pulled at the seat belt so hard
it kept jamming.

'Let me do it.' She reached across and slowly extended
the belt over him before clipping it shut.

'You didn't say that guy was going to be on the flight.'
Anil reversed out of the parking spot.

'I didn't know he would be.' Lina put a hand on his
thigh. 'He showed up with Fabio a couple of hours before
I was leaving. I don't see why it's such a big deal. I give
people a ride all the time. Ah – air conditioning, how
nice . . .' She adjusted the vents so the cold air was blowing
straight into her face. 'There isn't a single UN car at work
where the air conditioning system still functions.'

'I don't like the way he looks at you.' Anil's knuckles
were white on the steering wheel. 'It's like he assumes
something.'

Lina exhaled heavily and stared through the windscreen. 'I have no idea what you mean.'

'And what was that goodbye? Four kisses? Who does
that? It's either one on each cheek or three in total. But no,
this guy has his own extended version for you.'

Lina was surprised by the observation. She hadn't even noticed.

'And the way you become all apologetic around him, as though your life might not be good enough in his eyes.' He dodged potholes with neat, practised little swerves. 'Bloody roads seem to be getting worse. Soon they'll just be holes held together by a thin web of tarmac.'

'That's still better than the dust tracks everywhere in Sudan.' Lina hoped they could leave the topic of Hans behind.

'Why did you have to make out like going to Merc's is such a chore? And then suggesting that this car wouldn't be up to Hans's eco-standards – what was that all about? And that other guy – what the hell was he implying with his comment about the minimalist design of the plane? Getting a free ride and then criticizing the way the carrier looks. Bloody ungrateful. Who the hell do they think they are?'

'I don't know what you mean,' Lina repeated. 'I already told you I'd rather not go to Merc's.'

'You *never* want to go there.' Anil's mouth hung open in incomprehension. The tension between Lina and Merc, always palpable, had intensified after the incident at Regent's Park. Neither really bothered to make an effort with the other. Anil had accepted that the two were never going to be buddies, but saw no reason why they couldn't be at the same party once in a while. 'What's the big deal? Can't you put aside your own feelings and do it for me?'

'I'm here to be with you.' She ran a hand through his hair, letting her fingers caress the back of his head. 'I don't care about seeing anyone else, whoever they are and whatever birthdays they're celebrating.'

'If you want to be with me you'll come tonight.' He

pulled up in front of the great black gates at the top of the driveway to the Mayur residence. The image of a peacock, welded into the wrought iron bars, split in half as the gate was opened by a security guard.

Anil went straight to his room to change. Lina sat on the edge of the bed in the room that had become hers. Minnie kept telling her to redecorate in any way she wanted, even though Lina insisted she liked the space as it was. 'At least put some of your own stuff around – like family photos,' Minnie had urged.

Some signs of Lina's other life were scattered about. Amongst the satiny cream and purple cushions in front of the headboard was a fluffy pink mouse, called Boo, which her sisters had given her when she'd first left home to go to university. On the bedside table, under an old copy of *Prospect* magazine, was a leather-bound English translation of the Koran. Somewhere within its pages a card was still lodged, bearing the message Shareef had written six years ago for her eighteenth birthday. She rarely opened the Book these days, but she touched it often. Before going to bed at night she would press it to her forehead and take God's name.

Lina slid her toes along the back of each heel, easing off her shoes. A couple of little kicks had them flying through the air and landing on a royal-purple rug nearby. She circled her ankles, pointing and flexing her feet. They were swollen from the heat, the toes stuck together after being squashed too long in unyielding leather.

Her phone blipped, announcing a text message. She rose and padded towards her case, which one of the servants had left by the door. The marble tiles were cool under her soles. The message was from Hans:

Pls go 2nite. Hv pt smthng in yr bag. Side pkt.

A twist of dread in her stomach. What had he slipped in there? When? Her hand shook as she delved into the side compartment. She found a small metal object, a little bigger than a cigarette lighter – she realized it was a tiny combination camera and dictaphone.

'Lina?' Minnie came into the room. 'Do you need Mama Jo to iron anything?'

Lina dropped the gadget back into the bag and stood up to hug her. 'You look amazing.' She touched the shimmering pullah of Minnie's turquoise sari, which was draped in the Gujarati way, with the loose end of fabric hanging over one shoulder down the front. Sequins in all shades of blue, scattered with silver, covered the fabric in wave-like formations.

'What are you going to wear?' Minnie was surprised to see Lina still in cropped jeans, her hair pulled into a straggly ponytail. 'Shall I help you decide?'

Minnie opened the doors of the walk-in wardrobe where most of Lina's things were now stored. Much of what was in there had been bought for her by Anil or his mum. There was even a small safe at the back of one cupboard filled with the precious jewellery she'd been given.

Lina hung back while the other woman pushed hangers along a rail, looking for an outfit.

'What about this?' Minnie held up a lime-coloured lengha, which she'd bought for Lina during a recent trip to India.

Lina shook her head.

'Or this, then?' She dangled a red dress. 'I guess you'd rather wear something Western. I can give you some nice earrings to set it off.'

319

'I'm not sure, Minnie. By the way, I like your hair up like that.' Lina admired the elegant bun studded with sparkling gems.

'Do you?' Minnie patted it carefully. 'Freddie, my hair-dresser, came here this afternoon to do it for me. Such a shame you arrived so late, otherwise he could have done yours too.' She pointed at another potential outfit.

'I don't know . . .' Lina thought of the camera, then Hans, then Merc, then Anil, then the never-to-be-realized Millennium Development Goals. It was all too much. She ought to go. She couldn't.

Minnie was now waving a yellow sari at her.

'I've told so many people that you'll be there tonight. Everybody's saying this is going to be the best party ever held in Nairobi. Well . . .' Minnie winked. 'It might be – until we have your and Anil's wedding.'

Lina forced up the corners of her mouth even as her shoulders slouched. 'I'm so exhausted. I'm afraid I'll just spoil your fun by wanting to go home early.'

'Don't be silly. You'll forget your tiredness once we're there, that's what I think.'

'You haven't even had a shower!' Anil entered dressed in a white tuxedo.

Lina hardly noticed his irritation, so strong was the clench of desire across her senses. The perfect fit of the suit served to chisel his physique, emphasizing the strong shoulders, the long legs. He wasn't wearing a tie, but had the collars of both shirt and jacket turned up as usual. If Minnie hadn't been present, Lina wouldn't have been able to resist slipping her hand under the open shirt buttons at his throat and pulling his face towards her own.

Anil glanced from her to Minnie, who laid all the clothes she'd picked out on the bed.

'She can't decide what to wear,' Minnie said.

'Actually,' Lina's brow creased, 'I can't . . . I don't think . . . I'm not really in the mood . . .'

'Oh for G— we're not going over all this again, are we?' Anil shook his head.

Lina tried to coax him with her gentlest voice. 'An evening all to myself is just what I need. Then I'll be in perfect form for the rest of my stay.'

'I don't understand you!' His arms rose from his sides and then smacked down again.

'Look, Lina, see how you've upset him.' Minnie went towards her son, ready to dispense sympathy. She was rather put out by Lina's attitude as well. 'Just talk to her properly, Anil.' She patted his shoulder. 'I'm sure she can't say no to you.' She turned and gave Lina a little stage direction of a smile before moving towards the door. 'We'll be waiting for you two downstairs.'

Lina went and took both Anil's hands. 'Do you think it's easy to let you go off without me, looking like that?' She wrapped his arms around her waist.

'Why won't you come? We don't have to see anyone else for the rest of your time here.' He rested his chin on her head, fitted his palm into the dip of her back. 'I've booked us into one of the cottages in Karen for two nights from tomorrow.' Though she'd become more openly tactile, Lina still wasn't comfortable about sleeping with Anil in his parents' home. When she visited they often slipped off to a lodge or hotel for a few days. 'Give me one good reason why you're so reluctant – and tiredness doesn't count.'

The impatient pressure of Anil's fingers thrumming along her spine forced Lina to speak. 'It won't make any difference to Merc or his dad if I'm there or not.'

He stepped out of her embrace, his face and body slack with disappointment. 'It makes a difference to me.'

His arms stayed limp by his sides when she tried to hug him again. He left without another word or a backward glance. Lina followed, pleading with him not to be angry, but he ignored her.

Downstairs, Pravar and Minnie were waiting in the hallway by the main door.

'We're going to be late.' Pravar pushed up the grey sleeve of his wool-and-silk-blend jacket to check his watch.

'No one will notice. There are going to be so many people.' Minnie moved about, rearranging the odd rose in the two large vases on either side of the archway that led into the main living room. 'As long as we get there before the sit-down dinner starts.'

'We won't at this rate. No. Most definitely.' He went around the corner to the staircase, intending to shout for Anil, but spotted him coming down. 'There you are! We need to make a move.'

'Well, I'm ready. Let's go.' He walked past his father.

Upstairs, at the far end of the landing, Lina leaned over the banister, hands clenched over its metal railing, elbows digging into her ribs. Her mouth was tight with the urge to speak, but she didn't know what to say.

'So Lina's not coming.' Minnie knew it from the sullen set of his mouth.

'Why?' Pravar raised his voice.

Anil headed towards the front door. Despite his anger, he didn't want to criticize her in front of them.

'She's very stubborn, that girl. Yes. Completely.' Pravar's fingers began scratching at the air by his sides. 'No wonder you can't get her to set a wedding date – you

322

can't even convince her to come out for an evening!'

'It's not fair what she does to you, Anil.' Minnie went out to the BMW waiting just by the entrance. The driver had the engine running and the air conditioning on. A cold draught leapt at her as he opened the door to let her in. 'Her job is too demanding. That's what I think.' She sank into a cool leather seat.

'Who in their right mind would want to miss a do like this?' Pravar slid in beside his wife, ignoring her indications that he should temper his tone. 'Dignitaries from countries across Africa are coming especially, but Lina won't deign to join us. It's not normal, her behaviour. No. Not at all.' He leaned forward and prodded Anil, who had settled into the front seat. 'You need to stop playing the nice guy if you want to get her under control. Be a man. Give her an ultimatum – that'll force her into action.'

Anil started flicking through the tracks on the CD player.

'You're too nice, Neelu. She takes you for granted, I think.' Minnie tried to arrange herself so that her sari wouldn't get crushed.

'How long are you going to keep waiting around for her to commit?' Pravar's incomprehension was turning into outrage.

Anil kept his index finger pressed to the stereo, his eyes fixed on the fast-changing numbers as the system zoomed through its library of music.

'It's not easy. Her family seems to be very traditional.' Minnie looked out of the window as the car glided down the driveway to the gate. Though the garden was doused in darkness she knew where every plant grew. Near the gate, in the light of the lamp posts, was a giant cactus, its arms raised, like a menorah waiting to be filled with candles.

'Ah, her family,' Pravar said. 'That's just an excuse. Plenty of girls marry against their parents' wishes. What's so special about her that she can't?' He grabbed the headrest of Anil's seat with both hands and pulled himself up so that he was speaking right into his son's ear. 'Remember how when you were small you could only ever beat me at chess by cheating? Well, that strategy still stands: when the game isn't going your way – bend the rules.'

Anil pressed 'play' and turned up the volume. Pravar sat back, shaking his head, as the beat of a tabla filled the car. Anil closed his eyes and massaged his temples. The music, heard at that level in that small space, slapped at his ears and vibrated in his throat, inflaming the rebellion building up inside him. He knew he had to act, but he wasn't about to discuss it with Pravar, who treated everything like a transaction from which he had to emerge with the better deal.

It's Over

THE DRIVE TO KAREN took almost two hours. Anil wanted to detour through Lavington, so that he could show Lina the progress on his new project, a private residence. For much of the way they were caught in a scrum of hissing engines, hooting drivers and puffing exhaust pipes – all made worse by matatus whose attempts to dodge the traffic jams only made them worse.

Anil had his hand on the horn for most of the journey. At times, Lina wondered whether he was honking at her rather than the chaos outside. Her questions about the party were met with monosyllabic answers and prolonged stabs against the centre of the steering wheel. The resulting bellows were also accompanied by swearing.

'You don't have to pretend to be interested in what went on last night. I know you don't give a damn.' Anil's eyes swung between Lina and the road.

'I might not care about the party itself, but your experience of it matters to me. I want to know about that.'

He fixed his gaze ahead again. 'If you're really so interested in my experiences, you should come and share them with me.'

Lina's head dropped. She twisted the ring on her middle finger round and round. Eventually she said, 'How long are you going to punish me for missing the party?'

Anil's palm slammed at the horn. 'It's not about that –

and you know it,' he said. A moment later the car jolted, the engine stalling, as he was forced to brake because the matatu in front had changed lanes without indicating. 'Mjinga!' Anil yelled, lowering his window to shout more abuse.

The plot where Anil had been commissioned to build a house for one of his father's acquaintances was on almost two acres of gently sloping land thick with vegetation. The previous building, a bungalow with a red-tiled roof from colonial times, had been knocked down, and Anil had erected a two-storey U-shaped structure in its place. The building had no corners, and boasted windows that bent in deference to its organic curves.

'It looks like the house is reaching out to embrace the garden,' Lina observed.

'That's exactly what I wanted.' For the first time that day he smiled.

'So many windows. I love that. And you still have a lot of privacy because of all the trees.'

'My client's freaked out by those exact things.' Anil jangled the bunch of keys he was carrying. 'I almost designed the house around the trees. I wanted to cut down as few as possible. He thinks such big windows and screen of trees are a perfect invitation to thieves.'

'Well, he's got a point . . .' There was a reason why the city was nicknamed 'Nairobbery'.

'Yes, but he's also got an electric fence! Gideon wants to have grilles put at every window. Can you imagine? That would ruin everything. He won't budge, though. So we're looking into some sort of electronic alternative which could fold away. I've found a company in Germany that can make what we want, but it costs a fortune, and Gideon

326

refuses to pay more than what the standard grille would cost here.' Anil tried several keys in the lock of the temporary door which led into the house.

'What are you going to do?'

'I'm going to have to finance the difference myself.' Seeing Lina's surprise he added, 'This house is like my business card. It's got to stand for my new vision. I'm not having all my hard work ruined by an ugly security feature.'

The house wasn't conventionally divided into two floors: there were mezzanines and also vast chambers where the full height of the building was celebrated. Most rooms overlooked the south-facing central courtyard, which flowed into the larger garden. The windows on this side were all large, to let in lots of sunlight, keeping the house warm in the colder months and reducing the need for artificial lighting.

'I don't remember this bit being so open.' Lina walked a slow circle through one of the wings.

'It wasn't.' He couldn't conceal his pleasure that she'd noticed. 'I got rid of the wall that used to be here.' His arm swept an imaginary line. 'And I've put in a bigger window. That,' he said, pointing, 'frames the exact point where the sun sets.' The window was high up in the wall so that you could only see the tops of trees and sky through it. 'I wanted to create a space in which you could be bigger than yourself. Do you know what I mean?'

Lina's forehead wrinkled, her hands rested on the wide brown leather belt wrapped high around her waist over the white sheath of her dress.

'You know the way a person can rise to an occasion or a challenge? Surprise themselves by what's possible? Well, I'm interested in making spaces that can do that.'

Lina walked around, absorbing the scope of the house.

There was definitely harmony in it, and a limitless sense of possibility in the constant surprise of fluctuating height, expanse and light. 'I suppose you would want to try and live up to the beauty of this place.'

His mouth pressed into disagreement. 'That's putting it too strongly. It's more subtle – like playing squash with someone who's more talented – you improve, almost magically, at least for the duration of play. I believe architecture also has the power to raise our game, as it were.'

'It's very inspiring.' Lina went to kiss him, but he allowed only a brief peck. She couldn't tell if he was still annoyed about the previous night or simply excited about showing her the site. 'What has your client said about the changes?'

'I didn't even tell him. He's pretty much given me free reign apart from the stipulation for five bedrooms and a big kitchen.' Anil pinched the sharp corners of his collar as if he was pulling them to attention. His slim-fitted polo shirt was untucked over a sand-coloured pair of shorts.

'So he's got enough money to cover everything?'

'Oh, well, not exactly.' Anil looked sheepish. 'There's a budget, of course. But we're already way over thanks to those bloody grilles. But I need the freedom to be able to rip things down and start again. I have to get this right. I want people to forget that bloody Arrow. So I'm prepared to pay the extra. Or rather, my dad is.'

'Lucky client,' Lina said. 'And lucky you, to have Pravar's help.'

'I know. I never thought he'd be so supportive. Merc says he'd fork out anything to keep me in the country. I don't know.' Anil paused and rubbed his chin. 'I sometimes wonder if Merc's envious because I can practise my profession so freely here.'

'Because of your father's money.' Lina spoke quietly.

'Yes, due to that – but I'm also quite happy in this country.' He kept stopping to inspect the joins between every wall. 'There's more opportunity to make a real impact. Whereas Merc's got something against this place, and he'd prefer it if I felt the same way.'

'Merc holds a lot of grudges.' She regretted the comment immediately because it made them both think of what had happened the night before.

Anil seemed about to say something but began examining a doorframe instead.

'Come this way.' He drew her attention to the rooftop wind-catchers with vents on four sides to let heat out and fresh air in. They came to the first fired-earth wall he'd constructed. Only two had been made because the client was sceptical. But Anil had been determined to try the method. Specialists from Khiva in Uzbekistan had been flown over to pass their know-how on to local workers. 'Aren't they beautiful?' He patted the smooth, red-brown surface. 'Once I've perfected the technique I'm going to start on our house. I want the whole thing made this way.' The words were out before he had time to think. One part of him was annoyed that he'd let out this sign of his true feelings exactly when he was trying to punish Lina. But he also embraced this proof that she was integral to his being. He couldn't imagine any future in which she did not figure.

Lina pressed her palm against one of the walls, expecting to find it damp and yielding. But it was cool and solid and left no trace on her skin. 'It's amazing.'

'Soon everyone's going to want to construct like this.'

'Really? Even here? You told me they mostly associate mud with housing for the poor.'

'You're very negative.' Anil's tongue clicked.

'No!' She went towards him and almost tripped. There were lengths of pipe and scraps of other waste strewn over the raw concrete floor. 'I think what you're doing is great. It's just that I remember what you said about people's reactions to the idea of living in a mud house.'

'That's why I don't call it mud. It's fired-earth technology. Anyway, we'd better get on. I'm starting to feel hungry.'

'I haven't seen everything yet. We—'

'You can have a look another time. Maybe on the way back.'

They drove on in silence. After a while, Lina began telling Anil anecdotes about her recent span in Sudan. She'd started working with the Refugee Settlement team at the camp. Each day she spent a few hours at the screening centre, interviewing refugees to assess their eligibility and priority for resettlement in neighbouring countries. 'It's so hard to ascertain whether people's stories are true. They rarely have identification papers or any proof of where they come from. First, we have to verify whether people are genuine refugees or just poor locals who've slipped into the camp. Then it's all about trying to gauge whose need is biggest.' She tugged at a strand of hair and glanced sideways. Anil seemed to be listening. 'The other day this family came in – thirteen of them. The couple claimed that five of the boys were their sons. I was sure they couldn't be because the oldest alleged son looked about thirty, and the youngest was a toddler – and the mother seemed to be in her mid-thirties. Anyway, Jen, who was conducting the interview, asked the mother to name her sons in birth order. You could see immediately that the mother was thrown: she looked at the boys and stammered out their names, confusing two of them. So we sent the family out . . .' Lina paused as another round of hooting erupted without, as far as she could see, any provocation. Traffic on the Ngong Road was fairly sane for a Saturday afternoon.

'We began speaking to them individually, trying to cross-check their stories. I felt so awful, you know, like haven't these people been through enough, and now we're interrogating them? Jen's really good at it, though. She asked each member to speak in the dialect of the region that the father claimed they came from – of course half of them couldn't. She made them name the crops native to the area – again, most didn't have a clue. So she called the father back in and asked why his kids – even the older ones – knew nothing about the place they came from. Then the guy tried to backtrack, and admitted that only three of the boys were his sons, but the other two were cousins who were like sons because they had lost their own families. I'm not sure I would have been able to argue with that, but Jen sent him off, telling him to come back when he'd worked out exactly who constituted his immediate family.'

Still Anil did not speak. But he was using only one hand to steer the car, so Lina assumed he was a little more relaxed. The other hand rested lightly on the gear stick. Normally, Lina would have reached over and taken hold of it, but now she was afraid of spoiling the peaceful atmosphere. 'That happens all the time – groups being diced into smaller units which conform to our Western notions of what family is. Sometimes people get really upset.' She could almost hear the sharp, reverberating flares of anger from stones flung against the corrugated iron walls of the screening centre. 'They come and throw stuff at our building.'

'It's not safe there!' Anil hit the horn again. 'One of these days some crazy person could come in and attack you.'

'It isn't so bad. No foreigner working at our camp has ever been harmed.'

'That doesn't mean anything. But why should my opinion matter? I bet you've got people like that Hans,' he huffed out the name, 'applauding you.' His hand slammed down on the horn once more.

'What? He's not involved with any of the resettlement work. He's with a completely different organization, in another field altogether.'

'There seems to be a lot of overlap.' He was furious again, his toes clenched in his trainers.

'That's just because we're interested in the same issues. I'm also helping him with this disarmament initiative in South Sudan.' Her explanations steamed with guilt even though she'd done nothing wrong. She fumbled mentally for something that would placate Anil.

'He's a weirdo.'

'Talking of which . . .' Lina suddenly remembered something which she hoped might distract and amuse him. 'You'll never believe what that Khuram guy who my parents introduced me to did!' The twitch in Anil's face made her wonder whether to go on. 'He phoned my mum to tell on me – criticizing me for not communicating with him frequently enough. Isn't that the most ridiculous thing you've ever heard?'

He didn't reply immediately, just sucked in his cheeks. 'I can understand him wanting to complain. He's not exactly being treated fairly, is he?'

Now Lina had no answer. She looked out of the window and wished the journey would end quickly.

When they finally drove off Langata Road into the calm grounds of the Karen Blixen Cottages both were still silent and uneasy. They checked in and walked through the shady garden to their cottage. People were sitting outside, lingering at lunch under bottlebrush trees in spiky red bloom. Men in business suits conferred intensely while, at the next table, tourists lounged in shorts and bathing suits. Two little girls, one wearing bright orange armbands, the other with a crocodile-shaped inflatable swim-ring around her waist, chased one another across the lawn.

In the white quiet of their cottage Lina embraced Anil – draping herself around him from behind even before he'd set down their bags.

'I'm sorry.' She pressed her cheek to his back. Her hands began making circular motions from his stomach to his chest. He grabbed her wrists, stopping the action.

'I know that.' He stepped away and turned to face her. 'But it doesn't mean much, because I also know you'll do the same again.'

'I don't like to upset you.' She pulled in her lips, pressing them between her teeth for an instant. 'But it's true I'd rather not see Merc if I can help it. I'm not comfortable around him. I don't see why that should come between us.'

'It's not just Merc.' He sighed and gazed at the high wood-beamed ceiling as if considering the mound of other things that were troubling him.

'Can we sit down and talk about this?' Lina went towards the suite of armchairs in the adjoining room.

'Let's go outside. I need something to eat.' He hadn't even drunk a glass of water since getting up. He suddenly felt as if everything within him was shrivelling up: his brain, his stomach.

Lina followed him to the restaurant, praying that food would go some way towards restoring his mood. She didn't want to imagine what he meant by, 'It's not just Merc.'

They got a table close to the pool. Spray landed on Lina each time a kid jumped into the water, but she hardly noticed. Anil ordered without even checking the menu: a bottle of mineral water, a glass of white wine, a double espresso, a lobster thermidor and a rump steak with chips.

'Two main courses?' Lina spoke from behind the menu she was studying, even though she wasn't hungry. She, too, hadn't eaten that morning. She'd avoided going down to breakfast so she didn't have to see anyone. She'd been especially reluctant to face Pravar after the comments she'd overheard the night before.

'I can't decide which I want more, and I'm so hungry I could probably eat both. What are you having?' He squashed a chunk of bread into the small bowl of olive oil in the middle of the table.

Lina asked for the prawn cocktail.

'Tell the chef to hurry.' Anil pushed the sodden bread into his mouth while addressing the waiter. 'You'll be in for a big tip if he does. And can you bring that water and the coffee right away?'

'Thanks,' Lina added before the waiter hurried off. She reached out to wipe a drop of oil from Anil's chin. He continued to eat, tearing up bits of sourdough and steeping them in oil before cramming them into his mouth. When the water came he glugged three full glasses before finally leaning back in the canvas folding chair and exhaling heavily. Lina crossed her legs tighter, expecting that he would start on about whatever was troubling him. But instead, he sat up again, dropped two spoonfuls of sugar into his espresso and stirred it for ages. The scraping sound of the metal spoon against the ceramic cup seemed to get louder and louder. Soon it was all Lina could hear. Other noises – like the jazz band playing live, people chattering, birds calling – faded. She had a nagging suspicion that the outcome of his coffee drinking would be unpleasant. Ya Allah, she thought, please let things be OK.

Anil sipped slowly. He could almost feel his nerve endings fire up as the caffeine entered his system. All his thoughts and feelings since last night began to meld into resolution. He drained his cup, relishing the sweet last sip, thick with undissolved sugar.

'We can't go on like this, Lina.'

Ya Allah, *please*! She knew things weren't good whenever he called her Lina instead of Leenie.

'I don't know what you're trying to do.' He pushed his aviator glasses on to his forehead and set his elbows on the table. 'All your actions seem to contradict each other.' It was only as he said the words that their truth became apparent to him. At once, he felt a new clarity within, as though a space had been cleared. 'You talk about us being together, but nothing that you do seems to support that.' His head was tilted to one side, his eyes fixed on her. She was glad her sunglasses shielded her from his wounded gaze. 'You insist on working hundreds of miles away in a war-torn country when you could have a safer, better paid, but equally useful job right here near me. You want us to wait so that you have time to bring your parents around to the idea of our marriage, but in the meantime you won't let me near them and you allow them to arrange introductions to other men. You've decided you don't want anything to do with Merc, but I'm supposed to be open to seeing that Hans pop up left, right and centre. And then last night you refuse to come for the one occasion that matters to me.'

She swallowed, preparing to justify herself. But he went on.

'I've just gone along with everything you've wanted, hoping it'll make things easier for you and help you decide.'

She remained still, not even moving a finger to scare away the fly that was exploring the frame of her glasses.

'But you're no closer to securing our future than you were at the beginning. If anything, you've made things more difficult with all your—' He couldn't find an appropriate word. He wasn't sure there was one that could sum up her behaviour. 'We can't go on like this. So, I think—'

She held her breath, fearing what would come next.

'I need something definite from you. I won't go on in this haphazard way, playing along while you pretend and placate the rest of the world.' He reached over and took her hand. 'Forget all that shit,' he said. 'Let's just go and get married.'

Lina remained motionless. In all her imaginings of a proposal, she'd never anticipated that it would contain the word 'shit'. Anil let go of her hand and took off her sunglasses.

'I can't tell what you're thinking.'

Lina leaned her head to one side, as though she was listening out for something elusive. 'But how can we do it?'

'We'll fly to Vegas.' He grinned. 'It's simple.'

'Well I, um, I thought . . . I mean didn't we want, you know . . . wouldn't it be better if everyone supported us and was there?'

'Of course it would. Ideally. But it doesn't look like that's going to happen. So why should we wait?' He grabbed her hands. 'Let's just go now.'

'Now?' She squinted to shelter her eyes as a huge cloud pulled away from the face of the sun.

'Yeah, why not? Let's get on the next flight.' He chuckled, pleased with his idea.

'But I do have to be at work on Monday.' She felt the lameness of her statement in the face of his passion.

'Oh, forget work!'

'I can't just let people down.' She couldn't help coming up with objections, as if they were speed bumps that might slow down Anil's rush towards this new plan. 'They're expecting me. They need me. I would never leave without giving notice. I—'

'All right, all right. You can do things however you like. But I'm sure they won't quibble if you miss a few days next week. Tell them it was a surprise, I whisked you off to make an honest woman of you.' He stood up and pulled her out of her chair. Other guests turned to look as he picked her up and spun her around. 'We're getting married!' he shouted.

'Congratulations!' A man in a suit called back.

For a moment Lina gave in to his enthusiasm, thrilled by the happiness that brimmed in his voice and radiated through his fingers on to the skin of her arms. But then she thought of her parents. 'Anil!' Lina forced him to set her down. 'It would be much nicer if we could do things properly.'

Above them, the sun was quickly smothered by another cloud, and even the air seemed to darken.

Anil turned back towards the table where the waiter was setting down their food. 'Let's eat and then I'm going to get online and see when we can fly.'

'Don't you think we should maybe plan it better, take some more time?' She followed his example, picking up cutlery, putting a napkin on her lap; the rituals of dining provided a calm front behind which her mind could panic unobserved.

'What's to plan?' He spoke through a mouthful of steak. 'The great thing about this is that we don't need anything! We can just go and get married. You and me.' He stopped eating, took her face in his hands and kissed her. She clung to his lips, wanting to believe. 'All you need for a marriage are two willing people.' They'd lost sight of that. The sun nudged into view again, turning every colour a truer shade of itself.

But she couldn't let go of her doubts. 'You need your passport.'

'That's true.' He paused. 'I'll check flights first, then I can go home and pick it up.'

'What about your parents? What will you tell them?'

'Nothing. This is between you and me now.'

She nodded, but her shoulders slumped a little, making her collarbones protrude.

'They'll have to accept it. All of them. In fact, I'm sure this is the best way to deal with your family – give them a fait accompli and let them get used to it. They'll never agree to your marrying me as long as they think you might be dissuaded by their disapproval.'

She swallowed. 'What if—'

'I don't care. I'm tired of that kind of thinking.' Weariness threatened to grab all the mirth from his face.

'You're right.' Lina picked at her prawns while Anil finished his steak and went on to the lobster.

* * *

There was a flight leaving for New York the next afternoon. Anil decided they would take that and then get a connecting flight to Vegas. He booked the tickets, first class. The following morning he drove home to collect his passport and leave the car. He got the driver to drop him back at the cottages. When he returned to their room, Lina's suitcase was lying open at the foot of the bed, her things still spread around.

'What's going on? I've ordered a taxi to take us soon!' He picked some clothes out of the wardrobe and shoved them, hangers and all, into the suitcase.

Lina didn't answer, just stood there with her hands pressed to her mouth. She was wearing one of Anil's T-shirts, which she'd slipped on after taking a shower earlier. There was a long white mark down the front, from toothpaste that had dripped while she was brushing. Beneath the shirt's hem, the lace trim of her French knickers was visible.

'What the hell have you been doing? You promised to be ready by the time I got back.' If he knew what her limp posture and red eyes portended, he did not want to face it.

'I was talking to my parents.' More accurately, she had been crying down the phone, admitting she was still with Anil and pleading with her mum and dad to accept this. Shareef had told her that if she went ahead and married Anil, it would be their last conversation.

'Oh for fuck's sake! Let me guess – they refused to give their go-ahead, and you're now having second thoughts. Right?' His mouth bent into a crooked line.

'I'm sorry.'

'Why the hell did you have to contact them?' Anil had had a feeling he shouldn't leave her alone.

339

'I'm so sorry, Anil.' She slouched against the wall. 'I can't tell you how—'

He kicked her suitcase. The lid flew shut. 'This is sick! This is almost fucking incestuous. What normal person lets their parents rule their life? Why should they decide for you?'

'I don't know.' She stared at the floor. It was all wrong, an inversion of the natural order. But she couldn't hurt them – especially Shareef. She couldn't bear the flatness of his voice, couldn't ignore his warning that she was doing wrong in God's eyes. 'My dad—'

'How can your father's happiness be more important than your own? Than ours?' Just asking the question infuriated Anil. It was perverse. 'He's lived his life, had everything he wanted, and now he wants to decide how you should live, too? Can that be right?'

Lina shook her head. It did sound absurd. But there was another rationale at play: the obscure logic of the heart. In the past, she'd tried to give Anil an idea of her attachment to Shareef. He'd scorned her adulation, pointing out that what she'd experienced was just normal parenting. In any case, he'd insisted, whatever a parent did for a child it never earned them the right to rule that child's life.

'If I had a bit more time—'

'You don't need time, you need therapy!' Anil glared. 'Merc was right, this is all completely fucked up. I don't know what your parents have done to you, but it's . . . it's—' A fuse suddenly blew in him. He didn't want to argue any more.

'I'm sorry.' She started crying, and slid down along the wall, until she was sitting on the floor.

Anil put a shirt and a book into a sports bag. 'I'm going.

And if you don't come with me – that's it. We're finished.'

She remained propped against the wall, crying. She was terrified by the idea of him walking out for ever. At the same time, Shareef's last words hung on her like a noose: 'If you go with him then all I can say is Khuda Hafiz, may God protect you.'

He picked up the half-empty bag and stood over Lina. 'Are you coming?'

'Please.' She reached out and touched his calf. 'Let's just talk—'

'I don't want to talk any more.' His voice broke. 'If you really love me you'll get up and leave with me now.'

'Don't say that! You know I love you!'

'No I don't.' He started towards the door. 'Show me.' He pressed down the handle.

She tried to get up, but then slumped back again.

'Fucking great love this is.' He left, slamming the door so hard the lock broke.

'Anil!' Part of her went with him. She felt the wrench, like a midday shadow torn off. She saw herself running after him, falling into his arms. But the rest of her remained seated, glued to the floor with indecision, paralysed by pain. That old tug of war ripped open her heart.

IV

VI

Revelation

HE WAS DYING. He had no memory of getting to the taxi. If the pace of his heart was anything to go by, he must have made it in a furious sprint. How that muscle thrashed in his chest. He was dying. There was no strength left in him. He lay sprawled in the back seat, feeling as if he was attached to the car by a rope, being pulled along the burning tarmac of the road. He was dying. He had to remind himself to breathe. He took shallow, insufficient gulps. There wasn't enough air in the world to fuel his grief. His mouth stretched in a rictus of despair. He choked and coughed and gasped into the stale seats. The leather was molten. He was dying.

The taxi driver watched through the rearview mirror, getting up the nerve to issue a warning. 'Sah,' he said. 'There's a fine, you know, sah, for accidents? Twenty thousand bob.' That was probably nothing to men like this, he thought. They spent that much on a bottle of wine, but it would cover half his rent for a month. Though he wasn't sure cleaning up the puke would be worth it. 'Sah?' He pulled over and turned to his passenger. 'Are you sick?'

Anil shook his head. 'I've lost,' he said. 'I've lost someone.'

'Oh. Very sorry, sah.' The car moved on again.

At the airport Anil was surprised to see everything looked as it had always done: people were going about their business as if the world was still the same. He remained in the taxi for a while, trying to regain his composure. The driver waited. 'Take your time, sah. You know what they say? However long the night, the day is sho-ah to come.' Anil wiped his eyes and began to tell himself that Lina too would come. Their being together was as inevitable as the cycle of light and dark.

Before heading to the check-in counter he scanned the arriving taxis, to see if she was in one of them. There was no queue at the first-class desk. He asked the attendant to block the seat next to his. 'My partner is joining me. She'll be here soon.' During the security check his bag was singled out. An officer pulled out a bottle of face cream, it was more than 100 ml. Anil was told he couldn't take it on board. He couldn't even remember having packed it, but suddenly that glass bottle became infinitely precious, like the last relic of Lina, something he must preserve at all costs. He refused to let the officer throw it in with a heap of other offending liquids. Then he would have to check in his bag, the officer insisted. Anil pulled out some notes and passed them over discreetly. He was waved through.

In the lounge he kept an eye on the door, waiting for her to appear. He was the last to board the plane. Why he got on the flight at all, he couldn't have said. Maybe it was only to give her the chance to follow him. Even as he took his seat, he remained hopeful, still expecting her to show up, to burst on to the deck, flushed and panting, the way heroines did in the movies.

She stayed where she was after he had left, crying with a force that left no space for thought. Her mobile phone rang twice. Each time she lunged for it, hoping it might be Anil. Instead, her parents' home number flashed across the screen – they were no doubt checking to see if she'd gone ahead with her plan.

Then, all of a sudden, she was waking up on the floor of a dark room. The quiet was pierced by the call of a hadeda ibis: haa-haa-haa-de-dah! As if the night itself was cackling at her misery.

She crawled to the bedside table and fumbled for the light. He was gone. The knowledge caught at her heart like a hook. She noticed his iPod and remembered the last song they'd listened to. Lying naked together that morning, his fingers trailing through her hair. He'd translated the words for her, trying to impress her with his mastery of Urdu.

> *Life is just memory now.*
> *I heed each passing second only to measure*
> *The throb of your name in the pulse of Time.*

She walked around the room, in agony, yet still disbelieving. The imprint of his head was still on one pillow. She put out a hand, but withdrew it again, not wanting to change the impression with a touch. She went towards the bathroom, hitting her fists together. On the way she saw one of his shirts still hanging in the wardrobe. She stepped into the wooden box, wishing it was a coffin, and pressed the fabric over her face. The hook in her heart pulled harder. He was gone.

The next day she didn't want to fly back to Juba with Air Mayur as planned. It seemed wrong to go on enjoying Anil's hospitality. Lina phoned several colleagues to see if there was any NGO transport from Nairobi going towards Sudan. She didn't even care if it was a truck that took a day:

she just needed to get away from the city. But she was told a convoy of goods had left by road the day before, and the next plane was heading off at the end of the following week. The other option was to get a commercial flight to Juba. She soon found that the one flight out that day had already departed. She resigned herself to going back with Air Mayur one more time.

She arrived at Wilson Airport early, hoping the plane might already be there, and they could just go. Instead she was told the pilot was still on his way back from Mombasa. She waited on the ground floor of the control tower, a strange two-storey building with what looked like a blue-roofed pagoda stuck on top. She kept her sunglasses on and a tissue held to each cheek to soak up the tears that kept falling.

She did not know how much time passed, but eventually someone told her the plane was coming. As it landed and taxied Lina began walking towards it, expecting to be able to board and take off immediately. One of the attendants told her it would have to refuel first.

'It won't take long,' he added quickly when a moan slipped out of her. 'Here, madam, let me take your bag.' He picked up her suitcase.

Lina remained where she was, watching two men in overalls wheel stairs to the plane door. The next thing she knew Merc was coming down them wearing a light linen suit. He'd made a quick day trip to the coast to meet a local artist whose work he was thinking of exhibiting in the UK.

'Hey. You heading back to work?' He walked up to Lina, equally surprised to see her.

She nodded.

'Where's Anil?'

She shook her head, not trusting herself to speak.

'Lakini, the plane needs to refuel. Madam must wait some minutes,' the attendant explained.

Merc noticed her wet cheeks. 'Eh, give me that.' He took Lina's suitcase from the attendant. 'I'll help her.' With the other hand he steered Lina towards one of the nearby hangars.

They stopped just outside the building, and stood in the shade its timber frame threw on to the ground.

'Is everything OK?' Merc asked.

She looked like she'd stepped out of the eighties: skinny white jeans and a peach-coloured, three-quarter-sleeve cotton jacket on top of an over-sized navy T-shirt. The only thing about the whole outfit that matched was the white dribble of a stain on the shirt, which was as fluorescent as the jeans.

She opened her mouth and then shut it. What could she tell this guy? He'd never wanted her and Anil to be together.

There seemed to be only one explanation for her state and Anil's absence. 'Have . . . are you guys . . . is it over?' He couldn't even tell if Lina was looking at him from behind those dark glasses.

As soon as he said the last word she started taking huge snorting breaths and sobbing.

Merc put out a hand, but wasn't sure if he could touch her. They'd never been at all tactile with each other.

Lina leaned back against one wall of the hangar; her shoulders rolled forward, shaking.

For the first time ever, Merc felt not irritation, but pity for her. 'Sshhh. Ssshhh,' he said, letting his hand rub her shoulder.

After a while, she straightened up slowly and pulled off

her sunglasses. Her eyes were thin slits in their swollen lids. The paper tissues in her hands had disintegrated. 'He's gone.' Her voice was hoarse, tearing the words as they were spoken. 'He's left me.'

Merc's hand froze, then dropped back to his side. He'd never expected Anil would be the one to end the relationship. 'I know this won't give you any comfort now, but I really think it's for the best.'

Lina's expression didn't alter. Her face was numb from crying.

'And I'm not just saying that because of all the things we've argued about. You two were much too different – in every way. You get me?'

She shook her head, disagreeing but unable to explain.

Merc observed her, wondering whether to say what was on his mind. For years he'd held back, not wanting to betray his best friend. Anil would never have forgiven him for meddling. But now that the relationship was finished, he wouldn't be doing any harm, and maybe it would help Lina to know the truth.

'I always went on about your religion, but that wasn't the only reason I thought you two couldn't be together.' He played with the handle on her suitcase, pulling it up and down. 'It's your principles as well. The things you believe in are incompatible with him and his family.'

Lina looked away. She didn't need a lecture from Merc now. But his next words caught her attention.

'I know the Mayurs are unusually generous, but haven't you ever wondered why Air Mayur was so ready to fly you around at short notice?' He watched her closely.

She had thought about it, and even questioned Pravar a couple of times. But his answer had sounded plausible: he had more than twenty aircraft zipping around the country, there was a good chance at least one would be going close to her area at any given time.

'What about the strange cargo these flights sometimes had on board? Don't tell me that never struck you as odd.' His eyes narrowed.

'The aid?' Lina said. Those Red Cross boxes had been on many of the flights she'd taken out of Nairobi.

'Aid!' Merc exhaled sharply. How naïve was this woman? They painted fake signs on some old crates and she was taken in? 'Come on, Lina. Don't tell me you never suspected anything. You work for the UN, for fuck's sake! You know how aid is delivered – and it's not usually in small commercial aircraft like this.'

A horrible thought took shape in Lina's mind. She remembered Fabio's comment about the lack of any identifying features on the aircraft. It could not be. She shook her head. Not Anil's family. Not him.

Merc's lips puckered up and he inhaled with a long whistle. He was sure she must have had an inkling. Wasn't she always going on about the illegal arms trade, and the Kenyan government's involvement? 'Those planes carry weapons out of here.'

She covered her mouth with both hands as a convulsion passed through her body. If there had been any food in her stomach she would have vomited. She had to remind herself to breathe. Different ideas came together and then skittered apart in her mind. She gasped for air, as if it might help her think more clearly.

Sensing her bewilderment, Merc started to explain. Old weapons from the Kenyan State Armoury were being surreptitiously sold off. Pravar's company was flying the arsenal out to middlemen in central Africa. Merc had guessed what was going on from conversations overheard at his father's house. He was sure Anil had no idea – he'd never taken an interest in how Pravar made his money.

Merc then started to defend himself. 'I know you're probably wondering how I can know all this and not do anything about it. But I can't tell my father how to act. You get me? That's why I stay away.' He looked into the distance. The Nairobi skyline stretched out before them, Anil's Arrow the tallest building. 'I never wanted to live in this country. I thought Anil wouldn't be able to, either.'

'If he knew—' Lina whispered. She didn't believe Anil would be able to stand the place if he found out the truth.

'He doesn't want to know,' Merc said. 'He needs his dad's money to make his career. You get me? Who else would finance his quirky architectural projects?'

'So your father is the main one behind it all.' She thought of Hans and the device in her suitcase.

'Didn't you know that? I even thought you might be taking the flights to collect evidence.'

'Do you think I could do that to Anil?' He obviously had a pretty low opinion of her.

'You've been pretty rigid about sticking to your beliefs in other ways. I wasn't sure where you drew the line.' Merc couldn't look her in the eye.

'I could never use anyone in that way!' Her lips quivered.

'Well . . .' Merc slipped off his jacket and eased the collar of his shirt. The garment fitted so tightly it was a wonder the buttons didn't strain in their holes. 'Even if you had, it wouldn't have made much difference. There's pretty solid wrapping around the whole operation. My dad and Pravar are ostensibly sending the weapons to other legitimate governments. If the goods get sidelined along the way, how are they to blame?'

'I don't believe they can get away with it!' Lina said.

'You think the legal system in this country is going to hold them to account? You think the government here would cooperate if the International Criminal Court issued arrest warrants? You can forget it.'

An attendant came to tell them the plane was ready to board.

'She's just coming,' Merc said. He shifted so that he was facing Lina directly. 'In any case, this little racket is nothing in the bigger scheme of things. You know better than I do how China is giving the Sudanese government in Khartoum arms in return for oil. Stopping my father isn't going to make the slightest difference to what's going on in that country.'

She didn't answer.

'I'm just sorry that you've been the perfect cover girl for the operation. What better excuse could they have had than transporting UN staff to and from the area?'

'Oh God.' Lina clutched at her stomach.

'I'll take you to the plane.' Merc offered Lina one sturdy, veined arm and reached for her suitcase with his other hand.

She declined his assistance and took a few steps before stumbling. She would have fallen if he hadn't caught her.

'Oh God. Oh no, no. Oh God,' she kept repeating. Her legs wouldn't carry her forward, even though Merc was propping her up. He carried her back several metres, into the shade of the hangar, and she sank down on to the tarmac. She was breathing fast, almost hyperventilating.

'Do you want some water?' Merc didn't know what else to suggest.

She hardly heard the question, but nodded as a sort of reflex.

'I'll get it.' He dragged her suitcase back and left it beside her, dropping his jacket on it before going off.

Her mind seemed to have stalled – stuck like a record – going over and over the things Merc had said. All at once, she became aware of a ringing sound, and then of a slight vibration by her thigh. It was her phone. Anil? She reached into her pocket. What would she say? She had no idea, but she still wanted it to be him. Instead, the screen glowed with the names she least wanted to see: Ma & Baba. She dropped the phone into her lap. They could wait – and wonder, and suffer. The phone stopped, and then started up again a minute later. This time Lina didn't touch it, just let it buzz in the valley between her outstretched legs. She closed her eyes, let her head droop.

Then another noise startled her. It was a dim but high-pitched rumble that quickly grew into the unmistakable trumpeting of an elephant. Lina looked left and right trying to work out where the sound could be coming from. It seemed awfully close, and was getting louder with the frequency of – a ringtone! Somebody's mobile was going. By the time she'd worked out it had to be Merc's the ringing had stopped and started up a second time. She bent her legs to one side and shifted on to her knees so she could reach over for his jacket. Her wish, though it made no sense, was still that the caller might be Anil. In Merc's top pocket she found a wad of thousand-shilling bank-notes and a black American Express credit card. The phone was nestled in the inside pocket, next to a Mont Blanc pen. Lina held the pulsing piece of metal and plastic, from which the powerful call of the elephant was coming. A foreign number was displayed on the screen. Her heart pitched at the prospect that it might be Anil. But then the digits indicated it couldn't be. +44 – that was the international code for the UK. 121 – that was the code for Birmingham. 2417 – she dropped the phone. Her hands flew to her mouth. She blinked rapidly, tried to stop the trembling of her jaw by pressing her palms hard under it.

When the phone was silent once more she picked it up, unable to believe what she'd just seen. The phone began trumpeting again, announcing that a voice message had been received. Lina put the gadget to her ear. Next thing, she heard the voice of her father – distressed, abrupt: 'We need to speak. Everything has gone wrong. Because of you I didn't interfere. And now she wants to marry him. She's going to elope! God knows – she may already have done it. I need you to call me.'

She listened to the message again and then again. She must have heard it six times before Merc appeared in front of her, holding out a bottle of water. She passed him the phone, her father's voice still bleeding out of it.

Immediately, his brow moistened. His mouth began to worry, the lips sucking up against the teeth, moving around in circles, folding in and out. He slipped the phone into the back pocket of his trousers and then unscrewed the top from the bottle.

'You should have this.' He set it down beside her.

She was pale. 'Why is my dad calling you?'

He squatted down and ran his thumb along the leather seams of his brogues. He told her Shareef had first contacted him about two years ago, shortly after Lina had moved to New York.

'There's no way he could have got hold of your number. He never even knew you existed.' She suspected Merc was the one who'd got in touch with Shareef.

A muscle near Merc's left eye spasmed. 'I have no idea how he managed to contact me. Maybe you should ask him.' He didn't appreciate her implication that it was his fault.

Lina didn't believe Merc, but saw that she wasn't going to get anything out of him by arguing. 'OK, so *he* called. What did he want?'

'I'm not sure he knew. He was obviously having a moment of desperation. He asked for Anil. I told him Anil was in New York with you.'

Lina gasped. 'How could you?' She sprang forward and scratched at Merc's shirt. 'What right did you have?' she shouted into his face.

He took her by the shoulders and pushed her back against the hangar, slapping down her leg when she kicked him. 'I don't have to explain myself to you.' He brushed at his trousers, trying to get rid of the mark her shoe had left.

'I always knew you hated me.' Lina was crying again. 'But how could you do that to Anil?'

'Listen to you.' Merc stood up again and crossed his arms over his chest. 'Not a word against the father who started this mess in the first place.'

The full implications of that were becoming apparent to her slowly, like a tide that comes in hardly noticed and then threatens to drown you.

'If it hadn't been for me, you wouldn't have had such an easy time of it these last few years. I kept your dad off your back. I told him meddling wouldn't help.'

Lina stared at him, uncomprehending.

'He was ready to stop your allowance and force you back to Birmingham. But I said that if he waited he'd see the relationship wouldn't work out anyway.' Merc ran a palm over his smooth skull. 'You know as well as I do that Anil's used to getting what he wants. The only way he'd let you go was if he'd had enough – if he realized for himself

356

that any future with you was impossible. Like he has now.'
Merc shrugged.

'And where did I figure in this calculation of yours?'
Lina squinted up at him. 'Or didn't I count?'

'You?' He rubbed the toe of his shoe against some grass
that was growing out of a crack in the tarmac. The sun had
moved westwards and was to the side of them now. Its
long, low rays glanced off Merc's cheekbone. One side of
his face was glowing, the other shadowy. 'It's because
of you that everything's ended up like this. I knew you
would never be able to make a commitment to Anil. I
guessed it right from the beginning in the way you shilly-
shallied over everything. And I knew that being a
goody-goody you wouldn't be able to accept how his
family made their money.'

'You bastard!' Lina was overcome by another surge of
sobbing. 'How could you help my dad spy on me?'

Merc didn't answer immediately. He'd never thought of
it as spying. Shareef hadn't asked for specifics about what
Lina and Anil were up to. Indeed, they'd only ever spoken
once again after that first call – Shareef had got in touch
after Lina took the job in Sudan because he'd started
having doubts about Merc's theory. But, once again, Merc
had convinced him to wait a bit longer. This latest missed
call was a bit confusing. Shareef clearly wasn't sure what
was going on.

'Yes, your father stooped pretty low. He used me to
keep tabs on you. But you're in no position to be judging
others after lying non-stop for so many years. If you'd been
more courageous it could all have been so different. I'm
not surprised your father doesn't trust you. No one can.
Not Anil, not that German Mr Denim. You've let everybody down.'

357

Lina thought again of the device from Hans. If only she could have recorded all that Merc had said. 'Then you're not safe either.'

He put his hands in his pockets and laughed. 'You can't touch me. You won't.' He knew how her mind worked.

Revulsion for him coursed through her; she felt she might choke on it. 'You've ruined everything.'

'What the hell?' Merc bent down, took hold of her shoulders and shook them. Her head flopped back and forth, left and right, hair flying everywhere. The bottle of water tipped over, spilling on to Lina. 'When is your delusion going to end? This is all your own doing. If you had really wanted to be with Anil no one could have stopped you.'

'Let go of me!' She tried to push him away.

He stepped back. 'I've tried to help you, for fuck's sake. Isn't it better that you know all this? What if you'd actually married Anil and then found out?'

With such news there was no better or worse time: it would have been equally awful whenever she'd discovered it. The revelation had contaminated everything. But she didn't want Merc to have the impression he'd done her a favour. 'Nothing can ever change what I feel for Anil. I love him. I always will.'

'It's a pretty fucked-up kind of love.' Merc picked up his jacket and swung it over one shoulder. 'I'm going. You should, too. The plane's waiting.' He lifted her suitcase.

She made no effort to follow him, though she gathered up her phone and sunglasses.

Merc signalled to one of the groundsmen who came and took the suitcase from him. He turned back to Lina and, assuming she was too weak to heave herself up, offered to help.

She shook her head. 'I'm not going. I can't get on one of – those.' She raised a hand in the direction of the plane.

'Oh, for fuck's sake, Lina. What difference does it make now? You need to get the hell out of here. Come on.' He yanked her to her feet. There were dirty brown patches on her jeans from the dusty tarmac. Her phone and sunglasses fell to the ground.

'No!' She felt insubstantial, breakable, in his grip.

'Stop being stupid.' Merc picked up her things. 'The pilot's waiting and your bag is already on board.' The attendant was just going up the stairs into the aircraft.

'I can't.' She looked around, arms flapping. 'I won't go on one of these planes.'

'There's nothing on that aircraft. The pilot dropped some tourists at the coast when he picked me up. I saw them unloading, there's no cargo on board.'

Defiance energized her and she began running, calling out to the attendant to stop and give back her bag. He didn't hear and disappeared into the plane. She followed and Merc boarded behind her. When they entered the cabin, the attendant was just snapping shut an overhead compartment.

'I need my bag.' Lina panted. 'I'm not going.'

'Ati?' The attendant was confused.

Merc spoke to him in Swahili, telling him to ignore Lina. The man sidled past them and exited quickly.

Lina reached up to open the compartment where her suitcase was stored. She stood on her toes to pull it out, all the while ignoring Merc's exhortations that she was being foolish. As she tugged, the case slipped, hitting her on the head. She fell, crumpling into the aisle, the case bumping down on top of her. She was aware of her pulse, throbbing frantically at her temples, and behind that a more profound, primal thud in her brain. Then Merc was lifting her up, putting her in a seat.

'You have to go, and this is the best way. Just take this last ride.'

She could not fight any more. Her legs were shaking. She felt cold. Merc handed back her phone and sunglasses – one lens was cracked. He reached over and clicked her seat belt shut. Without another word, he left. A minute later the door of the plane was secured. She closed her eyes for the final trip.

2 October 1968

Yesterday I attended another rally against the Vietnam War. Nixon's promise to withdraw US troops has come to nothing. In fact, bombing has actually intensified in North Vietnam. When all those people gathered for the Peace Moratorium, I really believed it would make a difference. You and I were amongst the crowd who went and stood outside the US Embassy, thinking we were doing our bit against the war. Two years later, nothing's changed. What does democracy mean if a government can completely disregard the wishes of its people?

I say this now, but I can't pretend it has been my concern over the last few months. My own turmoil has obscured the world's. I only ended up in Grosvenor Square because friends dragged me along. Once there, I found myself shouting more vehemently than ever before. It was all the stifled anger about you, I think, giving force to my protest. I might have been at a demonstration against what you did. Mortifying, really, to have one's convictions eclipsed by petty personal feelings. But perhaps that's human nature: what's most immediate is most affecting. Always has been, always will be. Any compassion or dismay we might feel for another's plight can easily be overridden by our own needs, be it the simple urge for a caffeine kick or the complex commands of the heart.

It's the violation of trust that most tears at me. My confidence in you came from the way you behaved the day I took you to meet my parents, a year into our life together. All they knew of you was your profession, your Anglicized nickname and the fact that we had met at a party. I hadn't told them more because I knew they would refuse to see you, and I'd thought that if I could just get you in front of them, they would forget all their prejudices. But the minute they saw your colour they became oblivious to everything else.

There was no handshake for you, no exhortation to take the comfortable armchair, no cruise through the family photo album. They couldn't look at you, except to snatch furtive glances – as if you were an alien. And Mum didn't address you directly even once. I went into the kitchen to help her, leaving you alone with dad, who sat with arms folded across his chest while his right leg shimmied in disapproval.

Mum was putting the shortbread she'd set out back into its tin.

– I thought you said his name was Harry.

– It is.

– He doesn't look like a Harry.

She started laying out some Digestives instead.

– Since when have names come with physical provisos?

– You know what I mean. I'm surprised your dad let him in.

The teacups rattled under her trembling hands.

– First Lucas takes up with a blackie. And now you with . . . this. I don't know what we did wrong.

– Oh Mum. Why is something wrong just because you don't like it?

I took the tray from her.

– It's wrong because it's wrong! And your dad and

I have to hear it from strangers. After Lucas brought home his hussy the whole street was talking. That Mrs Polter stopped me at the shop. Not a word in ten years and then she says, How can you let your only son associate with such scum?

She'd told me that story countless times. I started walking towards the sitting room and she called after me:

– They'll be saying the same of you now.

The silence between you and Dad was set like jelly. Your attempts to converse with him had been met with grunts, twitches and monosyllables. My efforts were scarcely more productive. Mum poured the tea from the pot, added milk and doled out the second-class biscuits. And, suddenly, I saw these conventions for what they are: the tacking of social exchange, loosely and temporarily holding together a situation when the hemming force of sympathy is absent.

My parents then proceeded to behave as though you weren't in the room: talking about people you didn't know, ignoring all references I made to you. I was mortified. I don't know how you remained so composed. I couldn't see your eyes because we were seated side by side on the sofa, but you sat very upright, your sharp profile betraying nothing. Suddenly I couldn't stand it any more. I said:

– I think we should go.

Simultaneously we set down our half-drunk teacups. The untouched biscuits jutted off over the edge of the saucers like vulgar accessories. I went on:

– I don't feel very welcome.

We stood up and so did Dad, pressing down on the armrest to push himself up.

– You are always welcome, dear.

– You're embarrassing me, Dad.

– And you're humiliating us, dear.

Oh that false civility of his. I could see him quaking beneath its plastic veneer.

You stepped forward then, and said you'd wait outside for me. You bade a quick goodbye to my parents and left. Of course, once you were gone all traces of courtesy also disappeared. Accusations were fired like bullets: How dare you? Are you out of your mind? Spit flew from Dad's mouth. He kept using the words irresponsible, obscene and unacceptable. Each time I tried to interrupt he shouted: I don't want to hear it! Mum started crying. You've ruined everything, she said. The melodrama of it! Yet, even though I despised their views, their judgements were wounding. Dad warned me never to take you back there again. Family, he hollered, is not a cocktail to be concocted with exotica filched from the streets.

When I came and joined you at the top of the street, you pulled out your hanky and wiped my eyes. We started walking towards the tube station, your arm over my shoulder. I kept apologizing, but you stopped me.

– I'm not surprised by their reaction. My family would be the same if I told them about you.

– Who do parents think they are? To decide for their children? They don't own us.

You shrugged in your typical way: a slow rolling back of the shoulders, while easing your head from side to side, as if you were trying to release a crick at the base of your neck.

– We all have our notions of right and wrong. It's

only natural to want to direct the ones you love towards what you think is correct.

I turned to face you, and we stood looking at each other, the tips of our noses almost touching, our eyes exactly level – I liked to believe our being of equal height was a sign of providence: we have the same view of the world, I used to joke. How utterly wrong I was! You may have been the same height as me, but you turned out to be a smaller person.

I wasn't going to let my parents decide how I should live. Never . . . Our will is the only thing we have that's absolutely ours. Even our best thoughts are just echoes of received ideas and impressions. We are most ourselves when we truly follow our deepest impulses through to action. I knew then that I would bear anything to be with you. I wished aloud that it wasn't so complicated. You said:

– Such difficulties will always be there. What we ought to remember is that at the level of the heart, which is what counts most, I am just another you.

That seemed to me the most beautiful sentiment in the world. We might have been each other, standing – toe to toe, face to face, eye to eye – on a north London street that autumn day. At least we believed in the possibility, which is sometimes enough. Even now, I want to believe it: that I am another you. Surely, surely, at heart we are all the same? It's in the head that conflict starts. It is the mind that misconstrues.

In the end, though, faith, that long-term resident of your mind, invaded and conquered your heart. Then I was no longer another, but other.

Advice

SHAREEF WAS ALREADY AWAKE when the alarm rang. He hadn't been able to sleep since Lina's call the previous day. He'd made it clear that he would have nothing more to do with her if she went ahead and married Anil. He shuddered, his body in rebellion against what his head had decreed.

'Shareef?' Iman shook him gently. She was more punctual than he was with the prayers these days.

'You start.' He kept his back to her. 'I'll join you in a minute.' He didn't feel like talking to God right now. He was too upset. Was this the reward for following his faith?

Part of him wished he could somehow agree to what Lina wanted. People found ways around religious laws all the time. He thought of how some Jews cleverly circumvented the more impractical rules of Shabbat. They took all sorts of measures, right down to putting lights and TVs on timers so they wouldn't have the 'work' of pressing a button. But the most ingenious practice he'd come across was that of extending the eruv, or boundary, of their private space by running a wire from their homes to other streets or buildings, so that they could legitimately move around on Shabbat. Lina had told him that in New York such eruvim even extended from some Jewish houses to the United Nations building. Would that he could widen the parameters of Allah's law with a piece of wire!

But such compromises were impossible for him. Once you started making exceptions you devalued the whole belief system.

People tried it in Islam as well. The process of conversion, for example, could be a farce. He had no doubt that if one truly believed in Allah, it was sufficient simply to recite the shahada in order to become a Muslim. *'I bear witness that there is no deity worthy of worship but Allah, and I bear witness that Muhammad is His servant and messenger'.* But it angered Shareef when unbelievers said this kalimah just to obtain the badge of Islam to legitimize a marriage. That was why even a conversion by Anil was not an option. You had to come to Islam with the heart, not just the lips.

Shareef told himself to get out of bed, but his limbs remained immobile, one forearm covering his eyes. He was still in no mood to pray. It was the first Fajr he had missed in years. He rubbed the mark on his forehead. It wouldn't fade away now, even if he stopped praying altogether. He was branded as pious for life. No one would know if he never did another prostration. Except God. And Iman, who rose from her mat asking if he was ill. He didn't feel too good, that was for sure.

Shareef shifted on to his other side, sighing heavily. Such bad judgement. What had he been thinking when he had fallen in with that guy's proposition? He'd agreed not to let on that he knew Lina was still with Anil because Merc had assured him they were about to break up anyway. He'd gone through all their differences in detail – social, financial, religious, ethnic, philosophical – and claimed that the couple were struggling, and wouldn't be able to survive the tensions of their disparate worlds. He'd told Shareef Anil's parents were against the match as well, and none of Anil's friends liked Lina. And he'd also warned that interfering might be the one thing that would make them cleave to each other. 'I'm telling you, just leave it. This thing is going to unravel itself. You get me?' Those had been Merc's words. Unravel indeed. Looked more like they'd ended up knotted together.

Shareef felt the uneasy tug of shame at the hem of his conscience. Nothing had been achieved by following that avenue. Ya Allah, he thought, la ilaha ill Allah. There is no God but God. Al-Hakim, the Wise. Al-Alim, the Omniscient. The invocations worked like a key, unlocking a spirituality from which he had unwittingly sealed himself off. He pushed himself up, swung his legs over the side of the bed, and set his feet on the floor, before nudging them into a pair of woollen slippers. Astaghfirullah, silently he asked for God's forgiveness. As he went to wash his face and hands Shareef realized that he had set store by the wrong things. He had looked for solutions in the wrong place. The lesson – to be learned all over again – was to put his faith in God alone.

Anil arrived in New York and took a plane straight back to Nairobi again. By then he was already repenting his actions. The endless expanse of emptiness outside his window echoed what he felt inside. All those hours, suspended in mid-air, were a taste of existence without Lina. The fact of her absence pushed against him, so heavy it made his breath strain.

It was ridiculous that they should let themselves be kept apart. How had it come to this? Could he really be outdone by a non-existent being and a stubborn old man? He resolved to try again. His anguish began to abate the moment this intention declared itself.

As soon as he reached Nairobi again he tried to call

Lina. The satellite phone in Sudan didn't seem to be working – he got a long flat bleep each time he dialled. She might not even be there. Perhaps she was still in Nairobi – or maybe she'd gone back to her parents in the UK. He'd email her when he got home. He'd explain everything. There was no way she wouldn't agree.

Anil got the cab to leave him at the gate of the Mayur residence. He walked up the drive and went towards the back entrance of the house, hoping to slip in and freshen up without bumping into his parents. He entered the house, and was creeping past the kitchen when he heard Merc's voice. It was unmistakable: the thick, boisterous heft of his friend speaking in Swahili: 'If you've made it, Mama Jo, it's bound to be good.'

Then a grey rubber sole, with its red strip of branding running from the bottom up and round the back of the heel, hooked around the half-shut door pulling it open – and there was Merc.

'You're back!' He spoke with his mouth full, crumbs of rock cake on his lips. He had one of the warm, freshly baked little cakes in each hand. 'I was about to go – thought I'd missed you again. Where have you been, mazeh? You look like shit.'

Anil was unshaven and oily-faced. It looked as though he'd used his clothes to dry himself after a shower and then put them on immediately: his trousers were crumpled, and the collars on his shirt and jacket were flaccid, the corners curling.

Right then Anil decided he was never going to tell anyone about the abortive trip. 'Heavy night,' he said.

Merc finished one rock cake and extended his free arm over Anil's shoulders.

'Are you OK?'

'Why shouldn't I be?'

'What's that smell?' Merc bent towards Anil. 'You wearing perfume or something, mazeh?'

'It's probably the hotel shower gel.' Actually, it was the scent of Lina's face cream that Merc must have picked up. Anil hadn't been able to sneak the bottle past security in New York, so he'd liberally slathered the contents over his hands, neck and face before dropping it into a bin of similar products. For a while, the aroma had nursed his longing for Lina. Then he'd got used to it, catching only a slight, occasional whiff, which had tugged at his senses, strengthening his determination, making him adamant about being with her again.

'Doesn't suit you.' Merc wrinkled his nose.

Anil started walking again and Merc followed, stuffing the last cake into his mouth.

'So, come on, where have you been?' Merc expected Anil would now tell him about the break-up.

Anil didn't say anything.

A kink appeared across Merc's brow. 'I know you weren't with Lina because I saw her yesterday—'

Anil stopped. They were in the middle of the house, the circular staircase winding imperiously above them. 'Where?'

'At Wilson Airport.' Merc watched him closely. 'She was getting a flight back to Juba.'

'How was she?' Anil's hand ran along the strap of the bag hanging from his shoulder.

Merc rubbed his tongue over the ridges of his teeth. 'She seemed fine.'

'Fine?' Anil's voice rose without him realizing.

'Yeah – why? Shouldn't she be?'

Anil shook his head, nodded. 'So she's there now.' He'd

try the satellite phone again, see how she really was. She'd probably put on a brave face for Merc. Didn't want him gloating.

Merc noted the emphasis on 'there'. He had one hand on his hip while the other rubbed his chin. 'She was eager to get back. Keen to hook up with her crew of do-gooders, no doubt. She mentioned that guy who's always wearing a denim jacket.'

Hans! She'd been talking about *him*? After all that had happened? Hans? The bag slipped off Anil's shoulder and landed on the floor with a soft thud. 'What about me?' His eyes scanned Merc's face. 'Did she say anything about me?' His voice was unnaturally loud again.

'Why are you shouting, mazeh? What's the matter?' Now Merc had both hands on his hips. His fingers made little creases in the soft fabric of his trousers.

'Just tell me what she said!' Anil grabbed the collar of Merc's shirt.

'I thought I heard your voice!' Minnie hurried up, her long silk maxi rustling.

'Tell me!' Anil repeated.

'Nothing.' The word was forced out of a clenched jaw. 'She hardly said your name.'

'What's going on?' Pravar was just behind Minnie.

'We were just talking.' Anil let go of the shirt.

Merc ran a palm over the firework-pattern of creases on his chest.

'Where have you been, Anil?' Minnie started patting his cheeks and smoothing his hair.

'You're a mess,' Pravar said. He had a laptop, on which he'd been checking share prices, tucked under one arm.

You're one to talk, Anil thought. His dad wasn't wearing

his turban. He looked like a stocky Red Indian with his thinning hair in a sparse ponytail.

'Why are you having a go at Merc?' Minnie sniffed several times as a stale, sweet smell hit her nose. 'He's been worried about you. He was here yesterday as well, looking for you. I thought you were with Lina.'

'Since when do I have to account for my whereabouts every minute of the day?' Anil stepped away.

'Eh – don't take that tone with your mother.' Pravar raised his index and middle finger, pointing them at the ceiling. His voice echoed slightly in the large space. 'She's just concerned about you. We all are.'

'Well, I'm fine. I need a shower.' He picked up his bag again.

'I don't like the effect that girl has on you.' Pravar's top lip curled as though it was being pulled by some invisible thread. 'She ruined the evening on Friday, and now you come back from spending a few days with her looking like you've failed an obstacle course.'

Merc scratched the dip between his nose and upper lip. Now, he thought, Anil would announce that he was no longer with Lina, and shut Pravar up.

But Anil just hoisted his bag over his other shoulder, as if it was really heavy. He felt trapped by the triumvirate of disapproval.

'So what's the story, mazeh?' Merc tried again. 'Why weren't you with her?'

'I don't need this interrogation.' His eyes fixed on Merc.

'Why are you always the one running after her?' Pravar set the laptop on the third step from the bottom. 'If you left her alone for a while maybe she'd see what she's missing and come after you for a change.'

'You don't even know what's going on.' Anil

made a little U-turn and started up the marble stairs.

'As far as I can see, nothing is happening! No. Nothing at all!' Pravar threw his hands into the air. 'Stasis! That's the story of your life with her. Yes. Completely. And, believe me, nothing will change, if you continue like this.'

Anil continued to walk up, taking two steps at a time. He didn't need romantic advice from his father, of all people.

'You think all this waiting bullshit is going to work?' Pravar went after him.'You need to finish the relationship or do something to show her you're not going to hang around until the end of time. Otherwise, she's never going to decide. Oi! Anil. Listen to me.' Pravar panted to the top step. Minnie and Merc followed.

'This isn't one of your business transactions, Dad. You can't run people's hearts the way you do your companies.' Anil stood with one hand on the banister.

'Listen.' Pravar wagged a finger. 'I have only one rule for all circumstances: Don't let people treat you like a fool. If you want to be taken seriously, you have to show you're capable of tough action. Absolutely. My name is on the door. I decide who comes through it, and if I don't like the way they behave, I throw them out.'

'If you ask me, mazeh, I think it's high time you showed Lina the door,' Merc said.

'Yes, that would be the best thing.' Pravar slapped a palm against his own thigh.

'How can the girl go on respecting you, if you put up with all her maneno?'

'I've got things under control, OK?'

'The hell you have,' Merc said under his breath, 'you didn't even know where she was.' He went on, despite another reproachful glance from Anil. 'You're not in control of anything, mazeh, least of all yourself.'

'So now all of you know better than me how to live my life?'

'There are a hundred girls in this city who would marry you like this.' Pravar clicked his fingers. 'But you're fixed on one blockhead who's too scared of her family and her God to make any proper commitment. What's so special about her and her people? If we can accept the idea of you being with a Muslim, why can't they do the same?'

Anil's face twitched as though he was trying to ease an itch in his nostrils.

'Listen to your dad.' Minnie went up to Anil, her hands clenching and unclenching. 'He has a good idea, that's what I think. Tell him, Pravar.'

Anil sighed. He knew any plan hatched by his father was bound to be dodgy. Pravar outlined his preferred course of action. Anil remained impassive, while scepticism squirmed all over Merc's face. Minnie drummed her fingers against each other, her freshly manicured red nails reflecting light from the bulbs above.

'That will take ages,' Anil said when Pravar had finished.

'No – it doesn't have to, Neelu.' Minnie pawed him as if he was an animal that needed calming. 'I can start things rolling tomorrow. And it could all be finalized in a few weeks – depends on you, I think.'

'I don't see the point.' Merc's left thigh pressed against the shiny curves of the glass banister. 'Why set up such an elaborate ploy to trap Lina? It shouldn't be necessary.'

Anil chewed the insides of his cheeks. He didn't especially like Pravar's idea – but nor was he ready to give up on Lina. He tensed at the thought of what Merc had said about seeing her the previous day. She might be with that Hans right now. He shut his eyes, wincing unconsciously.

'So?' Pravar demanded.

'Don't do it.' Merc took a step towards his friend, as if he might be able to restrain him physically from making the wrong choice.

'What's the alternative?' Minnie cried. 'We have to do something!' She sidled closer to her son.

'Forget her. Nothing you do will work. Just forget her,' Merc urged.

'That's probably the better alternative.' Pravar joined the other two thronging around Anil.

'I can't forget her!' he shouted. His arms flew out to emphasize his vehemence, and one hit Merc.

Merc sprang back. 'You're a lost cause as far she's concerned.' He went to the staircase, perched on the handrail and slid down it, the way they used to when they were kids. 'A fucking lost cause!' he called from the bottom.

'He's right.' Pravar's tone was stern. 'Either you forget that woman or you take the course I've suggested.'

Anil took a deep breath. 'I'll do it.' What did he have to lose?

Eid

THE HOUSE WAS STILL saturated with the smells of celebration, even though Eid was almost over: aromas of fried foods, meaty curries and burning candles clung to the air. In the living room, a few guests lingered, too full to heave themselves off the sofa and out of the door. One dozed in an easy chair, hands cupped around his paunch, stains of lamb pilau on the sweater that was pulled over his white kurta pyjama. All of the other three men present, including Shareef, were similarly dressed in long tunics with matching baggy trousers. They lounged on the sofa, chatting and half-listening to the prayers being broadcast live from Mecca on a satellite TV channel.

Mariam wandered in, at Iman's instruction, and collected the empty teacups that were sitting on side tables or balancing on armrests. Behind her was Nasra, who had a big black bin-bag in one hand and was crouching down to pick up the torn wrapping paper and ribbon from all the presents that had been exchanged and opened earlier.

Back in the kitchen Mariam dumped the dirty crockery on the counter.

'Now can I go up to my room?' She unwound the salmon-coloured chuni that was looped around her neck, scratching at a spot where the embroidery on the garment had grazed her skin.

Iman looked around, checking whether there was anything else she could get the girl to do. Empty pans and platters lined the table where the buffet had been laid. The floor was scattered with grains of rice, the odd chickpea and a few shards of lettuce. 'First sweep around here, before we crush all this mess under our feet.'

Mariam's upper body flopped forward as though a huge load had been placed on her back. 'I've been working like a slave the whole day!'

'What-weh? And I've just been sitting around, have I? The food and presents all arrived miraculously out of nowhere, did they?' Iman shook her head. Small gold hoops swung at her lobes.

Mariam made a face but went to get the broom.

Iman returned to scraping leftovers on to one plate before handing dishes to Ruksana to be stacked in the dishwasher. Bending was still tricky: her coccyx remained tender, even though the fracture had healed.

'Don't be angry.' Ruksana flinched at the sound of metal banging against porcelain. 'We've had such a nice day. It's just a shame Lina isn't here.'

Iman sighed. Eid was the one occasion on which, she'd imagined, the whole family would always come together. And now, for the first time, Lina wasn't there. Possibly wouldn't ever be again.

Later, Iman asked Ruksana to join her for a walk to the small park nearby. Such gentle activity, more than anything else, helped the stiffness that sometimes built up in her lower back. She arched and rounded her spine a few times while Ruksana buttoned up Yusuf's jacket.

'You overdid it with the cooking, of course.' Ruksana gave her a sidelong glance as they headed down the street, Yusuf in tow holding both their hands. 'But I suspect the main reason for all your tension is the business with Lina.'

'When she agreed to the introductions I took it as a sign that she was over the other boy.' Iman pulled her shawl closer over her shoulders. 'I would never have believed she could pretend the way she has done. It's like she's two different people!'

'She's been divided in herself. Think of what she must be going through.' Ruksana pulled away some strands of hair that the wind had fixed to her lipstick. 'It's no wonder her actions seem confused.'

'Oh what-weh, Rocky, you're just like Shareef,' Iman complained. The sun hung low above them, pinned to the sky by chimneys. 'You make everything grey even when it's black and white. If he had really put his foot down . . .' She paused and stamped a heel. 'We wouldn't be in this position.'

'There's not much else he could have done, was there, Iman?'

'Other people manage to stop their daughters!'

'Yes, but how? With threats and violence and forced marriage? Is that what you want?'

'She refuses to speak to us.' Iman stared down at the footpath as they walked. 'For all we know she could be married!'

'You can't be sure—'

'Why else would she have cut herself off? I've begged Shareef to try and find out what's really going on, but he refuses. He's convinced Lina will inform us of the situation in her own time.'

'I think Shareef's being very magnanimous,' Ruksana said. 'Don't underestimate him. You must have faith, Iman. All this praying you've started doing, and still you can't leave things in God's hands. Remember the story of

Ibrahim and Ishmael in the Koran? Ibrahim was willing to sacrifice his son, but God intervened at the last moment and everything was OK.'

'What-weh?' Iman stopped. 'You think Shareef is being like Ibrahim?' It had never occurred to her to look at things that way.

'Well . . .' Ruksana tried to restrain Yusuf, who was running in impatient circles around them. 'I think he's able to let Lina go because he believes that Allah will bring her back.'

The explanation appealed to Iman. She was about to say more when some people they knew stopped and greeted them.

'And how is Lina?' one woman asked from behind a burka. Her eyes glinted through the slit in the black fabric swathing her body.

'They know something is up,' Iman whispered as they went on. 'Now that Lina lives abroad and hardly ever comes home. And because of all the introductions I've set up, which she somehow managed not to follow through with. People have become suspicious.'

'Soon something else will happen, and then they'll all be fixed on that. You know how it is,' Ruksana said. They walked into a tarmacked square, studded with a few trees, which served as a playground. In the far corner were the swings, Yusuf's favourite.

'Oh there's enough other stuff going on.' Iman started to elaborate, and then stopped herself. How could you talk about what was stewing in others' lives, when your own saucepan was leaking? 'I'm going to sit down,' she told her sister.

Iman headed to one of the benches. Why had this happened to them? Where had she gone wrong? Five times a day now, she put this question to Allah, asking for his guidance, pleading for his forgiveness; as if she could pray her way back to having an obedient child.

Confusion

THE LANDSCAPE WAS a palette of browns pitched against blue sky. Lina watched as the land cruiser she was in passed by yet another half-finished mud-brick building: a skeleton of walls with no roof, and gaps for doors and windows. She wondered if whoever was responsible for the construction got distracted halfway through, lost interest, or simply ran out of materials. There were countless similar structures all over South and West Sudan, apt symbols for the state of the country.

Since the break-up with Anil, Lina had kept volunteering to do all kinds of fieldwork in an attempt to get further away from the reality of her own life. She had spent the last week in Jonglei province doing an assessment of education facilities. Most donors were focused on meeting immediate humanitarian needs. Lina felt this was shortsighted. Education could give hope to children traumatized by the war. It would help to ease the transition back to ordinary life once the fighting was over. She'd therefore made it her mission to help on this front. The tiny UN budget had been supplemented by a generous donation from the Mayurs. She'd requested their help before Merc had told her about Pravar trading arms illegally. Afterwards she'd been uncertain about whether or not to use the money. Finally, she'd decided that it was justified because the need in Sudan was too great. It would be foolish to spurn anything that could improve conditions in the country.

So she and two colleagues had travelled around South Sudan with supplies of chalk, pens and notebooks. Their offerings were at once essential and irrelevant. People were being taught despite all the privations forced on them by circumstances. A crudely hung blackboard was all a place needed to turn it into a centre of education. In most villages, teachers had no textbooks and children learned without paper to write on. Lina had seen schools where kids of all ages sat cross-legged on the dusty floor, craning towards the teacher, tongues curled over upper lips in concentration. Sometimes, there were up to ninety students in a single class. One twelve-year-old boy, his eyes big with earnestness, said: 'I have learned to listen very carefully to the teachers. I write everything in my head.' Others admitted to hoarding cardboard whenever they could get hold of any, and separating the layers to use as paper for taking notes.

The voice of the driver, Garang, interrupted Lina's thoughts: 'We should be back in Juba within an hour.'

She had lost all track of time. Only the sun dipping in the distance hinted that evening was approaching. Otherwise, she struggled to recall what day it might be, or even which month. This was partly due to the state she'd been in since coming back from Nairobi three weeks ago. But the uniformity of conditions in this part of Sudan also confused her: there was always the same blistering heat. The locals were more attuned to its every fluctuation. This morning the guards outside her tukul had been huddled together, rubbing their hands, their faces obscured by winter jackets, hoods and scarves. Even now, in the jeep, several people were swathed in woollen vests and coats.

There had been a drop in temperature over the last days: from 45°C to 30°C. But for a non-desert dweller like Lina, the heat was still too intense. She couldn't wait to strip off her clothes and have a shower.

At the entrance of the compound, a tattered UN flag drooped. Lina was barely out of the car when Jen accosted her.

'Just in time! Get ready. The Médecins Sans Frontières guys are having a party tonight. We need to leave in half an hour.'

'I'm so tired.' Lina searched for the key to open the pad-lock on the door of her container.

'You'll be fine after freshening up.' Jen followed Lina into her room.

Lina threw her keys on the table and set her bag on the floor before flopping on to the bed. Above her hung the mosquito net, twisted into a knot. 'I missed this.' She poked it with her foot. A couple of the guest houses she'd stayed in during her trip hadn't had nets. 'Look at the state of me.' She pulled up her trousers and then her sleeves to show Jen the red bumps all over her skin.

'Why didn't you take one along?' Jen made a face.

'Stupidity. I expected better conditions.'

'*Better?* You should know by now that Juba is the most sophisticated place in the South. Things start to deteriorate as soon as you leave the outskirts of this city. I hope you're taking your malaria tablets.' Jen opened a cupboard and peered at Lina's clothes.

'What does Astrid want to borrow?' They went through the same ritual each time there was a social gathering.

Jen smiled, then pulled out a black top with ruched sleeves. It was the only smart piece of clothing Lina had with her, something she'd worn whenever she'd headed back to Nairobi. She wondered if she'd ever again step into that walk-in wardrobe in the Mayur house where all her nicer things were stored.

'Why doesn't she come and get it herself?' Lina yawned.

'Too busy painting her face. With four women to every guy here, a girl has to make an effort.' Jen closed the cupboard again. 'Sometimes I think I should write to the recruitment office and tell them they need to review their equal-opportunity obligations.'

'They do seem to have got a bit carried away with the positive discrimination.' Lina's eyes brightened momentarily.

'You're lucky you've got your Prince Charming in Nairobi.' Jen started meddling in one of the desk drawers.

Lina stared at the low ceiling, not seeing the three lizards lounging there. When she'd first arrived in Juba, she hadn't been able to sleep for fear that these creatures would crawl on her during the night. Now she scarcely noticed them, or the crickets that hopped amongst her possessions, or the hedgehogs in the compound. She even thought nothing of swallowing the odd insect that inevitably drowned in the local honey.

She scratched at one of her mosquito bites. None of her colleagues knew what was really going on in her personal life. She'd pretended to be ill several times over the last weeks and spent the days listlessly in her room, praying that the phone would ring or the computer would blip an alert about an email from Anil. But there had been nothing. All she was left with was the awful feeling that she'd made a bad mistake. She still wasn't sure exactly where her error lay. She was a ball of misery trapped in a cage that only Anil could open. She could not reach out to him herself – knowing what she did, and being quite aware that the knowledge had not changed her feelings or settled her loyalties.

'It's lucky for us, too,' Jen was saying. 'We wouldn't be able to wear your nice things if you were out to impress the guys here. Can I use some of this?' She raised a bottle of scent.

'Not that there's anyone I'd want to impress, anyway!' Lina rolled on to one side and watched Jen squirt perfume behind her ears and at her wrists.

'Of course, no one can compete with a Prince Charming who sends private planes for his princess! I think the guys don't make passes at you because they know what they're up against.'

Lina got up, went to the small table and took her laptop from one of the drawers. She hadn't yet told anyone that those flights had stopped for good. 'I need to check my email.' Ya Allah, she begged silently, let there be a message from him.

'That'll take ages! And you still haven't had a shower.' Jen looked at her watch.

'I'm not even sure if I'm going to join you.' Lina's computer hummed and flickered into action.

'You're coming. No arguments.' Jen poked her between the shoulder blades.

'You just want someone who's sober to drive you back later!'

'Exactly. You can't deny us our small pleasures in this place. I might have to go and raid Astrid's boudoir for some finishing touches.' Jen moved towards the door. 'She's the Queen of Accessories.' Astrid maintained a pretty high standard of grooming, despite all the privations of the place. 'We'll come back to get you at seven, OK?'

* * *

There was nothing from Anil. Instead, a message from Hans which she didn't open, and also several messages from friends and acquaintances in Nairobi expressing regret that she and Anil had broken up. '*I had no idea . . .*' one started. Another expressed shock – '*. . . can't believe he's already engaged to Preeti Devani*'. '*Hope you're OK*', they all wrote. Lina read this in disbelief, convinced that there must be some misunderstanding. But then the fact that Anil hadn't tried to contact her made her fearful it might be true. She rushed to the bag she'd flung at the foot of her bed and searched for the satellite phone. She dialled the number incorrectly three times before finally getting through to Anil's mobile. He answered almost immediately: 'Hi!'

At the sound of his voice, a confusion of relief and pain heaved through her. Contorting her face against the impulse to start sobbing, she spoke. 'I don't . . . I haven't heard from you.' She managed to produce some semblance of a sentence.

'Why were you expecting to?' His casualness made her feel worse. She couldn't know how his heart was charging, his brain tingling from the fact that she'd called.

She didn't answer, afraid that if she tried to say more she'd cry.

'So, um, what's going on?' He seemed distracted, as if he was doing something else at the same time. She couldn't have imagined he was gesturing to excuse himself from a table at the Muthaiga Country Club, where Preeti Devani and several other people were seated.

Unable to stand his indifference she began to weep. 'I saw . . . I had . . .' She was like an asthmatic having an attack, gulping and gasping. 'These emails.' The words were expelled roughly between breaths. 'They say. You. You're engaged. There's someone else. I read . . .'

'News gets around fast.' Anil made his way outside. So the gossips had done their work. He'd made a point of being seen with Preeti in public, knowing that word would quickly spread, and hopefully reach Lina, too. 'My parents arranged one of those introductions – like your family did. And, yeah, things have progressed quicker than expected.'

'It all sounds so . . . final.' Hearing him confirm the engagement made her feel their estrangement even more keenly. 'I didn't expect . . .' She heard the irrelevance of her own words. What *had* she expected? Not this. Not this. She pressed a hand over her mouth, blocking the cries that filled it.

'You thought I'd keep my life on hold for you even after you walked out on me?'

'I didn't!' Her breathing was as ragged as a curtain thrashing in the wind.

'Come on, Lina. You made yourself clear that day. Why have you called now?'

Yes, indeed, why? She had acted without thinking – again. Just followed her heart, which led her to one impasse after another. 'You have no idea what I'm going through! You've never understood anything! And now, after just a few weeks, you're ready to up and marry—' The betrayal seared. She doubled over, the phone still pressed to her ear.

'You left me no choice! I always had the raw deal in our relationship.'

'For God's sake!' Her speech kept being snapped by sobs. 'Anil! You've had it easy all your life.'

'Until I met you.' He was oblivious to the sidelong looks of golfers returning from their game for refreshment.

'If you agreed to marry me now nobody else would count. But no. That would be too simple.'

'There's no such thing as simple, Anil! That's what you've never understood.' The phone slipped from her hand and fell to the floor, switching itself off.

Anil stared at his handset, gave it a little shake. 'Lina? What are you saying?' When he realized she'd hung up he flung the phone into some nearby bushes.

'Lina?' Jen poked her head through the door. She'd expected to have to wait for Lina or chivvy her along – but there was no way she'd anticipated finding her choking with tears and hunched over her desk. Jen hurried into the room, a long chain of turquoise and black stones swinging from her neck.

Astrid came after her, high-heels clicking, wooden bangles jangling. 'Lina, what is it?'

Lina raised her head. Her skin was splatted with moisture, as though every pore was weeping.

'Are you ill?' Jen put a hand on her hot forehead, wondering whether malaria could have set in so quickly.

'You've had bad news?' Astrid had almost stepped on the satellite phone. She picked it up and set it on the desk beside the laptop, which was still lying open. 'Is it your boyfriend?'

Lina's mouth and cheeks began quivering.

'Oh no.' Jen gave her a hug. 'I'm so sorry. Has something happened to him?'

Astrid stood with one hand on her hip. 'He's been unfaithful, or?' She said this as if it was as normal as going for a walk.

Lina shook her head, nodded, the upper half of her body convulsed. 'He's marrying someone else.'

'What?' Jen knelt beside the chair and took Lina's hand.

'Just like that? Out of the blue?' Astrid gasped, then shrugged. 'So typical for a man.'

'How could he?' Jen squeezed Lina's fingers. 'He obviously doesn't deserve you.'

'No, for sure not. There's something better waiting for you, and we're going to start looking for it now.' Astrid picked up the towel that was hanging on one door of the wardrobe and passed it to Lina. 'Take a shower and then we can get out of here.'

'I'm not going anywhere.' Lina wiped her eyes on her arm.

'Well, then we'll stay with you.' Jen ignored Astrid's glare.

'No, you guys go. I'll be fine.' Stringy muscles stood out on Lina's neck from the effort of trying to stop crying.

'Doesn't make sense to sit around and feel bad.' Astrid made Jen move aside. 'Come on.' She pulled Lina up. 'You're better off being distracted than staying here and thinking non-stop on this guy.' There was no way Astrid was going to miss the MSF party. On the other hand, she wasn't keen to go on her own.

'Maybe Astrid is right. He's not worth moping over,' Jen said. They bundled Lina towards the shower room despite her protestations.

She did feel slightly better once she was washed and in fresh clothes – though she kept on crying. She caught sight of her puffy face in the mirror as she brushed her hair. 'I'm not fit to go out. Please. I don't mind being here alone. I'll probably go straight to bed.'

'OK.' Jen turned to Astrid, who was using the sharp end of a safety pin to separate her eyelashes, which had clogged together thanks to some lumpy, sand-contaminated mascara.

'This stupid desert of a place has ruined all my products,' Astrid muttered.

'Why don't we just sit with Lina for a bit and maybe go to the party later?' Jen proposed.

'Doesn't make sense. We'll be worrying about her the whole evening.' Astrid admired herself in the mirror and then looked at Lina. 'Trust me. You don't really want to be alone. You're going to get depressed if we leave you here. I know this exactly from my own experiences. You have to come.' She threw the pin back into her handbag and snapped it shut. 'I promise it's the right thing.'

All Lina could do was follow when the two women linked their arms through hers and led her out.

'My phone,' she said as Jen locked the door.

'You don't need it,' Astrid said. 'He won't call. And if he does you shouldn't speak to him anyway.'

Anil walked through the grounds of the country club, hands thrust into his pockets, chin tucked into his chest. He could hear balls being hit around the tennis courts nearby: a steady thwack, thwack, thwack. It matched the volley of thoughts inside his head.

What had Lina said at the end? He wondered if he'd misheard. The line was very scratchy. And maybe she hadn't hung up. The connection was so poor, their calls were regularly cut off. Perhaps she was trying to ring him back right this minute. He swung around and headed back towards the spot where he'd thrown the phone.

Above him the needle-shaped leaves of juniper trees lapped at the air. Still higher, clouds the colour of bruises scudded across the sky, in a fierce wind. He saw Preeti walk across the lawn towards him, her red dress like the lick of a flame burning through the landscape – and his conscience.

Anil pretended not to have noticed her. He realized his phone had probably landed in a rose bush. The flowers had fat, buttery petals tinged pink along the edges, as if they'd been sunburned. He bent over, peering through them in search of the silvery piece of metal that might reconnect him with Lina.

'Is everything all right?' Preeti touched his shoulder.

Anil crouched lower, out of her reach. 'I dropped my phone.' He might as well have told her to shut up and go away, so brutal was his tone.

She stood still, unsure what to do. 'Do you need help? Should I get someone?'

His response was to delve into the bush, pushing aside branches and swearing when the thorns clipped at his skin. Preeti went off to seek assistance, but by the time she returned with a waiter Anil was up, and brushing the mud from his hands and elbows. The knees of his ribbed pants were marked with round patches of soil.

Preeti didn't know what to make of him – this man who'd agreed to meet her with a view to getting married. He didn't seem at all interested in getting to know her. Each time he'd taken her out he'd spent more time chatting to other people. She'd only ever seen him in a group. It was as though he was afraid of being alone with her. And his mother claimed he'd once had a huge crush on her! There certainly didn't appear to be any residues of that. Preeti had some recollection of the summer that he'd tried to pursue her. Back then, she'd been too involved with someone else to give Anil a thought. Only now had she realized what a good catch he was. One of the most eligible bachelors in Nairobi, it was said. She could do a lot worse than end up hitched to him. Especially after the scandal she'd narrowly avoided. Not a hint of which, luckily, the Mayurs seemed to have heard.

'I've got to go.' There was no sign of a missed call from Lina on his phone. Anil picked a thorn from the pad of flesh on his palm, near his thumb. A ruby bead sprouted in its wake.

'Sssss.' Preeti winced. She spotted a few other scratches on his arms, all lined with delicate threads of blood.

Anil put the wound to his mouth and sucked it. Then he rubbed his palm on his trousers and set off towards his car. 'I've really got to go.' She was so taken aback he was impelled to add an apology. 'Sorry, but I do.' He started walking away.

'Will you join us for dinner later?' Preeti followed him.

'No.' He quickened his pace.

'And tomorrow? Are we still on for golf?'

'I don't think so.'

Janjaweed Juice

THERE WERE ABOUT twenty people in the MSF compound, only three of them male. Everyone was in the common kitchen and living space – a mud-brick building that had actually been completed for a change. A pool table filled one end of the room, and several people were gathered around that. The rest had split into little groups and were chatting over plastic cups filled with Janjaweed Juice, a potent local brew. No one could take a sip without grimacing.

'Are those real cornflakes?' Lina spotted two boxes of the cereal pushed into a corner on the wooden kitchen counter. Her mouth suddenly watered, craving their bland crunch. She hadn't eaten anything since a bowl of sorghum posho that morning.

'Can you believe it?' Celia, one of the MSF staff, nodded. 'It's been luxury here every morning this week. We've even got crisps.' She gestured towards the table where several bowls were set out.

'Please can I have some cornflakes?' Lina sheepishly put a hand in front of her face.

'Dude, we're all drinking Janjaweed Juice and you want, like, cornflakes?' A guy called Jason, whom Lina had just met, walked away in disdain, pushing a bottle of Juice into one of the pockets of his combat trousers. But Celia was already filling a bowl and pouring over some powdered milk.

'Where did you find this stuff?' Jen asked. Such items usually only appeared after someone had made a trip to Khartoum or Nairobi.

'Henry got the cornflakes.' Celia pointed to one of the guys playing pool. 'From the African Union troops, apparently.'

'Hold on a sec.' Jen stuck out her hip. 'The AU? The guys who don't have enough fuel for their cars or enough ammunition for their weapons? The guys who come to *us* asking for blankets? *They* have cornflakes?' She tugged at the necklace she'd borrowed from Astrid.

Everyone was more dressed up than usual: the women wearing skirts and lipstick, the guys freshly shaved and in clean shirts. Lina was the odd one out, in trousers and without a shred of make-up. She'd asked Jen and Astrid not to say anything about what had happened. A few people had asked if she was OK, and seemed to accept it when she said she was tired after her trip to Jonglei.

'That's the most delicious thing I've eaten in weeks!' Lina went to get a second helping. She felt better just from having a little food inside her. And her friends had been right: it did help to be among people rather than alone in her room, fixed on her interminable dilemmas. Although now – every muscle stiffened – they had ended, at last. She stopped eating. It didn't feel true. She recalled the emails, the subsequent phone conversation with Anil. Her whole being recoiled from the memory as a body might reject an implanted organ. She pushed away the bowl of cereal.

'Look at them.' Astrid tossed her head in the direction of the guys. All three were congregated around the pool table, handling cues and balls like they were the most exciting things in the world. 'You think they might make more of an effort with us.' She blinked rapidly, silver glitter sparkling over her thickly painted lashes.

'What do you expect?' Jen pulled a chair out from under the long wooden table and flopped into it. 'They've become lazy. With five of us to every one of them they seem to think we're the ones who need to seduce them. No doubt they'll roll up to one of us after drinking too much Juice and act like they're doing us a really big favour.' She peered into the bowls on the table. Two were half-filled with crisps, the other two contained freshly extinguished cigarette butts.

'I tell you.' Celia sat down as well, and the other women followed. 'Even their chat-up lines have deteriorated. I'm not saying any names, but two of those guys . . .' She indicated with her thumb towards the men at the back of the room, '. . . have tried to lure me back to their rooms with, "I've seen so much today, I just can't face sleeping alone." '

Laughter spouted around the table.

'So, did you go?' Jen asked, though all of them already knew how the proposition must have been received.

Celia spread her palms and held them up in surrender. 'Desperate times call for desperate capitulations.'

'They are even giving so terrible excuses when they don't want to see you.' Astrid set down her cup and started imitating. ' "I can't come for a while, babe, there's no fuel for the WFP plane." '

Jen joined in with, ' "I can't risk driving over because the wadi is too high and one of the cars almost tipped over trying to get out of here yesterday." '

' "There's a curfew in the town because of riots. I have to be in bed by eight," ' another woman said.

Celia shrieked and tapped the table a few times with

her cup to get the attention of the women collapsing into giggles around her. ' "I'll come see you next week, honey. I've just got to pass out food to ten thousand people first." '

'You're joking, right?' Jen could hardly talk she was laughing so hard. 'You made up that last one?'

Lina pushed her features into an expression of merriment, trying to blend in.

'Looks like all the fun is happening around this table.' The deep voice with a foreign lilt sounded familiar.

Those sitting with their backs to the speaker, including Lina, turned. It was Hans.

'Can I join you, ladies?'

They all sprang up to make space for him, except Lina. She had had no idea he was around. Her heart quickened. They hadn't met since Merc's disclosure. She'd emailed him less frequently since, too afraid of the implications of the information she was withholding. He winked at her as he sat down at the other end of the table, between Astrid and Celia. The conversation turned to politics. He'd just come from Darfur, where there had been more government attacks.

'Omar al-Bashir is giving oil to the Chinese in return for dollars and arms,' Hans said. 'His government is pocketing the cash and using the weapons against its own people.' He took a large sip of Janjaweed Juice and shivered as he swallowed. 'And the rest of the world doesn't give a damn.'

'It's too bad for your disarmament programme, neh?' Astrid aimed some broken crisps into her mouth, but they missed and landed on Hans's lap. 'Oh! Sorry!' She went at his thigh with both hands, as if to massage the crisps away.

Jen leaned against Lina and whispered, 'Did you see that? She practically threw those into his crotch!'

Lina mustered a half-hearted reply. 'I'm sure it was an accident.'

Hans had risen slightly to brush off his trousers – and Astrid's hands. 'Yah, my project is taking off very slowly.' His eyes travelled around the table and rested on Lina. 'Even I don't feel right about asking civilians to give up their guns with the Janjaweed on the loose.' His broad chest rose and fell as he took a deep breath and exhaled noisily 'Nobody would believe there's an arms embargo on this country. We've spotted Chinese-made Fantan jets in Nyala province, and Russian-made helicopters in Darfur. None of these transfers have been reported to the UN. Ask how they got there, and no one has a clue. '

Astrid moved her chair closer to his. 'It's all so stressy, neh? You need to relax a bit.'

'I'm OK,' Hans said.

'Always when you're around, Hans-Schatzie, the conversation is getting so heavy. You need to let yourself think on other things.' She linked arms with him.

'Reality is hard, Astrid.' Hans extricated his limb. 'If you'd rather not look on it maybe you should have gone to work for a fashion magazine.'

'Such a tone! Come on!' Astrid's blusher-enhanced cheekbones protruded. 'Don't pretend to be superman. We all need a break sometimes.' She sidled up to him again.

'That monster Bashir should be forced to step down.' Celia had to raise her voice slightly because someone had increased the volume of the music.

'I can't see how that'll happen. The world isn't interested in getting more involved here—'

'Why not? There's oil, after all,' Jen interrupted. As Hans

began answering she pressed up to Lina again and murmured, 'I don't think Astrid's got a chance. He keeps looking at you!'

Lina gave her a little kick under the table.

But Jen wouldn't stop. 'It's true. You're one of the few around here who hasn't given in to him yet—'

'Jen!' Lina hissed. Hans did have a reputation as a bit of heartbreaker, but she was sure he had no interest in her. And besides, he knew she was with Anil. Except – reality struck again – she wasn't. Not any more. She held her breath and tensed every muscle, willing herself not to cry.

'Yah,' Hans was saying. 'The Chinese get a third of their oil from this continent and Sudan is one of the main suppliers. That's why China blocks international attempts to intervene in the crisis here.'

'All this depressing stuff.' Astrid pouted. Her red lips were begging for contact with him. 'You need to have some fun or you're going to burn out.'

'I'd like to take a break, but there's no time.' He rolled the sleeves of his shirt up twice over the cuffs of his denim jacket. Astrid's eyes lingered on his sturdy wrists, his strong hands. 'I read an Oxfam report recently in which it was predicted that by 2010 half the world's population could be living in states that are experiencing violence or are at risk from it.'

'I really hope what's going on here doesn't get ignored.' Celia pushed her fringe out of her eyes. 'All the time, while I'm out in the field, I meet people who believe help is on the way. They say, "The white man will come."'

'It's true.' Hans nodded. 'I also hear this very often, "The white people will help us." But I almost feel embarrassed when they say it. Look how long we're taking!' His eyes happened to rest on Lina again. 'Something's got to change. We need a breakthrough.'

Astrid cooed some German into his ear.

Jen prodded Lina and whispered again, 'I bet she's telling him he shouldn't sleep alone tonight!'

Lina forced a smile, despite the stomach cramps she could suddenly feel. She hoped Astrid would immediately make off with Hans, so that she wouldn't have to speak to him herself.

'Are you OK?' Jen asked.

'I shouldn't have come.' Lina had gone pale.

'Take a sip of this.' Jen handed over her cup of Janjaweed Juice.

'You know I don't drink!' Lina turned her face away.

'Think of it as medicine. It'll help. Just try some.' Jen pushed the cup under her friend's nose.

Lina was about to refuse again when there was a black-out. A collective groan filled the room, followed by fumbling as people reoriented themselves. Then the soft sound of smooching permeated the darkness.

'That seems like the right game for these conditions,' one of the guys drawled.

There was laughter and people moved to light candles and refill their cups.

'I bet Astrid jumped on him the second the lights went out,' Jen whispered.

'Ssshh!' Lina was sure everyone would hear now that the music had stopped. She was feeling nauseous, veering between emotions. A little whimper escaped from her. Next thing Jen had the cup of Juice at her lips.

'Drink,' she urged. 'It'll make you forget everything.'

Lina took a sip. The inside of her mouth shrivelled up.

It tasted like the pink liquid dentists give you to rinse out your mouth, mixed with petrol. The fume of it went up her throat and into her nose like acid steam. She felt as though her nostril hairs were being singed. And then heat spread through her chest and belly, in a healing diffusion, almost spiritual. She was glad it was dark and no one could see her face contorting.

'And?' Jen asked.

'Is that how all alcohol tastes?' Lina kept hold of the cup, swilling around the liquid that was left.

'No. This stuff is something else.'

Their eyes adjusted to the dimness.

'You can have the rest. There's only a sip or two in there.' Half the mug remained. 'I'll get myself some more.' Jen went to fetch another drink.

Lina rose from the table and groped her way towards the window, wishing she hadn't come to the party. Perhaps the evening could have provided the levity she needed to counter her mood, but Hans's presence meant the whole thing had become a strain. Outside, she could see the outline of the UN jeep. She would have driven back to their compound if she hadn't been afraid of doing so alone. Especially since she could hear gunfire in the distance. Not that this was any reason to be especially alarmed. It was a rare night when she wasn't woken, at some point, by it: either single sporadic shots from rifles, or continuous machine-gun rounds that shuddered into the air. Such weapons were so much a part of daily life here that they were even used to signal morning prayers during Ramadan. Guns, guns, guns! Lina exhaled heavily. She was never allowed to forget about them. Each shot might have been ringing out from her conscience. She took another sip of Janjaweed Juice.

'You've been very quiet this evening.' Hans put a hand on her waist.

Lina jumped. She'd assumed he was in Astrid's grip.

'I haven't heard from you in a long time.' He stood with his back to the wall by the window. In the candlelight only his profile was visible to Lina.

'I've been so busy.' She tucked her hair behind her ears. The cornflakes threatened to travel back up the way they'd gone down. In a panic she drained most of her cup and immediately broke into a fit of coughing. Hans slapped her on the back as if she was choking. She felt the burn of the alcohol right down her gullet and deep in her head. It was strangely pacifying. 'So much has happened.' She blinked rapidly.

'Yah, it gets like that sometimes.' He suddenly moved forward and kissed her on both cheeks. 'But there should always be time to greet a friend properly, or?'

'Of course. Sorry.' Lina pecked him back. 'I've been too caught up in my own thoughts.'

'Something special on your mind?' He came a little closer.

If Jen had been nearby she would have sent a teasing 'I told you so' Lina's way. But Lina was too caught up in her own problems to detect any ulterior motives in Hans.

'Just – lots of things.' Her tongue felt heavy and swollen. She wondered if it had something to do with the Juice.

'I was surprised that you didn't even reply to my messages. I sent an email to say I'd be here this evening.'

'I've been away.' She mentioned her trip to Jonglei.

'I was thinking maybe you were trying to avoid me.' He looked at the floor, one corner of his mouth pulled into a wry smile.

Lina was grateful for the window ledge, which she was leaning on with her elbows. Her legs alone might not have held her up. Maybe he already knew! Maybe he was testing her! 'Why would I do that?'

He caught her gaze again. 'I don't know. I'm glad it's not so.'

'Are you OK otherwise?' Lina asked.

'A little tired.' He rubbed one eye.

'Working too much?'

'The work I don't mind. It's more the feeling of not making much real headway. We're no closer to signing an international arms-trade treaty. America refuses to be a signatory. And without them on board no one else takes it seriously.' His fingers tensed around some invisible hard object. 'At a local level we make just dribs and drabs of progress.'

Lina drank the last of her Juice. The drink dabbed at her senses, blurring them so that she was soon cradled in a benign web of sensations, no one feeling dominating.

'I've started a group,' Hans was saying, 'to lobby the Olympic committee to drop shooting as a competitive sport. The less outlets there are legitimizing the use of guns, the better.'

'It sounds like you're shooting forward on all fronts.' Lina blinked, suddenly unsure of what she'd heard and whether she'd already replied. 'On all fronts. You're really shooting.'

Hans paused. 'There's a big mismatch between the scale of the problem and the rate at which we're dealing with it.'

'You're too hard on yourself.' Lina burped and then tittered, covering her mouth with one hand.

There was another short silence before Hans went on. 'We are making gains. We'll get there in the end.'

'I hope you do.' She felt quite buoyant. 'You really do. You do. You have to.' She registered a strange look on Hans's face but didn't pause to think about it because someone was asking if their drinks needed topping up.

'Just a tiny drop. A drop.' She held out her cup. 'That's enough!' She jerked it away from the pouring bottle and some of the liquid slopped to the floor and Hans's boots.

'Oh sorry! So sorry. Sorrreeee.' She knelt, intending to wipe them, but lost her balance and ended up sitting on the floor. She giggled and drank again, clenching her teeth as the Janjaweed Juice went down.

'Are you all right?' Hans squatted, his gaze shifting between her face and the dripping cup she was holding.

'I only wanted a little bit. Just an eensy weensie teenie weenie minnie miney bit . . .' Miney . . . Minnie . . . She remembered Anil and felt herself swell with sadness again. Hoping to counter this she took another swig of the medicine Jen had prescribed. But her body couldn't handle any more and she ended up spitting it back into the cup.

Hans took the plastic receptacle from her.

She stretched out on the floor and nestled her head on her arm. 'Lie down for a minute.'

For an instant he thought she was asking him to spread out on the floor beside her. But then she repeated, 'I need to. Lie down. Just for a minute.'

'What's happened?' Jen came up with several of the other women. 'Oh, shit.'

Lina's head had rolled to a strange angle, her mouth was open and her eyes were shut.

'Can you carry her?' Celia looked at Hans. 'Will you bring her to my room? She shouldn't be here like this.'

Hans picked Lina up and took her to Celia's room, which was along the corridor in the same building.

'I'll stay with her.' Jen pulled a sheet over Lina's body. She was shivering slightly.

'No, don't worry. I will – I've had enough of the party anyway.' Hans sat down on the other side of the bed. 'Really. I'll take care of her.'

It was after midnight when Anil landed at Juba airport. The place was almost empty, most of the lights were out, and a grumpy officer was dozing at immigration. Anil had his first sense of foreboding when several men pressed forward, asked if he needed a taxi, and quoted grossly inflated prices when he stated his destination. Thank goodness he'd had the foresight to bring some dollars. As he drove through the night in one of the cabs, Anil realized he had no idea if they were going in the right direction. The vehicle was speeding along a dusty road with headlights dimmed and hazard lights flashing. Anil couldn't guess what this combination signalled. He tried not to think about being kidnapped or murdered. The only other person who knew of his whereabouts was the pilot, who'd been instructed to wait in the aircraft.

Hardly any of the streetlights were working. In the hazy glow of those that did Anil could see the tangled threads of electricity cables. They were hanging from pylons leaning at such extreme angles, it was a wonder they didn't collapse. Shadowy low-rise buildings cowered against an emptiness that threatened to steal right into the soul. Motorbikes buzzed past like oversized bugs, their fumes merging with the dust from the road to leave a smoky fug across the area. Anil was disconcerted that this was where Lina had chosen to work.

'City centre?' he asked the driver, trying to gauge where they were.

The driver's head bobbed in a figure of eight. 'There – market.' He pointed towards a pit of blackness.

Now, Anil thought, would be a good time to own a gun. He wished he'd agreed to the one his father had urged on him. Such a weapon would probably make no difference to the circumstances, but it would – he saw this as an advantage for the first time – have boosted his confidence considerably.

He'd spent the whole flight rehearsing what to say to Lina. It was to be a passionate avowal of his love, complete with quotes from their favourite qawwalis. He was picturing the reunion when the car pulled up in front of a large gate.

'UN.' The driver gestured to the flag. Then he raised four fingers and pronounced, 'Forty dollar.'

'Wait.' Anil climbed out of the vehicle. He wasn't going to pay a cent until he was sure he'd been brought to the right place. He went and shook the gate. 'Hello?'

Peeling white paint stuck to his palms. He grimaced and kicked at the gate, as if to punish the metal for trying to pass on a contagious disease. He rubbed his hands against each other, trying to brush off the oily specks. 'Hey! Hello! Is anyone there?' His words flared against the cold air.

The driver hooted, and soon a man wearing a woollen cap and wrapped in a blanket came out. He said something Anil didn't understand, but the driver, who was leaning out of the window, replied.

'I'm here to see Lina Merali,' Anil persisted. 'She's with the UN.'

'Ah, no.' The man behind the gate shook his head. 'Bukra. Inshallah.'

'What?' Anil turned to the driver.

'He say come tomorrow.'

'I can't come tomorrow! Tell him I need to see her right now!' Anil rattled the gate.

Another short exchange between the two Sudanese men ensued.

'Nobody here. He say UN people gone to MSF.'

'Where's that?'

The driver did a snaking movement with the arm that was hanging over the side of the window. 'I take you. Forty dollar more.'

'Fine.' Anil got back in.

Five minutes later they stopped in front of another gated compound. Anil paid the driver and asked him to wait.

'Forty dollar.' The man grinned, making Anil wonder if 'forty' was the only number he knew in English.

A guard wearing a parka jacket and ski gloves let Anil in.

He went straight towards the building with the most lights on. He noted the rudimentary nature of the structure. With its low ceilings and small windows it reminded him of a military barracks. The smell of cigarettes and spirits pinched at the back of his throat when he stepped in. A group of people were sitting around a table playing cards. Two of the guys had crew cuts that made them look like American marines. A woman eyed him from behind a fan of six cards. Her thick black eyeliner was smudged, and specks of silver glitter sparkled at the corners of her eyes.

'Hi, sorry to interrupt.' It was unsettling to have so many people staring at him. Anil could almost feel the collective gaze stroking his leather jacket, fingering the cashmere scarf around his neck. 'I'm looking for Lina . . . Merali? Is she here?'

His eyes flitted around the room, taking in the tacky plastic furniture and the cheaply framed Matisse prints on the walls. A couple were slowly dancing to some barely audible jazz. Two women were curled up on the sofa, one of them braiding the other's hair. The kitchen counter was covered with empty bottles and gaping crisp packets full of salty crumbs. These were the last throes of some kind of party, Anil realized. So Lina had come here after their conversation. She'd been too busy having fun to answer his calls.

'Are you Anil?' A butch-looking blonde set down her cards and rose from the table. 'I'm Jen,' she said when he nodded. 'Lina's resting. She wasn't feeling well.'

Anil was so glad to hear this that concern gushed out of him in tones of joy. 'Really? What happened? Where is she?'

Jen walked around the table. 'I'll take you to her. She's in Celia's room – this way.'

Jen pushed at the door, which was open just a fraction. 'Lina?' Her low voice barely penetrated the room, just as the weak light from the corridor threw in an ineffectual triangular gleam. A flat, sour smell filled the air, as if someone had been sick. Clothes were scattered all over; hanging off bedposts, drawer-knobs and the handles of the built-in wardrobe. Anil was at the foot of the bed before he realized there were two people on it. Jen switched on one of the bedside lamps and Anil recognized the larger of the prostrate figures as Hans. He was lying on his back, one hand under his head, the other draped over Lina whose back pressed into his side. A jolt went through Anil's body, as if he'd misjudged the height of a step.

The brightness made Hans stir. His eyes squeezed open reluctantly. 'What's going on?' He propped himself up on his elbows and blinked the room into focus.

'I should be asking you that. What the fuck are you doing with my girlfriend?' Anil hauled him off the mattress. 'Get away from her!'

Hans stumbled and fell to the floor. He started to speak, but Anil yelled, 'Shut up!' Then he kicked Hans twice in the ribs.

'You've got the wrong—' Jen pulled on Anil's arm, trying to get him away from Hans who was curled up on the floor groaning.

'Leave me alone!' Anil jerked away.

He went to Lina's side of the bed, bent over and shook her. 'Lina?'

She moaned. Anil caught a whiff of alcohol.

'Lina?' It came out louder, more roughly.

She turned over, but didn't wake up. The sheet slipped as she moved, exposing her bare midriff and thighs. Flimsy scraps of lilac underwear seemed to be all she had on.

Anil backed away, shaking his head, breathing heavily. He turned and ran out of the door, through the main room – knocking over a chair and startling everyone – before heading back out, into the night. The cold slapped his face, shocking him to a standstill. He froze – one leg in front of the other, left hand in a fist, the right covering his mouth – like a puppet suspended mid-motion. His thoughts zoomed in and out of clarity. At the gates the taxi was still waiting, engine switched off, hazard lights flashing an on-off orange beam.

Suddenly the short-haired blonde was there, waving some garments in his face.

'It's not what you think,' Jen said. She talked fast, the

words clipped by her rough voice and an accent he couldn't place. Fragments of what she said stood out, as if they had been expressed in bold and underlined: '. . . drank too much . . . passed out . . . vomited . . .'

No, he wanted to say, Lina doesn't drink – then he recalled the smell that had come off her. His mouth pulled into a grimace.

'. . . in no state . . .' Jen was saying, '. . . back tomorrow . . . OK?'

She looked up at him, waiting for an answer. He was handsome all right, but this volatile man was nothing like the Prince Charming they'd all imagined and joked about. She wondered what was really going on with Lina. Most people who did their kind of work were running away from something. You came out to help other people and you ended up fucking yourself up even more.

Anil's gaze shifted between the taxi and the building. During his hasty journey to Juba he hadn't once considered that his mission might fail. He squeezed his eyes shut and pressed a palm either side of his head.

'I don't think she should be disturbed until tomorrow,' Jen repeated.

Anil began toying with the zip on his jacket, pulling it up and down. One moment the device's tiny silver teeth were aligned in a neat row, the next they fell apart in a sinister, mouthless grin. Jen was right, Lina wasn't in good condition. But, that might, in fact, work to his advantage. He stomped past Jen and re-entered the building. All chatter ceased when he passed through the main room, but no one tried to stop him. Lina was alone in the bedroom. There was no sign of Hans.

Anil knelt down, put a hand on her clammy cheek. 'Lina. Look at me.'

Her eyeballs rolled under their lids. He went on calling her name.

It was like dragging her back from oblivion – her lids would manage to spring apart for a second before smacking shut. And then the whole effort of prising them open would begin again.

'Lina!' He patted both her cheeks.

She lurched awake, rising off the bed slightly before flopping back down. This time her eyes stayed open.

'Anil.' Her tone was low and dry, like an autumn leaf crackling underfoot.

He reached for some clothes hanging on a nearby chair. Amongst them were a baggy yellow shirt and pair of lime-green leggings. He began pushing Lina's limbs into the garments.

'We're getting out of here.'

She frowned. Memory had become a tunnel she couldn't fathom. At the far end was the faint glow of her arrival at the MSF compound that evening, then a length of emptiness up to the point where she now was.

'Can you walk?' He helped her sit up and set her legs on the floor.

She rose, but immediately wobbled back down again. A few dry retches racked her body. She lay back on the bed. Anil realized he would have to carry her. She sank against him, finding succour against his chest, inhaling the scent of his neck.

This time when he passed the crowd on the way out, it was clear they had been talking about him. Everyone glared disapprovingly, but only Jen intervened, asking Lina if she really wanted to go. The marine-types stood on either side of Jen, ready to grab Lina if the need arose.

Eventually, Lina's quiet insistence that she was OK made them back off.

Anil instructed the taxi to go back to the UN compound first so they could collect Lina's passport. She drifted asleep during the short ride, and he had to wake her so the guard would let them in. She was more alert during the next stage of the journey. Every pothole they drove through jumbled her thoughts. There was no sequence to them, nor did they cohere into words. Instead, she experienced waves of dread. It started when Anil blurted, 'That German was in bed with you.'

Her response was automatic. 'Nothing happened.' It was a conviction that went beyond the gaps in her memory to the core of who she was.

Anil's jaw worked furiously, as if he was chewing on his doubt. 'I'm never leaving you alone again. We're going to Nairobi, and from there we'll fly to England with my parents and make your family agree to our marriage.' His silhouette against the car window almost blended into the darkness outside. 'We should have done this years ago. They won't be able to keep objecting if they actually see for themselves how much we love each other.'

Lina's fingers dug into Anil's palm. She dared to believe he might be right. Yet, at the sight of the aeroplane with its peacock emblem on the tail, she felt, once more, the grip of dread. She had to resist the impulse to retch as she took the window seat. Outside, pale threads of colour were starting to weave through the night sky.

'There's one thing . . .' She turned to Anil, lines of worry extending from her eyes right across the narrow bridge of her nose.

He'd been about to click his seat belt shut – his breath caught mid-inhalation, like silk snagging over sharp metal.

'No . . . no, it's nothing . . .' She couldn't say more.

He didn't probe, just slipped his fingers through hers, gripping so tightly her knuckles hurt.

The thin outlines of Juba disappeared within a minute of take-off, snatched into the fist of the night. As they rose through wisps of cloud Lina began to pray silently, repeating the same phrase over and over: Ya Allah, let everything be OK.

On your last morning, you went around the flat checking every drawer and cupboard. You'd stored all that you weren't travelling with at a friend's, claiming you didn't want to clutter up Lucas's place. I asked if you were searching for a particular item.

– No, I want to make sure I haven't forgotten anything.

– You're acting like you're never coming back!

– Well, I'm not. Neither of us will be.

– I'm still here for a few days. I can take anything that you've forgotten.

– I just want to make it easier for you. You'll have enough stuff to manage.

– Stop fussing. Come sit down and have a bite. I've cooked for you.

For once you didn't tease me about the meal. Usually you joked that 'assembling' was the more appropriate word for my efforts. The only dish you really liked was my French toast. Real cooking was what your mother did in Delhi. And, no doubt, your new wife is well-trained in the marathon endeavours that your favourite cuisine seems to entail. You told me just the base of a dish could take an hour to prepare: the roasting of spices, frying of onions and slow cooking-down of tomatoes. Well, I hope you choke on all those slave-labour sauces, the way I have on the choice you force-fed me.

413

Anyway, you weren't hungry, understandably. I would have lost my appetite too, at the last, critical stage of an emotional swindle like yours.

– I'm really going to miss you.

You held me tight, as you said those words, the way you had done many times over the last weeks. The way, I realize now, one might hold something treasured that is soon to be relinquished. Even our love-making had slowed down, intensified. Once, with the soles of my feet pressed to your cheeks you'd said: I wish I could memorize every part of you. For what? I had wondered. You didn't answer with words, but continued to make your mental map of me, pushing your hands into my flesh, coaxing it to yield up every secret. Everything is most precious in the moments before you lose it.

– At least you'll be in a new environment. I'll be waiting back here amongst all the familiar people and places. I'll notice your absence everywhere.

You took a deep breath and said:

– But I'm going to miss you for ever.

It might have been the start of our little game, the one where we each insisted, to infinity, that our feelings were stronger than the other's. I was sitting opposite you, my elbows on the table, my chin in my hands. Between us the untouched cauliflower cheese sat under its veil of melted cheddar. I pushed it to one side and reached out to take your hand.

– I already miss you, and you're not even gone yet.

– I miss you when you're in a different room. I don't know how I will cope, missing you from such a distance.

There was something in your voice, a faint tremor, that scared me.

– Delhi is not so far. And a month isn't that long. We can write to each other. I've never had a letter from you. It'll be romantic.

Another deep breath. You squeezed my hand tighter.

– Sel, I'm not coming back.

– What?

– I can't come back . . . to you.

It didn't sink in. I thought maybe you were going to live there – hence the last-minute decision to give up the flat – and you were going to ask me to come as well.

– I don't think it can work. There are too many complications.

I kept staring at you, my mouth slightly open, still not able to comprehend. It was like seeing a film with the wrong subtitles: the image didn't match the words. I remember being surprised that I was still sitting in my chair, because I had the sense of falling, sinking, under a weight of dread. The smell of the cauliflower was suddenly repugnant and I retched.

– Sel?

You got up and came over to me.

– Here, come here.

You half-carried half-walked me to the sofa, where I sat forward, staring at the floor, my arms crossed over my stomach.

– Oh god, Sel. I'm sorry. I'm so sorry.

My throat constricted. It was hard to speak. But I forced out a question:

– Why are you doing this?

– I have to. There's no other way.

You were standing before me. All I could see were your black shoes, freshly polished. For a second I thought I might be sick over those shoes. But the convulsion passed through me without bringing up my breakfast.

I managed to keep up a strange charade of civility. Whether this was just the Englishness in me, or a reflection of the fact that we had always spoken to each other gently, I don't know. In any case, I remained hunched over as you went on, delivering some rehearsed speech.

– No two people, however much they care for each other, can live in the bubble of their love. We all come with too much history to be remade entirely by love. At first, I thought that was possible, but I've come to realize that I can't simply cut myself off from the past. I know I haven't seen my family for years, but that doesn't mean I've forgotten them or their expectations. They will always be there, even if I don't want them to be. Just as your family and their disapproval will. This seems acceptable to you now – it was to me for a while – but one day it might not be. And then there will only be regret.

I started to try and persuade you. It was like a reflex. A consequence of my belief that sound argument can win the day. At that point, I still imagined I could influence you:

– I'm not sure what a life would be worth if there was nothing to regret at the end of it. Regret is a measure of how much or how little you dared. I would rather have dared too much than too little. Wouldn't you?

– There are some risks that don't just have consequences for this life.

– This life is all we can be sure of! I don't see the

416

point of deferring happiness for some future promise of salvation. Unless – are you saying you're not happy with me?

– This has nothing to do with you, Sel. In letting you go I know that I'm giving up a good part of myself; a part that I'll probably never recover. But I cannot live with contradictions any more. I can't act one way and think another.

I didn't understand. I looked up then and saw you wiping your eyes with the back of your hand. It was the only real hint of grief that you gave.

– This is wrong in god's eyes.

You made a wide arcing gesture with your arm. And it seemed to me like you were saying that all the things we had shared were suddenly rendered worthless because they lacked the seal of religious approval. That's when I started to get angry, when the feeling blew up in me like a ball and began its furious, furtive bouncing.

– All of a sudden that's a problem? Why haven't you brought this up before?

– I've always made it clear that my family would never accept you.

You might have been a magician, pulling non-sequiturs, like ribbons, out of thin air.

– But you haven't even told them. I thought that's what you'd do while you were at home this time. How can you assume what their reaction will be?

– They won't accept you. My parents are too old and conservative to change their minds. Yours didn't.

– Yes, but that didn't stop me, did it? If everybody always listened to their parents the word progress would be defunct. And anyway, that's got nothing to do with

417

what you just said about god. Why didn't you mention him before, if he was such a problem?

You knelt down in front of me and sat back on your heels. You put your hands on my knees. I used to call them healing hands. There was always such strength in your touch, such comfort. When I had any pain – period cramps or a headache – just the pressure of your palms on the afflicted spot could bring relief.

– God is not the problem. Don't say it like that.

Suddenly I was getting instructions on how to talk. You had never tried to influence the way I dressed, ate or behaved.

– OK, so what is? All this time, I never interfered with your faith. I didn't have the impression it was an obstacle between us. I tolerated everything: the fasting, the halal food, the praying.

– That is it, you see. It is not a question of tolerance. It has to do with respect. I do not feel you have accorded this to my faith.

You were getting all formal, as though you were talking to a stranger.

– Of course I respect you!

You looked away, and I could tell that my answer had confirmed something that made you sad.

– And as far as your family goes, I always believed you'd be strong enough to choose us.

– For a long time there's been something in me that isn't reconciled to us being together. I thought, I hoped, it would go away. But it's just got worse. And now it's become clear to me that our relationship is not right in god's eyes.

– Why? Because I'm not a Muslim?

I sat up and leaned against the back of the sofa, my

arms still encircling my waist, my fingers clutching at the wool of my sweater.

– That's part of it.

– So it's not enough in god's eyes that two people love and take care of each other? What kind of god says that we have to be the same denomination to deserve each other?

– It's not a question of denomination. You do not even believe. And that's why you'll never understand. I know for you my faith has just been something on the periphery, but for me it is at the centre of my being. It is who I am, it is the essence of me. You don't see that, and you can never share it. This is a source of pain to me. How can I be with someone who cannot appreciate that core of my existence? And in future, if we had children, how would we raise them? I can find no answers to these questions which satisfies me.

– So that's it? You can find no answer, so it's over? Didn't you think we might have found an answer together? Isn't that what it means to be a couple?

You shook your head.

– You misunderstand me.

– No, I think I've grasped it pretty well. You're saying that because we don't believe in the same god, all the things we have in common don't count. The things that have united us all these years – the books, music, values, friends, ideas, dreams, experiences, politics – none of that is enough. Suddenly a shared faith is the most important thing. That's right, isn't it?

Your hands slipped from my knees into your lap. You stood up again.

– This is not how I wanted things to end.

– Oh no? Well, I'm sorry it's not going exactly to

plan. You managed it all so smoothly until now, didn't you?

– This has been the hardest decision of my life, Sel. I've thought about it for a long time. I've been praying for guidance. I know, now, by the grace of god, this is what I must do.

– What do you mean a long time? How long?

You didn't look at me. Very quietly you made your admission.

– From the beginning.

I was speechless.

– Right from the start I was struggling with myself. I knew it was wrong in god's eyes. First I tried not to think about it, then I tried justifying it to myself in all sorts of ways.

– You should have told me. I had a right to know.

– I never doubted my love for you. I'm talking about the kind of doubt that implicates the soul. It's an uncertainty that comes from knowing you are not being true to god and therefore not true to yourself. God has made laws for us to follow.

The way you aggrandized your struggle, giving it these cosmic proportions! I had never heard you speak in such a manner, making religion so personal. In the theological discussions we had sometimes had, with each other or friends, you were always cleverly evasive.

– This country has laws for us to follow. Breaking the odd one doesn't make you a bad citizen. And, in fact, civilization is built on the foundation of laws that were challenged and broken.

– Faith is different. You can't say: I believe but I'm not going to do this or that. God and the laws are one.

– What you say doesn't make sense.

You spoke quietly, patiently, as was your custom.

– It is hard for someone like me to explain the mysteries of the divine.

Oh, the cop out! Always easy to fudge questions about god by claiming he's too complex.

– You could at least do a better job of explaining the mysteries of your own behaviour! Why have you waited until you're just about to leave before telling me all this?

– Because I knew you would try to change my mind. And I wasn't sure I'd be strong enough to resist.

– You seem pretty commonsense-proof to me.

You looked at your watch.

– I should go.

My voice broke.

– How can you do this?

Yours trembled – until you spoke his name. Then certainty gilded your words.

– It is the right thing. It is god's will.

Who is your god to decide for me? I wanted to shout. It was like god was your wife and I had been your mistress: a fleeting indulgence, easily renounced.

– He knows best. There is a bigger picture. It is not only for this life or this self that our actions count.

– Oh shut up! Shut up! I don't know you. What are you saying!

You brought me some tissues and said goodbye without a touch. Your last words were spoken as you stood in the doorway, about to depart:

– Please forgive me. It is god's will.

I heard the door shut. I sat alone in that room, which you had cleared of all our belongings, so I was surrounded by blank walls and empty shelves. After a while, I don't know how long, the door opened again and Lucas was there. You had phoned him on the way to the airport and told him to come to me. That was just like you, to be kind even at your cruellest. No doubt your god would have approved.

Persuasion

LINA STOOD ON THE pavement and watched Anil drive away in a rented black Mercedes. They'd arrived at Heathrow Airport early that morning and headed straight to Birmingham. Minnie and Pravar had been dropped off at the Hyatt Hotel before Anil had reluctantly brought Lina to her parents' house. She'd insisted on seeing them alone first. It would be too much of a shock if she just appeared with the Mayurs after not even talking to her family for the past month. Anil wasn't keen on the idea. He'd kept Lina close to him in the forty-eight hours since they'd left Juba, afraid to let her out of his sight even to use the toilet. He thought she was making excuses when she argued about needing a day to prepare her parents to meet him. In the end, he'd agreed to give her a few hours with them.

The street looked the same: long rows of brick houses with their short driveways sloping down to the main road. The tarmac was still dimpled in places, the larger holes filled with water from a recent shower. Globules of fuel, which must have trickled from leaking vehicles, gleamed like iridescent eyes in the puddles. Lina checked her watch. It was midday, though you wouldn't have known it from the muffled light: the sun was bandaged in thick wads of cloud. At six in the evening the Mayurs would finally meet the Meralis. Goosebumps rose like hackles under the long silk sleeves of Lina's blouse. She walked towards the front door of her parents' house. Now that Anil was gone, fear bolted from the back of her mind, where his confidence had kept it in check, to become the focus of all her thoughts. Once again, he had tried to harness their future. When they were together it felt manageable, but as soon as she was on her own, her grip became unsteady, her sense of direction flawed. Her fingers shook as she pressed the doorbell.

Iman started to weep when she saw her daughter. She pulled Lina in, pressing the girl to her bosom, squeezing her repeatedly, as if to make sure she was really there. Lina wanted to dissolve into her mother's embrace, the soft promise of forgiveness in her flesh.

'I knew you would come back. I knew it.' Iman tilted her head back so she could look at Lina. 'When did you arrive? Are you hungry? Do you need to rest? Yarhamukallah, God have mercy on you, you're so thin.' She ran the tips of her thumbs over Lina's cheekbones and felt her happiness begin to wane. Suffering was corroding her daughter's face, imprinting it with untimely lines and shadows. 'Where are your things?' Iman looked around. 'Did you get a taxi? Why didn't you phone and tell us you were coming-weh? We could have collected you from the airport. How long are you here for?' Questions spilled out, inadequate defences against her growing apprehension.

'I'm not sure, Ma.' Lina pushed the door shut with the two-inch heel of her tan-coloured nubuck boots. 'It depends.'

'On what?' Iman pulled at the scarf that had slipped from her head.

'Can you call Baba and ask him to come home? I'd prefer to speak to you both at the same time.' Lina didn't know how the words came out so evenly, when her heart seemed to have taken up residence in her stomach and was cartwheeling frantically through that hollow cave.

Iman went automatically to the phone, which hung off the wall around the corner, near the staircase. She could guess what was coming and she didn't want to face it alone.

Lina remained in the entrance hall. She breathed deeply, picking through the strands of smell, which, knotted together, made for the unmistakable scent of home. Her eyes took in the furniture, as one might search the face of an old friend, for traces of change. Every detail found its reflection in memory. Even the flowered wall-paper seemed an extension of her consciousness, the background against which many moral struggles had been enacted. Home. The suffocating comfort of the place. It made one part of her want to forget the world and curl up on the sofa, while another bit longed to run away.

As soon as Shareef was back Lina, without any prelim-inaries, announced that Anil and his parents were waiting just a few kilometres away, and would come that evening to ask for her hand in marriage.

'What-weh!' Iman rose from the kitchen table where they'd all assembled. 'Bismillah! Those people are not entering this house. They lead you astray, and then they think they can walk in and claim our hospitality? No way! Tell her, Shareef.'

Shareef sat straight-backed, as if he'd been tied to the chair. 'Your mother's right. There's no point in such a meeting.'

'We've set a date for a wedding.' Anil had forced her to pick a day before they left Nairobi, and Minnie had im-mediately instructed an event organizer to start making arrangements. All the things Lina had agreed to now struck her as details from a stranger's life. And yet, she was using them to batter her parents. She wondered, as she already had so many times since leaving Juba, if she was still under the influence of the Janjaweed Juice. 'I want you all to be there.'

'Astaghfirullah!' Iman clutched at the cotton of her kameez, between her breasts.

Shareef said nothing.

'It's in Nairobi. At the end of next month.' Lina threw out the slips of information as if they were crumbs to beckon birds.

'I can't listen to this any more!' Iman pressed her palms to her ears and spun around twice, as though she was being assaulted from all sides.

'Iman!' Shareef shouted. Lina stiffened and even Iman was shocked into silence. 'This hysteria will get us nowhere. If you can't be reasonable I'll speak to Lina alone.'

'This is no time for reason.' Iman turned to Lina, her lips trembling. 'I will never meet those people, do you hear me? Never.' She left the kitchen, slamming the door.

Shareef crossed his arms and looked down at his feet in their black Oxfords. The outside of each heel always wore away first. They were due for another stint at the cobbler.

'Do you remember?' he said eventually. 'When you were little you loved stepping into puddles because you thought you would end up in the sky?'

She nodded slowly as the memory returned, of splashes, wet socks, the dripping hems of dresses, and a mother's perpetual exasperation.

'It is a little bit like that now, I think, the illusion of this so-called love. What you imagine you will get from marrying this man, and what you will actually have . . .' He did not finish but placed a hand over his mouth so that his nose rested in the tender dip between the thumb and index finger.

'How can you know that?' Lina recalled that he'd spied on her through Merc. The thought of his meddling made her sick. She pulled at the cuffs of her sleeves until they half-covered her hands. The thread at the shoulder seams of her shirt stretched taut. 'Don't you trust my judgement?'

'In the Koran it says something about how it can happen that you will hate a thing which is good for you, or you will love a thing which is bad for you. You cannot always distinguish, but God can. That is why we have His word to direct us. As the Book says, God's guidance is the true guidance.'

'I want you to meet Anil. At least give me that. You can't have a fair opinion about a person you haven't met.' Under the table, her nails dug into the silk fabric of her shirt.

Shareef blinked rapidly, disturbed by the hardness of her tone. 'Lina, he could be a prince, he could be a saint – it wouldn't make a difference. My opinion of him doesn't matter, it is God's will that counts.'

Lina wished he would stop dragging God in left, right and centre. God didn't matter to her right then, it was *him* that mattered – *his* approval, *his* understanding. She craned her neck towards him. 'I've tried to be without Anil and it doesn't work!'

'You haven't gone about it the right way.'

Lina rose abruptly. 'How do you know?' And the next sentence was out before she was aware that she'd decided to say it: 'A bit of spying doesn't make you an expert on my relationship!'

Shareef's mouth opened, then closed, and began

working as though there was something he couldn't crack between his teeth.

'I know you used Anil's friend to keep an eye on me.' She went and stood right in front of him. 'How long did you know and not say anything?'

'Almost as long as you've been deceiving us.'

She turned away, pressed a hand to her mouth. Here it was again – the urge to cry – when she'd been relying on the numbness of the last few days to persist.

Shareef noted the chink of weakness in her demeanour and saw his chance. 'I wouldn't tell you to give up that man if I didn't think – no, if I wasn't one hundred per cent certain – you would find happiness again.' He indicated that she should sit down. 'I also loved someone who was not a Muslim. I met her at university, the way you did Anil. We were together for a while, almost as long as you two. I thought I couldn't live without her. She seemed to be my soulmate.' He stopped and willed his heartbeat to slow down. He hadn't spoken about this to anyone ever before.

'Wha . . . who was she?'

'She was an English lady, a literature student. We were different, but there was something very strong between us. Yet, even though I loved her, I had a feeling from the beginning that the relationship wasn't right. I kept thinking I could live with her not being Muslim – not having a faith at all, in fact – but eventually I saw that it wasn't possible.'

'Because of your family?' She leaned across the table.

'Of course they would have disapproved, but I never told them. I knew there was no point.' He still hadn't looked at Lina. He drew invisible squiggles across the table with an ink-stained finger. Family had never really been the determining factor. He could have borne being ostracized. Her love had meant that much to him. He'd thought it could compensate for all that he might lose.

Lina imagined him renouncing his love. How could he have done it willingly, without family pressure? He couldn't have loved her enough, she thought.

'I gave up her up because of Allah. I saw that I couldn't be a good Muslim and live with a woman who didn't believe in God and couldn't even start to understand what He meant to me.' It hurt to remember, even though he thought he'd done the right thing. He kept tracing the grain of the wooden table. The past, he realized, was etched in him as finely and irrevocably as those lines in the wood.

He definitely didn't love that lady enough, Lina felt. She watched him closely. 'Does Ma know?'

'No.'

That was when she caught it – a hint of feeling – in the quietness of his no and the flickering of his eyelids.

'Why?'

'It wasn't important any more.' How could he have told Iman at the beginning, when he made her the butt of his resentment for what he'd lost? And how could he have revealed it later, when knowing might have ruptured the new intimacy that had started to develop?

Lina studied her father. Why wouldn't he look at her while he spoke? All she could see was the black mark on his forehead drilling into her like a third eye.

'I'm only telling you this to show you that it's possible to love again, to love better, to be happier.' He didn't tell her how he'd wondered for years if he would ever again know real joy. That it had come unexpectedly with her birth – a pang and then a jolt and then a long rush, like recognizing a favourite tune and being able to sing along without thinking. 'Nothing can compare to what I have now with all of you, our family.'

'What was her name?'

He caught her eyes, as if by accident, startled by the question. 'Oh, that doesn't matter any more.'

'But what was it?' She wanted to hear him say it, to see if his tone remained the same.

'It's really senseless to go digging up all these details. I just wanted to show you that I understand—'

'Why don't you want to tell me, Baba?'

He inhaled, as if to draw the name up from the crevice where it was buried. It had existed only in his thoughts for decades, and took some summoning before arriving at his lips. Slowly, he exhaled her identity: 'Selina.' He could almost feel her skin in its sound.

He did love her. Lina heard it in his whisper. She saw it in the way his whole face was compressed with emotion. He really loved her. Her confusion deepened. She'd never questioned her parents' feelings for each other. Despite their differences of opinion and temperament, they were a strong unit. And yet, from what Shareef had just told Lina, it was clear that their union was hard-won, their understanding based on things unrevealed.

'That's why I'm telling you,' Shareef was saying. 'The only way is to make a clean break.' He'd been almost clinical in the way he had abandoned Selina, trying not to leave a trace of himself behind, and eliminating all reminders of her from his own possessions. He'd almost managed not to shed a tear when he'd said goodbye to her. Though minutes later, at the bottom of their street, he had broken down completely. He'd been caught out, despite his precautions. Several weeks afterwards, he had put on a shirt and come across a button that she'd sewn back on, the thread a different shade of blue from that which criss-crossed the others. He'd stood there, holding that tiny round piece of plastic, pressing the flesh of his fingers against it, trying to squeeze out a hint of her touch. He would have swallowed the button if he'd believed it might give him the sensation of being in her arms again.

'A quick, clean break,' he repeated, 'is the only way.' And not just that, he had then taken the most drastic measure to prevent himself from slipping back. During his trip home to India, right after the split with Selina, he'd married Iman, as his parents wished. His only condition was that she couldn't join him immediately in the UK. He'd cited financial reasons, but in truth he couldn't abide the idea of being close to another woman. Yet committing himself to Iman had been the best way to handcuff himself to his resolution. Otherwise, the temptation to contact Selina again might have been too great.

'But how can you be sure you did the right thing, Baba? Even if you say you're content now, maybe you would have been even more satisfied if you'd followed that other life? How can you ever know?' Lina was certain that if she left Anil she would be plagued for ever by the thought of the life she might have had with him.

'When you follow God's will then you know what you do is right. His guidance is the true guidance.' He didn't admit that he had sometimes doubted this. Before Iman came to live with him, there had been days when he'd had to call in sick at work because he was too miserable to face the world. He had shunned God on those days, refused to pray – as if this might hurt Allah, as if He was just sitting around waiting to be worshipped. Shareef's faith had been tested, no question. Much more, in fact, than it had been while he was actually in the relationship. But God had remained steadfast, and in the end Shareef had cleaved to His dependability.

'You are the proof that I chose well,' Shareef told Lina. 'Whatever you do, it won't change the fact that I had you, and that was a great gift.'

Lina's eyes filled up. It felt as if several pairs of hands were clawing at her heart. That familiar tug of war, each side pulling on her with equal force. 'Maybe I won't be as lucky as you, Baba. Maybe I won't find someone like Ma.'

'Put your faith in God. He will not let you down. He is All-Merciful, All-Compassionate.'

If he had said something else it might have been different, but the repetition of his pious platitudes suddenly disgusted her. He wouldn't even *allow* for the possibility of being wrong! It was this she rebelled against, his unflinching certainties about *her*. She folded her hands and pressed her thumbs against her lips.

Shareef spread his palms across the table and used them to push himself up so he was standing again. He glanced at the illuminated digits of time on the microwave. It was half past one. 'You'd better call those people and tell them not to come.'

Lina thought of Anil waiting, felt the pressure of all the promises she'd made, the preparations that had commenced. 'I still want you to meet him.'

Shareef moved so fast the chair fell to the floor. He strode around to where she was seated. 'What was the point of the conversation we just had? Didn't you hear what I said? I want nothing to do with that family!' He thumped a fist on the kitchen counter. The nearby ceramic salt and pepper holders jumped and rattled. 'If you insist on keeping up your connection to them, then you can leave now.' He pointed at the door.

Lina didn't move. She kept looking ahead, and began to speak as though she was addressing someone who was seated opposite her. 'If you don't agree to let the Mayurs visit I'll tell Ma about Selina.'

Shareef gasped.

The audibility of his shock spurred Lina on. 'It's only fair. You've always been such an advocate of fairness.' She got up and faced him. 'You have to allow me this.'

'The past doesn't matter.' He pulled at his collar. 'Your mother knows me. She knows what we are together. Nothing you say can change that.' He was convinced of this – and yet, he did not want it tested.

Lina was so propelled by the force of her daring that she couldn't stop. 'Let's see.' She went towards the door.

'Wait, Lina!' Shareef stopped her hand touching the doorknob. He bit his bottom lip, took several long breaths. 'Even if they come, it won't change my mind.'

'You can't know that in advance.' She couldn't imagine how he could meet Anil and not like him.

'Aaaah! Have you lost your mind?' Shareef was yelling again. 'You're willing to sacrifice us just to have that infidel and his family here? There are limits, Lina! Maybe you should just leave this house now. For good.'

She could hardly follow his order, given the way he'd managed to wedge himself between her and the door. How she despised him in that moment! Contempt pinched up all her features, lengthening her thin face. Shareef could tell that his outburst had only hardened her resolve.

'I can't pretend. I won't be a different person with those people.' His voice rang with warning. 'It will be a show, nothing else. If that is what you want . . .'

'I want you to be fair, Baba.'

Their eyes locked, each measuring the resistance in the other.

'You should tell Ma that they're coming,' Lina said.

Iman was in the front room, seated on the sofa, with an ironing board open in front of her and a basket of laundry by her feet. She hadn't managed to iron anything. The machine sat on its metal slot on the board, puffing out steam, and a sheet lay untouched, covering the board's legs in a crumpled cascade. She was concentrating too hard on trying to catch what was going on in the kitchen. Only the occasional rise in tone assured her that father and daughter were still talking. It all sounded far too moderate for Iman's liking.

The hiss of the iron felt more appropriate to the circumstances. Each time she heard it Iman felt as if her own emotions were being acknowledged. She reached for the handle and began to move the hot metal along the creased cotton. How quickly the fabric became smooth! Iman worked faster, drawing comfort from the simple transformation. Maybe normality could be restored after all.

Then she heard a roar from Shareef. She put down the iron. As he hollered on she was consoled – that he was no longer rebutting Lina with mild logic – and also frightened. What could have evoked such a reaction from him? She was wondering whether to go to the kitchen when Shareef came into the sitting room. He rolled his shoulders a few times, cricked his neck. He checked his watch, touched his belt and rocked on his heels. Then his gaze rested on the join between the panels of wallpaper just above her head.

'Shareef? What's going on?'

His nose and mouth twitched like an animal sensing danger. He became aware of a funny smell, and wasn't sure whether it was the scent of his own cowardice or something external. Iman noticed it, too, and hastened to lift the iron off the sheet on which she'd left it sitting. There was a V-shaped brown burn in the middle of the fabric. The machine itself seethed with the singed scraps of cotton that had stuck to it. Iman stared at the damage while Shareef flapped around, pulling the iron's plug out of the socket.

'Why did you have it so hot? You always go overboard.' He lifted the iron and put it to one side. 'Damn thing's ruined! We'll have to get a new one. And you can throw that bloody sheet away as well. Such a waste. Why did you have to do all this now?' He grabbed the sheet and balled it up in his arms.

Iman's posture went floppy with incomprehension. Shareef headed out to dump the sheet in one of the big bins outside the front door.

'It was a mistake,' she said when he returned.

'I don't care. Let it all burn.' His arms rose and fell. 'What good is fresh laundry? A clean shirt doesn't make you think more clearly. Ironed sheets on a bed don't guarantee you'll sleep better.' He picked up the iron and had an urge to hurl the damned contraption to the floor. Instead, he wound the lead around his hand in a rough spiral.

'Where's Lina?' Iman didn't like the way anger was twisting his features.

Shareef folded up the ironing board. Then he picked it up, together with the iron. 'Better put these away.' He slipped out again and Iman heard him shoving the items into a cupboard. She also caught the sound of Lina moving about in the kitchen – the kettle coming on, dishes being washed. She didn't know what to make of the contrast between that homely clatter and the abrasive noises her husband was producing. He re-entered the sitting room, closed the door and leaned heavily against it.

'Shareef?' Her voice was full of suspicion.

His eyes darted towards her and then fell to his feet. 'It looks like those people are coming after all.'

'What-weh?'

'Best to get it over and done with.'

'You agreed?' Iman slumped against the back of the sofa. 'Tobah!'

'I say let Lina see the two families in one room.' Shareef still wasn't able to look her in the eye. 'If words can't drill sense into her, then this meeting might.'

'I won't do it, Shareef, I tell you.' Iman sat forward, hands pressed between her legs. 'I will not take part in any such get-together. Do you hear me?'

'Well – there's no way out now. They'll be here in a few hours. Six o'clock, Lina said.'

'How could you allow this?'

'I tried saying no and it didn't make a difference.' His voice, though low, was loaded with aggression. 'Lina's ready to marry that man. This meeting is the last opportunity to . . .' He swallowed. 'Maybe to influence her. So they're coming.'

'Then I'm going.' Iman pushed herself off the sofa.

'Where?' Shareef's gaze jerked into line with hers.

'Somewhere. Anywhere.' She grabbed at her braid and pulled the end repeatedly through one palm. There was no one she could visit, of course, because that would involve revealing the dramas that were being played out in her own house. She'd have to walk around, or go to the cinema or maybe just drive somewhere and sit in the car. Anything would be preferable to facing those people. 'You can handle this on your own, since you're too weak to put an end to it.'

Shareef's hands rolled into fists. 'Iman, your not being present won't alter the fact of their coming. Please!'

Iman's chin quivered. She wished Lina had never come back. It would have been better not to have seen her at all than be dragged into such lunacy.

'Come on, Iman!' Shareef grasped her by the upper arms. 'We have to face this together. How will it look if we don't present a solid front?'

'I don't care!' She pushed him off with her elbows. 'I'm more concerned about Mariam and Nasra. They'll be home from school by then. Had you even thought of that? They shouldn't witness such idiocy.' She'd have to phone them, delay their return somehow.

Shareef fell to his knees in front of her, his arms encircling her hips. 'Iman, please. I can't do this without you.' He squeezed her thighs. 'Just stay by my side. You don't even have to speak. I just need you to be close. Please, Iman, do this for me.'

Face to Face

Although Iman had started off by saying that she wasn't going to do anything to mark the visit, a couple of hours before the Mayurs' arrival she'd started to clean downstairs as though a health inspector was coming around. And then she'd begun preparing food as if for a great celebration. It wasn't out of any feelings of generosity towards *them*. She just didn't want to give a poor impression of her family. The perversity of her mixed feelings appalled her. Even prayer couldn't entirely calm her down and dim her rage. She felt better while she was actually praying, but as soon as she stopped all her worries boiled up again.

'Can I help with anything?' Lina came into the living room. It was spotless. Even the pile of Shareef's ever-accumulating newspapers had been removed. Iman was plumping up the cushions one last time. She was handling them roughly, almost pummelling each one.

'Don't you think you've done enough already?' Iman snapped.

The doorbell rang.

They came in carrying heaps of gifts. Lina started to feel ill the moment she saw all the booty. She wasn't aware that they had prepared to this extent. She had to excuse herself and run to the bathroom. When she got back to the living room they were already seated. Minnie was talking to her sisters, while the men were having a tense conversation about real estate. Trust Pravar to have turned the topic to money right away, Lina thought.

Pravar had taken the single armchair. He sank back into it, running his hands over the worn velvet fabric on the armrests. As he talked his eyes settled on the accidentally mismatched socks that were visible where the man's trousers had ridden up.

Lina hastened to the kitchen to assist her mother. Iman's every act brimmed with force. She set down the jar of tea bags with a thump, closed the cupboard with a bang, grabbed a tray as though it was a shield to be wielded in self-defence. She ignored Lina's offers of assistance and flew around the kitchen as though someone was timing her.

'I can see why you fell for him. But you should have known better,' she remarked eventually.

Without a word, Lina picked up the tray of food and carried it to the other room. When she came back Iman was wiping her eyes.

'You don't know what you're putting us through.' Iman pulled her chuni over her head, tucked it behind her ears, and then looped the ends around her neck.

Lina couldn't think how to respond. The only thing still holding her together was the look of reassurance Anil had given her when he'd walked in. His presence alone gave her confidence. He was wearing a suit, as was Pravar. And Minnie, of course, was typically well-turned-out. In fact, they were a bit overdressed for the occasion and the location. She couldn't help noticing how out of place they looked in her modest home, as if they were too glossy to fit in. And those flowers they'd bought! She felt annoyed all of a sudden, because they were so pristine: a flawless arrangement in their own glass vase. They made the rest of the room feel shabby. Why couldn't Anil just have bought a bunch of chrysanthemums at a petrol station, the way normal people did? Such ostentation would only make her parents uncomfortable. Iman would probably accuse them of trying to bribe her. Which, knowing Pravar, they probably were.

Out in the street passers-by noted the flashy new Mercedes parked outside the Merali house. One particularly inquisitive neighbour – the one who always asked Iman how Lina was doing – stole up to the front window to take a peek. Through the mesh of the white net curtains she saw two families having tea together. Mouths moved energetically – though more from chewing than talking. It looked like a typical introduction – except – one man was wearing a turban! The woman scurried away to spread what she'd seen.

Indoors, the sounds of appreciation for Iman's cooking were making her soften slightly, against her inclination.

'Mmmm. These must be the best mince koftas I've ever eaten.' Anil helped himself to a fourth one. 'Mum, you have to get the recipe from Iman.'

Lina winced as he used her mother's name. She knew her parents would hate being addressed so informally. She should have warned Anil in advance. But then again, the list of 'don'ts' that she'd given him was already long enough. He'd remarked that there was probably less protocol for visiting the president of the USA.

'Yes, they're very good.' Minnie balanced the plate on her lap. 'The BSE scare doesn't seem to have put people off eating beef. Even at the hotel they had a special steak menu as a lunch offer. Very strange, I think.'

'That's probably because it's cheap.' Pravar spoke through a mouthful. He was eating heartily despite a huge portion of spare ribs at lunch. He'd deliberately chosen the pork, as if it would somehow arm him before entry into a Muslim household. 'They've got special offers on it now to tempt everyone and keep the beef industry afloat.'

Iman was riled by the implication that she'd bought the mince because of the low price. 'We don't buy our meat at the supermarket, anyway. It has to be halal.' She might have been daring them to stop eating. Pravar did, in fact, halt his chewing for a moment. 'Anyway, you can't get such diseases from halal meat,' she went on.

'Ma.' Mariam rolled her eyes.

'What?' One side of Pravar's mouth stretched upwards. 'You think all disease drains out with the blood when you kill animals your halal way?'

Lina shot Anil a panicked glare. He also seemed uncomfortable with his father's comment.

'I don't know the science of it.' Iman tossed her head. 'But I've heard that is the case.'

'Who told you?' Shareef asked.

'Mullah Aazim. He shops at the same halal place as us.'

'Ach.' Shareef waved a hand. 'That's nothing to take seriously.' Aazim's view on a lot of things was pretty questionable.

'Well, he said it,' Iman insisted. 'He also told me he'd seen a story in the paper about how sales of halal meat are up in Russia. Even non-Muslims there prefer that now because they believe it carries less of a risk.'

'People sometimes get funny ideas. I wouldn't believe everything you hear.' Shareef hoped she would drop the subject.

Iman's eyes narrowed. First he insisted that she be

present to support him, and then he put her down like that in public.

'I think if any of us are destined to catch such a disease then we'll get it whatever we believe.' Minnie pushed the cushion on her left further behind her back, and tried to forget the hole she'd spotted in its cover. 'Fate – there's nothing you can do to change it. That's what I think.'

There was a short silence, and then Anil cleared his throat. 'I guess fate may be partly what's brought us all into this room together. I want to thank you both, Shareef and Iman, for agreeing to see me and my parents. I understand that this isn't easy for you. I hoped that if you saw me and Lina together . . .' He glanced at her, but she was staring at the floor. 'You'd see how serious we are. We want to spend our lives together. We've already set a date for the wedding. It's difficult for Lina to be doing all this without your approval, so I'm here to ask you, please.' He turned to Shareef, who was sitting beside him. 'Give us your permission to get married. And please say you'll join us for the celebrations in Kenya. I've already reserved flights for all four of you and Khala Rocky and her son. If you say yes I'll confirm everything.'

The directness of the appeal caught Shareef off guard. He quickly swallowed the food in his mouth. On the other side of the room Iman drew in a sharp breath. She hadn't expected such an open plea, either. It was embarrassing to be put on the spot like that in your own front room. She hoped Shareef would spell out an irrevocable no. She wanted these people out of her house as soon as possible. Especially Pravar, with his snooty glances, looking around the place as if he'd been transported to an Islamic version of Disneyland. She wished Mariam and Nasra weren't there, witnessing the whole debacle.

Lina felt her limbs might lock solid with tension. She wondered if everyone could hear her heart thumping.

'Every father wants the best for his child,' Shareef said.

'Yes. No. Absolutely. That's why we are here. For Anil's sake. To support him.'

Shareef nodded. 'The thing is, it's not in my hands to decide this.' He happened to glance at Iman.

'Ha ha!' Pravar grinned. 'It's the same in my house. Someone else wears the trousers, at least as far as the kids are concerned.'

'It is not in any human hands.' Shareef spoke quietly. 'What is possible and what is not has already been decided by God.'

'We should not put a question mark where Allah has put a full stop,' Iman added.

Another silence descended. Lina did not dare look up. Beside her Nasra pressed her fingers down on top of the sweets Iman had made, and then turned over her hand to see if the silver foil had come off on to her fingertips.

'I respect Lina's faith. I would never try to stop her from practising. She's free to teach our children what she believes.'

Shareef kept smoothing the corners of his moustache.

Anil put his plate down between his feet, and clasped his hands together. He had to will himself to stay calm, to keep the exasperation out of his voice. 'You want Lina to be happy and that's what I wish for, too. She will pass from your care into mine.'

Shareef started to roll his shoulders. They moved slowly, as if against some great force.

Pravar sat up. 'I personally don't see the point of going over and over the same point. The question is simple: Will you accept that your daughter is marrying my son?'

Minnie and Iman both shifted on their seats. Lina's clothes felt too tight, despite their bagginess. Anil sensed that his father's forthright tone wasn't the right counterpoint to Shareef's gentle machinations.

'I cannot answer that question. It is not for me to say. The law is there. It is laid out clearly in the Book. I have promised only to follow the law.'

'And Lina?' Pravar pulled her out of passivity. 'Does she follow this *law*? Presumably not, seeing as she's with my son. Yes? No?'

Lina's eyes darted over all their faces. She could see the expectation there, the impatience. 'What matters to me, right now,' she said, 'is to have the go-ahead from you.' She looked at Shareef.

'Very funny situation.' Pravar threw his hands into the air. 'You say you can't decide, she says she can't decide. You say God is responsible, she says you are responsible. This is impossible. Completely. No? Absolutely. Yes? So why are we here?'

Anil wondered if it might have been better to come without his parents. Pravar was too brazen. This wasn't Kenya, where you just threw your authority around and then sealed the deal with kitu kidogo. 'I've waited all these years for Lina,' he said. 'I won't be put off now.'

Pravar jerked his head in Lina's direction. 'Why can't the girl decide for herself?'

'Of course she is free to do that. She has always been,' Shareef said.

'And you would accept whatever she does?'

'We would have to. But all decisions have consequences. To accept does not mean to condone.'

'Well.' Pravar stood up. 'There's nothing else to say then, is there?' He wasn't going to stand for any more insinuations about his family's unworthiness. 'The date is set – chosen by Lina herself. I guess you lot won't be there to enjoy it. I hope you will, at least, accept our gifts today. We came with goodwill and the best intentions.' His wrists moved in expressive circles. 'Show them, Minnie, what we've brought.' He seemed confident, as if he had one last trick up his sleeve.

'Oh, it's not much. Just a few things for the girls.' She explained that the flowers were for Iman, and the bag of luxury chocolates for them all. Then she handed Mariam and Nasra each a bag. The girls peered, but dared not delve into the bags because of the warning stare Iman was directing at them. Finally, Minnie gave Lina a small black bag with the word '*Precious*' embossed across one side in silver letters.

'This is too much.' Lina tried to refuse the gift. She knew '*Precious*' was the jeweller Minnie always bought from in Nairobi.

'How can you say that when you don't even know what's in there?' Minnie's teeth flashed into view. 'For all you know it could be a chocolate egg.'

'Even that would be too much. You didn't have to do all this.' She glanced at Anil, who was biting on his cheeks.

'Open it, then,' Pravar ordered. He was standing over everyone now.

Lina lifted a box out of the bag and began to unwrap it. She suspected it was an ostentatious ring that she'd be asked to slip on as a token of allegiance. She started to panic about how she should respond. The box almost fell out of her hands as she pulled away the last of the ribbon. She took the lid off. Her heart almost stopped when she saw the diamonds gleaming within.

'Take it out. Let's all have a look,' Pravar said.

She drew out the chain. It was a long strand of platinum strung with diamonds. No! It was not a necklace, she realized, but a tasbih! She gasped and heard several more gasps around her. The stones glinted, throwing out sparks the way a wet dog shakes off water. Lina dropped the tasbih back into the box. Her mouth was open, but she didn't know what to say.

Pravar gazed around with satisfaction, pleased at the incredulity on all the Meralis' faces. This, if anything, would bring them around.

'That tasbih is supposed to be a symbol.' Anil spoke up. 'It's a sign of our respect for your faith. We – I will never interfere with that faith. I will only support Lina in it. I don't want to take anything away from her – only to give.'

Shareef stole a glance at Iman. He could tell what she thought from her pose: her straight back, and the angle of her chin. She wanted to tell them to take their wretched rocks and get the hell out. He was also dismayed by the over-the-top gesture. He supposed that such extravagance was just the Mayur family's way. What touched him was Anil's earnestness, his love for Lina was obvious in his words and bearing. Try as he might, Shareef couldn't be indifferent to that.

'You are a fine young man.' Shareef put a hand on Anil's shoulder. He sensed Iman tensing across the room. 'Lina is lucky to know you. I think I might have misled you in letting you come here today. Perhaps you thought you could persuade me to support your wish to be with my daughter. My mind was never the one I expected to be altered by this meeting. I had hoped only that it would help Lina see things more clearly. The choice is still hers.' Then Shareef directed himself at Pravar. 'You have been too generous—'

'Ah, this is nothing.' Pravar waved nonchalantly. 'We could give Lina the world.'

'Yes, I see that you could take very good care of her. I hope you will not misunderstand me when I say that we cannot accept your kindness. These presents – I'm sure Lina will agree regardless of what she decides . . .' He waited for her confirmation, which came with a few dips of her chin. 'These presents obligate us beyond our capacity to reciprocate. I must ask you to take them back.'

Nasra, who'd been covertly spying out the contents of her bag, let out a sound of disappointment.

'It doesn't make any difference to us whether you give them back or throw them in the bin!' Pravar's face reddened. 'Either way, it's a slap in the face.' His eyes rested accusingly on Anil for an instant.

'At least let the girls keep their gifts,' Minnie interjected. 'There's nothing much in those.'

'You misunderstand me. It is not your generosity I'm rebuking, it is my own limitations that I'm pleading. I am not in the habit of taking where I cannot give back.'

'Well, your daughter should have thought of that before she took my son's heart!' A pin at the crest of Pravar's turban caught the light and flashed. 'I think our business here is done.' He dashed from the room and let himself out of the front door.

Anil and Minnie quickly rose too.

'He gets very emotional,' Minnie tried to explain. She knew that Pravar was upset because he'd expected the tasbih to seal the deal, and he'd taken it personally that his money hadn't done the trick. She said a hasty goodbye and hurried after her husband.

'And now, Lina?' Anil came and stood next to her.

The vacant glaze that had been there when she'd come

447

to consciousness in the MSF compound had returned to Lina's eyes. 'I need to say goodbye.'

'Ya Allah!' Iman twisted around, her face puckered with pain.

Lina took a step towards her, but Shareef came between them. His visage was like a plaster cast of itself, cold and hard.

'Just go, if you're leaving.'

'Baba.' The corners of her mouth turned down, her bottom lip protruded.

He remained stiff, implacable. 'Just go.'

V

In the Line of Fire

IN A LOW TIMBER structure, on the outskirts of one of the camps for internally displaced people in South Sudan, Sheikh Jibal Obkik placated a family whose son had been arrested earlier that day for being in possession of a gun. There was a strict no-guns policy in UN-run camps. Anyone caught with a weapon was handed over to the police – a fate dreaded by all because the officers were believed to collude with various militias, and were feared for their cruelty. The male family members and Sheikh Jibal were all seated on chairs in a circle. Lina and the translator, Wani, who was converting the Arabic into English, were at the back of the room on a bench.

Lina scribbled notes for the report she would later write on how disputes in the camp were arbitrated. Despite her efforts to focus, she was following the proceedings only sporadically: her concentration was like a ball that keeps rolling off the surface on which it has been carefully balanced. There were just two weeks to go, now, before her wedding. The day after tomorrow she would fly to Nairobi and arrive just in time for the revelry. Ten days of celebration would mark the run-up to her union with Anil. And hardly anyone who really mattered to her would be there. Lina tapped the inner soles of her trainers together. Thin puffs of dust rose off them. She gave herself a shake and forced her attention back to the scene in front of her.

Dahab, the father of the boy who'd been arrested, was defending his son.

'What are we supposed to do? Everybody around us has guns.' He meant everybody outside the camp. 'How can we protect ourselves?' Dahab was a frail old man. His clothes were too large for his frame. The shoulder seams of his green shirt hung halfway down his upper arms. His hands shook as they rested on the walking stick which stood between his legs.

Sheikh Jibal clicked his tongue. 'If I let your family keep their weapon, then your neighbours would want one, too, and pretty soon everybody would be insisting on their right to self-defence.' He was the only one wearing a jalabiya, but the long white robe alone was not what distinguished him. It was his manner that made him stand out: the consideration with which he listened, the assurance with which he spoke. If only such men had been in charge at every camp. The UN tried to allow people to maintain their traditional customs and structures as far as possible, it made life much easier for everyone. But not all the appointed leaders could be impartial or resist bribery.

'Maybe it wouldn't be such a bad thing if every man has his own gun,' Dahab said.

'Ay, and then?' Sheikh Jibal remained calm but firm. 'You yourself know how many rivalries there are in this place. Soon we would have fighting going on right here – in the space where we are supposed to be protected.'

'But we're not, are we?' One of the other elders interrupted. 'This is what we're saying: they come from outside with guns and kill us.'

'Ay, we can keep discussing, but you all know the rules, and they can't be changed.' Sheikh Jibal rose and started shaking hands with all the men. 'I'm sorry about your boy.

But there's nothing I can do now. Just remember, those who have guns end up killing.'

'Ay, and those who don't have guns end up dying.' Dahab shook his head before leaving.

Lina watched him go, disturbed by his statement. There were no easy answers in this place. She thought of Hans. They had bumped into each other once since that awful night in the MSF compound. The encounter had been awkward, both of them embarrassed by something that hadn't happened. She felt more like a fraud around him than ever. Truth be told, she felt false, full stop.

'Lina, are you finished?' Wani nudged her.

Sheikh Jibal was standing by the door, waiting to see if she had any questions.

'Almost.' She pretended to make some final jottings. Later she'd have to ask Wani to talk her through what had happened so she could do a proper write-up.

All of a sudden there was the sound of shots being fired outside. Lina dropped the notebook and Sheikh Jibal peered out of the hut. He slammed the door shut and shouted something in Arabic.

'He's saying to get down!' Wani told Lina. The two of them ran and crouched in a corner, behind the chairs and benches. They heard more shots. Then the sound of horses and people running.

After a minute, Sheikh Jibal looked out again and rushed from the hut.

'Where's he gone?' Lina whispered as the door banged shut. She was now lying flat, her elbows pressed into her sides, her forehead against the earthen floor. Beside her Wani was in almost the same position, though his head was turned towards the entrance.

'Probably to check on his family.'

There were more shouts, cries, shots. Chickens squawked. Goats bleated. Donkeys brayed. Children shrieked. A soundtrack from a slaughterhouse.

'Janjaweed.' Wani could tell from the curses being hollered outside.

'You! Black women, we will exterminate you, you have no God! We are your God! Your God is Omar al-Bashir!'

Lina also understood some of the cries: 'You blacks, you have spoilt the country! We are here to burn you.'

She started to pray. Bismillah al-rahman al-rahim. Silently repeating those same words over and over. Her jaw kept trembling, causing her teeth to chatter like a small bag of stones being shaken around. She thought of Anil – how she might never be with him. Ya Allah, let me live to see him again. She thought of her family – they hadn't spoken since the day she'd left Birmingham. Even her sisters were afraid to communicate because Shareef had threatened to disown them, too, if he found out they'd been in touch with Lina. She'd refused to believe in the finality of their estrangement, telling herself her parents' attitude would soften. Now, for the first time, she faced the fact that she might never see them again. She was hounded by regret for the cruelty – hers and theirs – of the last encounter. Ya Allah, give me a chance to repair those bonds.

Outside, about two hundred armed men were storming through the camp. The horses on which they rode kicked up orange flames of dust. Most of the riders headed straight for the grain depot, shooting anyone who got in their way. There they stole sacks of millet. Others roamed the camp alleyways, rounding up cattle. Within ten minutes they were riding off again, their loot loaded on to their beasts, several dwellings left burning in their wake.

'I think they are gone,' Wani said as quiet descended.

Lina hadn't moved apart from giving involuntary shivers and convulsions of fear. She was still too scared even to lift her head.

Wani crawled to the window and peeked out. 'They have gone.'

He came and helped Lina on to a chair. Every one of her limbs was still trembling. They were deciding what to do when a ringing sound made them both jump.

'My phone,' Lina said. It was in her bag, which was on the bench where she'd been seated before. One of her colleagues was calling around to check that everyone was OK. Lina was told to stay where she was until someone came to get her. But Wani was impatient to go and verify that the people he knew were not hurt.

'I'll come with you.' She was afraid of staying alone in the hut.

She followed him down one of the dusty streets. The place felt strangely deserted, though some men were starting to emerge and grope cautiously through the aftermath of the attack. At one point, Wani, who was walking ahead of her, turned abruptly and tried to make her do the same. But she'd already seen what he had. Lying on the ground a few metres away was a body twisted into a heap. A wooden walking stick lay beside it, the hooked end protruding from under one leg like a broken smile. The man's green shirt was soaked with blood. It was Dahab.

'He needs help!' Lina fumbled for her phone. 'We've got to get someone here. He needs attention!' Her legs gave way. Her knees dug into the dry soil. But she kept searching for her phone.

Wani knelt beside her. 'It's too late, Lina. Too late.'

A younger man was already prostrated by the body, weeping.

Lina didn't want to believe it. She recalled the old man's last words: 'Those who don't have guns end up dying'.

It was only after Lina was collected from the camp and taken back to the staff base that she began to get a clearer idea of what had happened that afternoon. Apparently police had pursued the attackers, but been ambushed. African Union forces were alerted, but could not mobilize in time. Two UN cars were unaccounted for, radio calls were still going unanswered – there had been several passengers in each vehicle. As the evening wore on, it became clear that there were half a dozen other casualties in the camp. There were also rumours that five women had been abducted.

The attack in itself wasn't unusual. Such incidents happened regularly across the region, and small skirmishes took place in the vicinity almost every day. Staff were told to expect them, and given training in emergency response procedures. But the audacity of this one was shocking. It had all happened so quickly, yet the time Lina had spent lying face down in the hut had felt interminable. She suddenly realized that that was what camp residents experienced on a regular basis. No wonder they wanted guns. She had to remind herself that if there had been more guns, it would have meant more deaths. And that could not be justified, even if some of the dead were Janjaweed.

'You OK, Lina?' Jen put a mug of tea in front of her.

'She's still in shock,' another colleague said.

They were all in the common room at the staff headquarters: a little compound of bungalows situated about half an hour's drive east from the main camp.

Lina recognized the faces around her, heard their voices, felt someone take her hand – and at the same time, she had the sense that she wasn't in the room. She was still on that street, recognizing Dahab's body. What if he had been killed by one of the guns brought over from Nairobi in a plane she'd flown on? Did that make her guilty? Was she indirectly responsible for his murder? Questions, which she had avoided since the decision to marry Anil, dashed to the front of her mind. She was complicit. There was no getting around it. She was implicated by all she knew, and all she had not done.

The two jet skis slashed long white trails across the water, like zips being opened along the back of the sea. Anil was half-standing as he revved his machine up to maximum speed. Behind him Merc was shouting something. Anil could hardly hear over the noise of the engine and the slap of water against the jet ski.

A few minutes earlier they'd been at a bar on the beach for Anil's stag party. JT had asked Merc what he was going to say in his best man's speech and Merc had revealed that he hadn't written it yet. The guys had all launched into reminiscence, dragging up old incidents involving Anil's humiliation, and offering them to Merc for his speech.

'Hey, it's not that I'm short of material.' Merc took a long sip from his bottle of Tusker. 'I just don't want to waste time on something that probably won't be necessary. You get me?' He still couldn't believe Lina and Anil were back together for good. Things had been a little cool between him and Anil ever since he'd called his friend a lost cause. Nor had Merc met Lina since that day at Wilson Airport. Merc was sure she hadn't mentioned their discussion to Anil – otherwise he would certainly have heard something from his friend by now. On the other hand, he doubted Lina could wed Anil without saying a word about the arms trafficking. Something weird was going on. 'Who knows if this wedding will really take place?'

JT drew in a breath like a whistle and looked from Anil to Merc.

'The great Tiresias speaks,' Anil shook his head. 'Why don't you save your optimism for your own nuptial prospects?'

'Mazeh, I have no such designs. I'm with Herbert Spencer on that one.' He raised his beer. ' "Marriage: a word which should be pronounced mirage." ' Especially by his poor friend, who had been plodding towards this Fata Morgana for years.

The other guys, half of them with gold bands on their ring fingers, cheered and clinked their bottles against his. Only Anil sat with his eyes narrowed and his drink rooted firmly to the table.

'I do actually have the first line of my speech,' Merc admitted. He pretended not to want to share it, but then gave in to the chorus of insistence. 'It's simple: I never believed this day would come.' Silence fell over the table. The smack of waves flopping on to the beach suddenly seemed louder. 'I may well have to improvise the rest on the day, because it's true, I won't believe it until I see it. You get me?'

Anil stood up. 'Sometimes you're a cynical bastard. I need a break from this doom and gloom.'

As he headed off Merc calmly took another swig. 'That Lina's got him like a terminal disease.'

Anil walked towards the ocean, kicking up sand and feeling it slide through his toes. A serpentine fringe of seaweed traced the tidemark along the beach. Merc's words skewered his own unvoiced fears. Extravagant celebrations were due to commence in a few days, and Lina had hardly been involved in any of the planning. 'I've never known a girl so uninterested in her own wedding,' Minnie had commented.

Anil had then noticed the jet skis tied to the small jetty, bobbing on the water like space-age swans. He'd decided to go for a ride.

'Shit!' Back at the table Merc had sprung up. 'The guy's totally lewad and he's getting on a jet ski.' They'd all had too much pombe for that kind of thing. He'd run down the beach towards his friend, shouting at him to wait. Anil had been arguing with the attendant, refusing to wear the life jacket he was trying to give him.

'It's too hot, bwana. I'm just going for a short spin.'

Then, as Merc was trying to stop him, Anil had just taken off. So Merc had leapt on to one of the other jet skis and followed, similarly disregarding calls to put on a life jacket.

'Mazeh! Slow down! You're going out too far!'

Anil turned to catch what Merc was saying. He was close now, just a couple of metres behind. They were both going so fast that the machines kept bouncing out of the water and flying through the air.

'You've always had it in for Lina,' Anil yelled.

'That's because I know more about her than you do!'

'What?' Anil swerved towards his friend. He was now riding against the waves. Surf hit him in the face like tear gas. He squeezed his eyes shut for an instant.

'She hasn't told – Shit! Anil! Watch out! Look!'

Anil faced forward again and saw a motorboat coming towards them out of nowhere. 'Turn! Go—' Merc continued to call.

Those were the last words Anil heard from his friend's mouth.

Pravar called Lina in Sudan to tell her there had been an accident. He refused to give her any details, saying only that Anil was in hospital and his condition was stable.

'Can I speak to him?'

'No one can. He's in a medically induced coma, because of the trauma. They're going to start bringing him out of it tomorrow. I'm sending a plane to get you,' he announced.

'I ca—' Her heart clanged. Apart from the night when Anil had come to get her from Juba, she hadn't flown with Air Mayur since Merc had told her about the arms trafficking. She could just go tomorrow, with the UN plane, on the flight she'd originally booked in order to attend her wedding. The flight which, ever since the attack on the camp, she'd been debating whether to take or not. But Anil . . .

'It'll be there in three or four hours,' Pravar was saying.

'I . . . OK.' She had to go. She had to be there when Anil woke.

Her worry for him eclipsed the guilt of using Air Mayur again. Even as she wrote a quick report on the attack, she found herself thinking of him. Usually, when she was working, it was her other life that seemed unreal. The worst afflictions of the West were padded by comforts. If news of friends' affairs, divorces, job difficulties, illnesses and disobedient children came through, the problems seemed like presents she could have gift-wrapped and given to the brutalized folk around her.

When the Air Mayur plane took off for Nairobi, she looked down and saw the camp fading to a speck.

She imagined women down there queuing for the day's food and water rations, and she remembered her mother saying: 'Finish what's on your plate, Lina. There are children elsewhere on this planet who are starving.'

'How does my finishing help them?' ten-year-old Lina had wondered out loud.

A look had passed between the parents, one of those impenetrable exchanges. Then Shareef had spoken, 'It helps *you*, to know, to remember, always, how lucky you are.'

As the plane rose above the clouds, Lina was sure that luck, happiness, love – all the things that mattered – could not be measured in relation to anyone else's experience. The private sphere is bigger than the public. It always has been. That is why lovers can rejoice during a war, why a birth is celebrated during famine, why siblings play heedlessly in fields where their ancestors were maimed. Even those on opposite sides of a public divide can end up defying convention or risking death out of their own personal conviction. The past is dotted with acts of humanity, instants of individual benevolence, between seeming enemies: Tutsi and Hutu, Muslim and Hindu.

Lina held this thought with a kind of shame, knowing what she did: that the public can eclipse, degrade and destroy the private. This had been proved countless times while she was working in Sudan. The women she met, who had fled from their homes, and arrived with nothing except the growing seed of the men who had raped them. The fathers, who had seen their daughters violated. The wives, whose husbands had been murdered in front of them, hacked by machetes as if they were blades of grass. The children, forced to collaborate in the slaughter of their own parents. These were histories crueller than anything she would ever experience. They haunted her, turned her sick with sadness at the monstrosity of mankind. They were the causes to which she'd dedicated her life – and yet, they seemed to fade in the face of her own personal crisis.

She wondered how many kinds of truth there were. How many layers of reality? And how anyone was supposed to decide which one mattered most. She tried to push away the feeling, even as it claimed her. She was full of fear about Anil – what had happened to him? What would the future bring? How would she tell him what she needed to? These worries tore at her worse than any atrocity. Cringing, wanting to tear apart the words as they formed, she thought: the world, finally, is what lies closest to your heart.

At the Aga Khan Hospital Pravar greeted Lina with a brief wave before continuing with a heated conversation on his mobile phone. Minnie, however, kept one of her hands firmly locked in Lina's while giving her an update outside Anil's room. She snivelled while she spoke, stopping frequently to blow her nose. 'It was an accident. They were drunk. Boys will be boys. And those two were always messing around. So this happened. It's simple to say now that they should have been more careful. But it's always easy to know better afterwards. I just wish they had been luckier . . .'

'They?'

'It was him and Merc on jet skis, the others were on the beach. It was an accident. And Merc – didn't make it.'

Lina's hands slapped over her mouth. Several thoughts hit her in quick succession: Merc was dead. Poor Anil. Merc was dead. There was no way the wedding could go ahead now. The last thought contained a shameful measure of relief.

'The police are investigating. They have to – for insurance and whatnot. But it's clear it was an accident. It's completely clear, I think.'

Lina nodded.

'Go talk to him now.' Minnie pushed her towards the door. 'Maybe you can make him see sense. He keeps blaming himself.'

Anil's left side was swathed in casts and bandages. His leg – the same he'd smashed the knee of falling down the stairs at the Arrow – was slightly upraised on a couple of pillows, the toes peeking out of a cast that extended up to his thigh. His arm was also in plaster. There was a bruise on his left temple. There were other bruises, which couldn't be seen, all over his body and his heart.

'Anil,' Lina whispered, not sure where to touch. Her fingers grazed the palm of his right hand.

'You're here.' He looked so tired. There were lines in his face that she'd never seen before. His hair seemed to have greyed as well. His hand closed over her fingers.

She didn't know what to say. 'Does it hurt?'

'Not enough.' His mouth grew thin. 'I should have been the one who died.'

'Anil! Don't say that!'

'It's my fault.' His voice was dull.

'It was an accident, Anil. Don't do this to yourself.' Maybe she was culpable, too. Hadn't she prayed countless times for something that would take the decision to marry Anil out of her hands? Hadn't she wished endlessly that it might all be settled without her having to make a choice?

'My own friend.' Tears rolled from his eyes. 'My best friend. I killed him.'

'Anil.' She looked around desperately as if there might be some reassurance lying around that she could pick up and offer him. She caught sight of Pravar watching them through the window in the door.

'I put us in the situation. I got on the jet ski without a life jacket and he followed me.'

Pravar stepped in and shut the door behind him. 'You better stop talking like this. You hear me? Yes? No?' He stood by the side of the bed, wagging a finger. 'These officers are hanging about trying to find someone to blame, and they just need to hear your self-pity to nail you.'

'I can't deny the truth.'

'Talk to me about the truth when you're holed up in Nairobi Prison. You just say you can't remember anything when they ask – OK?' He hovered over his son. 'That lump on your head is enough to prove concussion. Yes. Definitely.' He had no patience with Anil's moping. The boy had survived the accident only to emerge into a shark pool of accusations and threats. Merc's father was understandably anxious to establish what had happened to his son. Even though Samuel Ojielo claimed to believe Anil was innocent and that he simply wanted to 'establish the facts', Pravar didn't trust him. These people always had agendas. It didn't matter how entwined their business interests were, Pravar knew Ojielo's loyalties were ultimately with his family and his tribe.

The owners of the motorboat, meanwhile, were trying to sue. They'd already got a statement from the water-sports attendant confirming that the boys were drunk and neither was wearing a life jacket. Pravar's people had since bribed the man to give a counter-statement asserting otherwise, but there was no telling which way things might go. All three parties were paying the police, so Pravar was doubly suspicious, despite the chuckled guarantees that the head investigator was giving him. If he'd been sure that the case would go in favour of whoever paid the most, he wouldn't have been so worried. But Merc's dad was a government minister and the motorboat owners were wealthy Luos, so there was no predicting what might sway the officers – greed, clan loyalty or the promise of presidential goodwill.

'I have to go to a meeting now.' Before leaving, Pravar brought his face level with Anil's and briefed him once more on how to behave.

Anil was subdued after his father's departure. 'The funeral's tomorrow,' he said a while later. 'I want to go. You have to help me.'

'How can you go? You can't walk!' She wasn't even sure he could sit up.

'I'll go on a stretcher, if I have to. It's the least I can do.' He didn't care that his broken ribs cut like blades with every breath, let alone the tiniest move. 'You've got to make sure they don't sedate me.' He'd overheard his father telling Minnie they'd just get the doctor to 'put him out for a while' if he continued to insist on attending the funeral. He knew Pravar was perfectly capable of this. 'Promise that you'll stay here and accompany me.'

'If that's what you want.' She shifted from one foot to the other. 'If you think you can cope.'

'I'll manage. It'll be good practice anyway, for the wedding.'

Her heart seemed to stop. 'You can't . . . you don't mean . . . we're still going ahead?'

'It's the only thing that makes me feel it might be worth living.'

Her heartbeat kicked in with a ferocity that made her dizzy. She pulled up one of the chairs and sat down near the bed. 'Is it the right thing, though? Might be better to wait.' One hand went to her chest, where a hard lump was forming.

'What will waiting change? The preparations have been made. We might as well do it.' The green shadow of unshaven hairs across his jaw made him look even worse.

'But you're not really strong enough. You won't be able to attend all the functions.' The first event had been due to take place the following night, but it had been cancelled, in deference to Merc.

'I never wanted all that fuss, anyway. It was more for my mum. All these people that have been invited, I don't even know most of them. I'm glad I have an excuse to miss most of it. The wedding itself is what counts. I'll be at the registry for that.' Somehow. Even if he was still confined to a horizontal existence. His brows pulled together suddenly and his mouth contorted in pain.

Lina, gripped by her own doubts, didn't notice. 'What about me?'

He took several slow breaths before answering. 'You can do whatever you like. Go party, or hang out with me in this palace of thrills. Some of your friends are coming over, aren't they?'

She nodded. Isabel would arrive in two days.

'So you'll get busy.'

'I guess so.' She knew of only one thing she had to do. It would be more demanding than the full sum of her life's efforts so far. The blood pounded in her head. She looked at the tubes surrounding Anil. They looped over and into him, like limp, tangled music staves. She rose quickly and went to his bed. She kissed his forehead, pushed her fingers through his hair. It felt rough and sticky.

'All knotty.' Lina ran her long nails through it.

'Haven't washed it since the accident.' His mouth twisted.

'Shhhh.' Lina pressed her lips to his. 'Don't think about that now.'

He closed his eyes and sucked in his cheeks as though he was trying to hold himself together. 'Merc said something before he . . . before I . . . before . . .' He took a deep breath. 'He said he knew you better.'

Lina's hands slipped down to grip the metal frame of the bed.

'He didn't get a chance to finish . . . But he sounded so sure. I feel like he knew something I don't.'

Lina held his gaze, unblinking, as if this was a staring competition she had to win. 'How could he know me better than you? No one knows me like you do.'

'He was so sure.' Anil remembered the defiance in Merc's voice – its determined urgency had overriden the rev of the jet ski engines.

'Certainty was Merc's trademark, wasn't it? He always thought he knew best.' Even her shock at his untimely death couldn't eradicate the dislike that had built up over the years.

'He thought we'd never get married.'

She began blinking rapidly. Blood throbbed through her hands. She wondered if the acceleration of her heartbeat would vibrate through the metal of Anil's bed and shake him to recognition of the truth she was still trying to deny.

'He said you wouldn't be able to do it.'

'I'm here now, aren't I?' She spoke so gently that he couldn't have guessed how hard the words were to say.

Departure

'W̲ᴇ'ʀᴇ ʟᴏᴏᴋɪɴɢ ʟɪᴋᴇ ꜰᴏᴏʟꜱ.' Pravar paced their bed-room, arms hanging, his short fingers catching at the air as if they were itching to grab hold of something. 'A wedding in which no one gets married.' What nonsense. It was like having a film without actors.

'What do you mean? They will be married on Saturday.' Minnie folded up her heavy sari carefully. She thought of all the new clothes piled up in Lina's room, outfits that she'd had made for her in India and that now wouldn't be worn for the ceremonies. Same with all Anil's stuff, the new suits and sherwanis – the latter would probably sit unused for ever. She couldn't imagine him finding cause to put on one of the elaborately embroidered long jackets on any other occasion.

'Atch.' Pravar batted away her certainty. 'I wouldn't bet on anything. No way. Too much has gone wrong in the last week. Makes me think this match is doomed. Didn't I tell you?' He stopped and pointed at his wife.

'Well, at least it looks like we're getting to a decent end now.' She put the sari into a protective bag.

'A decent end!' Pravar rolled his eyes. 'The groom is an invalid, the best man is dead, and the bride looks like she's ready to run off!'

Minnie sat down on the bed. 'You don't think she will?'

'I don't know what to think.' He didn't trust the girl. 'She certainly looks a mess.'

'A lot has happened, Pravar. And she must be upset that her family isn't here. That's not easy for any girl.' Minnie remembered how much she'd missed her dead father at her own wedding. 'She wouldn't back out now. Not after everything that's happened, and with Anil in such a state.'

Pravar shook his head. He wasn't sure. Yesterday, he'd seen Lina in the garden, crying and talking on her mobile. Why not use one of the house phones? There was one in every room. Why go and hide out in the garden? If she was still trying to convince her ignorant parents to come around it was a bad sign. He'd already asked the driver, Kamau, who took her everywhere, to keep an eye on her and report immediately if anything suspicious went on. So far Kamau had only related that she cried a lot. Not a fact that needed verification. It was clear from the daily state of her face. Yes. Completely. You'd think they were torturing the girl, instead of giving her a dream wedding.

'I just hope Anil's well enough to sit in a wheelchair, at least, by Saturday,' Minnie was saying. It had been terrible to see him brought to Merc's funeral on a stretcher, like a second corpse.

'Anil's not the one we need to worry about. He's so obsessed with that girl I doubt anything could stop him now.' Pravar started pacing again, but quickly came to an abrupt halt. 'I want you to keep an eye on Lina. Yes. You must insist that she starts showing her face at the functions from tomorrow night.'

'Well, tomorrow she has to. It's the mendhi. She'll agree, don't worry. She's good like that, I think.'

'She bloody agrees to everything with everyone. That's the problem. Absolutely. Yes.'

469

* * *

Lina showed Isabel into one of the Mayurs' guest-rooms, where Minnie had said she could stay. Her friend's mouth fell open as she looked around.

'This place is like a modern Versailles. You can bet I'll be here for all my holidays after you're married.'

Lina stood by the huge French windows that led on to the balcony. 'If I get married,' she said.

Isabel came out of the walk-in wardrobe she'd been busy examining. 'You're not still having doubts? *Lina!*'

'I wish Anil had a different family.'

'What?' From where Isabel was standing she could only see Lina's reflection in the windows: a barefoot silhouette with stooping shoulders in a turquoise sundress. 'I bet he wishes the same about you.'

On another day Lina might have laughed.

'Wow! Look at the size of this bathroom. It's almost bigger than my flat!' Isabel turned from the doorway. The expression on her friend's face made her modify her tone. 'What a waste of space.' She came to stand by Lina, and slid open one of the windows. A huge jacaranda tree loomed in front of the balcony. Below it, people were running back and forth, carrying flowers, trolleys laden with glasses, piles of starched napkins. There would be three hundred guests in the grounds soon. The fever of preparation filled the air. 'You know, Leenie, sometimes I think if you really loved him enough you would have been married to him by now. Something's holding you back, and I can't believe it's just your parents or your God,' Isabel said.

'You're right.' Silent shudders began racking Lina's body. She raced to the bathroom and began retching over the toilet. Isabel saw her coughing up a transparent sort of mucus streaked with blood.

470

'Lina?' She helped her friend to the sink. 'What is it? Are you sick?'

Lina washed her face and rinsed her mouth. She allowed herself to be led to the long low stool by the foot of the bed. When she'd calmed down a bit she told Isabel about Pravar's connections to the illegal-arms trade.

'How long have you known this?'

'About three months.' Lina could have told her the exact number of days.

'How could you let things get to this stage?' Disbelief made Isabel's voice sound deeper.

'I thought I might find a solution.' Lina's arms hung limply.

One part of her knew it was love for Anil that had brought her this far. But another bit wondered if it could perhaps be, as her parents insisted, because she hadn't stayed within God's bounds? 'No one was ever lost on a straight road,' Shareef had told her. 'God had laid out the way: walk as He directed, and you would never lose direction'.

'For a while I told myself that maybe if I set up a charitable foundation in Nairobi and used Pravar's money to good ends it would be a way of undoing, or at least, making up for, the awful ways he amassed his wealth.'

'I don't know if bad money can ever be made good just because it's given to charity.'

Lina nodded, remembering the attack on the camp and the death of Dahab.

'I can't believe you haven't talked to Anil about this.'

'He needs his father's money! He hasn't earned any-thing from his architecture yet. He makes a loss on every project because of his fussiness, and Pravar foots every bill. Until he establishes himself he's totally dependent on his dad. That's his career, his passion. I don't want to ruin it.'

'You can't marry him!' Isabel declared.

'I need to find some way of not going ahead which won't hurt Anil.' Lina fiddled with the hem of her dress.

'Will you get real!' Isabel's arms flew into the air. 'That's impossible. He's going to be devastated, and there's no way you can avoid that. You just have to figure out when you're going to tell him. Today? Tomorrow? Or when you're in the registry office?'

'*I can't.*' How could she desert Anil now? When his best friend had died? When he'd warned her that he might not cope if she let him down again? 'It's not a good time. If we could just delay everything—'

'*Lina!* The longer you leave it, the worse things will get. You need to make a decision once and for all.' It occurred to Isabel that breaking up now might in fact be advantageous. At least Anil was in no state to rush after Lina and restart things.

Lina squinted up at her friend. 'Will *you* tell him?' she whispered.

Isabel was stunned. 'No way!'

'Well, I can't do it. I can't. I can't!' Lina was shivering with refusal.

'Well, the other option is to leave. Get out of the country.'

'How can I just run off?'

Isabel assumed her friend was wondering about the practicalities of getting away. 'You'll have to go without a word to anyone here. I'll help you, of course. You can come to my place in London.'

Lina didn't say anything.

'Well?'

'I don't know.'

Isabel felt like shaking her. Every day in her job, Lina encountered some of the worst things in the world, and yet she couldn't face up to the problems in her own life. 'For goodness' sake, Lina! Be honest with yourself! You can't go on like this.'

Anil, buoyed up by morphine, lost all sense of how time was passing. He slept a lot and when he woke up his first thought was always: Is Lina here? Mostly she was. Then she would lie next to him, balancing precariously on the thin ledge of spare mattress, kissing him constantly and telling him that he smelt too medical.

This morning she was especially tender, he could feel her love in every movement she made. Tomorrow they would be married. If only Merc was around to see how wrong he'd been. Anil stroked Lina's palms, tracing the filigree patterns of mendhi that stained her skin. The mendhi was a rich earthy red-brown. 'Apparently the strength of a couple's love is reflected in the depth of the colour.'

'And if it's an arranged marriage?' Lina burrowed into his side.

'Then it's an indication of how deeply they will come to love each other.' He was happy to indulge in these superstitions for today.

'We don't need such signs. No colour could adequately suggest how much I love you.' She pressed her nose behind his ear and kissed his neck repeatedly. 'I wish I could squeeze you.' She laid an arm over his torso. She wanted to lie on him and press against his body: feel every dip and roundness of his flesh, each protusion of bone. Imprint him against herself.

'You'll be able to soon.'

Her lips ached from desire, from a need that no amount of kissing could satisfy. She didn't refrain from caressing him even when the nurse walked in. Only Isabel's arrival made her stop.

'We have to go, Lina, you'll be late for the appointment at the beautician.'

Minnie had booked her in for a last-minute face treatment.

'I'm coming.' She slid off the bed but hugged Anil again, making up for the gentleness her arms had to exercise by rubbing her cheeks hard against his, running her nose along his forehead.

'See you later.' Anil smiled.

Lina's mouth pulled into a shape meant to match his. At the door she stopped. 'Bye—' Halfway through uttering the word she was back for one more cuddle.

'Lina! The driver's waiting.' Isabel tapped a high heel against the tiled floor.

Again Lina pulled herself away and made it out of the room before dashing to Anil for a last hug.

'What's up with you today?' Anil laughed, enjoying the extravagance of her affection.

'I love you so much.' There was a quiver in her speech. 'You know that, don't you?' Without thinking she grabbed at one of the plastic pill containers on the bedside table. Her hand closed around it, clasping it as though it was a lifeline.

'I know it because I feel the same,' Anil said.

'Lina!' Isabel's call was loaded with exasperation and apology.

'You better go.' Anil waved. 'I'll see you tomorrow, at the registry.'

This time when Lina came out of the room Isabel

grabbed her and marched her out of the hospital. A few people turned to look at the crying woman being led along the corridors with a rattling box of pills in her right hand.

The beautician rang Minnie to say Lina had missed her appointment. She immediately called Kamau, who revealed that he was sitting in the car park at Sarit Centre waiting for Lina and her friend. He'd been there almost two hours. Two hours? Minnie wondered how they could keep him hanging around so long, forgetting that she frequently did the same, for longer. She tried contacting Lina, who didn't answer her phone. In a panic she dialled Pravar's number.

'I told you that girl was going to do a runner!'

'But all her stuff is still here.' Minnie had wandered into Lina's room. With the phone at her ear she opened cupboards and drawers. 'Even the suitcase.'

'That doesn't mean a thing. The bitch!' Pravar fumed. 'I'll call some of my people and get them to check passenger departure lists at the airport.'

Lina was expecting to be caught and stopped. She and Isabel passed through customs like criminals outwitting a search party. Her limbs felt brittle, as if they were a bundle of sticks that she was being forced to carry around. Her surroundings seemed far away, even Isabel, who was steering her, seemed distant. Regret had settled, like a wide gulf, between Lina and life.

Isabel, sure that Pravar had Kamau keeping tabs on Lina, had insisted that they lose him. They'd got Kamau to drop them at Sarit Centre, asking him to wait while they shopped. Then they'd crossed to the other side of the mall and taken a cab to the airport. On the way Lina had wanted to stop by the hospital again, to see Anil once more. But Isabel had refused to let her. 'It's too risky. And anyway,' she'd said, 'it won't make a difference now.' So Lina was left with an already fading memory of the last contact with Anil: her fingers in his hair, her palm on his cast, the greying blue of the wound on his forehead. The collars of his pyjamas had been upturned that morning for the first time since the accident.

Ever since the last kiss she'd been thinking of all the time she'd wasted at the beginning, the years it had taken before she'd allowed proper intimacy between them. She wished she could go back and do it all differently. She wished she'd given in to his attempts at canoodling in the back of every taxi they'd sat in. She wished she could hold his hand in all the public places where she'd fobbed him off. She wished she could go back and live the time with him again – live it all better, more fully. If she had taken advantage of every opportunity for a caress or an embrace, gone to see him more often instead of worrying about the cost, made work less of a priority – maybe she wouldn't now feel this gaping desolation.

'I want to die,' she whispered, staring out of the plane window. The pill bottle was still lodged in her palm. Her fingers were frozen around it. She hadn't been able to let go of it even when passing through security. If her grip on it loosened she would also fall apart. Ya Allah, let me die. She thought of Anil and felt only love. For her parents there was only anger. Towards Pravar a strong disgust. She suddenly wished Merc had never told her the truth. Her feelings and actions hardly made sense. What had she done? She could barely recall the thoughts and steps between each stage of her betrayal. That's what it was! She had forsaken her love. Ya Allah, let me die.

'I want this to stop.' This sadness, this life. She wished it would all end.

Isabel squeezed her hennaed hand.

'The pain will subside, with time,' Isabel said, as if grief was a nuclear element. In that case, Lina's would have a half-life of billions of years. Certain forms of sadness feel fresh for ever, no matter how ancient their origin.

How long? Lina closed her eyes. Ya Allah, let me be at that point – twenty, fifty, a hundred years from now. Let me be at the point where this is over.

Letters

Anil returns from the toilet and slides back along the banquette to his corner seat at Café Lafin. As he does so, his feet rub against a package that has been sitting on the floor by his table. It's a present he's brought along for Lina. He pushes the parcel further under the seat and thinks of Merc, who was indirectly responsible for the creation of its contents. After the argument in front of Minnie and Pravar, he'd sent Anil a set of cards depicting four scenes painted by Botticelli. They illustrated a story from Boccaccio's *Decameron*.

In it, Anil recalls, the nobleman Nastagio, rejected by his beloved Paola, is wandering alone in a forest when he comes upon a terrible scene where a knight and his dogs chase, catch and then disembowel a naked woman. Nastagio can do nothing to stop them. When they have finished, the woman rises, whole again, and the chase continues. The knight explains to Nastagio that he committed suicide for love and that this is his punishment – and also that of the woman who repeatedly rejected him. He has been fated to chase and destroy her, and therefore himself, for eternity. Nastagio then invites his own indecisive lover and her family to witness this scene. As a result, Paola agrees to marry him.

In a note accompanying Botticelli's beautifully haunting depiction of this story, Merc had written:

That could be you. I mean the sorry knight. Watch out.

Anil had shown the cards to Lina before they'd left for the UK to ask for her parents' blessing. 'That's not us,' she'd said, turning the image over.

Later, Anil had had the idea of asking Kilempu to sculpt an interpretation of the story of Nastagio as one of his wedding presents to Lina. At first the artist had refused, claiming he didn't do Western rip-offs. Nor had he had much sympathy for the subject: 'I myself have never understood the appeal of marriage. It can't hold together a bad match or improve a good one. Eh? Are we together?' But eventually Anil had persuaded Kilempu that the symbolism of the story was universal. The artist had then taken so long with the work that by the time it was completed Nastagio and the knight had seemed irrelevant to Anil's life.

Except maybe they weren't. Anil slumps against the banquette as if he's been pushed. It suddenly occurs to him that he is both those characters: the condemned knight and the aspiring Nastagio. All the outward trappings of normality and success have obscured this. Mostly, he's even been able to keep the truth from himself. Though at moments, in the thrall of certain qawwalis, he has faced and even enjoyed his weakness, because the grace of art is that it ennobles those who love too much. In life we might despise them, but in art we revere them.

Anil feels angry all of a sudden – at himself, at her. At life! Why is he here? Why is he still waiting? Because he can't let go, because he wants the happy ending as hewn out of wood by Kilempu on the fourth tablet of the Nastagio story, which lies wrapped up at his feet. Because he's always got what he wanted. Because, because – he loves her. Still. Always.

Lina stops a few metres from Café Lafin. Her body is sweating, trembling – as if she's done a marathon. She takes a tissue from her bag and wipes her forehead and upper lip. Ya Allah. She says a short prayer and feels her equilibrium slightly restored, though she's still not sure if it's right to be here. It was the letters that prompted her to contact Anil. After years spent blocking off all feelings for, and memories of him, a collection of words had undone her defences. So she had followed her instincts and asked for a meeting. The decision had been made easier by the fact that Shareef had passed away, and Lina was divorced from the man she'd eventually married five years after leaving Anil.

Shareef certainly wouldn't have blessed a resumption of her old alliance with the other side. And, of course, there was the question of whether Anil would want to see her, after what she'd done to him. Since her departure from Kenya the night before the wedding, he'd never been in touch. At one level this was no surprise – she had hurt him too deeply. But another part of her couldn't accept that he wouldn't try and get hold of her. Anil never quit, that was his greatest vice and most extraordinary quality. But his silence over the years showed that he must have given up on her. And Lina believed she had lost the right to approach him, had forfeited it the day she stole out of his life with yet another lie.

Then she'd found the letters in Shareef's little study. Two years after his death, when Iman decided to move to London, Lina had gone home to help her mother pack up the old place. Iman hadn't touched any of Shareef's things

480

since his sudden demise. Even the stacks of old news-papers still lay around the house, supplemented by new ones, because Iman wouldn't cancel his subscription, and went on accumulating the news as though he might come back to catch up on it all.

In the drawers of his desk, Lina had come across a large A4 envelope. In it there had been more sealed envelopes held together with a rubber band. There was also a letter from a solicitor. It explained that the enclosed letters, all addressed to Haree Merali, had been found amongst the papers of the deceased Ms Selina Mary Turner. Selina? That Selina? The letter went on to explain that the executor of Ms Turner's estate had requested that the letters be for-warded on to the intended recipient. Lina pulled the rubber band off and examined them. There were stamps on some, and the address of Shareef's old law firm in London. Her finger brushed over the name Haree. She had never heard anyone call him that.

Lina read through the official letter again. At the top of the page she spotted a new detail, mention of the literary estate of S. M. Turner. Her mouth fell open. She recalled the day when Shareef had picked up a book she was read-ing: *I Am Another You*. That was by S. M. Turner, wasn't it? The story was still vivid in her mind: the seemingly ideal couple torn apart because one of them insisted their union was against God's will. Was it an account of what had happened between Shareef and Selina?

Lina remembered how she'd absently remarked that the author had recently committed suicide. A few minutes later Shareef had disappeared and locked himself in the bathroom, claiming to be ill. Iman had been obliged to drive her to the train station instead. Lina sat with the letters in her lap and her head in her hands, thinking of how she had unwittingly delivered a blow to her father. Why had he kept the letters if he had never intended to read them? The abruptness of his death had left so many things unfinished.

Going through the letters was like living through her ordeal with Anil again. Each memory they brought up had been agonizing, like a broken limb being jerked by a chain. She could hear Anil in so many of Selina's words. And when she read the last letter, she understood what she'd tried to suppress for years – that she still loved him. There was some relief in accepting the inevitability of this fact. Nevertheless, the feeling surprised her because, right then, she had believed she was finally in love with someone else. Not the sort of compromised love that had characterized her marriage, but something that filled her whole being with delight. She had met Nadeem, a professor of theology, at a conference called 'Build your own Ark', about harnessing religion to help educate people about climate change. He was a practising Muslim, and a fanatic recycler, who fancied himself an incarnation of Bob Dylan when he picked up the guitar. Being with Nadeem had made her believe that maybe God really did know best, a notion she had struggled with, despite trying to pray her way past it. She'd started imagining spending the rest of her life with Nadeem.

Started – until those letters turned up and dispelled all her assurance. She'd read the last one so many times she knew it verbatim now. It summed up her fate better than any fortune-teller could have, and explained the exigencies of her heart more precisely than any shrink might. Its power made her want to share it with Anil. She had finally had an excuse for reaching out to him, a way of showing him what she felt.

It's in her clutch bag now, the piece of paper that's led to this juncture. She tucks the bag under one arm and walks to the café entrance, ready to face the past and the future.

Meeting

S HE ENTERS. He knows it's her by the shoes, which he spots first because, for some reason, he's looking down the moment she comes through the door. Beautiful high-heeled leather pumps the colour of camel hide. Each step she takes is like a note, and as she approaches they become a bar and, all of a sudden, he can feel the old music of longing straining through his being. She is before him now, in a chocolate-brown trench coat, a whorl of matching silk at her neck. Her hair is short! A soft, feathery cut that's parted on the side and falls softly over her ears. He slides along the banquette, away from the table, and stands to greet her.

'Anil.' She meets his embrace. His hands close around the tops of her arms and she takes hold of his just above the elbows. Each presses a cheek to the other, once on each side. Their lips make kissing sounds – he gets her ear, she his sideburn. She seems somehow taller; he doesn't have to bend quite as much to hug her. They hold each other with the measured intensity of friends consoling each other at a funeral.

His smell! The crispness of aftershave mingled with the low-pitched, sour musk of his body. It fills her senses like a song, and makes her body ache to move again in a once familiar rhythm.

They stand for a moment, just looking at one another,

seeing how age has touched both their faces with its signature shadows and creases. He's put on a little weight, she realizes. It's clear in the fullness around the cheeks and chin.

Is she happy? he wonders, because he can find no signs that suggest otherwise in her features; even the scar on her lip is well-disguised today, painted over with taupe lipstick. Only the faint, dusk-coloured smudges under her eyes hint at some mystery, which the rest of her radiance tries to eclipse.

'The hair suits you,' he says.

'Do you like it?' She lets go of him and ruffles the layers. 'I had it done a couple of years ago.' Without thinking she goes to sit on the banquette perpendicular to his, so they are beside each other at the table, the way they always used to be.

'What will you drink?' He signals to a waiter as she sets down her bag and shrugs off her coat. Underneath she's wearing a knee-length wrap-around dress. The print on the jersey material resembles milky coffee swirled through with streams of cream. She's still slim. Under the folds of fabric her body moves with quiet confidence.

'I don't know, what are you having?' She looks at the empty cups before him and pulls down the ends of her lips apologetically. 'Or should I say, have you had?'

'I'd like another Irish coffee.'

'Oh God, I haven't drunk one of those in . . . gosh, yes, well . . . a while.' Since she was last with him. 'Maybe I'll try one again? Yes. Why not?' She smiles, and he sees that her teeth are a little yellow.

He turns to the waiter. 'Two Irish coffees, please.' And without her prompting he asks for the alcohol to be left out of one.

'Lots of extra cream instead.' They recite this in unison, and then look at each other, seeing a slight blur, as though all the instances of their saying this together have suddenly been superimposed across the moment.

'Some things don't change,' Lina says after the waiter has gone.

'No. Like your being late.' He raises his eyebrows.

'You don't know how bad I feel. Really, I had arranged everything. I was determined to get here by five – before if possible. But, I don't know if you've heard the news?'

He nods.

'I had to walk quite a bit of the way here. I'm sorry.' She shrugs.

'The world always seemed to be conspiring against us. And now this terror alert, today of all days.'

She, too, saw it as a sign – one of the many there have been over the years, suggesting that they could never – should never – be together.

'Merc was right.' Anil folds his hands. 'Do you remember how he used to say this terrorism problem would never go away?'

'He was right about a few things.' But not us, she hopes. Please not us.

'And wrong about a lot of stuff too! Anyway . . .'. He brushes at the air. 'It's silly to think that such events are omens especially aimed at us. You could read premonitions into everything, if you tried.'

'I don't know. God has his ways of talking to us.'

Anil swallows the sarcasm that tingles in his mouth, itching to question her statement. 'I was starting to wonder whether you'd make it. Luckily, I got your text.'

'Would you have left?'

'I'm not sure.' Of course he wouldn't. 'You're still well within your worst record.'

'Oh God, don't remind me.' She puts her elbows on the table and drops her face in her hands, trying to imagine which incident he might be referring to.

'The time you kept me waiting for almost six hours.' Strictly speaking that's not the record-breaking incident. It's nothing compared to his lifelong wait, the self-imposed sentence, one part of him held suspended – forever willing her back – while the rest ostensibly got on with things. 'Do you remember that? It was my birthday, and we were supposed to have lunch together. I spent the whole afternoon sitting in that place – what was it? Turino's?'

'I don't know why you always insisted on hanging on for me. You should just have left. It would have served me right.' She remembers him phoning her, getting angrier with each call and yet stubbornly sitting there, refusing to eat anything until she arrived.

'You kept saying you were on your way. I believed you.'

'You always waited. You never let me off the hook.' She looks down and repositions her cutlery, pushing it to the right-hand edge of the table, as though she's clearing a space for something. She used to think his patience was selfless, a generous and noble act of love, until Isabel described it as a strategy. She'd said that Anil knew Lina would never be able to relax as long as she was aware that he was hanging on for her somewhere. That's why he had never let her renege on any commitment. Not once had he made things easy by telling her to forget what she'd promised and not worry. It had meant that she was constantly tormented by the guilt of letting him down, and the need to compensate. Only after she and Anil finally broke up

487

had Lina come to see that his constancy was a form of control. And still, she realizes, he has a grip on her. She stops herself from apologizing once more for her lateness.

'I was the one on the hook,' he says.

She smiles, sighs through her nostrils. 'You never let me go.'

He studies her, wondering what she means. Does she know he's never stopped wanting her? Is she claiming he still has some hold on her? Blaming him? Is she asking to be released? 'I had to. You made me, in the end.' She'd done it when he was at his lowest: his body broken, his heart already mangled by the death of Merc. He can't even remember the days after she jilted him. They'd pumped him up with painkillers that muffled the impact by keeping consciousness at bay as well. But facing reality wasn't easy, even after a medically induced three-week delay. Of course, part of him had wanted to contact her as soon as he was well enough, but he'd been too full of anger and hurt. And then he'd had Pravar in the background, threatening to disinherit him if he went anywhere near Lina. The warning in itself wouldn't have stopped Anil, but he'd felt too broken to fight for her again. He'd stayed at home for a couple of months, hardly leaving his room. Then one day he'd got up and started work in a frenzy, as if nothing had ever happened. At some point soon after that, he'd got married, because it had seemed like the next logical thing to do. 'You were the one who decided. For both of us.'

He doesn't understand, she thinks. And she doesn't know how to explain without accusing him. Perhaps it's not even important any more. 'How have you been?' she says. It's the most inadequate question, the words unable to contain all that has happened.

'Good. You?'

'Fine. Really OK. Yes. Alhamdullilah. Praise be to God.' Her crossed hands rest on her upper arms. Her fingers are topped by works of art: nails smooth and shiny, with the delicate white moons of a perfect French manicure.

Anil watches her, noticing everything: the repeated invocations of God's name, the little mole that's appeared above her left eyebrow, the faint lines that mark the skin on her neck, the tiny, peeping head of a safety pin peering out of her cleavage, where it holds together the overlap of her dress at the deep V-neck. This can't be what we have to tell each other, after so many years – can it? He doesn't want to hear that all is well, that life just went on, and maybe even got better. He'd like to see evidence of some irreparable damage, to hear that nothing was as good after they separated, to find regret embalmed in every syllable she utters.

'I heard about that prize you won. I can't remember the name . . .'

'The Pritzker?'

'Yes.'

'Well, you contributed to where I ended up. Remember how you used to push me to incorporate more eco-aspects in my work?'

She nodded. 'They call you the Man of Mud, don't they? Because of the way you've used earth in construction.'

'Hardly revolutionary. It's one of the oldest construction materials. I took a good idea and improved it a bit. That's all. People thought it couldn't work in Europe. I've shown it can.'

'I was so happy for you when I saw it in the papers.' A shorter strand of hair keeps falling into her eyes, and she keeps pushing it back. 'I can't believe nobody from India or Africa had ever won it before, and now you're the first person who can sort of fly the flag for both those regions. I wasn't surprised, though. I always knew you'd be very successful.'

'Depends how you measure success.' His eyes flicker briefly across the room, but he doesn't heed the filled-up tables, the clink of wine glasses on the air.

He's the same, she thinks: still wanting to qualify each statement. 'Well, you have everything. Don't you?' She's hoping he doesn't. She prays that there's still something missing – her! – despite all he's attained. 'You've achieved the peak in any architect's career – it's the equivalent of the Nobel, isn't it? And then you've got a great family and wealth and health. Haven't you? I always hoped you'd get whatever you wanted to make you happy.'

He leans back and crosses his arms over his chest, irritated by her benevolence, this pseudo-generosity, ready to give him the world without the one thing that counts – that still counts! This is what most exasperates him. His desire for her is like a curse. He won't let on, though, that nothing he's achieved has compensated for that forced loss, whose impact still reverberates in him. He refuses to be hurt by her again. Even though her request for this meeting has made him hope for a reconciliation, he's learned too well that hope can contain the seeds of its own destruction. 'Yes, I suppose I do have all that I could wish for. I've had to work bloody hard for it.' He suddenly realizes just how difficult it has been: the constant exertion, the drive to outdo himself again and again and again. And all for the secret hope – he admits it to himself for the first time – that she might hear of his endeavours, and remember him, and long for him, and maybe even come back. The futility of these motives hits him, the idiocy of a life planned – albeit subconsciously – around the possibility of a return to the past. His mouth curls into a thin twist.

Lina thinks he's still grumpy because of her lateness. She's wondering how she can placate him when the waiter arrives with their drinks.

'Is that what you call extra cream?' Anil eyes the inch-high white layer trembling above the hot, black depths of one coffee. The waiter looks confused. '*Extra* cream, that means at least half of the cup's contents should be cream. Could you make it again? Properly, this time.'

'I don't mind. It's fine for me.' Lina raises a hand to take the cup off the waiter's tray.

'No it's not. I know you wouldn't be able to drink it without more cream. You'd find it much too strong.' Anil turns back to the waiter. 'Just bring us a fresh one.'

'Thank you,' she adds.

The waiter apologizes and retreats.

'The service in this country is awful.'

An old panic rises up in Lina again – that familiar, long-dormant anxiety about Anil's bad moods and how she can alleviate them. 'Are you OK?' She's surprised by his brusqueness towards the waiter.

'Yes.' His arms are still twined over his chest.

She sees that the cufflinks at his wrists are embossed with the image of a peacock. Beneath the black double-breasted shirt – only Anil would be wearing something like that on an ordinary day – his stomach bulges a little over the belt of his trousers. He really has put on weight.

'What about you?' he says, his gaze so intense that she feels the sweep of it, as if his fingers are running along her skin. 'You haven't said much about yourself. You look great. Life must be good.'

'It's not bad.' She's not really sure where to start, what to tell.

'How's your dad?'

Her face changes. There's a little tremble in her lip, as though the scar is vibrating. 'He's . . . he passed away.'

'Oh no. I'm sorry.' He bends forward, puts a hand on her forearm. Is this why she's come to see him? Could it be that now . . . ? 'When did he—?'

'About two years ago. It feels like—'

Two years! His hand withdraws and goes to rub his forehead, as though the words are stones released from a slingshot, and have struck him right between the eyes. Why didn't she contact him sooner?

'. . . and it was totally unexpected, and I don't know. You just never imagine that . . . a car accident.'

What does this mean for us? He wants to ask, but forces himself to keep pace with her.

Their drinks arrive again. This time the proportion of cream to coffee is skewed the other way, but Anil hardly notices.

'It seems so unfair, because he was completely well otherwise and still working.'

'He wasn't the type to stop, was he?'

'I mean, he didn't go to the office any more, but every day people came to the house to get his advice. Drove my mother mad. Now she misses all that.'

'Is she still living in Birmingham?'

'No, she moved to London, and stays with Khala Rocky now. It made sense, I live here, both my sisters are also here.'

Were they the 'we'?

'How are *your* parents?' She reaches for a cube of brown sugar and plops it into her coffee.

'They're both fine.' The fingers of his right hand vibrate against the tabletop.

'They must be so proud of you.' She can picture Minnie mentioning Anil's achievements at every opportunity, while pronouncing the accolades incorrectly. 'Does your mum still throw those amazing parties?'

He nods and wonders where they're going. He wants to know every little detail of her existence. But this talk could lead to nothing. And yet, he's afraid to push, to ask outright why they are here. In case. In case it's not the reason he wants it to be.

'What's your father up to these days?' She tries to keep her tone neutral. The thought of that man still riles her. She'd sent him an anonymous letter after breaking up with Anil, warning that Air Mayur was being watched, and that he should end all the 'goods delivery' flights to neighbouring countries. It had been a cowardly move, and she had no idea whether it had made any difference. But she'd felt compelled to do something.

'Playing a lot of golf.'

'Every day?' Her eyebrows arch.

'Pretty much.' He can't understand this interest in the minutiae of his family's life. 'I guess he deserves it. He worked hard. It wasn't easy to make him retire.'

'So, um, have you taken over his, uh, empire?' There's a queasiness in her stomach.

'Me?' He laughs, and she finds her own face mimicking the motion. She feels again the old sensation of being destined to reflect and share his moods. 'No way! Most of the companies have been sold off.'

'Oh.' She plays with a strand of hair. 'What about Air Mayur?'

He frowns. 'That went ages ago. There was some

493

conflict with Merc's dad over it. I don't know the details. I think it might have had something to do with me and the accident . . .' A bolt of pain twitches across his features. 'Ojielo and my dad never worked together again. Anyway, you know I was never interested in that world. My dad's got people running what's left of his business.'

'He was very good about supporting your career.'

'Yes. I guess I wouldn't be where I am without him. But I'm glad I don't need to rely on him for anything any more.'

'Mmmm.' Lina savours a sip of coffee.

She licks her lips, and Anil feels his insides flip in a way he didn't know was still possible. And then guilt pulses through him. He thinks of his wife, Deepa, and their children. There have been other women since he wed her, several brief affairs. He doesn't think she knows. He never made a real effort to love her – couldn't. He'd still been obsessed with Lina when they married, and didn't believe it was possible to feel the same way about anyone else. More to the point, he hadn't wanted to. But something has developed between him and Deepa over the years. Perhaps it simply has to do with the passing of time and the bond of children, but he feels, all of a sudden, grief at what he's prepared to do to her for the sake of Lina. 'So, do you live around the corner from your mother?' All these trivialities! He only wants to understand what's inside her heart, but he no longer has the right, or perhaps the courage, to inquire directly, and so must arrive there through surreptitious probing.

'No.' She'd like to elaborate, but doesn't know how. Isn't sure what she can reveal without wounding or misleading him. Was it really a good idea to meet? She hadn't expected that even the air between them would be so charged. She feels both comfortable and awkward. It would be easy to slip into being with him. Like driving in the city of her youth after a long absence – there'd be an instinct for the right direction. She could get to where she wanted, though perhaps by a different route. But there's something that still stands like a roadblock across every path. She watches Anil as he bends down to drink his coffee and drains most of it in one long sip, his neck thrust out over the table like a tortoise. Same old habit. It almost makes her smile. 'But I see her quite regularly, at least once a week. The kids love her. And I think she likes seeing them more than she does me.'

'Kids?'

'Boys. Two boys. Mashallah.' She reaches for her bag. She's searching for a photo of them to show him when she suddenly decides – No. It doesn't make sense to share this core of her world that has nothing to do with him. Their connection – hers and Anil's – has always been intensely personal, necessarily exclusive of others. She cannot bring her sons into this chaos of contradictory feelings and unclear meanings. Her love for them is fierce. It's the strongest emotion she's developed for anyone since leaving Anil – or is it? Her heart raps sharply, like someone at a window trying to check if anybody's in. This is why she's really here: to see if the new call of her heart can survive exposure to the old. A frisson of astonishment passes through her – because it looks like the old feeling has once again eclipsed everything else. She rummages in her bag, pulls out a tissue, and pretends to blow her nose. 'And you?'

'Three girls and one boy.'

'Four! I – we – you always wanted four.' She looks away, remembering how they had planned a family and named every child.

He seems to relax somewhat as he tells her their names and ages.

She fights to keep her face straight as she recognizes that two of the girls bear the names they once selected for their imagined children. Should I tell him about the boys? she wonders. For they, too, have names picked decades ago under a hot Kenyan sun.

One of Anil's hands runs over the wallet in his trouser pocket, where he has some pictures of his kids, but he doesn't show her, either, because the expression on her face is unreadable. She doesn't recognize the names, he thinks. She hasn't picked up on the first real hint he's thrown her.

And she, seeing a flicker of puzzlement cross his face, doesn't share her thoughts.

'How lovely that you have girls. Sounds like a perfect family,' Lina says.

'Looks like we've both ended up with perfect families.' He has to keep the bitterness out of his voice.

'Well.' Lina shrugs. 'I'm divorced. But my boys are perfect. Subhanallah. God is glorious. They really are.'

Hope surges through Anil again, like a shot of amphetamine. It even renders him temporarily impervious to the God references that keep punctuating Lina's speech like bad grammar. Gone is his former ambivalence towards religion. Experience has left him full of contempt for it. He no longer even wears a kara. 'Oh. Has it been long?'

Lina notices the change in his tone and posture. She hesitates before admitting, 'Almost three years now.'

Three years! Again, he's thrown. Why has it taken her so long to get in touch? Maybe it still takes her ages to make any kind of decision.

He looks angry, and Lina's not sure why. She clasps her hands together and sits back, trying to work out how she can extricate herself from any misunderstanding without doing more damage. Oh Baba, she thinks, you were right. You can't go back. Some feelings can't survive exhumation. They flare, burning with the white brilliance of magnesium, threatening to annihilate you once more.

Silence stacks up between them like empty crates.

'I don't know why we're here,' Anil eventually says, sighing.

'I wanted ... I found ... there's something.' Her thoughts tumble over one another. She takes a deep breath. 'I made a discovery which I wanted to share with you.' She starts telling him about the letters and their link to the book. 'Remember that novel Merc gave us?' She'd read it again and been shocked by the parallels between the letters and the novel. '*I Am Another You* is the story of Selina and my dad.'

Anil was silent.

'Those letters made me see things differently. I've spent all these years wondering why . . .' Why I couldn't forget you, she thought. 'Why some things are impossible to get over. After I read those I realized . . . I understood . . . better. I mean, I am what I am because of you.' That little pi symbol creases into shape between her brows. 'It's like what you said about my contribution, in a way, to the kind of the architecture you do. You've influenced every single aspect of me – from my work, to my interests, to the way I dress. Of course I can never be free of you, you're part of me for ever. You're always there, even if you're not.' Her clumsy rationale is no less true for being improvised, though Lina senses it is consoling her more than it does Anil.

He's still looking at her blankly, if not in disbelief.

'I'm not being very clear, am I? I can't put it better than Selina did.' She opens her bag and takes out the letter. 'I would like you to have this.'

He takes the envelope and turns it over once.

She's about to ask him to read it now, in front of her, when he crushes it into the pocket of his trousers.

Anil feels like a great stone has been rammed down his throat and pushed to the pit of his stomach. 'This is why you wanted to see me?'

The magnitude of her misjudgement leaves her pale. 'I wanted . . . I was . . . I needed . . .' She inhales and exhales slowly. 'I wanted to share what I found.'

He looks down at the table and nods, like he's confirming something to himself. How can I have let her do this to me again? He could understand his father wanting to disown him for being such a sentimental idiot. He feels like disowning himself. But damn him if he's going to let her see that! There is power in self-restraint, he reminds himself, as he ducks and reaches under the table, clenching his teeth against the urge to declare his feelings. He remembers Merc telling him that once you stop wanting something, not having it doesn't matter. That's his problem! He's never stopped wanting her. By the time he's upright again his features have drooped into a sulk. 'I've got something for you, too.' He puts a package on the table, and slides it towards her.

'Oh, Anil! Oh no, why?'

'It's nothing,' he says, meaning it's everything. His apparent indifference belies his curiosity about whether she'll recognize the image, despite Kilempu's free interpretation.

She unwraps the wooden carving and runs her fingers

498

over the surface. It's the final wedding scene from Botticelli's illustration of a story from the *Decameron*. She remembers what precedes this happy ending. She bites her lip. Anil could not have hurt her more if he'd disembowelled her with a sword the way the knight does his unpossessible maiden. Why has he given her this? As revenge? To show that he got a happy ending despite her? Or is he trying to suggest something else? She's afraid to look at him. What have we done to each other? Her heart shrinks from the question. Maybe they are just like that wretched pair in the story, condemned to make each other suffer for ever. The tragedy of it exhausts her. She slumps forward. Anil thinks she's taking a closer look at the carving when, in fact, she is giving up, abandoning herself, as never before, to what comes next. No more weighing up and wondering, just acquiescence. She raises her eyes to meet Anil's, ready to find her fate in his gaze. Whatever sign he now gives she will accept, whether it is rebuke or devotion.

His face is hard. Sometimes, when hope is desperate, it has the semblance of anger. In Lina's bewildered expression, Anil reads ignorance. She has not grasped the significance of the gift! He can't help resenting her for not remembering. It's as if she's refused to acknowledge the existence of something as indisputable as air.

Unsettled by his behaviour, unsure how to respond, Lina starts folding the paper back over the carving again. He doesn't want me any more! He no longer loves me! It takes every effort to keep her breath steady and her eyes dry. Reversing the direction in which her blood flows couldn't be more difficult. She feels the tension from her ear lobes right down to her toes, while she tries to orient herself. She thinks of her sons, her work, Nadeem, her family – *this* is who she is, what she has chosen. Why does Anil still have the power to make her forget? Ya Allah! Give me the strength to face my weakness. Ya Allah, help me. *To God belongs the East and the West; wherever you turn, there is the face of God.* She is grateful that at every crux there is one immutable truth at which she can clutch. He is always there. He will not burden us beyond what we have the capacity to bear. Ya Allah, I am at my limit. Ya Allah, help me. She prays that He will free her from this crisis with the instantaneity of the hypnotist's click. But God's grace might be a blood transfusion, so imperceptibly does it work. Meanwhile Anil is still watching her, waiting. She braces herself, as might a weightlifter before hoisting a record-breaking load. 'This is beautiful. Thank you,' she says.

'It's nothing.' He shrugs. This encounter, this stilted conversation, this life – all of it is suddenly pointless because, it's clear, she does not care for him as she once did. He'd like a drink, but doesn't want to keep sitting with her. He imagines himself at the bar in three strides, down-ing a cold whisky. Instead he picks up the small tumbler of water that accompanied his coffee and finishes it in a swig. 'I should go.' He starts to get up.

'Me, too.' She rises slowly and puts on her coat and scarf.

He can no longer stand her inaccessible closeness, can't abide the heft of his unrequited feelings. He pulls out his wallet and drops too much money on the table.

As they walk towards the door she notices him bend quickly and press his fingers over his kneecap for a moment. She wonders if he still suffers because of that jet-ski accident. How she has scarred and tormented this man. Astaghfirullah. She feels drained. Would it be possible to

500

measure all that they have done to each other? The damage and the improvements? Has one outweighed the other? Or are the qawwals right that even the wounds of true love are a kind of gift?

Outside it is raining: a shower so fine as to be almost unnoticeable, like spray from a perfume bottle. The streets are emptier, the traffic quieter, the daylight dimmer. To both it feels like an age since they were last out in this world. Anil keeps his hands in his pockets, as though that's the only place they're safe. Lina grips the carving as if it's a mast. They hesitate. Neither knows which words will make an ending – if indeed words can finalize anything.

'Please don't forget to read the letter.'

The bloody letter. He can feel it chafing against his left palm like sandpaper. How can she offer him such a pitiful coda? An old letter of her father's. The man who kept them apart.

She steps forward and presses her cheek against his. Before he can respond, she's moved back.

'I'm going that way.' She points.

It's Anil's direction, too, but he inclines his head the opposite way. 'Well, I'm headed there.'

She swallows. Her lips part, then press against her teeth, then part again. Her eyes zig towards his left trouser pocket and swiftly zag away.

'Do you want it back?' He pulls the letter out. The folded paper protrudes from his fingers, limp as an old banknote.

'No!' Her hands leap behind her back. 'It's yours now.'

She whips around because her eyes are full. She starts walking away, along a street watered by tears to a blur of moving shapes. She focuses on setting one foot in front of the other. At every step, she silently recites, one of God's ninety-nine names. Al-Alim, The Omniscient. Al-Hakim, The Wise. Al-Hafiz, The Preserver. Al-Bari, The Rightful. Al-Haqq, The Truth. It is on the strength of His existence that she moves. By pulling on His word, as on a rope, she manages to progress across the pavement instead of collapsing. Allahu Akbar. God is Great. But He cannot halt the agony in her heart. He cannot stop her wishing things were otherwise.

The desire to run after her is so strong Anil has to grit his teeth and press his heels into the ground. He wills her to slow down or turn. All he needs is a tiny show of hesitation, the merest hint of doubt. Stop! Look at me, he silently pleads. But she walks on.

So this is it.

He's never really believed it could be over. Perhaps this has to do with the inconclusive ways in which he and Lina have previously parted – inconclusive because his heart hasn't kept pace with circumstances. But, now, that old muscle has stayed in step with events, and he suddenly understands the awful, empty, irreparable nature of what is happening. He sees it will spread, like red wine spilled on white linen, to every corner of what remains, and become the continuum along which all else must proceed: the stained tablecloth on which life is served up and must be consumed every day.

Every day. That unit is incomprehensible. All the measurements that make sense of existence no longer have any meaning. How long since the first time they met, the last time they kissed? How long since he divined her spirit in the poetry of the qawwals? How long since her absence fired the motor of his will, fuelling the relentless drive towards fame? How long has he been standing on this street? A hundred years, a day, a minute?

People are hurrying past, stepping around Anil as if he's a tree growing out of the pavement. A tall man with blond dreadlocks and a rucksack brushes past roughly and calls out an apology without looking back. Anil realizes that one of his arms is still extended, that the yellowing sheet of paper is hanging from him, like a scab that's ready to drop off. He unfolds it and begins to read.

19 June 1969

A year has passed and I have not heard anything from you. I, too, made no approach. These musings, ramblings, I have kept to myself. Sending them to you now seems more pointless than ever. But I won't rule out the possibility that I might, some day.

I found the photos of us recently, in a hardback copy of my favourite novel. It was strangely appropriate, though you cannot, I'm sure, have known how. I guess you just shoved the pictures in without thinking. But on the page where they were wedged was a quote I'd underlined while reading: *Remembering is a disease I suffer from*.

We are, all of us, thus afflicted. My own symptoms persist. Even as I studied the photos, greedily reacquainting myself with forgotten details of your face, the old anger bopped up, making me tear the images in half and throw them away. Only the impact of events recedes, the experiences themselves remain forever embedded in us. The past recurs in the smell of burning sugar; hints of it linger in the sound of certain words; or it unexpectedly takes shape in the back of a stranger's head. Worst of all are the thoughts that form in the silence of the night, when the truth is hardest to ignore and one's own culpability is undeniable. Then regret consumes me, and I feel the bitterness rise in my throat. But, even in the worst moments, there is this consolation: that you, too, can never forget.

Because the heart is a black box.

Every conquest, loss or rejection leaves its trace. We love according to what the heart has been taught. We love in the shadow – sometimes benign, sometimes malevolent – of every disappointment, betrayal or fulfilment. We love – and no god can control the feeling or mitigate the consequences.

He looks up the street and starts to run, the rectangle of the letter flapping in his hand like a dog-eared, war-torn flag – of surrender.

Acknowledgements

As research for this book I spoke to people who work for NGOs, some of whom have been based in Sudan. I am grateful for all the impressions I received. I was inspired by several blogs written by aid workers, in particular the author of 'Sleepless in Sudan'. Oxfam's reports on the Millennium Development Goals and the Arms Trade were very helpful to me as well.

Thanks to Agam, for help with different kinds of local lingo. And to my friend Amar, for general advice and feedback.

Thank you, Seema – my authority on all things medical and my favourite source of funny stories.

Thanks to Madeline, Kate, Vanessa and all the other people at Transworld Publishers who have been involved with this book.

Huge thanks to my lovely editor, Jane, for pushing me, but also accepting my limits. For being so generous in every way, and really caring about me and my writing.

A big thank-you to my agent, Zoe, who is wonderfully astute and makes my writer-self feel safe and understood. Thanks also to Mohsen and everyone else at Rogers, Coleridge & White who has helped me.

Very special thanks to Eve, for all the inspiring conversations and frank suggestions.

Finally, thanks – though that word is hardly adequate – to Matti, the lucid core of my heart.

Ishq & Mushq

Priya Basil

'An enticing debut novel by a much-vaunted young novelist'
GLASGOW HERALD

WHEN SARNA SINGH leaves the lustrous green hills of Uganda for England, rows of cramped old houses were not what she was expecting. Husband Karam has brought her to Clapham Common, hoping that the greenery will remind her of Kampala. But Sarna is convinced they have moved to England so he can visit his secret London lady friends. She has a devastating secret of her own. How long before Sarna's web of deceit destroys her own family?

Against a backdrop that spans Partition from India, Elizabeth II's Coronation and Churchill's funeral, to the present day, Priya Basil's explosive family drama is passionate and moving.

'With a verve for the colour of life, this book . . . surprises with its underlying wisdom'
GOOD HOUSEKEEPING'S 6 Great Reads

'Brilliantly woven . . . clever and often funny'
CANDIS

'The product of a deft hand that mixes engrossing narrative with unexpected dashes of magical realism'
INDIA TODAY

9780552773843

The Poet's Wife

Judith Allnatt

IT IS 1841.
Patty is married to John Clare:
Peasant poet, genius and madman.

Travelling home one day, Patty finds her husband sitting, footsore, at the side of the road, having absconded from a lunatic asylum over eighty miles away. She is devastated to discover that he has not returned home to find her, but to search for his childhood sweetheart, Mary Joyce, to whom he believes he is married.

Patty still loves John deeply, but he seems lost to her. Plagued by jealousy, she seeks strength in memories: their whirlwind courtship, the poems John wrote for her, their shared affinity for the land. But as John descends further into delusion, hope seems to be fading. Will she ever be able to conquer her own anger and hurt, and reconcile with this man she now barely knows?

'Affecting and beautifully written'
THE TIMES

'This novel will have you reaching for the nearest copy of John Clare's powerful poems'
DAILY MAIL

9780552774437

My Name Is Salma

Fadia Faqir

'Exquisitely woven, laced with humour and social awareness'
LEILA ABOULELA, author of *The Minaret*

WHEN SALMA BECOMES pregnant before marriage in her small
village in the Levant, she is swept into prison for her own
protection and her new-born baby is snatched away.

In the middle of the most English of towns, Exeter, she rebuilds
her life and settles down with an Englishman. But deep in her
heart the cries of her baby daughter still echo. She decides to go
back to her village to find her. It is a journey that will change
everything – and nothing.

'A beautiful book, written in vivid, tender prose, about
creating a new world when you have lost everything
that matters. Salma is unforgettable'
MAGGIE GEE

9780552773621

Aphrodite's War

Andrea Busfield

THE ISLAND IS divided, but one man's love will never be compromised . . .

Cyprus, 1955 – a guerrilla war is raging and four Greek brothers are growing up to the familiar sounds of exploding bombs and sniper fire.

Determined to avenge the death of his elder brother and to win the heart of his beloved Praxi, young Loukis joins a cell of schoolboy terrorists operating in the mountains. But when his cohorts blow themselves up in a freak accident, he returns home in shock, yearning for the warm embrace of his family – and of his sweetheart.

But his adored Praxi is now married to someone else, and playing at her feet is a young toddler . . .

9780552776349